A Regency Collection

CHRISTINE MERRILL — A Regency Virgin's Undoing

LOUISE ALLEN — A Regency Rake's Redemption

ANN LETHBRIDGE — A Regency Courtesan's Pride

DIANE GASTON — A Regency Gentleman's Passion

ANNE HERRIES — A Regency Lord's Command

CAROLE MORTIMER — A Regency Lady's Scandal

MARGARET McPHEE — A Regency Captain's Prize

SARAH MALLORY — A Regency Baron's Bride

AMANDA McCABE — A Regency Officer's Wedding

CARLA KELLY — A Regency Earl's Pleasure

ISABELLE GODDARD — A Regency Earl's Pleasure

ELIZABETH BEACON — A Regency Rebel's Seduction

A Regency

Officer's Wedding

CARLA KELLY

Published in Great Britain 2016
by Mills & Boon, an imprint of Harlequin (UK) Limited,
Eton House, 18-24 Paradise Road, Richmond, Surrey, TW9 1SR

A REGENCY OFFICER'S WEDDING © 2016 Harlequin Books S.A.

The Admiral's Penniless Bride © 2011 Carla Kelly
Marrying the Royal Marine © 2010 Carla Kelly

ISBN: 978-0-263-91769-7

052-0516

Harlequin (UK) policy is to use papers that are natural, renewable and recyclable products and made from wood grown in sustainable forests. The logging and manufacturing processes conform to the legal environmental regulations of the country of origin.

Printed and bound
by CPI Group (UK) Ltd, Croydon, CR0 4YY

The Admiral's Penniless Bride

CARLA KELLY

Carla Kelly has been writing award-winning novels for years—stories set in the British Isles, Spain and army garrisons during the Indian Wars. Her speciality in the Regency genre is writing about ordinary people, not just lords and ladies. Carla has worked as a university professor, a ranger in the National Park Service and recently as a staff writer and columnist for a small daily newspaper in Valley City, North Dakota. Her husband is director of theatre at Valley City State University. She has five interesting children, a fondness for cowboy songs and too many box elder beetles in the autumn.

Prologue

1816

The last five years had been a hard school. When Sally Paul had left the Bath employment registry with a position near Plymouth as lady's companion, but only enough money to ride the mail coach, she had known she was heading towards pinch pennies.

As she neared the Devonshire coast, Sally owned to some uneasiness, but put it down to the fact that, after Andrew's suicide, she had sworn never to look on the ocean again. Still, times were hard and work difficult to come by. No matter how pinch penny the Coles might prove to be, she was on her way to employment, after six weeks without.

Such a dry spell had happened twice in the past two years, and it was an occupational hazard: old ladies, no matter how kind or cruel, had a tendency to die and no longer require her services.

Although she would never have admitted it, Sally hadn't

been sad to see the last one cock up her toes. She was a prune-faced ogre, given to pinching Sally for no reason at all. Even the family had stayed away as much as they could, which led to the old dear's final complaint, when imminent death forced them to her bedside. 'See there, I *told* you I was sick!' she had declared in some triumph, before her eyes went vacant. Only the greatest discipline—something also acquired in the last five years—had kept Sally from smiling, which she sorely wanted to do.

But a new position had a way of bringing along some optimism, even when it proved to be ill placed, as it did right now. She never even set foot inside the Coles' house.

She hadn't minded the walk from the Drake, where the mail coach stopped, to the east edge of Plymouth, where the houses were genteel and far apart. All those hours from Bath, cramped in next to a pimply adolescent and a pale governess had left Sally pleased enough to stretch her legs. If she had not been so hungry, and as a consequence somewhat lightheaded, she would have enjoyed the walk more.

All enjoyment ended as she came up the circular drive, noting the dark wreath on the door and the draped windows proclaiming a death in the family. Sally found herself almost hoping the late member of the Cole family was a wastrel younger son given to drink who might not be much missed.

It was as she feared. When she announced to the butler that she was Mrs Paul, come to serve as Mrs Maude Cole's companion, the servant had left her there. In a moment he was back with a woman dressed in black and clutching a handkerchief.

'My mother-in-law died yesterday morning,' the woman said, dabbing at dry eyes. 'We have no need of you.'

Why had she even for the smallest moment thought the matter would end well? *Idiot*, she told herself. *You knew the moment you saw the wreath.* 'I am sorry for your loss,' she said quietly, but did not move.

The woman frowned. *Maybe she expects me to disappear immediately*, Sally thought. *How am I to do that?*

She could see that the woman wanted to close the door. Five years ago, at the start of her employment odyssey, Sally might have yielded easily. Not now, not when she had come all this way and had nothing to show for it.

'Mrs Cole, would you pay my way back to Bath, where you hired me?' she asked, as the door started to close.

'There was never any guarantee of hire until I saw you and approved,' the woman said, speaking through a crack now. 'My mother-in-law is dead. There is no position.'

The door closed with a decisive click. Sally stood where she was, unwilling to move because she had no earthly idea what to do. The matter resolved itself when the butler opened the door and made shooing motions, brushing her off as if she were a beggar.

She told herself she would not cry. All she could do was retrace her steps and see if something would occur to her before she returned to the Drake. She did not feel sanguine at the prospect; she was down to her last coin and in arrears on any ideas at all.

What was it that Andrew used to say, before his career turned to ashes? 'There isn't any problem so large that it cannot be helped by the application of tea.'

He was wrong, of course; she had known that for years. Sally looked in her reticule as she walked. She had enough for one cup of tea at the Drake.

Chapter One

The Mouse was late. Admiral Sir Charles Bright (Ret.) was under the impression that he was a tolerant man, but tardiness was the exception. For more than thirty years, he had only to say, 'Roundly now', and his orders were carried out swiftly and without complaint. True, copious gold lace and an admiral's stars might have inspired such prompt obedience. Obedience was second nature to him; tardiness a polar opposite.

Obviously this was not the case with The Mouse. For the life of him, he could have sworn that the lady in question was only too relieved to relinquish her old-maid status for matrimony to someone mature and well seasoned. During their only visit last month, The Mouse—Miss Prunella Batchthorpe—had seemed eager enough for all practical purposes.

Bright stared at his rapidly cooling cup of tea, and began to chalk up his defects. He did not think of forty-five as old, particularly since he had all of his hair, close cut though it was; all of his teeth minus one lost on the Barbary Coast;

and most of his parts. He had compensated nicely for the loss of his left hand with a hook, and he knew he hadn't waved it about overmuch during his recent interview with Miss Batchthorpe. He had worn the silver one, which Starkey had polished to a fare-thee-well before his excursion into Kent.

He knew he didn't talk too much, or harrumph or hawk at inopportune moments. There was no paunch to disgust, and he didn't think his breath was worse than anyone else's. And hadn't her older brother, a favourite commander who helmed Bright's flagship, assured him that, at age thirty-seven, Prunella was more than ready to settle down at her own address? Relieved, even. Bright could only conclude that she had developed cold feet at the last minute, or was tardy.

He could probably overlook Miss Batchthorpe's plain visage. He had told her this was to be a marriage of convenience, so he wouldn't be looking at her pop eyes on an adjoining pillow each morning. He could even overlook her shy ways, which had made him privately dub her The Mouse. But tardiness?

Reality overtook him, as it invariably did. One doesn't live through nearly three decades of war and many ranks by wool gathering. She might have decided that he simply would not suit, even if it meant a life of spinsterhood. He knew even a year of peace had not softened his hard stare, and the wind- and wave-induced wrinkles about his mouth were here to stay.

Whatever the reason for The Mouse's non-appearance, he still needed a wife immediately. *I have sisters*, he thought to himself for the thousandth time since the end of the war. *Oh, I do.*

Fannie and Dora, older than he by several years, had not intruded much in his life spent largely at sea. They had corresponded regularly, keeping him informed of family marriages, births, deaths and nit-picking rows. Bright knew that Fannie's eldest son, his current heir, was an ill-mannered lout, and that Dora's daughter had contracted a fabulous alliance to some twit with a fortune.

He put his current dilemma down to the basic good natures of his meddling siblings. Both of them widowed and possessing fortunes of their own, Fan and Dora had the curse of the wealthy: too much time on their hands.

Fan had delivered the first shot across the bows when he had visited her in London after Waterloo. 'Dora and I want to see you married,' she had announced. 'Why should you not be happy?'

Bright could tell from the martial glint in her eyes—Wellington himself possessed a similar look—that there was no point in telling his sister that he was already happy. Truth to tell, what little he had glimpsed of Fan's married life, before the barrister had been kind enough to die, had told him volumes about his sister's own unhappiness.

Dora always followed where Fan led, chiming in with her own reasons why he needed a wife to Guide Him Through Life's Pathways—Dora spoke in capital letters. Her reasons were convoluted and muddled, like most of her utterances, but he was too stunned by Fan's initial pronouncement, breathtaking in its interference, to comment upon them.

A wife it would be for their little brother. That very holiday, they had paraded a succession of ladies past his startled gaze, ladies young enough to be his daughter and older and desperate. Some were lovely, but most wanted in the area he craved: good conversation. Someone to talk to—there was the sticking point. Were those London ladies in awe of his title and uniform? Did they flinch at the hook? Were they interested in nothing he was interested in? He had heard all the conversations about weather and goings on at Almack's that he could stomach.

Never mind. His sisters were determined. Fan and Dora apparently knew most of the eligible females in the British Isles. He was able to fob them off immediately after his retirement, when he was spending time in estate agents' offices, seeking an estate near Plymouth. He had taken lodgings in Plymouth while he searched. Once the knocker was on the door, the parade of lovelies had begun again, shepherded by his sisters.

Bemusement turned to despair even faster than big rabbits made bunnies. *My sisters don't know me very well*, he decided, after several weeks. The last straw came when Fan decided that not only would she find him a mate, but also redecorate his new estate for him, in that execrable Egyptian style that even *he* knew was no longer à la mode. When the first chair shaped like a jackal arrived, Bright knew he had to act.

Which was why he now awaited the arrival of Miss Prunella Batchthorpe, who had agreed to be his ball and chain and leave him alone. Dick Batchthorpe, his flagship commander, had mentioned her often during their years together. Something in Bright rebelled at taking the advice of two of the most harebrained ladies he knew; besides, it would be a kind gesture to both Dick, who didn't relish the prospect of supporting an old maid, and the old maid in question, who had assured him she would keep his house orderly and make herself small.

As he sat in the dining room of the Drake, with its large windows overlooking the street, Bright couldn't help feeling a twinge of relief at her non-arrival, even as he cursed his own apparent shallowness. Miss Batchthorpe was more than usually plain.

He heard a rig clatter up to the front drive and looked up

in something close to alarm, now that he had told himself that Miss Batchthorpe simply wouldn't suit. He stood up, trying not to appear overly interested in the street, then sat down. It was only a beer wagon, thank the Lord.

Bright patted the special licence in the pocket of his coat. No telling how long the pesky things were good for. Hopefully, his two dotty sisters had no connections among the Court of Faculties and Dispensations to tattle on him to his sisters. If they knew, they would hound him even more relentlessly. He would never hear the end of it. He hadn't survived death in gruesome forms at sea to be at the mercy of managing women.

Bright dragged out his timepiece. He had waited more than an hour. Was there a legally binding statute determining how long a prospective, if reluctant, groom should wait for a woman he was forced to admit he neither wanted, nor knew anything about? Still, it was noon and time for luncheon. His cook had declared himself on strike, so there wasn't much at home.

Not that he considered his new estate home. In its current state of disrepair, his estate was just the place where he lived right now. He sighed. Home was still the ocean.

He looked for a waiter, and found himself gazing at a lovely neck. Had she been sitting there all along, while he was deep in his own turmoil? In front of him and to the side, she sat utterly composed, hands in her lap. He had every opportunity to view her without arousing anyone's curiosity except his own.

A teapot sat in front of her, right next to the no-nonsense cup and saucer Mrs Fillion had been buying for years and which resembled the china found in officers' messes all across the fleet. She took a sip now and then, and he had the distinct impression she was doing all she could to prolong the event. Bright could scarcely remember ever seeing a woman seated alone in the Drake, and wondered if she was waiting for someone. Perhaps not; when people came into the dining room, she did not look towards the door.

He assumed she was a lady, since she was sitting in the dining room, but her dress was far from fashionable, a plain gown of serviceable grey. Her bonnet was nondescript and shabby.

She shifted slightly in her chair and he observed her slim figure. He looked closer. Her dress was cinched in the back with a neat bow that gathered the fabric together. This was a dress too large for the body it covered. *Have you been ill, madam?* he asked himself.

He couldn't see her face well because of the bonnet, but her hair appeared to be ordinary brown and gathered in a thick mass at the back of her head. As he watched what little he could see of her face, Bright noticed her eyes were on a gentleman at a nearby table who had just folded his newspaper and was dabbing at his lips. She leaned forwards slightly, watching him. When he finally rose, she turned to see him out of the dining room, affording Bright a glimpse of a straight nose, a mouth that curved slightly downward and eyes as dark brown as his own.

When the man was gone from the dining room, she walked to the table and took the abandoned newspaper back to her own place. Bright had never seen a lady read a newspaper before. He watched, fascinated, as she glanced at the front page, then flipped to the back, where he knew the advertisements and legal declarations lurked. Was she looking for one of the discreet tonics advertised for female complaints? Did her curiosity run to ferreting out pending lawsuits or money owed? This was an unusual female, indeed.

As he watched, her eyes went down the back pages quickly. She shook her head, closed the newspaper, folded it neatly and took another sip of her tea. In another moment, she was looking inside her reticule, almost as though she was willing money to appear.

More curious now than ever, Bright opened his own paper to the inside back page, wondering what had caused such disappointment. 'Positions for hire' ran down two narrow columns. He glanced through them; nothing for women.

He looked up in time to see the lady stare into her reticule again. Bright found himself wishing, along with her, for something to materialise. He might have been misreading all the signs, but he knew he was an astute judge of character. This was a lady without any funds who was looking for a position of some sort.

Bright watched as the waiter came to her table. Giving him her prettiest smile, she shook her head. The man did not move on immediately, but had a brief, whispered conversation with her that turned her complexion pale. *He is trying to throw her out*, Bright thought in alarm, which was followed quickly by indignation. *How dare the man!* The dining room was by no means full.

He sat and seethed, then put aside his anger and concentrated on what he was rapidly considering *his* dilemma. Maybe he was used to the oversight of human beings. *You do remember that you are no longer responsible for the entire nation?* he quizzed himself silently. *Let this alone.*

He couldn't. He had spent too many years—his whole lifetime, nearly—looking out for this island and its inmates to turn his back on someone possibly in distress. By the time the waiter made his way back to his table, Bright was ready. It involved one of the few lies he ever intended to tell, but he couldn't think any faster. The imp of indecision leaped on to his shoulder and dug in its talons, but he ignored it.

With a smile and a bow, the waiter made his suggestions for luncheon and wrote down Bright's response. Bright motioned the man closer. 'Would you help me?'

'By all means, sir.'

'You see that lady there? She is my cousin and we have had a falling out.'

'Ah, the ladies,' the waiter said, shaking his head.

Bright sought for just the right shade of regret in his voice. 'I had thought to mollify her. It was a quarrel of long standing, but as you can see, we are still at separate tables, and I promised her mother...' He let his voice trail off in what he hoped was even more regret.

'What do you wish me to do, sir?'

'Serve her the same dinner you are serving me. I'll sit with her and we'll see what happens. She might look alarmed. She might even get up and leave, but I have to try. You understand.'

The waiter nodded, made a notation on his tablet and left the table with another bow.

I must be a more convincing liar than I ever imagined, Bright thought. He smiled to himself. *Hell's bells, I could have been a Lord of the Admiralty myself, if I had earlier been aware of this talent.*

He willed the meal to come quickly, before the lady finished her paltry dab of tea and left the dining room. He knew he could not follow her; that went against all propriety. As it was, he was perilously close to a lee shore. He looked at the lady again, as she stared one more time into her reticule and swallowed. *You are even closer than I am to a lee shore*, he told himself. *I have a place to live. I fear you do not.*

Early in his naval career, as a lower-than-the-clams

ensign, he had led a landing party on the Barbary Coast. A number of things went wrong, but he took the objective and survived with most of his men. He never forgot the feeling just before the jolly boats slid on to the shore—the tightness in the belly, the absolute absence of moisture in his entire drainage system, the maddening little twitch in his left eye. He felt them all again as he rose and approached the other table. The difference was, this time he knew he would succeed. His hard-won success on the Barbary Coast had made every attack since then a win, simply because he knew he could.

He kept his voice low. 'Madam?'

She turned frightened eyes on him. How could eyes so brown be so deep? His were brown and they were nothing like hers.

'Y-y-yes?'

Her response told him volumes. She had to be a lady, because she had obviously never been approached this way before. Better drag out the title first. Baffle her with nonsense, as one of his frigate captains used to say, before approaching shore leave and possible amatory adventure.

'I am Admiral Sir Charles Bright, recently retired from the Blue Fleet, and I—' He stopped. He had thought that might reassure her, but she looked even more pale. 'Honestly, madam. May I…may I sit down?'

She nodded, her eyes on him as though she expected the worst.

He flashed what he hoped was his most reassuring smile. 'Actually, I was wondering if I could help *you*.' He wasn't sure what to add, so fell back on the navy. 'You seem to be approaching a lee shore.'

There was nothing but wariness in her eyes, but she was

too polite to shoo him away. 'Admiral, I doubt there is any way you could help.'

He inclined his head closer to her and she just as subtly moved back. 'Did the waiter tell you to vacate the premises when you finished your tea?'

The rosy flush that spread upwards from her neck spoke volumes. She nodded, too ashamed to look at him. She said nothing for a long moment, as if considering the propriety of taking the conversation one step more. 'You spoke of a lee shore, Sir Charles,' she managed finally, then shook her head, unable to continue.

She knows her nautical terms, he thought, then plunged in. 'I couldn't help but notice how often you were looking in your reticule. I remember doing that when I was much younger, sort of willing coins to appear, eh?'

Her face was still rosy, but she managed a smile. 'They never do though, do they?'

'Not unless you are an alchemist or a particularly successful saint.'

Her smile widened; she seemed to relax a little.

'Madam, I have given you my name. It is your turn, if you would.'

'Mrs Paul.'

Bright owned to a moment of disappointment, which surprised him. 'Are you waiting for your husband?'

She shook her head. 'No, Admiral. He has been dead these past five years.'

'Very well, Mrs Paul.' He looked up then to see the waiter approaching carrying a soup tureen, with a flunky close behind with more food. 'I thought you might like something to eat.'

She started to rise, but was stopped by the waiter, who set a bowl of soup in front of her. She sat again, distress on her face. 'I couldn't possibly let you do this.'

The waiter winked at Bright, as though he expected her to say exactly that. 'I insist,' Bright said.

The waiter worked quickly. In another moment he was gone, after giving Mrs Paul a benevolent look, obviously pleased with the part he had played in this supposed reconciliation between cousins.

Still she sat, hands in her lap, staring down at the food, afraid to look at him now. He might have spent most of his life at sea, but Bright knew he had gone beyond all propriety. *At least she has not commented upon the weather*, he thought. He didn't think he could bully her, but he knew a beaten woman when he saw one, and had no urge to heap more coals upon her. He didn't know if he possessed a gentle side, but perhaps this was the time to find one, if it lurked somewhere.

'Mrs Paul, you have a complication before you,' he said, his voice soft but firm. 'I am going to eat because I am hungry. Please believe me when I say I have no motive beyond hoping that you will eat, too.'

She didn't say anything. He picked up his spoon and began with the soup, a meaty affair with broth just the way he liked it. He glanced at her, only to see tears fall into her soup. He held his breath, making no comment, as she picked up her soup spoon. She ate, unable to silence the little sound of pleasure from her throat that told him volumes about the distance from her last meal. For one moment he felt enormous anger that a proud woman should be so reduced in victorious England. Why should that surprise him? He had seen sailors begging on street corners, when they were turned loose after the war's end.

'Mrs Fillion always makes the soup herself,' he said. 'I've eaten a few meals here, during the war.'

Mrs Paul looked at him then, skewered him with those

lovely eyes of hers, so big in her lean face. 'I would say she added just the right amount of basil, wouldn't you?'

It was the proud comment of a woman almost—but not quite—at her last resources and it touched him. She ate slowly, savoring every bite as though she expected no meals to follow this one. While she ate, he told her a little about life in the fleet and his recent retirement. He kept up a steady stream of conversation to give a touch of normalcy to what was an awkward luncheon for both of them.

A roast of beef followed, with new potatoes so tender that he wanted to scoop the ones off Mrs Paul's plate, too. He wanted her to tell him something about herself and he was rewarded after the next course, when she began to show signs of lagging. Finally, she put down her fork.

'Sir Charles, I—'

He had to interrupt. 'If you want to call me something, make it Admiral Bright,' he said, putting down his fork, too, and nodding to the flunky to take the plates. 'During the war, I think the crown handed out knighthoods at the crack of a spar. I *earned* the admiral.'

She smiled at that and dabbed her lips. 'Very well, Admiral! Thank you for luncheon. Perhaps I should explain myself.'

'Only if you want to.'

'I do, actually. I do not wish you to think I am usually at loose ends. Ordinarily, I am employed.'

Bright thought of the wives of his captains and other admirals—women who stayed safely at home, tended their families and worried about their men at sea. He thought about the loose women who frequented the docks and serviced the seamen. He had never met a woman who was honestly employed. 'Say on, Mrs Paul.'

'Since my husband…died, I have been a lady's companion,' she said, waiting to continue until the waiter was out of earshot. 'As you can tell, I am from Scotland.'

'No!' Bright teased, grateful she was no longer inclined to tears. She gave him such a glance then that he did laugh.

'I have been a companion to the elderly, but they tend to die.' Her eyes crinkled in amusement. 'Oh! That is not my fault, let me assure you.'

He chuckled. 'I didn't think you were a murderer of old dears, Mrs Paul.'

'I am not,' she said amicably. 'I had been six weeks without a position, sir, when I found one here in Plymouth.'

'Where were you living?'

'In Bath. Old dears, as you call them, like to drink the water in the Pump Room.' She made a face, which was eloquent enough for him. She sobered quickly. 'I finally received a position and just enough money to take the mail coach.'

She stopped talking and he could tell her fear was returning. All he could do was joke with her, even though he wanted to take her hand and give it a squeeze. 'Let me guess: they were sobersides who didn't see the fun in your charming accent.'

She shook her head. 'Mrs Cole died the day before I arrived.' She hesitated.

'What did you do?' he asked quietly.

'I asked for the fare back to Bath, but she wouldn't hear of it.' Mrs Paul's face hardened. 'She had her butler shoo me off the front steps.'

And I am nervous about two silly sisters? Bright asked himself. 'Is there something for you in Bath?'

She was silent a long moment. 'There isn't anything anywhere, Admiral Bright,' she admitted finally. 'I've been sitting here trying to work up the nerve to ask the proprietor if he needs kitchen help.'

They were both silent.

Bright was not an impulsive man. He doubted he had ever drawn an impulsive breath, but he drew one now. He looked at Mrs Paul, wondering what she thought of him. He knew little about her except that she was Scottish, and from the sound of her, a Lowland Scot. She was past the first bloom of youth and a widow. She had been dealt an impossible hand. *And not once have you simpered about the weather or Almack's*, he thought. *You also have not turned this into a Cheltenham tragedy.*

He pulled out his timepiece. The Mouse was now nearly three hours late. He drew the deepest breath of his life, even greater than the one right before he sidled his frigate between the Egyptian shore and the French fleet in the Battle of the Nile.

'Mrs Paul, I have an idea. Tell me what you think.'

Chapter Two

'You want to marry *me*?'

To Mrs Paul's immense credit, she listened without leaping to her feet and slapping him or falling into a dead faint.

She thinks I am certifiable, Bright thought, trying to divine what was going on in her mind as he blathered on. He was reminding himself of his least favourite frigate captain, who spoke faster and faster as the lie grew longer and longer. *Dash it, this is no lie*, he thought.

'You see before you a desperate man, Mrs Paul,' he said, wincing inside at how feeble that sounded. 'I need a wife on fearsomely short notice.' He winced again; that sounded worse.

He had to give her credit; she recovered quickly. He could also see that she had no intention of taking him seriously. Her smile, small though it was, let him know precisely how she felt about his little scheme. *How can I convince her?* he asked himself in exasperation. *I doubt I can.*

'Mrs Paul, I hope you don't think that through England's darkest hours, the Royal Navy was led by idiots.'

Her voice was faint, mainly because she seemed to be struggling not to laugh. 'I never thought it was, Admiral,' she replied. 'But...but why on earth do you require a wife on fearsomely short notice? Now that you are retired, haven't you leisure to pursue the matter in your own good time?'

'I have sisters,' he said. 'Two of 'em. Since I retired last autumn, they have been dropping in to visit and bringing along eligible females. They are cornering me and I feel trapped. Besides, I am not convinced I want a wife.'

The look she gave him was one of incredulity, as though she wondered—but was too polite to ask—how a grown man, especially one who had faced the might of France for years, could be so cowed by sisters. 'Surely they have your best interests at heart,' Mrs Paul said. She seemed to find his dilemma diverting. 'Do you require a...a nudge?'

'That's not the issue,' he protested, but he admitted to himself that she did have a point. 'See here, Mrs Paul, wouldn't you be bothered if someone you knew was determined to help you, whether you wanted it or not?'

She was silent a moment, obviously considering his question. 'May I be frank, Admiral?'

'Certainly.'

'There are times when I wish someone *was* determined to help me.'

She had him there. 'You must think me an awful whiner,' he admitted at last.

'No, sir,' she said promptly. 'I just think you have too much time on your hands now.'

'Aha!' he exclaimed, and slapped the table with his hook, which made the tea cups jump. 'It's my stupid sisters who have too much time! They are plaguing my life,' he finished, his voice much lower.

'So you think proposing to me will get them off your back?' she asked, intrigued.

'You are my backup, Mrs Paul.'

Oh, Lord, I am an idiot, he thought. She stared at him in amazement, but to her credit, did not flee the dining room. *Maybe you think you owe me for a meal*, he thought sourly. *Humouring a lunatic, eh?*

'Backup? There is someone else who didn't deliver?' she asked. Her lips twitched. 'Should I be jealous? Call her out?'

She had him again, and he had to smile. In fact, he had to laugh. 'Oh, Mrs Paul, I have made a muddle of things. Let me explain.'

He told her how in desperation because his sisters would not leave him alone, he had contacted the captain of his flagship, who had a sister withering on the matrimonial vine. 'I made her an offer. It was to be a marriage of convenience, Mrs Paul. She needed a husband, because ladies… er…don't seem to care to wander through life alone. I was careful to explain that,' he assured her. 'She agreed.'

He looked at the lady across the table from him, amazed she was still sitting there. 'It *is* foolish, isn't it?' he said finally, seeing the matter through her eyes. 'I have been stewing about in this dining room for hours, and the lady has not appeared. I can hardly blame her.' He looked at his hook. 'Maybe she doesn't care overmuch for hooks.'

Mrs Paul put her hand to her lips, as though trying to force down another laugh. 'Admiral, if she cared about you, a hook wouldn't make the least difference. You have all your teeth, don't you? And your hair? And surely there is a good tailor in Plymouth who could—' She stopped. 'You must think I am terribly rude.'

'No, I think you are honest and…dash it, I have all my hair! I did lose a tooth on the Barbary Coast—'

'Careless of you,' she murmured, then gave up trying to hold back the mirth that seemed to well up out of her.

Her laughter was infectious. Thank goodness the dining room was nearly empty by now, because he laughed along with her. 'What is the matter with my suit?' he asked, when he could talk.

She wiped her eyes on the napkin. 'Nothing at all, Admiral, if only this were the reign of poor George III, and not the regency of his son! I realise you have probably worn nothing but uniforms for years. Many men would probably envy your ability to wear garments from the turn of the century, without having to resort to a shoehorn. I am no Beau Brummell, Admiral, but there is a time to bid adieu to old clothes, even if they do fit.'

'I was never inclined to add pounds,' he said, trying not to sound sulky. 'A tailor would help?'

'Perhaps, but he won't solve your problem of sisters,' she said sensibly. 'Suppose I agreed to your…er…unorthodox proposal, and you fell in love with someone? What then?'

'Or suppose you do?' he countered, warmed that she still seemed to be considering the matter.

'That is unlikely. I have no fortune, no connections, no employment. I had a good husband once, and he will probably suffice.'

She spoke in such a matter-of-fact way that he wanted to know more, but knew he didn't dare. 'Did you tease him as unmercifully as you have teased me? "Careless of me to lose a tooth?" Really, Mrs Paul.'

'I was even harder on him, sir,' she said in good humour. 'I knew him better and everyone knows familiarity breeds content.'

You're a wit, he thought in appreciation. 'I have no skills in searching for a wife, Mrs Paul. I never thought to live that long. I will blame Napoleon.'

'Why not?' she said, her voice agreeable. 'He had his own trouble with wives, I do believe.' She leaned forwards. 'Admiral, I know nothing of your financial situation, nor do I wish to know, but surely a visit to Almack's during the Season would turn up some prospects that would satisfy even your sisters.'

Mrs Paul obviously noted the look of disgust on his face, but continued, anyway. 'If you'd rather not chance Almack's, there is church. Unexceptionable ladies are often found there.'

'You'd have me endure sermons and make sheep's eyes at a female in a neighbouring pew?'

She gave him such a glance that he felt his toes tingle. 'Admiral! I am merely trying to think of venues where you might find ladies—suitable ladies! Were you this much trouble in the fleet?'

'This and more,' he assured her, warming to her conversation. *By God, you are diverting*, he thought. 'Mrs Paul, do you ever talk about the weather?'

'What does the weather have to do with anything?' she asked.

'Good books?'

'Now and then. Do you know, I read my way through the family library of the lady I worked for in Bath. Ask me anything about the early saints of the church. Go on. I dare you.'

Bright laughed out loud again. 'Mrs Paul, mourning is well and good, I suppose, but why hasn't some gentleman proposed recently? You are a wit.'

He wished he hadn't said that. Her eyes lost their lustre. 'It is different with ladies, sir. Most men seem to want a fortune of some size, along with the lady.' She looked in her reticule again and her look told him she was determined to turn her wretched situation to a joke. 'All I have in here is an appointment book, the stub of a pencil and some lint.'

The last thing you want is pity, isn't it? he told himself. 'So here we are, the two of us, at point non plus,' he said.

'I suppose we are,' she replied, the faintest glint of amusement returning to her eyes.

'And I must return to my estate, still a single gentleman, with no prospects and a cook on strike.'

'Whatever did you do to him?'

'I told him my sisters were coming to visit in two days. They order him about and demand things. Mrs Paul, he is French and he has been my chef for eleven years, through bombardment and sinking ships, and he cannot face my sisters either!'

'What makes you think matrimony would change that?' she asked sensibly. 'They would still visit, wouldn't they?'

He shrugged. 'You have to understand my sisters. They are never happier than when they are on a mission or a do-gooding quest. With you installed in my house, and directing my chef, and having a hand in the reconstruction, they would get bored quickly, I think.'

'Reconstruction?' she asked.

'Ah, yes. I found the perfect house. It overlooks Plymouth Sound, and it came completely furnished. It does require a little...well, a lot...of repairs. I think the former owner was a troll with bad habits.'

Mrs Paul laughed. 'So you were going to marry this poor female who has cried off and carry her away to a ruin?'

Bright couldn't help himself. He wasn't even sure why

he did it, but he slipped his hook into the ribbons holding Mrs Paul's bonnet on her head. She watched, transfixed, as he gave the frayed ribbon a gentle tug, then pushed the bonnet away from her face, to dangle down her back. 'Are you sure you won't reconsider? I don't think you will be bored in my house. You can redecorate to your heart's content, sweet talk my chef, I don't doubt, and find me a tailor.'

'You know absolutely nothing about me,' she said softly, her face pink again. 'You don't even know how old I am.'

'Thirty?' he asked.

'Almost thirty-two.'

'I am forty-five,' he told her. He took his finger and pushed back his upper lip. 'That's where the tooth is missing. I keep my hair short because I am a creature of habit.' He felt his own face go red. 'I take the hook off at night, because I'd hate to cut my own throat during a bad dream.'

She stared at him, fascinated. 'I have never met anyone like you, Admiral.'

'Is that good or bad?'

'I think it is good.'

He held his breath, because she appeared to be thinking. *Just say yes*, he thought.

She didn't. To his great regret, Mrs Paul shook her head. She retied her bonnet and stood up. 'Thank you for the luncheon, Admiral Bright,' she said, not looking him in the eyes this time. 'I have had a most diverting afternoon, but now I must go to the registry office here and see if there is anything for me.'

'And if there is not?' It came out cold and clinical, but she didn't seem to be a woman searching for sympathy.

'That is my problem, not yours,' she reminded him.

He stood as she left the table, feeling worse than when he waited for The Mouse. She surprised him by looking back at him in the doorway, a smile on her face, as though their curious meal would be a memory to warm her.

'That is that,' he said under his breath, feeling as though some cosmic titan had poked a straw under his skin and sucked out all his juices. It was an odd feeling, and he didn't like it.

With each step she took from the Drake, Sally Paul lost her nerve. She found a stone bench by the Cattewater and sat there, trying to regain the equilibrium that had deserted her when she was out of Admiral Bright's sight. The June sun warmed her cheek and she raised her face to it, glorying in summer after a dismal winter of tending a querulous old woman who had been deserted by her family, because she had not treated them well when she was able and could have.

Let this be a lesson to me, Sally had thought over and over that winter, except that there was no one to show any kindness to, no one left that being kind to now would mean dividends later on, when she was old and dying. Her husband was gone these five years, a suicide as a result of being unable to stand up to charges levelled at him by the Admiralty. The Royal Navy, in its vindictiveness, had left her with nothing but her small son, Peter. A cold lodging house had finished him.

She sobbed out loud, then looked around, hopeful that no one had heard her. Even harder than her husband's death by his own hand—mercifully, he had hanged himself in an outbuilding and someone else had found him—was her son's death of cold and hunger, when she could do nothing but suffer alone. She had been his only mourner at his pauper's unmarked grave, but she had mourned as thoroughly and completely as if a whole throng of relatives had sent him to a good rest.

There was no one to turn to in Dundrennan, where her late father had been a half-hearted solicitor. The Paul name didn't shine so brightly in that part of Scotland, considering her father's younger brother, John, who had joined American revolutionaries, added Jones to his name and become a hated word in England. This far south, though, it was a better name than Daviess, the name she had shared with Andrew, principal victualler to the Portsmouth yard who had been brought up on charges of pocketing profit from bad meat that had killed half a squadron.

She had no other resource to call upon. *I could throw myself into the water,* she told herself, *except that someone would probably rescue me. Besides, I can swim, and I am not inclined to end my life that way. I could go to the workhouse. I could try every public kitchen in Plymouth and see if they need help. I could marry Admiral Bright.*

She went to the registry first, joining a line by the door. The pale governess who had shared a seat with her on the mail coach came away with nothing. The bleak expression on her face told Sally what her own reception would be. The registrar—not an unkind man—did say Stonehouse Naval Hospital might still be looking for laundresses, but there was no way of knowing, unless she chose to walk four miles to Devonport.

'It's a slow season, what with peace putting many here out of work. You might consider going north to the mills,' he told Sally. When she asked him how she would get there, he shrugged.

Dratted peace had slowed down the entire economy of Plymouth, so there was no demand for even the lowliest kitchen help in the hotels, she discovered, after trudging

from back door to back door. One publican had been willing to hire her to replace his pots-and-pans girl, but one
look at that terrified child's face told Sally she could never
be so callous. 'I won't take bread from a baby's mouth,'
she said.

'Suit yourself,' the man had said as he turned away.

Evensong was long over and the church was deserted.
She sank down wearily on a back pew. When her money
had run out two days ago, she had slept in Bath's cathe-
dral. It had been easy enough to make herself small in the
shadows and then lie down out of sight. St Andrew's was
smaller, but there were shadows. She could hide herself
again.

And then what? In the morning, if no one was about,
she would dip her remaining clean handkerchief in the holy
water, wipe her face and ask directions to the workhouse.
At least her small son was safe from such a place.

There were several prayer books in their slots. Sally
gathered them up, made a pillow of them and rested her
head on them with a sigh. There wasn't any need to loosen
her dress because it was already loose. She feared to take
off her shoes because she knew her feet were swollen. She
might never get them on again. She made herself comfortable on the bench and closed her eyes.

Sally opened her eyes with a start only minutes later.
A man sat on the end of the row. Frightened at first, she
looked closer in the gloom at his close-cut hair and smiled
to herself. She sat up.

He didn't look at her, but idly scratched the back of his
only hand with his hook. 'The Mouse still hasn't turned
up.'

'You have probably waited long enough,' Sally said
as she arranged her skirt around her, grateful she hadn't

removed her shoes. 'I don't know what the statute of limitations is on such a matter, but surely you have fulfilled it.'

He rested his elbows on the back of the pew, still not looking at her. 'Actually, I was looking for you, Mrs Paul. The waiter informed me that you left your valise in the chair.'

'I suppose I did,' she said. 'There's nothing in it of value.' She peered at him through the gloom. 'Why did the waiter think I was your responsibility?'

He glanced at her then. 'Possibly because earlier I had told him you were my cousin, and we were on the outs, and I was hoping to get into your good graces by buying you dinner.'

'That was certainly creative, Admiral,' she said.

'Dash it all, how am I supposed to approach a single female I have never met before?' he said. She couldn't help but hear the exasperation in his voice. 'Mrs Paul, you are more trouble than an entire roomful of midshipmen!'

'Oh, surely not,' she murmured, amused in spite of her predicament. She glanced at him, then stared straight ahead towards the altar, the same way he stared.

There they sat. He spoke first. 'When you didn't come out of St Andrew's, I thought you might not mind some company.' His voice grew softer. 'Have you been sleeping in churches?'

'It…it's a safe place.'

He hadn't changed his position. He did not move any closer. 'Mrs Paul, my sisters are still meddlers, my chef is still on strike, I can't get any builders to do what they promised, the house is…strange and I swear there are bats or maybe griffons in the attic.'

'What a daunting prospect.'

'I would honestly rather sail into battle than deal with any of the above.'

'Especially the griffons,' she said, taking a deep breath. *Am I this desperate? Is he?* she asked herself. *This man is—or was—an admiral. He is either a lunatic or the kindest man in the universe.*

'What say you, Mrs Paul?' He still didn't look in her direction, as though afraid she would bolt like a startled fawn. 'You'll have a home, a touchy chef, two dragons for sisters-in-law, and a one-armed husband who will need your assistance occasionally with buttons, or maybe putting sealing wax on a letter. Small things. If you can keep the dragons at bay, and keep the admiral out of trouble on land, he promises to let you be. It's not a bad offer.'

'No, it isn't,' she replied, after a long pause in which she could have sworn he held his breath. She just couldn't speak. It was beyond her that anyone would do this. She could only stare at him.

He gazed back. When he spoke, he sounded so rational she had to listen. 'Mrs Paul, The Mouse isn't coming. I want to marry you.'

'Why, Admiral? Tell me why?' There, she had asked. He had to tell her.

He took his time, exasperating man. 'Mrs Paul, even if The Mouse were to show up this minute, I would bow out. She's a spinster, and that's unfortunate, but she has a brother to take care of her, no matter how he might grumble. You have no one.' He held up his hand to stop her words. 'I have spent most of my life looking after England. One doesn't just chop off such a responsibility. Maybe it didn't end with Napoleon on St. Helena and my retirement papers. Knowing your dilemma, I cannot turn my back on you, no more than I could ever ignore a sister ship approaching a lee shore. You need help. I need a wife. I don't think I can make it any plainer.'

'No, I suppose you cannot,' she murmured, but made

one final attempt to make the man see reason. 'Admiral, you know nothing about me. You truly don't.' It was on the tip of her tongue to tell him, but she found she could not. *Coward*, she thought.

He looked at her then, and his face was kind. 'I know one thing: you haven't wittered once about the weather. I suppose marriages have started on stranger footings. I don't know when or where, but I haven't been on land much in the past twenty years.'

'I suppose they have,' she agreed. 'Very well, sir.'

Chapter Three

Sally didn't object when the admiral paid for a room at the Drake for her, after suggesting the priest at St Andrew's might be irritated to perform a wedding so late, even with a special licence. And there were other concerns.

'I must remind you, sir, I'm not The Mouse. I cannot usurp her name, which surely is already on the licence,' she pointed out, embarrassed to state the obvious, but always the practical one.

Admiral Bright chuckled. 'It's no problem, Mrs Paul. The Mouse's name is Prunella Batchthorpe. Believe it or not, I can spell Batchthorpe. It was Prunella that gave me trouble. Prunella? Prunilla? A coin or two, and the clerk was happy enough to leave the space blank, for me to fill in later.'

'Very well, then,' Sally murmured.

She was hungry for supper, but had trouble swallowing the food, when it came. Finally, she laid down her fork. 'Admiral, you need to know something about me,' she said.

He set down his fork, too. 'I should tell you more about me, too.'

How much to say? She thought a moment, then plunged ahead. 'Five years ago, my husband committed suicide after a reversal of fortune. I ended up in one room with our son, Peter, who was five at the time.'

She looked at the admiral for some sign of disgust at this, but all she saw was sympathy. It gave her the courage to continue. 'Poor Peter. I could not even afford coal to keep the room warm. He caught a chill, it settled in his lungs and he died.'

'You had no money for a doctor?' he asked gently.

'Not a farthing. I tried every poultice I knew, but nothing worked.' She could not help the sob that rose in her throat. 'And the whole time, Peter trusted me to make him better!'

She didn't know how it happened, but the admiral's hand went to her neck, caressing it until she gained control of herself. 'He was covered in quicklime in a pauper's grave. I found a position that afternoon as a lady's companion and never returned to that horrid room.'

'I am so sorry,' he said. 'There wasn't anyone you could turn to?'

'No,' she said, after blowing her nose on the handkerchief he handed her. 'After my husband was…accused…we had not a friend in the world.' She looked at him, wondering what to say. 'It was all a mistake, a lie and a cover-up, but we have suffered.'

Admiral Bright sat back in his chair. 'Mrs Paul, people ask me how I could bear to stay so many years at sea. Unlike my captains who occasionally went into port, I remained almost constantly with the fleet. We had one

enemy—France—and not the myriad of enemies innocent people attract, sometimes in the course of everyday
business on land, or so I suspect. My sisters have never
understood why I prefer the sea.'

'Surely there are scoundrels at sea—I mean, in addition
to the French,' she said.

'Of course there are, Mrs P. The world is full of them.
It's given me great satisfaction to hang a few.'

She couldn't help herself; she shuddered.

'They deserved it. The hangings never cost me any sleep,
because I made damned sure they were guilty.' He looked
into her eyes. 'Mrs Paul, I cannot deny that I enjoyed the
power, but I have never intentionally wronged anyone.'

*Too bad you were not on the Admiralty court that con-
victed my husband*, she thought. *Or would you have heard
the evidence and convicted, too?* She knew there was no
way of knowing. She had not been allowed in the chambers. Best put it to rest.

'I have the skills to manage your household,' she told
him, when he had resumed eating. 'I'm quite frugal, you
know.'

'With a charming brogue betraying your origins, could
you be anything else?'

'Now, sir, you know that is a stereotype!' she scolded.
'My own father hadn't a clue what to do with a shilling,
and he could outroll my *rrr*'s any day.' She smiled at the
admiral, liking the way he picked up his napkin with the
hook and wiped his lips. 'But I am good with funds.'

'So am I, Mrs P.,' he said, putting down the napkin.
'Napoleon has made me rich, so you needn't squeeze the
shillings so hard that they beg for mercy! I'll see that you
have a good allowance, too.'

'That isn't necessary,' she said quickly. 'I've done with

so little for so long that I probably wouldn't know what to
do with an allowance.'

He looked at his timepiece. 'Past my bedtime. Call it a
bribe then, Mrs P. Wait until you see the estate I am foist-
ing on you!' He grew serious quickly. 'There is plenty
of money for coal, though.' With his hook, he casually
twirled a lock of her hair that had come loose. 'I think
your fortunes have turned, my dear.'

It was funny. The hook was so close to her face, but
she felt no urge to flinch. She reached up and touched it,
twining the curl further around it.

'My hook doesn't disgust you?' he asked, startled.

'Heavens, no,' she replied. 'How did you lose your hand?
And, no, I'm not going to be frippery again and suggest
you were careless.'

He pulled his hook through the curl, patted it against her
cheek and grinned at her. 'You do have a mouth on you,
Mrs Paul. Most people are so cowed by my admiralness
that I find them dull.'

'I am not among them, I suppose. After your taradiddle
about being my cousin, I think you are probably as faulty
and frail as most of humanity.' She sat back, amazed at herself for such a forthright utterance. She had never spoken
to Andrew that way, but something about Charles Bright
made him a conversational wellspring as challenging as
he was fun to listen to.

'Touché!' He looked down at his hook. 'I was but a first
mate when this happened, so it has been years since I've
had ten fingernails to trim.'

She laughed. 'Think of the economy!'

He rolled his eyes at her. 'There you go again, being a
Scot.'

'Guilty as charged, Admiral.'

'I wish I could tell you it was some battle where

England's fate hung in the balance, but it was a training accident. We were engaged in target practice off the coast of Brazil when one of my guns exploded. Since it was my gun crew, I went to lend a hand.' He made a face. 'Poor choice of words! The pulley rope that yanks the gun back after discharge was tangled. I untangled it at the same time it came loose. Pinched off my left hand so fast I didn't know it had happened, until the powder monkey mentioned that I was spouting. Mrs P, don't get all pale on me. We had an excellent surgeon on board, almost as talented as the smithy who built me my first hook.'

'You never thought about leaving the navy?'

'Over a hand? Really, madam.'

'How do you keep it on?'

She was hard put to define his expression then. She could have sworn there was something close to gratitude in his eyes, as though he was pleased she cared enough to ask such a forwards question.

'Apart from eight-year-old boys, you're the first person who ever asked.'

'I'm curious.'

'I'll show you later. There's a leather contraption that crosses my chest and anchors to my neck.' As she watched, he tilted his head, pulled at his neckcloth and exposed a thin strap. 'See? If ever my steward is gone or busy, you might have to help me get out of it. Are you any good at tying neckcloths?'

'I've tied a few,' she said.

'Good. You might have to tie more. Beyond that, I'm not too helpless.'

'Helpless is not a word I would ever use in the same breath with your admiralness.'

'What a relief that is, Mrs P,' he said. 'Where were we?'

'Something about you?'

'Ah, yes. I was born forty-five years ago in Bristol. My father was a successful barrister who could not understand why I wanted to go to sea. He made arrangements and I shipped aboard as a young gentleman at the age of ten. My older sisters are Frances—I call her Fan, or Fannie—and Dora, who follows where Fannie leads. Both married well and both have outlived their husbands, which means I am ripe for meddling from them.' He shuddered elaborately.

'Any interesting avocations, now that you are retired?'

'Not yet. Mrs Paul, your eyelids are drooping.' He stood up. 'I will retire now and leave you to your chamber. Do you think nine of the clock tomorrow morning is too early to bother the vicar at St Andrew's?'

'I should think not.' She looked up at him, a frown on her face. 'You don't have to go through with this, you know.'

'I believe I do.' He bent down then, and she thought for one moment he was going to kiss her. Instead, he rubbed his cheek against hers, and she smiled to feel whiskers against her face. It had been so long. 'Mrs Paul, you need help and I need a wife. I promise you I will cause you no anxiety or ever force myself on you without your utmost consent and enthusiasm, should you or I ever advance this marriage into something more...well, what...visceral. Is that plain enough?'

It was. She nodded. Then he did kiss her, but only her cheek.

'Very well, then, Admiral. I will be an extraordinarily excellent wife.'

'I rather thought so,' he said as he went to the door and gave her a little bow. She laughed when he kissed his hook and blew in her direction, then left the room.

'You are certainly an original,' she said quietly. She sat at the table a few minutes longer, eating one of the remaining plums, then just looking at the food. It was only the smallest kind of stopgap between actual dinner and breakfast, but she had not seen so much food in front of her in years. 'What a strange day this has been, Admiral,' she whispered.

She didn't sleep a wink, but hadn't thought she would, considering the strangeness of her situation. She spent much of the night debating whether to tell her future husband that her married name was Daviess, but decided against it, as dawn broke. He knew her as Mrs Paul, and what difference could it make? She had resolved several years ago not to look back.

When the 'tween-stairs girl made a fire in the grate and brought a can of hot water, Sally asked for a bath, hoping the admiral wouldn't object to the added expense on his bill. When the tub and water came, she sank into it with pleasure.

She left the tub after the water cooled. With a towel wrapped around her, she pulled out the pasteboard folder from her valise and extracted her copy of the marriage lines to Andrew Daviess, and his death certificate, reading again the severe line: 'Death by own hand.' Poor, dear man. 'Andrew, why didn't you think it through one more time?' she asked the document. 'We could have emigrated to Canada, or even the United States.'

With a sigh, she dried herself off and stood a moment in front of the coal fire. The towel fell to the floor and she stood there naked until she felt capable of movement. She looked in the mirror, fingering her stretch marks and frowning over her ribs in high relief when she raised her arms. 'Sally, you'll eat better at Admiral Bright's estate,' she told her reflection. 'You are just an empty sack now.'

She was in no mood to begin a marriage with someone she did not know, but there didn't seem to be anything else to do. She dressed quickly, wishing she had a better garment for the occasion. She shook out a muslin dress from the valise, one she had worn many times, and took it and the pasteboard folder downstairs. She left the dress with the parlour maid, asking that someone iron it for her, then let herself out of the Drake.

It was still early; no one was about in the street except fishmongers and victuallers hauling kegs of food on wheelbarrows. From her life in Portsmouth as Andrew Daviess's wife, she knew he had been efficient in his profession, even up to the shocking day he was accused by the Admiralty of felony and manslaughter in knowingly loading bad food aboard ships. In the months of suspended animation that followed, she had seen him shaking his head over and over at the venality of his superior, whom he suspected of doctoring the all-important and lucrative accounts to make the errors Andrew's alone. He could prove nothing, of course, because his superior had moved too fast.

And finally Andrew could take it no longer, hanging himself from a beam in their carriage house, empty of horses since they could no longer afford them and pay a barrister, too. He left no note to her, but only one he had sent to the Lord Admiral proclaiming his innocence, even as his suicide seemed to mock his words.

Now the whole matter was over and done. She knew that by marrying the admiral, who had no idea what a kettle of fish he had inherited and with any luck never would, her life with Andrew Daviess was irrevocably over.

When she arrived at St Andrew's, the vicar was concluding the earliest service. She approached him when he finished, explaining that in another hour, she and a gentleman would be returning with a special licence.

'I am a widow, sir,' she said, handing him the pasteboard folder. 'Here are my earlier marriage lines and my late husband's death certificate. Is there anything else you need from me?'

The old man took the folder and looked inside. 'Sophia Paul Daviess, spinster from Dundrennan, Kirkcudbrightshire, Scotland, age twenty-two years, 1806'. He looked at Andrew's death certificate, shaking his head, so she knew he had read the part about 'Death by his own hand'. He handed the document back. 'A sad affair, Mrs Daviess.'

'It was.'

'And now you are marrying again. I wish you all success, madam.'

'Thank you, sir.' She hesitated. 'For reasons which you must appreciate, I have been using my maiden name, rather than my married name.'

He walked with her to the door. 'I can imagine there has been some stigma to a suicide, Mrs Paul.'

If you only knew, she thought. 'There has been,' was all she said.

'Those days appear to be ending. I'll look forwards to seeing you again in an hour.' The vicar held out his hand. 'If you wish, I can enter this information in the registry right now, so you needn't be reminded of it during this next wedding.'

It was precisely what she wanted. 'Thank you, sir.'

As she returned to the Drake, she looked up to the first storey and saw the admiral looking out. He waved to her and she waved back, wondering how long he had been watching and if he had seen her leave the hotel.

When she came up the stairs to the first floor, he opened

his door. 'You gave me a fright, Mrs Paul, when I knocked on your door and you weren't there. I reckoned you had gone the way of The Mouse, and that would have been more than my fragile esteem could manage.'

'Oh, no, sir. I would not go back on my word, once given,' she assured him.

'I thought as much,' he said, 'especially after the 'tween-stairs maid said you had left a dress belowdeck to be ironed.' He thumped his chest with his hook, which made Sally smile. 'What a relief.'

'I went ahead to the church with my marriage lines and Andrew's death certificate. I thought he might want to see them and perhaps record them. Such proved to be the case.'

'So efficient, Mrs Paul,' he murmured. 'I shall be spoiled.'

Not so much efficient as ashamed for you to see that certificate, she thought. *Oh, seek a lighter subject, Sally.* 'That's it, sir. I will spoil you like my old ladies—prunes in massive amounts, thoroughly soaked for easy chewing, and at least a chapter a day of some improving literature such as, such as…'

'I know: "The prevention of self-abuse during long sea voyages",' he joked, then held up his hand to ward off her open-mouthed, wide-eyed stare. 'I do not joke, Mrs P! You would be amazed what do-gooders in the vicinity of the fleet think is important.'

She laughed out loud, then covered her mouth in embarrassment that she even knew what he was talking about.

'I was a frigate captain then. I preserved a copy of that remarkable document and asked all my wardroom mates to sign it. The purser even added some salacious illustrations, so perhaps I will not let you see it until you are forty or fifty, at least.'

She couldn't think of a single retort.

'What? No witty comeback?' There was no denying the triumph in his eyes.

'Not to that, sir,' she admitted. 'Perhaps I will not read you improving chapters of *anything*.'

She was spared further embarrassment by the 'tween-stairs maid, who brought her ironed dress upstairs and shyly handed it to her. Admiral Bright gave the little girl a few coins before she left.

Sally went into her own room and put on the dress, but not before wishing it would magically turn into a gown of magnificent proportions. *Just as well it does not*, she scolded herself as she attempted to button up the back. *I don't have the bosom to hold it up right now.*

She also remembered why she hadn't worn the dress in ages. By twisting around, she managed to do up the lower and upper buttons, but the ones in the middle were out of reach. She stood in silence, then realised there was nothing to do but enlist the admiral. She knocked on the door. She felt the blush leap to her face, even as she scolded herself for such missish behaviour, considering that in less than an hour, she was going to marry this man.

'Admiral, can you possibly tackle the buttons in the middle of this dratted dress? Either that, or call back the 'tween-stairs maid.' She looked at his hook and frowned. 'Oh, dear. I forgot.'

Admiral Bright was obviously made of sterner stuff. He came into her room and closed the door behind him. 'What? You think I cannot accomplish this simple task? Who on earth do you think buttons my trousers every morning? Turn around and prepare to be amazed.'

She did as he said, her cheeks on fire. He pressed the flat curve on his hook against her back to anchor the fabric, then pushed each button through, his knuckles light against her bare skin.

'No applause needed,' he said. 'Turn around and stop being so embarrassed.'

She did as he said. 'You're going to wish The Mouse had showed up.'

'No, indeed, madam. I have something for you, and you will have to manage this yourself.'

He took a small sack out of his coat front and handed it to her. 'I got this in India. It should look especially nice against that light blue fabric.'

Holding her breath, Sally took out a gold chain with a single ruby on it.

'You can breathe, Mrs Paul,' he advised. She could tell by his voice how pleased he was with her reaction.

'I wish I had something for you,' she whispered as she turned the necklace over in her hand.

'Considering that this time yesterday, you thought you were going to be tending an old lady with skinflint relatives, I am hardly surprised. Come, come. Put it on. I can't help you with the clasp.'

She did as he said, clasping the fiery little gem about her neck where it hung against her breast bone. Suddenly, the old dress didn't seem so ordinary. She couldn't even feel the place in her shoes where the leather had worn through.

'It's not very big, but I always admired the fire in that little package,' he told her, half in apology, partly in pride.

She could feel the admiral surveying her, and she raised her chin a little higher, convinced she could pass any muster, short of a presentation at court. All because of a little ruby necklace. She touched it, then looked at Admiral Bright. 'You deserve someone far more exciting than me,' she said.

He surprised her by not uttering a single witticism, he whom she already knew possessed many. 'You'll do, Sally Paul,' he said gruffly and offered her his arm. 'Let's get spliced. A ruby is small potatoes, compared to the favour you're doing me of shielding me for evermore from my sisters!'

Chapter Four

They were married at half past nine in St Andrew's Church, where some three centuries earlier, and under different ecclesiastical management, Catherine of Aragon had knelt after a long sea voyage and offered thanks for safe passage. Sally could appreciate the mood and the moment. When the vicar pronounced them husband and wife, she felt a gentle mantle of protection cover her to replace the shawl of lead she had been carrying around for years. She couldn't have explained the feeling to anyone, and she doubted the admiral would understand. She was too shy to expand on it, so she kept the moment to herself.

Truth to tell, she hoped for better success than Catherine of Aragon. After the brief ceremony, when the young vicar chatted a bit mindlessly—obviously he hadn't married a couple with so little fanfare before—Sally couldn't help but think of her Catholic Majesty, gone to England to marry one man, and ending up a scant few years later with his brother, Henry.

* * *

She mentioned it to the admiral over breakfast at the Drake. 'Do you not see a parallel? You came here to marry The Mouse, and you ended up with the lady's companion. Perhaps Catherine of Aragon started a trend.'

The admiral laughed. 'If it's a trend, it's a slow-moving one.' He leaned forwards over the buttered toast. 'What should I call you? I've become fond of Mrs P, but now it's Mrs B. And I had no idea your name was actually Sophia, which I rather like. How about it, Sophia Bright?'

She felt suddenly shy, as though everyone in the dining room was staring at the ring on her finger, which seemed to grow heavier and heavier until it nearly required a sling. 'No one has ever called me Sophia, but I like it.'

'Sophia, then. What about me? You really shouldn't persist in calling me admiral. Seems a bit stodgy and you don't look like a midshipman. Charles? Charlie?'

She thought about it. 'I don't think I know you well enough for "Charles". Maybe I'll call you "Mr Bright", while I think about it.'

'Fair enough.' He peered more closely at the ring he had put on her finger in the church. 'It's a dashed plain ring.' He slid it up her finger. 'Rather too large. H'mm. What was good enough for The Mouse doesn't quite work for you.' He patted her hand. 'You can think about my name, and I can think about that ring, Sophia.'

Now I am Sophia Bright, where only yesterday I was Sally Paul, she thought as she finished eating. *No one will know me.* While he spoke to the waiter, she looked over at her new husband with different eyes. There was no denying his air of command. Everything about him exuded confidence and she felt some envy.

He was certainly no Adonis; too many years had come and gone for that. His nose was straight and sharp, but his lips were the softest feature on his face. Such a ready smile, too. He reminded her of an uncle, long dead now, who could command a room by merely entering it. She began to feel a certain pride in her unexpected association with this man beside her. After the past five years of shame and humiliation, she almost didn't recognise the emotion.

He had no qualms about gesturing with his hook. If he had lived with the thing since his lieutenant days, then it was second nature, and not something to hide. She looked around the dining room. No one was staring at him, but this was Plymouth, where seamen with parts missing were more common than in Bath, or Oxford. *This is my husband*, she wanted to say, she who barely knew him. *He is mine*. The idea was altogether intoxicating and it made her blush.

He had hired a post chaise for the ride home. 'I…we… are only three miles from Plymouth proper. I suppose I shall get a carriage, and that will mean horses, with which I have scant acquaintance,' he told her. 'It's going to be hard for me to cut a dashing figure atop a horse.' He shrugged. 'I wouldn't know a good horse if it bit me…which it will, probably.'

Sally put her hand to her mouth to keep in the laugh. With a twinkle in his eyes, the admiral took her hand away. 'It is a funny image, Sophia,' he said. 'Go ahead and laugh. I imagine years and years of midshipmen would love to see such a sight. And probably most of my captains, too.'

He fell silent then, as they drove inland for a mile, over the route she had taken on foot only yesterday. *How odd*, she thought. *It seems like years ago already, when I was Sally Paul.*

He was gazing intently out the window and she wondered why, until the ocean came in sight again and he sat back with a sigh. *He misses it*, she thought, *even if it is only a matter of a few miles.*

'You miss the ocean, don't you?'

He nodded. 'I thought I would not. After I retired, I spent some weeks in Yorkshire, visiting an old shipmate far inland—well, I was hiding from Fannie and Dora. What a miserable time! Yes, I miss the ocean when I do not see it.' He looked her in the eye. 'Did you ever meet a bigger fool?'

'Probably not,' she replied, her voice soft, which made the admiral blush—something she doubted he did very often. 'It it amazing what revelation comes out, after the ring goes on.'

'I suppose you have deep, dark secrets, too,' he told her, good humour in his voice, as if he could not imagine such a thing.

He had come closer to the mark than was comfortable, and she wished again she had told him her real married name. It was too late now. She would have to hope the matter would never come up. Sally returned some sort of nonsensical reply that she forgot as soon as it left her lips, but which must have satisfied the man. His gaze returned to the view out the chaise window.

'I do have a confession,' he said, as the post chaise slowed and turned into a lane which must have been lovely at one time, but which now was overgrown and rutted.

It can't be worse than my omission, she thought. 'I'm all a-tremble,' she said, feeling like the biggest hypocrite who ever wore shoe leather.

He chuckled, and touched her knee with his hook. 'Sophia, I promise you I do not have a harem in Baghdad— too far from the coast—or an evil twin locked in the attic.' He didn't quite meet her gaze. 'You'll see soon enough.

How to put this? I didn't precisely buy this property for the manor.'

He had timed his confession perfectly. The coachman slowed his horses even more on the last turn, and then the estate came into view. What probably should have been a graceful lawn sloping towards a bluff overlooking a sterling view of Plymouth Sound was a tangle of weeds and overgrown bushes.

The admiral was watching her expression, so Sally did her best to keep it entirely neutral. 'It appears you could use an entire herd of sheep,' she murmured. 'And possibly an army equipped with scythes.'

She looked closer, towards the front door, and her eyes widened. She put her hand to her mouth in astonishment. Rising out of a clump of undergrowth worthy almost of the Amazon was a naked figure. 'Good heavens,' she managed. 'Is that supposed to be Venus?'

'Hard to say. You can't see it from here, but she seems to be standing on what is a sea shell. Or maybe it is a cow patty,' the admiral said. He coughed.

There she stood, one ill-proportioned hand modestly over her genitals. Sally looked closer, then blushed. The hand wasn't over her privates as much as inside them. The statue's mouth was open, and she appeared to be thinking naughty thoughts.

'I think this might be Penelope, and her husband has been gone a long time,' Sally said finally.

She didn't dare look at the admiral, but she had no urge to continue staring at a statue so obviously occupied with business of a personal nature. She gulped. 'A very long time.'

'No doubt about it,' the admiral said, and he sounded like he was strangling.

I don't dare look at him, else I will fall on the floor in a fit of laughter, and then what will he think? Sally told herself. And then she couldn't help herself. The laughter rolled out of its own accord and she clutched her sides. When she could finally bring herself to look at the admiral, he was wiping his eyes.

'Mrs Bright, you would be even more shocked to know there was a companion statue on the other side of the door. Let me just say it was a man, and leave it at that.'

'Wise of you,' she murmured, and went off in another gust of laughter. When she could muster a coherent thought, Sally realised it had been years and years since she had laughed at all, let alone so hard.

'What happened to…ah…Romeo?' she asked.

'My steward—you would probably call him my butler—whacked him off at the ankles. I suppose he hasn't had time to get around to the lady.'

The admiral left the post chaise first. She took his hand as he helped her out. 'I can scarcely imagine what delights await me indoors,' Sally said.

'Oh, I think you can,' was all he would say, as he put his hand under her elbow and helped her up the steps. 'Careful now. I should probably carry you over the threshold, Mrs Admiral Sir Charles Bright, but you will observe the front steps are wobbly.'

'I shall insist upon it when the steps are fixed.'

'Oh, you will?' he asked, and then kissed her cheek. 'Hopefully, our relationship will continue after your first view of the entry hall.' He opened the door with a flourish. 'Feast your eyes, madam wife.'

The hall itself appeared dingy, the walls discoloured from years of neglect, but the ceiling drew her eyes upwards immediately. Her mouth fell open. She stepped back involuntarily and her husband's arm seemed to naturally encircle her waist.

'At the risk of ruining my credit with you for ever, Sophia, I saw a ceiling like this once in a Naples bawdy house.'

'I don't doubt that for a minute!' she declared, looking around at a ceiling full of cupids engaged in activities the statue out front had probably never even dreamed of. 'Over there...what on earth...? Oh, my goodness.' Sally put her hands to her cheeks, feeling their warmth. She turned around and took her husband by the lapels of his coat. 'Mr Bright, who on *earth* owned this house?'

'The estate agent described him as an earl—the sorry end of a long line of earls—who had roughly one thing on his mind. Apparently, in early summer, the old roué used to indulge in the most amazing debaucheries in this house. After that, he closed up the place and retreated to his London lodgings.'

She couldn't help herself. She leaned her forehead against her new husband's chest. His arms went around her and she felt his hook against her waist. 'There had better be a very good reason that a man of sound mind— I'm speaking of you—would buy such a house, Admiral Bright.'

'Oh, dear,' he murmured into her hair. 'Not two minutes inside your new home and I am back to "admiral".' He took her hand. 'Yes, there is a good reason. Humour me another moment.'

She followed where he led, her hand in his, down the hall with its more-than-naughty inmates high above, and out through the French doors into the garden, which was as ill used as the front lawn. Beyond a thoroughly ugly gazebo was the wide and—today—serene expanse of the ocean. It filled the horizon with a deep blue that blended into the early summer sky. Sea birds wheeled and called overhead and she could hear waves breaking on the rocks below. In the distance, a ship under full sail seemed to skim the water as it made for Plymouth.

The admiral released her hand. 'One look at this and I knew I would never find another place so lovely. What do you think, Sophia? Should I tear down the house and rebuild?'

She turned around and looked at her new home, sturdy with stone that might have once been painted a pastel; elegant French doors that opened on to a fine terrace; wide, floor-to-ceiling windows that would be wonderful to stand behind, when the day was stormy and still the ocean beckoned.

'No. It's a good house. Once a little—a lot—of paint is applied.'

'My thoughts precisely. I got it for a song.'

She had to smile at that. 'I'm surprised the estate agent didn't pay *you* to take it off his hands! Have your sisters been here?'

'Once. Fannie had to wave burnt feathers under Dora's nose, and they were gone the next morning before it was even light. I confess I haven't done anything to the house since, because they assured me they would never return until I did. Until now.' He sighed and tugged her over to the terrace's stone railing, where they sat. 'It worked for a few months, but even these imps from hell weren't strong enough to ward off the curse of women with too much time on their hands. Fannie is planning to redecorate in an Egyptian style, and Dora tags along.'

'When?'

'Any day now, which is why my cook is on strike and...' He put his hook to his ear, which made her smile. 'Hark! I hear the thump-tap of my steward. Here he is, my steward through many a battle. John Starkey, may I introduce my wife, Mrs Bright?'

Yesterday, she might have been startled, but not today. From his peg leg to his eye patch, John Starkey was everything a butler was not. All he lacked was a parrot on his shoulder. If he had opened his mouth and exhibited only one, lonely tooth, she would not have been surprised. As it was, he had a full set of teeth and a gentle smile, even a shy one. She looked from the admiral to his steward, realising all over again that these were men not much used to the ameliorating company of women.

But his smile was genuine. She nodded her head. 'Starkey, I am delighted to make your acquaintance. Is this the strangest place you have ever lived?'

'Aye, madam.'

'But you would follow the admiral anywhere, I take it.'

He looked faintly surprised. 'I already have, Mrs Bright,' he replied, which told her volumes about a world of war she would never know. It touched her more than anything else he could have said.

'Starkey answers the front door, polishes my best hook— and any other silver we might have lying around—decants wine with the best of them and never considers any command too strange,' the admiral said. 'Starkey, the naked woman in the front yard will have to go. Lively now.'

'Aye, aye, sir.' He knuckled his forehead. 'I ran out of time.' He bowed to them both and left the terrace. In a few minutes, Sally heard the sound of chopping.

'I'm low on servants,' he told her as he got off the railing and started for the French doors. She followed. 'That will be your task. Go back to Plymouth and hire whomever you think we need.'

She walked with him slowly back down the hall, neither of them looking up. He paused before a closed door. 'This is my—our—library.'

'Wonderful! I was hoping the house had one.' Sally started forwards, but the admiral neatly hooked the sash on the back of her dress and reeled her in.

'Over my prone and desiccated corpse, Sophia,' he said. 'If you think *these* cherubs are…ah…interesting, you'll be fair shocked by the walls in here. And the books. And the busts.' He winced. 'I've never seen such a collection of ribaldry under one roof. The earl seemed to prefer illustrations to words.'

'My blushes,' Sally said.

'Mine, too, and I consider myself a pretty normal navy man.' He laughed softly. 'The old earl has me beat! I looked through one book and found myself darting glances over my shoulder, hoping my mother—she's been dead nearly forty years—wasn't standing close enough to box my ears and send me to bed without any supper.' He removed his hook from the back of her dress. 'I'm not a man who believes in book burning, but I'm going to make an exception, in this case. We'll make an evening of it.'

He continued down the hall, and she followed, shaking her head. He stopped before another door. 'Speaking of meat…this is the way belowdeck to the galley.' He straightened his shabby coat. 'In case you are wondering, I am girding my loins. My cook is down there—don't forget he is on strike.'

Sally stared at the door, and back at her husband. 'Is he *that* terrifying?'

'Let us just say he is French.' He peered closer. 'Right now, you are probably asking yourself how on earth you let yourself be talked into marriage to a certified lunatic and life in a house of, well, if not ill repute, then very bad art.'

He started to say something else, but he was interrupted by a crack from the front entrance and the sound of bushes shaking. 'I think Penelope has more on her tiny mind now than Odysseus's continued absence,' Bright murmured. 'I will choose discretion over valour, and not even ask what you think of all this.'

You would be surprised, Admiral, she thought. *I have never been so diverted.* Sally took his arm and opened the door. 'I think it is time I met your cook.'

Chapter Five

'His name is Etienne Dupuis, and I won him with a high card after the Battle of Trafalgar,' the admiral whispered as they went quietly down the stairs. 'He was the best cook in the fleet, but he can be moody at times.'

'This is one of those times, I take it,' Sally whispered back. 'Why are we whispering?'

'He told me if I ever allowed my sisters here again, he would leave me to Starkey's cooking and return to La Belle France.'

'And would he?'

'I don't intend to find out.' His lips were close to her ear, and she felt a little shiver down her spine. 'Let us see how charming you can be, Mrs Bright.'

They came into a pleasant-sized servants' hall. Thankfully, there were no cupids painted on these walls, but all was dark. The Rumford didn't look as though there had been a fire lit for several days.

'I think we're too late,' she whispered, not minding a

bit that the admiral had pulled her close. 'See here, sir, are you more afraid than I am?'

'Absolutely,' he told her. 'You didn't know you had married the coward of the Blue Fleet, did you? Good thing there was no Yellow Fleet. Stay close, Sophia. He threw a cleaver at me once.'

'Goodness! In that case, I think I should stay far away!'

He took her hand and towed her further into the kitchen. 'Etienne? I want you to meet my wife. She is the kindest creature in the galaxy.'

Sally smiled. 'You don't even know me,' she whispered into his shoulder.

'I think I do,' he told her, raising her hand in his and kissing it. 'You've been here twenty minutes at least, and you haven't run screaming away from this den of iniquity I purchased. I call that a kindness. Etienne? She's nothing like my sisters. Can we declare a truce?'

The admiral nodded towards the fireplace and a high-backed chair, where a little puff of smoke plumed. The man in the chair—she could see only his feet—didn't move or say anything. He cleared his throat and continued to puff.

'He's more than usually stubborn,' Bright whispered.

'He sounds very much like the old ladies I tended,' Sally whispered back. She released her grip on the admiral. 'Let me see what I can do.' She couldn't help herself. 'What is it worth to you, sir?' she teased.

Before he spoke, the admiral gave her such a look that she felt her stomach grow warm. 'How about a wedding ring that fits?' he asked at last, with the humorous look she was used to already, the one that challenged her to match his wit.

'Solid gold and crusted with diamonds,' she teased. 'And an emerald or two.'

Sally picked up a chair at the servants' table and put it down next to the high-backed chair. She seated herself, not looking at the little man. 'I'm Sophia Bright,' she said.

There was a grunt from the chair, but nothing more.

'Honestly, how can my husband even imagine you can work in this place, with no pots-and-pans girl, and no assistant? What was he thinking? And his sisters? That's more than even a saint could endure. I shouldn't be surprised if you have already packed your valise.'

Another puff. Then, 'I have been thinking long and hard about packing.'

'I could never blame you,' she said, shivering a little. 'Do you have enough bed covering down here? I believe it would be no trouble to find a proper footstool for your chair. I will go look right now.'

That was all it took. The little man got up from his chair and bowed. 'Etienne Dupuis at your service, Lady Bright. Bah! What would I do with a footstool?'

'Make yourself more comfortable?' she asked, keeping her voice innocent. 'And I will worry about you, shivering down here in the dark.'

In a moment, the chef had pulled down the lamp over the table, lit it and sent it back up. He shook coal into the grate and lit it, then turned to the Rumford. 'Would madam care for tea?'

'I'd love some, Etienne, but I know you are a busy man and it isn't time for tea yet. Besides…weren't you about to pack?'

'I will make time,' he said, bowing graciously again and ignoring her question. 'I shall have Starkey serve tea on the terrace.'

'That is so kind of you,' she said, not daring to look her

husband in the eyes. She could see that he had not moved from where she had left him. 'Perhaps some tea for the admiral, too.' She leaned closer in a conspiratorial manner. 'Poor man. It's not his fault that he has such sisters.'

'I suppose it is not,' the chef said, busying himself in the pantry now. 'They order me about and tell me what to do in my own kitchen! Me!'

Sally tisked several times and frowned. 'Not any more, Etienne. I am here.'

'You think you can stop them?' he asked, waving his hands about.

'I know I can,' she answered simply, mentally shouting down every qualm rattling around in her brain. 'There are no limits to what I would do to preserve the sanctity of your kitchen.'

Dupuis stopped and blew a kiss in her direction. He looked at the admiral. 'Sir! Wherever did you meet such a gem?'

'In a hotel dining room, Etienne. Where else?'

The chef laughed and smiled in conspiratorial fashion at Sally. 'He is such a wit.' He made a shooing motion with his hands. 'Zut, zut! Upstairs now!' He drew himself up. 'Etienne Dupuis will produce!'

Sally clapped her hands. 'You are everything my darling husband said, and more! In future, perhaps you would not mind showing me at the beginning of each week what you plan for meals? Just a little glimpse.'

He bowed elaborately this time. 'I will bring my menus upstairs to your sitting room each Monday. And you might be thinking of your favourite foods.'

Lately it has been anything, Sally thought. *I am just partial to eating again.* 'An excellent arrangement,' she said. 'This, sir, is your domain.' She nodded to him, turned on her heel and rejoined her dumbfounded husband. 'Come, my dearest, let us return to the terrace. I believe I saw some wrought-iron chairs there.'

With a smile, Bright held out his arm to her. 'Amazing,' he murmured. 'My dearest?'

'He is French and we are newly married. Do you have a better idea?'

The admiral glanced back at the chef, who was watching them, and put his arm around her waist. 'I rather like it. Sophia, peace is suddenly getting interesting. I thought it never would.'

What he said, whether he even understand or not, went right to her heart. She impulsively put her hands on his shoulders. 'I do believe I understand you now.' She said it softly, so Etienne would not hear. 'You've been at loose ends.'

He would have backed off, but she had him. His eyes narrowed. 'You're sounding a little like my sisters, Sophia.'

'I probably am,' she answered, on sure ground. 'I am a female, after all. *They* reckoned you needed a wife. *I* reckon you just need a purpose. The war is over.'

It sounded so simple that Sally wondered if he would laugh at her nonsense. To her horror at first, tears filled his eyes. 'My goodness,' she said softly, when she recovered herself. 'I'm not so certain you knew that.'

He said nothing, because he couldn't. She took a handkerchief out of her sleeve and quickly wiped his eyes. 'There now. We will have to brush old leaves and bird droppings, and heavens knows what else, off those chairs.'

The admiral said nothing as they walked down the hall, but he refused to release her hand, even when Etienne was not around to watch. On the terrace, he sized up the situation and found a piece of pasteboard to brush off the leaves from two chairs. He indicated one with a flourish and she sat down.

That's what it is, she thought, as she watched him tackle the wrought-iron table. *He needs a purpose. I do hope he doesn't regret his hasty marriage already, because I still need a home.*

He sat down beside her. 'I have never seen anyone deal so quickly with Etienne, and I have known him for years. How did you know what to do?'

'I believe I discovered the key when I was lady's companion to what I will charitably call crotchety old women. All they ever needed was someone to listen to them. I listened.' She put her hand on the admiral's arm. 'Don't you see? In all his years of war and loss, and humiliation, I suppose, at being won in a card game, Etienne's refuge has been his kitchen. If something threatens it, he goes to pieces.'

The admiral looked at her, making no move to draw away from her light touch. 'I should just humour him?'

'What do you lose by humouring him? I doubt he makes many demands.'

He reflected a moment. 'No, he never has, really.' He leaned forwards. 'How do you propose to keep my sisters out of his kitchen?'

'I'll bar the door if I have to,' she replied. Challenged by this man, she leaned forwards, too, until their noses were nearly touching. 'This is my house, too, now, unless you've changed your mind already.'

She sat back then, suddenly shy, and he did the same, but with a half-smile on his face. 'Change my mind?' he said. 'When you have declared that you will be a buffer for my chef, and probably even for me, as well? Only an idiot would change his mind.'

He closed his eyes and turned his face to the sun. 'Peace,'

he said finally. 'Sophia, I have missed out on everything in life because of Napoleon—a…a…wife, family, children, a home, a bed that doesn't sway, clean water, fresh meat, smallclothes not washed in brine, for God's sake, neighbours, new books from lending libraries, Sunday choir—you name it. I didn't know how to court, so look what I did.' He opened his eyes, looked at her and hastily added, 'About that, be assured I have no regrets, Sophia. One doesn't become an admiral of the fleet without a healthy dose of dumb luck.'

She was silent a long moment, looking out to sea, wondering what to make of the events of the past two days that had changed her life completely. 'Perhaps my luck is changing, too.'

'Count on it, wife.'

She was not so confident to take his assurance for fact. The last five years had shown her all too clearly how swiftly things could change. But then, she reasoned later, why could they not change for the good, too? Maybe the admiral was right.

They spent a pleasant afternoon on the terrace, drinking Etienne's fragrant tea and eating the biscuits he brought out later, warm and toasted from the Rumford, which must have sprung back to life as soon as they had left the kitchen.

Sally was content to sit on the terrace, even in its shabby, unswept state, because the view was so magnificent. Also, she had no wish to enter the house again. As she sat, she began to think about the ramshackle garden in front of her.

'Herbs would be nice,' she commented.

'Herb's what?' he teased.

She rolled her eyes. 'Were you this much trouble to your sisters when you were young?'

'Probably.' He looked where she was looking. 'Funny. All I see is the ocean and you see the land.'

'Herbs right there in that closest weedy patch. Lavender, thyme, rosemary. Etienne will thank me. I would put roses there. The possibilities are endless.'

Clouds gathered overhead. When the rain began, the admiral held out his hand to her. 'Looks like we are forced to go inside. May I suggest the bookroom? I think it is a place the old earl seldom entered, because he never decorated there.'

He was right; the bookroom was bereft of statues or cupids behaving badly. After indicating a chair, he sat down at the desk and took out a sheet of paper. Sally moved closer and uncapped the inkwell. The admiral nodded his thanks, then took up the pen and rested his hook on the paper to anchor it.

'First things first, Sophia. Name it.'

'More servants. I will ask Etienne what sort of staff he requires. We should have a downstairs maid, an upstairs maid and a 'tween-stairs girl. Gardeners. Would Starkey like a footman?'

'Probably. We need painters with copious buckets of paint.' He stopped and leaned his elbows on the desk. 'Sophia, how to we find these people? On board ship, I spoke and everyone jumped.'

'We need a steward—someone who knows the area who can find these people for us.'

He wrote, still frowning. 'Starkey might think I am infringing on his territory. Still, how do I find a steward?'

Sally thought a moment. 'We pay a call on your neighbours.'

'What, and poach from them?'

'You are a trial, Admiral. I wish I had known this yesterday.'

His lips twitched. 'I'm not doing this on purpose. I'm out of my depth here.'

'I repeat: tomorrow we will visit your closest neighbours. You will leave your card, explain the situation—I am certain they are already well aware of what this house looks like—and throw yourself on their mercy. If you are charming, they will provide assistance.'

'And if I am not?'

'You *are* charming, Mr Bright.' She felt her cheeks grow warm when he looked at her. 'Do you even know who your neighbours are, sir?'

'The one directly next to us is an old marquis who seldom ventures off his property. A bit of a misanthrope, according to the real estate agent.'

'Any other neighbours?'

He gestured vaguely in the other direction. 'Across the lane is Jacob Brustein and his wife, Rivka. He's the banker in Plymouth who partners with William Carter. Or did. I think Carter has been dead for years, but the name always gave Brustein some clout. My sisters were appalled.'

She considered this information. 'Tomorrow morning, we will visit your neighbours.'

He looked at his list. 'Don't you need a maid to help you with your clothes?'

Sally shook her head. 'The dress you saw me in, in the dining room, one cloak, a shawl, a nightgown and this blue dress constitute my wardrobe.'

He dipped the pen in the inkwell. 'One wardrobe for the lady of the house and suits for me. Then you will need a lady's maid. A laundress, too?'

She nodded, feeling the pinch of poverty again, even

though she sat in a comfortable room. 'I'm sorry to be a burden.'

He waved the list to dry the ink. 'Burden? Look at all this sound advice you have given me.' He reached across the table for her hand. 'Sophia, pay attention. I am only going to say this once, since the subject of money seems to embarrass you. As much as I disliked Napoleon, I grew rich off of him. This paltry list won't make much of a dent. It won't, even when I add a carriage and horses, and a coachman, and someone to clean—whatever you call it—from the stables.'

'Try muck.'

The admiral tipped back his chair and laughed. 'Very well! Muck. I can see that your principal task will be to smooth my rough edges.'

'Very well, sir.'

Starkey knocked on the door, then opened it. 'Dupuis wanted me to tell you that dinner is served in the breakfast room. I have covered the scabrous paintings.' He closed the door, then opened it again. 'Penelope and Odysseus are gone,' he intoned. 'Or maybe she was Venus and he a typical sailor.'

Sally stared after him. 'This place is a lunatic asylum,' she said, when Starkey closed the door.

'Not quite, dear wife. You have a worse task ahead, one I won't even bother to immortalise on paper. You must find me something useful to do.'

That will be a chore, she thought, as she removed her clothes that night in the privacy of her own bedroom. Starkey had made the bed at some point in the evening and lit a fire in the grate, which took away the chill of the rain that continued to fall.

Dinner had been sheer delight. On short notice, Etienne

had prepared a wonderful onion soup and served it with homely pilot bread, a menu item she remembered well from the days when Andrew would bring home his work and pore over the Royal Navy victual list, as she sat knitting in their tidy bookroom.

She had felt shy at first with Charles, spending so much time in the company of a man she barely knew, but who was utterly engaging. Thinking to put her at ease, he started telling stories of life at sea—nothing designed to horrify her, but stories of travel to lands so far away she used to wonder if they were real, when she was a child. He told them with gusto, describing the purgatory of being a 'young gentleman', a thoroughly unexalted position below midshipman, when he was only ten.

She must have looked askance at such a rough life for a mere child, because he stopped and touched her hand. 'Don't worry. I will never send our children to sea so young.'

He had continued his narrative, probably not even aware of his inclusion of her in his life, and she knew better than to say anything. She found herself listening to him with all her heart, filled with the pleasure of something as simple as conversation. She realised she had been hungry for it, after years of tending old women who liked to retire with the chickens. A lady's companion didn't quite belong in the servants' hall, and certainly not in the master's sitting room. There had been too many nights spent in solitude, with too much time to miss her son and agonise over her husband's ruin. This was different and she relished the admiral's company.

He had said goodnight outside the door to her chamber. 'I'm across the hall, if you need anything,' he said, then turned smartly on his heel, looking every inch the commander, and probably not even aware of it.

You don't know what else to be, do you? she thought, closing the door. *As for what I need, it isn't much, Admiral. When you are destitute, you quickly discover how much you don't need, or you die.*

She sat cross-legged on her bed, bouncing a little, pleased to feel the comfort of a mattress thicker than a bandage. She had hung on to the mirror-backed hairbrush Andrew had given her one Christmas, and applied it, after she had taken all the pins from her hair.

She turned over the brush and looked seriously at her face, noting the anxious eyes and thin cheeks, and wondering again why Admiral Bright had even paused to look at her in the dining room. All she could think was that the poor man was desperate for a wife, and when The Mouse didn't materialise... Well, whatever the reason, she would do her best to smooth his passage on land.

She was in bed and thinking about pinching out the candle when he knocked.

'Sophia, I forgot something. Stick your hand out the door.'

Mystified, she got up and opened the door a crack. 'Why on earth.:.?' she began.

He had taken off his coat, removed his neckcloth and unbuttoned his shirt; she could see the webbing of straps against his neck that bound his hook to his wrist. He held out a piece of string.

'I'm determined to do something about that ring that you kept taking on and off during dinner. Did it end up in the soup?'

What a sweet man you are, she thought. 'You know it didn't! I can surely just wrap some cloth around it and keep it from slipping off,' she said. 'You needn't...'

'Mrs Bright, I won't have my wife stuffing cloth in her

ring. What would our unmet neighbours think? Besides, it was my choice for The Mouse. Somehow, it just isn't you.'

She opened her mouth to protest, but he gently laid his finger across her lips. 'Mrs Bright, I am not used to being crossed. Retired I may be, but I like my consequence. Hold out your ring finger like the good girl I know you are. Lively now.'

She did as he said. How could she not? He handed her a small stub of a pencil and draped the string across her finger.

'I don't have enough hands for this,' he muttered. 'Just wrap it around and mark the right length.'

Sally did, touched at his kindness. Their heads were close together, and she breathed in his pleasant scent of bay rum again. 'There you are, sir.' She handed him the marked string and the pencil.

He stepped back. She stayed where she was, her eyes on his brace. 'May I undo that for you?'

'Why not?' he said, leaning down a little. 'Do you see the hole in the leather? Just twist and pop out the metal knob. Ah. Perfect. I can do the rest, but it's hard to grasp that little thing.'

'That's all?' she asked.

'Simple enough with two hands, eh? Oh, you can undo my cufflinks, too. This pair is particularly pesky.'

She handed him the cufflinks. 'Goodnight, sir. Let me know if you need help in the morning.'

He smiled his thanks and went back to his room, closing the door quietly behind him.

She fell asleep easily after that, making it the first night in years she had not rehearsed in her mind all the anguish and humiliation of the past five years. 'Trust a houseful of naughty cupids and vulgar statues to distract me,' she murmured to herself. 'Lord, I am shallow.' The notion made her smile and she closed her eyes. 'Pretty soon I will think I actually belong here.'

She woke hours later because she knew she was not alone in her room. She lay completely still, wondering, then turned over.

Staring at her from the other pillow was a face so wrinkled that her mouth dropped open. He was watching her and grinning, and there didn't seem to be a tooth in his head. She tried to leap up, but he grasped her wrist and gave it a slobbery kiss.

'It's been a long year, missie,' he said.

Sally screamed.

Chapter Six

Retired though he was, Admiral Bright knew he was destined never to sleep at night with both ears at rest. Not even when he resided on his flagship, and had little role in the actual workings of it—leaving that to his captain—could he sleep calmly at night. No, it was worse then, because his command was an entire fleet and he held even more lives in his hands.

He was out of bed before his wife even finished the scream, looking about for something to help her, from what, he had not a clue. Nothing wrong with his reflexes. By the time she screamed again, he had found his cutlass in the dressing room. Frustrated with a missing hand, he shoved the cutlass under his arm and yanked open the door.

Simultaneously, her door opened, too. He heaved a quick sigh to see her on her feet, even though her eyes were wide with terror, and something more. She threw herself into his arms and the cutlass clattered to the floor. She was awfully easy to grasp and hold on to, much as he already was beginning to suspect she would be.

'What in God's name…?' he began. He tried to pick up the cutlass, but she wouldn't turn him loose. He patted her. She felt sound of limb, so he left the cutlass where it lay, and held her close, not minding a bit.

She burrowed in closer, babbling something that sounded like words; her brogue didn't help. He put his hand on her chin and gave her a little shake, which brought her up short.

'Hey, now. Slow down. You're all right.'

He was gratified to know that all his years of command weren't a total waste. She stopped talking and took a deep breath, then leaned her forehead against his chest.

'I think I killed him! And he's so old!'

He blinked. He couldn't have heard her right. 'Sophia?' he asked. 'What did you say?'

With an exasperated exclamation, she left his embrace, took his hand and tugged him into her chamber. 'Admiral, he was just…there! His head on the other pillow! I thumped him with my candlestick, but when I took a closer look…I've murdered an old man!'

'Good God,' was all he could think to say.

She climbed on her bed, affording him a marvellous glimpse of her legs, then flattened out on her stomach and peered over the edge on to the side closest to the wall. She looked back and gestured to him impatiently, so he joined her, lying there with his feet dangling over one side, looking where she pointed. A true antique lay on the floor, tangled in the bedclothes. His eyes were closed and a bruise rose on his forehead.

'Do you think he's dead?' Sophia whispered.

Maybe the old man on the floor heard her, because he groaned and opened his eyes. 'Was it something I said?'

he managed to croak. 'You never did anything like that before.'

Bright glanced at Sophia, who stared at the old fellow. 'Who...who...on earth are you, and what were you doing in my bed?'

The man held up his arm and Bright helped him into a sitting position. 'Listen here, this is my wife's bedroom,' Bright said. 'I think I've a right to know what is going on.'

The man gently touched the knot on his forehead, winced and looked at the two of them, watching him from the bed. 'This is the right house, and I know this is June 10th. What, pray tell, are you two doing here?'

Bright looked at Sophia, who had gathered herself together into a tight ball on her pillow. 'My dear, maybe you were right about this being a lunatic asylum.'

The old man began to wave his arms about. 'For God's sake, help me to a chair,' he insisted. 'Do I have to remind you it is June 10th?'

Sophia took one arm and Bright took the other, and walked him to a chair by the fireplace, where he sat down gratefully. 'I could use some water,' he said.

Bright had to smile when Sophia picked up the carafe at her bedside and started to sprinkle the old gentleman with it.

'No! No! You silly piece! I want to drink it!' he declared, his voice still weak, but testy. 'It's June 10th!'

'June 10th?' Bright echoed. 'Is June 10th the night when lunatics and drooling idiots in Devon come out of the moor? This is a private dwelling and you have accosted my wife.'

The man stared at them, looking from one to the other and back again, like a tennis match in the court of France. 'This is the manor of Lord Hudley, is it not?'

'No, it is not. I bought it two months ago from his estate.'

The little man seemed to deflate further before their eyes. 'His estate? He is *dead*?' He choked out the last word in a way that sounded almost theatrical.

'These six months or more,' Bright said. He pulled up the other chair and gestured for Sophia to sit in it. After a long look at the old man, she did. 'I believe he died in Venice after too much vino, which landed him in the Grand Canal, with nary a gondola in sight.'

'That would be totally in character,' the old gentleman said. 'I wonder why I was never informed?'

'Are you a relative?' Sophia asked.

Even in the dim light, Bright could see that her hands were shaking. He put his hand over hers and she clutched him.

Bright wasn't sure the old boy heard her. He sat back and closed his eyes again. 'Hudley's gone?'

'I fear so,' Bright said gently. 'Now, if you wouldn't mind tell us the significance of June 10th?'

The little man seemed to gather his tattered dignity about him like a dressing gown. 'You can't imagine how I used to look forwards to June 10th.'

'Perhaps I could, if I had any idea what June 10th *was*.'

'Hudley held the most amazing debauches here,' the old man said, his voice almost dreamy. He glanced at Sophia, who glared back. 'This is *my* bedroom, missy! Hudley always had my favourite Cyprian tucked right in here.'

Sophia gasped. Bright glanced at her, amused, as her mouth opened and closed several times. He looked back at the old fellow, new respect in his eyes.

'I know this is rude, but how old *are* you?'

'Eighty,' he said with some dignity, and not a little pride.

'I have been attending Hudley's debauches for forty years, every June 10th.' His eyes got more dreamy, obviously remembering some of the more memorable ones. 'Do you know—are you aware—that a Cyprian can swing from the chandelier in the library?' He held up a cautionary finger. 'But only one unencumbered with clothing. Small feet, too.'

'I don't doubt you for a minute, sir.'

What a prodigious old sprite, Bright thought in astonishment. He could feel Sophia's eyes boring into the back of his nightshirt. *I'm going to be in such trouble if I don't cease this line of enquiry*, he thought. 'I doubt seriously we will ever need to test the strength of the chandelier,' he said, knowing how lame he sounded. 'Perhaps we should introduce ourselves? I am Sir Charles Bright, retired admiral of his Majesty's Blue Fleet. This is my wife, Lady Bright.'

The old man inclined his head as graciously as though he addressed his retainers. 'I am Lord Edmonds, and I live in Northumberland.'

No wonder you looked forwards to a visit to Devonshire, Bright thought. *I would, too, if I lived in Northumberland. You probably dreamed about this all year.* 'I suppose that would explain why you never heard of Lord Hudley's demise.'

Lord Edmonds was in the mood to reminisce. 'Sometimes one, sometimes two, sometimes—'

'That will do, Lord Edmonds,' Bright interrupted, grateful that the dark hid his flaming face and unwilling to look Sophia in the eye.

Edmonds was unstoppable. 'You're a navy man. Don't tell me you never...'

He floundered, but was rescued by an unexpected source. 'Lord Edmonds, more to the point right now, how did you get into this house?' Sophia asked, her hands folded demurely in her lap now, and looking far too fetching in her nightgown, with hair all around her shoulders.

Thank the Lord the old boy was diverted. Maybe he could also see in Sophia what was not lost on Bright. 'Simple, my dear. Hudley secreted keys all over the terrace. I found my key—mine is under the little statue of Aphrodite with her legs...well, you know...out by the roses.'

'Oh,' Sophia said, her voice faint. 'And there are keys everywhere?'

'Everywhere,' Lord Edmonds agreed cheerily. 'We never had trouble getting in.'

This was the moment when Charles Bright had his first brush with what one of his captains—after a trying time ashore with a pregnant wife—used to call 'marriage politics'. The fact that he recognised the moment made Bright's heart do a funny thing. He knew his ship's surgeon would call such a thing impossible, but he felt his heart take a little leap. Nothing big, but there it was. *I can laugh because I want to, and this antediluvian roué is harmless*, he thought, *or I can think of Sophia, and that sudden intake of breath. Choose wisely, Admiral.*

He took a deep breath, knowing that if he laughed, he might as well have waited another day or two for The Mouse. 'Lord Edmonds, that worries me. Would you mind spending the night here—in a different room, of course— and walk around the gardens with me in the morning?' He touched Sophia's cheek, humbled at her tears. 'I...I won't have my wife alarmed like this again.'

He swallowed and looked at the woman making herself so small in the chair next to the old man. 'My dear, I will never let anything like this happen again.'

She only nodded, because Bright could tell she couldn't speak. The fear in her eyes reminded him how little he knew about women. Bright had no qualms about thanking the Lord for small favours to a man who, mere days ago, would have laughed. *I just learned something*, he thought, as he smiled at her with what he hoped was reassurance. *Pray I remember it.*

'I can recall some of them,' Lord Edmonds said.

'Very well, then. How about you and I go belowdecks and see if my chef won't mind providing us some tea? You might as well go back to bed, Sophia,' he said. 'I'll find a bedroom for our...uh...guest.'

'Oh, no,' she declared, getting to her feet. 'I'm not staying up here by myself!'

Etienne didn't seem surprised by his early morning visitors; Bright hadn't thought he would, considering the odd hours they were both familiar with from life in the Channel Fleet. He rubbed his eyes, looked Lord Edmonds over, and even provided some ice chips in a towel for the bump on his head.

Sophia had retreated to her room long enough to find a dressing gown as shabby as her nightgown and twist what looked like a wooden skewer into her mass of hair, pulling it back from her face. He found his own dressing gown, and she had kindly tied the sash without being asked.

She stuck right by his side down the stairs, which gave him the courage to drape his handless arm across her shoulder, hoping it wouldn't disgust her. It didn't. She let out a long breath, as though she had been holding it, and gave him a quick glance full of gratitude.

They sat downstairs in the servants' hall for more than an hour, listening to Lord Edmonds, more garrulous by the minute, describe in glowing detail some of the more memorable revelries in the quiet building. As the clock chimed three, he gave a tremendous yawn. 'I am ready to hang it up,' he announced. His eyes turned wistful. 'Forty years. My dears, when you live in the land of chilblained knees and sour oatmeal, a toddle down to Lord Hudley's was always an event to look forwards to.' He winked at Sophia, who by now was smiling. Glancing back at Bright, he said, 'She's a tasty morsel. Where did you find her?'

'In a hotel dining room,' Bright said, which seemed to be the best answer. Sophia laughed, which told him he had chosen right again.

Lord Edmonds looked at them both, obviously wondering if there was a joke unknown to him, then shrugged. 'I just need a blanket and a pillow,' he said, then brightened, ever the optimist. 'You could let me sleep in the library.'

'Absolutely not,' Bright said firmly. 'My steward has already prepared you a chamber in the room next to me. After breakfast in a few hours, you and I will tour the grounds.' He held out his hand and wiggled his fingers. 'I'll thank you for your key now.'

Lord Edmonds sighed, but surrendered the item. He followed them up the stairs, muttering something about 'how stodgy today's youngsters are', which made Sophia's shoulders shake. 'He thinks we are young people,' she whispered to Bright. 'Should we be flattered?'

'I know *I* am,' he whispered back. 'Sophia, you must admit he is a prodigious old goat, to think he was going to thrill some Cyprian! Pray God I am as hopeful, at age eighty.'

'I don't have to admit anything of the kind,' she shot back. 'I hope you two finds lots of keys tomorrow morning!'

He left Sophia at her door and escorted Lord Edmonds to his. He stood in the middle of the hall, uncertain what to do. The evening had already turned into something disturbingly similar to watch and watch about when he was a lieutenant: four hours on and four hours off, around the clock, at the good pleasure of the gods of war. He looked at Sophia's door, wondering if she would sleep.

There was a wing-back chair in the hall, rump sprung and removed from one of the bedchambers. He pulled it to Sophia's door and sat in it, making himself comfortable with his cutlass across his lap. No telling what a randy old goat would do, he reasoned, especially one so intimately acquainted with a ne'er-do-well like Lord Hudley.

He settled himself and closed his eyes.

'Is that you, Charles?'

She sounded like she was crouching by the keyhole.

Charles, eh? he thought, supremely gratified. 'Aye, Sophie, my fair Cyprian.'

She opened the door a crack. 'I think I am safe enough,' she said, but he caught the element of doubt in her voice. 'And I am not your "fair Cyprian",' she added, for good measure.

He winked at her and closed his eyes. When she still stood there, he opened one eye. 'Sophia, it's been many a year since anyone has questioned me.'

'I'm not one of your lieutenants!' she flared.

Temper, temper, he thought. *It makes your eyes awfully bright.* 'That's true,' he said agreeably. 'You're oceans prettier. Goodnight, Sophie. If you stand here arguing with me in your bare feet, I will only conclude that war was more peaceful than peace.'

She let out her breath in a gusty sigh. 'This is a strange household.'

'I can scarcely wait to see what tomorrow brings.'

She surprised him then, padding back inside her room, then returning with a light blanket. She tucked it around him, cutlass and all, all without a word. The door closed quietly behind her.

* * *

When Sally awoke, the rain was gone. She lay there a long moment, her hands behind her head, relishing the quiet. She was hungry, but without the familiar anxiety. She sniffed. Etienne apparently didn't let his Gallic origins get in the way of an English breakfast. Of course, he had been cooking in the fleet since Trafalgar. She could dress at her leisure, and go downstairs to breakfast on the sideboard. There were no demanding old ladies, no employers to dread, no fears of being turned off and no quarrels about her begrudged wages.

She lay there, knowing she would give it all up for one more moment with Andrew, before the Lords of the Admiralty hounded him to death; another chance to walk with Andrew, Peter between them, as they held his hands and skipped him across puddles. She thought about the two loves of her life, then did something she had never done before: she folded the memory into her heart and tucked it away. There was no pain this time, only a certain softness in knowing how well she had loved, and how hard she had tried.

Sophia dabbed her eyes with the sheet and sat up, listening to voices on the lawn. She went to the window and threw open the casement to look out on the glory of the ocean. She rested her elbows on the sill, eyes merry as she watched Lord Edmonds—looking small and frail in the morning light—and her husband walk among the overgrown bushes, stopping now and then to retrieve keys.

What had frightened her so badly last night made her smile this morning. 'You didn't really have to sleep outside my door last night, Charles,' she said out loud, knowing he couldn't hear her. 'But thank you, anyway.'

She turned around and stopped, while the tears came to her eyes again. She must have slept soundly, because the blanket she had tucked around her husband was draped over the foot of her bed. The cutlass lay inside the entrance to her room, as though daring anyone to disturb her. She put the blanket around her shoulders, wishing for that elusive scent of bay rum. All her thoughts yesterday had been of how foolish, how weak she had been to allow a good man to feel so obligated that he would marry her, when he probably could have done so much better.

Her thoughts were different this morning. She relished the notion that of all the people in the world, she had encountered someone who cared enough to help her.

She went to the window again, this time to look at her husband only, walking and listening to an old man. She closed her eyes and opened them. He was still there; she hadn't imagined him.

Chapter Seven

Lord Edmonds would probably have stayed all week with very little encouragement, but he was gone before lunch, sent on his way in a post chaise which Starkey had engaged, after a short walk to Plymouth.

Bright escorted Lord Edmonds to the chaise and helped him in. He returned to stand beside her on the step, put his arm around her for obvious show and waved to the old bounder.

'That's it, that's it, go away, Lord Edmonds,' he said out of the corner of his mouth as he smiled and waved.

'You're quite good at that,' she commented. 'You know, looking as though you are sorry to see him leave.'

'I've had plenty of practice with any number of members of parliament and lords in their chamber who thought they knew more about the management of the fleet than I did,' he told her. 'And lately, my sisters have given me ample reason to wish them to the devil.'

She turned to go back inside and stopped. 'I can't face that hallway again.'

'I can't, either. Let's go down to the beach.'

She went with him in perfect agreement. He helped her down the wooden steps to the sand below, where the tide was out. As she watched, perched on a well-placed rock, he went to the edge of the tide and threw in ten keys, one at a time, sending them far out to sea.

'They'll sink in the sand or be carried further out,' he told her, wiping his hand on his trousers. He sat beside her on the rock, waiting a moment before he spoke, as though choosing his words. 'During our walk in the garden, I had told the old rascal that we were newly married. He wondered why we were sleeping in separate chambers.'

'Oh, dear,' she murmured.

'I politely told him it was none of his business. Still… are we going to lie to my sisters? I own it makes me uneasy to prevaricate any more than I already have. Any thoughts?'

It was on the tip of her tongue to tell him her real last name, and what had caused her to use her maiden name. One or two breathless sentences would explain the matter, except that she knew the moment for confession has passed. Anything now would paint her as the worst sort of opportunist, and she couldn't face more recrimination, not after the last five years. 'No thoughts, really,' she said, feeling the blush and slow burn of the hypocrite scorch her breasts and face. Maybe he would put it down to the delicacy of the subject.

'I had planned to tell Fannie and Dora precisely why I was marrying The Mouse, but that would have caused The Mouse humiliation. I know. I know. I should have thought of that before I hatched this silly scheme. Maybe it shows you the level of my desperation.' He turned to look at her directly. 'So what are we? Long-lost lovers, or a marriage of convenience? Do we lie or tell the truth?'

She wondered if he was reading her mind, because his eyes had hardened in a way that gave her the shivers. She couldn't look at him.

He sighed and returned his gaze to the ocean. 'I just gave you my admiral look, didn't I? I fear it is second nature, Sophia. If I tell the truth, that's just humiliation for you, isn't it?'

She nodded, thinking of times in the past five years she had been humiliated, from the ringing denunciation of her late husband by the Admiralty lords, to the quick glances of former friends, only to have them avoid her, until she disappeared into cheap lodgings.

He was waiting for her to say something. 'I think you should tell the truth,' she said, her voice low. 'Just get it over with. Maybe they will leave you alone then. That's what this is all about, isn't it?'

He seemed struck by that notion, which surprised her. 'I suppose it is,' he said finally, and he sounded disappointed, as though something had changed, but she couldn't see it. 'I'm sure you are right. Still…'

After a long, long silence, he nudged her shoulder. 'Maybe I can manage one more lie,' he said at last as he stood up and offered her his arm again. 'Why should you be embarrassed again?'

'I don't mind,' she told him.

'You should,' he said. 'After all, you're the wife of a retired admiral now and someone of consequence.'

'I'm a penniless lady's companion!' she said, feeling anger flare, where before there had been embarrassment. 'Who are we fooling, when it is just the two of us?'

He stopped then, took her hand from his arm and clapped his arm around her shoulders for a brief moment, as though trying to squeeze a little heart into her. 'No, you're Lady Bright. Humour me. Lady Bright. Sounds perky, doesn't it?' He grew serious, matching her mood. 'We'll think of something.'

When? she wondered as they went into the house. She made a point to look up at the ceiling, with all the naughty cupids. *This kind man has married me. I need to start proving my worth*, she told herself. She returned her gaze to the man beside her. 'Charles, it is time we took the bull by the horns. This house must be painted, and soon.'

'I know. The neighbours, is it?'

'The neighbours. We will visit them and ask for advice. We will throw ourselves on their mercy and see if we can poach a bailiff.'

'Madam, why didn't I think of that?'

'Simple,' she told him. 'You are used to commanding people. Now it is time to grovel and plead for help. I am going to change into my one other dress and my ugly but serviceable walking shoes.'

'Just near neighbours,' he told her a half-hour later, as they went down the front steps.

Sally peered into the bush by the front door. Penelope the Statue was now recumbent, and Starkey was busy on her with a sledgehammer, pounding her into smaller chunks to haul away. 'That's a good start,' she said. 'We are moving towards respectability.'

'I wonder if lemon trees would grow in this climate,' her husband said as they walked down the weed-clogged lane. 'I would like lemon trees flanking the door.'

'We can ask our nearest neighbour.' Sally pointed to the end of the lane. 'The banker?'

'Yes. The estate agent apologised over and over for that particular neighbour. He feared I might take exception to settling in the vicinity of a Jew. I assured him I could stand the strain. Hypocrite!'

They came to the end of the lane. 'Now we stop and look both ways,' he said, amusement in his voice. 'Such a quiet neighbourhood! Come, my dear, let us visit our neighbour.'

The lane was far tidier than their own, which the admiral pointed out to her with some glee. 'I expect the man would like our rutty mire to look more like his entrance. I think the estate agent had it all wrong, Sophie dear; *we* are the liability.'

'Speak for yourself, Charlie,' she teased, happy to see him in more cheerful spirits.

'Let us be on our best behaviour. You say Jacob Brustein, founding father of Brustein and Carter, is banker to half the fleet? I love this man already.'

He knocked on the tidy door, then pointed to the small box beside the door. 'It's a mezuzah, Sophie. If we were Jewish, we would put a finger to our lips and then touch it.'

Sally looked around with interest and envy. While not as large as the ramshackle house across the road, it was everything the admiral's was not. From the honey-coloured stone, to the trellis of yellow roses, to the delicate lace of the curtains in the front room, she saw perfection. *I am too impatient*, she thought, as she watched a cat in the window stretch and return to slumber. *This effect is achieved over the course of many years.*

The door was opened by a pleasant-looking housekeeper. The admiral removed his hat. 'I am Admiral Bright and this is my wife, Sophia. We have come to call on Mr Brustein, if he is available to visitors.'

'Come inside, please,' she said, opening the door wider. Sally could hear the faintest of accents. 'I will see.'

The housekeeper left them standing in a hall lined with delicate watercolours. 'This is elegant,' Sally whispered.

'Makes our place look like an exhibitioner's hall,' the admiral whispered back. 'At least the parts that don't look like a brothel.'

'Hush,' she whispered, her face flaming. 'Behave yourself.'

A moment later she heard footsteps, light but halting, and turned to see a leprechaun of a man coming towards them, leaning heavily on a cane, his face lively with interest. He wore a suit even older than her husband's, and a shawl around that. White hair sprang like dandelion puffs around his head, except where it was held in place by a skullcap. As he came close, she saw that he barely came up to her shoulder. She curtsied; he gave her an answering bow.

'Well, well. It's not every day that an admiral comes to call,' he said, his accent slightly more pronounced than the housekeeper's. 'And his pretty lady.'

Charles bowed, then held out his hand. 'Sir, I am lately retired and I think I am your nearest neighbour. Admiral Bright at your service. This…um…pretty lady is my wife, Sophia.'

'Charming. Admiral, you have an account with me.'

'Along with most of the fleet, I think,' Bright said. 'Two months ago, I bought that excuse for an estate that has probably been offending your eyes—not to mention your sensibilities—for decades.'

The old man nodded. He gestured them into the sitting room, where Sally had seen the lace curtains. The cat in the window opened one eye and then the other, then left the window to twine around Jacob Brustein. He gently pushed the cat away with his cane. 'Go on, Beelzebub. If you trip me up, I'll be less than useless.'

Sally picked up the cat, which went limp in her arms and started to purr.

'He is the worst opportunist in Devon,' Brustein said, indicating the sofa. 'But he brings me mice every day, thinking I am unable to catch my own. One cannot ignore benevolence, in whatever form it takes.'

They sat. Jacob nodded to the housekeeper, who stood at the door, and she left. 'You have come calling?'

'We have indeed,' Bright said. 'My wife assures me that is what people do on land. Since I have spent the better portion of twenty years at sea, I must rely on her notions of what is right and proper.'

Brustein turned his kindly gaze on her. 'Then you are probably in good hands.'

'My thoughts precisely,' Bright replied.

Sally was spared from further embarrassment by the arrival of the housekeeper, this time with tea and small cakes. She set the tray down in front of Sally, who looked up to smile, and noticed tears in the housekeeper's eyes. *I wonder what is wrong?* she thought. She glanced at the old man, who seemed to be struggling, too. Uncertain what to do, she asked, 'Wou-would you like me to pour, Mr Brustein?'

He nodded and wiped at his eyes.

'I hope we have not come at a bad time,' Bright said. 'We can come another day.'

With that, Brustein took out a large handkerchief and blew his nose vigorously. He tucked it back in his coat, and settled the shawl higher on his shoulders. 'This is an excellent day. You will understand my emotion when I tell you two that you are my first neighbourhood visitors.'

Sally gasped. 'Sir, how long have you lived here?'

'More than thirty years, my dear.' He indicated the tray in front of her. 'Would you pour, please? As for the cakes...' he shrugged '...I suppose it is too early for such things.'

It was, but Sally decided she would tug out her fingernails by the roots, rather than embarrass the man. 'They are very welcome, Mr Brustein.' She picked up the teapot, determined not to barter with the old fellow's dignity for one second. 'One lump or two, sir?'

Brustein looked around elaborately. 'The housekeeper would insist I get nothing but one. Since I do not see her, three.'

She did as he asked, then looked at her husband, who watched Brustein with a certain tenderness in his eyes that surprised her. 'And you, Charles?'

He shook his head. 'None. Just tea. And one cake.'

Their host noticed this exchange. 'You have not been married long, if your wife does not know your tea habits, Admiral.'

'True,' Bright said, accepting the tea from her. 'Peace allows a man certain privileges he never enjoyed before, or so I am learning, eh, Sophie dear? No one ever visited you? Well, the old rogue across the road was no bargain, so you were none the poorer there.'

'People have always been willing to bank with us,' Brustein said, after a sip. 'But visit?' He shrugged.

'I'm embarrassed for my other neighbours,' Bright said. 'Shame on them.'

Brustein shrugged again, holding his hands out in front of him in a gesture more eloquent than words. 'But you are visiting me now, are you not?'

'We'll come back, too,' Sally chimed in. 'I like your house.' She laughed. 'I like any house that doesn't have naughty cupids on the ceiling!'

Brustein's eyes widened. 'I had heard rumours.'

'All true,' Bright said. 'I assure you that I bought the scurrilous place for the view!'

Between the two of them, Sally and her admiral spent the next few minutes describing—in muted tones—the result of one old rogue's hobbyhorse. The tea level lowered in the pot and the cakes vanished one by one. When they finished, Brustein told them of his arrival in England in 1805 from Frankfurt-am-Main at the request of his cousin, Nathan Rothschild, who had begun his British sojourn in Manchester as a cloth merchant.

'When Nathan got into the London Exchange, he needed more help, but I found life more to my liking in Devonshire.' Brustein sat back, and Sally was quick to position his ottoman under short legs. 'Thank you, my dear. Admiral, she is a treasure!'

'I know,' Bright said softly, which made Sally's face go warm. 'And she blushes.' He smiled at her, and was kind enough to change the subject. 'Do you still go into the office, sir?'

'Once in a while. I have turned the business over to my sons, David and Samuel. William Carter died several years ago, and we bought out his family. We'll keep the respectability of the Carter name, though.'

He pulled out a pocket watch then, and gave the Brights an apologetic glance. 'I must end this delightful gathering,' he said, the regret obvious in his voice. 'My wife, Rivka, is not well, and I usually spend most of my morning with her. She will wonder where I have gone.'

'We wouldn't dream of keeping you any longer,' Sally said quickly.

The Brights stood up. Brustein struggled to join them, and the admiral put a hand under his elbow to assist. Jacob Brustein took his arm with no embarrassment.

'You're a good lad,' he said. 'Can the fleet manage with-out you?'

'It had better,' Bright said, pulling up the shawl where it had slipped from the old man's narrow shoulders. 'More shame on me if I didn't lead well enough to make a smooth transition.'

Brustein hesitated at the door to the sitting room. 'I wonder—could you both do me a small favour?'

'Anything,' Sally said and Bright nodded.

'My Rivka, she is confined to her bed. It would mean the world to me if you could visit her in her room.' He patted Sally's hand. 'For years, she would prepare tea and cakes for visitors who never came.'

Sally could not help the tears that started behind her eyelids. *I did not think I had another tear left, after all that has happened to me*, she thought in amazement. 'Nothing would make us happier,' she replied, as soon as she could talk.

Helped by one of them on each side of him, Brustein led them upstairs and into an airy room with the windows open and curtains half-drawn. A woman as small as he was lay in the centre of her bed, propped up with pillows. Brustein hurried to her side and sat down on the bed, taking both her hands in his. He spoke to her in a language that sounded like German to Sally. The woman opened her eyes and smiled.

'Ah, we have company,' she said in English. She glanced at her husband, her eyes anxious. 'You gave them tea and cakes?'

'Delicious tea and cakes,' Bright said.

Sally took his hand, because his voice seemed almost ready to break. 'Your husband was the perfect host,' she said.

Rivka Brustein indicated the chair. 'Sit, pitseleh, sit,'

she whispered, looking at Sally. 'Tell me about your new home.' Her gesture was feeble, but she waved away her husband. 'Jacob, show this handsome man your collection of globes. I want to talk to the nice lady.' Her soft voice had a measure of triumphant satisfaction in it that lodged right in Sally's heart. Wild horses couldn't have dragged her away.

Twenty minutes was all Rivka Brustein could manage. Her eyes closed and she slept. Gently, Sally released her hand and put it on the snowy coverlet.

She opened her eyes. 'You'll come back?'

'I'll come back.'

'Will you read to me?'

Why weren't the old ladies I tended as sweet as you? Sally thought, as she blew Rivka a kiss from the doorway. 'I'll bring a book you will enjoy,' she said, wondering if anything in her own library—the one the admiral had declared off limits—was fit to read. 'I'll find something.'

Rivka slept. Sally closed the door quietly behind her.

Chapter Eight

'Thirty years, and no one from this neighbourhood has ever visited,' the admiral murmured as they left the Brustein manor. He looked back at the house to Jacob, who stood in the door. 'I have to wonder now what revelations are waiting for us at our other nearest neighbour's domain.' He patted her hand, which was crooked in his arm. 'You're a good girl, Sophie.'

'I am as shocked as you,' she said. 'Such a nice old couple.' She looked ahead to the much more substantial estate barely peeking through the foliage. 'Who lives here?'

'We will probably be above ourselves here, so mind your manners,' he teased. 'The estate agent told me Lord Brimley resides here through the summer. He is a marquis, no less.' Bright stopped. 'The name rings a bell with me, but I cannot remember why. Brimley. Brimley. Perhaps we shall see. Are you game for another house?'

She nodded. 'This is certainly more enjoyable than trying to avoid staring at walls in our...your...house.'

He started walking again, then gave her a sidelong look. 'You were right the first time, Sophie. For all its warts, it is our house.'

I wish I felt that way, but you are kind, she told herself. She wished her face did not feel so hot. Hopefully, the admiral would overlook her embarrassment. 'That notion will take some getting used to.'

'Indeed it will.' He sighed. 'And we are no further along towards solving the dilemma of finding mechanics to remodel.'

'And paint,' she added. 'Gallons of paint.'

He chuckled and tucked her arm closer. 'Paint, aye. If I were on my flagship, I would bark a few orders to my captain, and he would pass my bark down the chain of command until—presto!—it was painted.'

Lord Brimley's estate loomed larger than life, compared to the more modest Brustein manor. They walked slowly down his lane, admiring the faux-Italian ruin that looked as though it had been there since the Italian Renaissance. 'D'ye think Michelangelo did a ceiling inside the gazebo?'

She nudged him. 'You know he did not!'

'Rafael, then. Perhaps Titian?'

'Oh, you try me!'

He laughed and tucked her hand closer. 'Let us behave ourselves.' He leaned down to whisper in her ear as they climbed the shallow steps to the magnificent door. 'Now if this is a house of the first stare, the butler will open the door even before we… Ah.'

Sally couldn't remember when she had seen so much dignity in a black suit. Instinctively, she hung back on the last step, but the admiral pulled her up with him.

'I am Admiral Sir Charles Bright, recently retired,' her

husband said, not in the least intimidated by the splendour before him. 'This is my wife, and we have come calling upon Lord Brimley. I have recently purchased the Hudley estate, which abuts this one.'

The butler ushered them in, but did not close the door behind him, as if there was some doubt they would be staying long. Bright gave her a sidelong wink, which sorely tried her.

'I will see if Lord Brimley is receiving callers,' the butler said. He hesitated one slight moment, as if wondering whether to usher them into an antechamber, at the very least. He must have decided against it. He unbent enough for a short bow and turned smartly on his heel.

'We don't rate the sitting room,' the admiral whispered. 'I think mentioning "Hudley estate" might have been my first mistake. Perhaps I should have added that Penelope and Odysseus are no longer in heat at the front entrance.'

Sally gasped and laughed out loud. 'Admiral Bright, I cannot take you anywhere!'

He merely smiled. 'Madam wife, I am a pig in a poke. I thought it best not to mention the fact until after our wedding. Imagine what surprises await you.'

She would have returned a sharp rejoinder, except the butler returned and indicated in his princely way that they should make themselves comfortable in the sitting room.

'Our fortunes seem to be shifting ever so slightly,' Bright murmured when the butler left them alone there. 'Brimley. I wish I could remember.'

They waited a long while, long enough for Sally to overcome her terrors and walk around the room, admiring the fine paintings. When the admiral began sneaking looks at his timepiece, the door opened to admit Lord Brimley himself. She glanced at her husband, but saw no recognition in his eyes.

'I am Brimley,' the man said, inclining his head towards them. 'Admiral Bright, accept my condolences in the purchase of that miserable estate.' He smiled at them both, but there was no warmth in his eyes. 'I can only assume that since you have a wife—and a lovely one, I might add—that you intend to paint the rooms.'

'I do, my lord, since I wish to keep my wife,' Bright said. 'As a seaman not long on land, though, I am a bit at a loss how to find workers.'

'You need a proper steward.'

'My wife thinks I need my head examined,' Bright said frankly. 'But the view…oh, the view. Can you see the ocean from your estate?'

The marquis did not answer for a long moment. Sally watched in surprise and then consternation as a whole range of emotions crossed his face. 'I rejoice, Admiral, that I cannot,' he said finally, as though each word was tugged from his mouth by iron pincers.

She glanced at her husband, noting his frown. He opened his mouth to speak, but nothing came out.

'The ocean is not to everyone's taste, I imagine,' she said, filling the awkward void.

'It is not to mine.'

The embarrassing silence was filled by the return of the butler and a maid, who deposited a tray on the small table between them. The marquis indicated Sally should pour, and she did.

They sipped their tea. When the silence was nearly unendurable, the marquis turned slightly to face Admiral Bright. 'You do not know who I am?' he asked, his tone frigid.

'My lord, I do not.'

'Perhaps you will know this name: Thomas Place.'

Admiral Bright set down his tea cup with a click. 'I know that name as well as my own, my lord. Was he your son?'

'My only child.'

'Lieutenant Thomas Place, Viscount Malden,' Bright murmured. He stood up and walked to the window and back again, the marquis's eyes on him. 'He made sure that none of us would use his title, so he was Mr Place to me. I had to bark at him a time or two, but he was a good lad. I was his captain.'

'I know you were, Admiral,' the marquis said, rising to join Bright by the window. 'I have followed your career with some interest.' He looked at Sally, and she could see only infinite sorrow in his eyes now. 'Lady Bright, I hated your husband for nearly twenty years. Until three years ago, as a matter of fact.'

Sally looked at both men, her eyes wide. She tried to interpret her husband's expression, except that there was no expression now, only the uncompromising gaze of a man caught off guard and righting himself by the greatest of efforts. She rose, or tried to, except that the admiral had returned to her side and was gently pressing down on her shoulder with his one good hand.

'No fears, my dear,' he said and leaned down to put his cheek next to hers, for a brief moment. She found the sudden gesture reassuring beyond words and relaxed. He lightened the pressure on her shoulder, but did not remove his hand.

'Say on, my lord,' he said, his voice firm and very much in command.

As Sally watched, horrified, the marquis seemed to wilt before her eyes. Her husband must have noticed it, too, because he returned to the man by the window and put his hand under his arm to support him. Without a word, he led the marquis back to his seat. Sally did rise then, and went to sit beside Lord Brimley. *If he were one of my old ladies, I would do this*, she thought, as she quickly removed her bonnet, set it aside and took a napkin from the tray. As he watched her, his eyes dull, she dipped it in the tea and dabbed gently at his brow. 'There now, my lord. Do you wish me to summon your butler?'

Her simple act seemed to rouse him. He shook his head. 'No. No. Bedders would only act like my old maid aunt, and worry me to death.'

'Your wife then, my lord? Should we summon her?'

'My dear, she is dead these past three years. And that is what I need to tell your husband.' He patted the seat on the other side of him. 'Sit down, lad,' he ordered, as though there were many more years between them.

'I...uh...I really don't know what to say, my lord,' Bright began, looking mystified.

'Of course you do not. You never knew us.'

They were both silent. Sally yearned to jump into the conversation. She fought down a fierce urge to defend her husband, an urge so strong that it startled her, considering the briefness of their acquaintance. She looked down and noticed her hands were balled into fists. She glanced up at her husband, who had been watching the gesture, again with that unreadable expression.

The marquis spoke, looking at her. 'Lady Bright, my son served under your husband on the...the *Caprice*...was it not? I thought I would never forget. Considering how many years have rolled over the matter, perhaps it is not so surprising.'

'The *Caprice*. My first command. We took the ship to the Antipodes. We were not at war with France or Spain then, and our assignment was to ferry a naturalist—one of Sir Joseph Banks's protégés—to find something called a fairy tern.'

'You were successful, I believe, at least according to the last letter I ever received from my boy.' The marquis's voice broke on the last word, and Sally felt her heart turn over. She took his hand. He offered no resistance to her touch.

'Yes. We accomplished our orders and were returning to Plymouth,' Bright said. 'We needed to take on food and water, so we docked at Valparaiso, not knowing that Spain and England were at war again.'

He paused and gazed out the window for a long moment. 'And there my boy died in the fight that followed, as you clawed your way out of the harbour,' Lord Brimley said. He looked at Sally then. 'Do you have sons, my dear?'

'None living,' she whispered. Bright reached across the marquis to touched her hand.

'I am sorry for you both,' Lord Brimley replied. 'I know the feeling. If I thought I could do it and not collapse, I would summon Bedders to fetch the letter of condolence your husband wrote to me, twenty-three years ago. I can quote it: "I am relieved to be able to inform you…"'

He could not go on, but Bright could. '"…that your son's death was quick and painless."'

The words hung in the room like a powerful stench. The old man raised his head again. 'Was it a lie? Did you lie to me at such a moment?'

Sally let out the breath she had been holding, her eyes on her husband. She could almost hear the tension in the room humming like a wire stretched taut and snapped.

'I did, my lord.'

The marquis must have been holding his breath, too, because it came out in a sudden whoosh that made Sally jump. 'I thought you had, and I hated you for it. I thought you a coward for not having the courage to tell the truth about the last moments of a sterling lad dearer to my heart than any other creature on earth.'

Bright said nothing. He looked at the floor as though wishing it would open and swallow him. It was Sally's turn to reach across the marquis and touch his hand.

'Do you want me to tell you?' he said finally.

'I thought I did,' the marquis admitted. 'When I heard you had retired—oh, yes, I have followed your career—I wanted to ask.' He shook his head. 'Not to confront you or berate you, mind you; not after what happened three years ago. But just to know.'

'What changed your mind three years ago?' Bright asked.

'My wife died,' the marquis said simply. 'Naturally I was at her bedside through the long ordeal.' He looked at Sally, tears in his eyes. 'She was a dear old girl. Do you know what her last words to me were?'

Sally shook her head. He turned his attention to the admiral. 'Look at me, Bright! Her last words on this whole earth were, "Thank God my boy did not suffer. Thank God!" With a smile so sweet, she slipped from my life.'

He cried then, grasping both their hands. 'I knew it was a lie, but that lie had sustained my dear one through years of what probably would have been unbearable torment, had she known the truth. I had no idea, until that moment. I decided then that I would not hate you any longer, Sir Charles.'

The quiet in the room was unbroken until the butler opened the door quietly, then closed it. The marquis sat back then, patting their hands. 'I never thought to have this moment to tell you, at least until the estate agent shared the news of the estate sale. He thought I would be pleased to have good neighbours. And I am.'

Sally looked at her husband, astounded at his composure. *Who is this man I have married on such short notice?* she asked herself again.

'I don't know what to say, my lord,' Bright said at last. 'Would you like me to tell you how he died? I have never forgotten.'

The marquis gave him a shrewd look. 'I doubt you have ever forgotten how any of your men died.'

'I have not,' Bright said simply, with the smallest catch in his voice.

'I thought I wanted to know. For years, I thought I did.' The old man shook his head. 'Now I think it does not matter. He is at peace.'

Bright nodded. 'Let me tell you that he was brave. My surgeon and I sat with him throughout the entire ordeal. That is no lie. He suffered, but he did not suffer alone. Mercifully, towards the end, he went into a coma and was no longer conscious. Any of us in the fleet would have envied the conclusion, my lord, and that is no lie.'

The marquis nodded, and sipped his tea in silence. When he spoke again, he addressed the admiral in a kindlier tone. 'Look here, lad. What you need is a good steward to make all those onerous arrangements.' He made a face. 'I have been in that house a grand total of once, and never took my wife there. You are obviously married to a tolerant lady.'

'I am realising that more as each day passes,' Bright said, with a sidelong look at Sally that pinked her cheeks. 'I fear my credit will not last for ever, though, no matter how charming she thinks I am. A good steward, eh?'

'Yes, indeed.' He leaned towards Bright. 'If you don't think I am an old meddler, I may have such a fellow. He's been the under-steward here for several years and I think he is chafing to advance. May I send him your way? On approval, of course.'

'My lord, I would be honoured.' He touched Sally under the chin with his hook, which made her smile. 'And my dear lady would be relieved.'

The marquis turned almost-fatherly eyes on her. 'Lord, how she blushes! I didn't know anyone blushed any more.'

They stayed a few more minutes. The admiral shook his head at staying for luncheon. 'We have overstretched our welcome, Lord Brimley,' he said in apology. 'I did want to meet my neighbours, though.'

'And you will both return, I trust,' the marquis replied as he rose to his feet. He smiled at Sally, taking her by both hands. 'Can you not convince your husband to stay for luncheon?'

Sally looked at the admiral, but he shook his head. 'Not this time, my lord. Please do ask us again, though.'

Bright was silent after they left, looking neither right nor left until they were out of sight of the manor, and any prying eyes. When they turned the bend in the lane, he suddenly sank to his knees. His hat fell off as he leaned forwards. Astonished, Sally knelt beside him, her hand across his back. To her horror, he began to sob.

There was a roadside bench not far from the lane. Murmuring nonsensicals to him, she took him by the arm and helped him there, where he leaned back, his face pale and bleak. 'You couldn't manage one more minute there, could you?' she asked.

He shook his head as the tears streamed down his face. He seemed not to mind that she saw them. *What do I do?* she asked herself, and then knew the answer. Without a word, she gathered him close to her, saying nothing because she had no words to ease his pain, only her body. She held him close and smoothed down his hair.

'You haven't forgotten one of them, have you?' she asked.

He shook his head, unable to speak. She sat there, the admiral as tight in her arms as she had ever held her son. As she breathed the pleasant scent of his hair, it occurred to Sally that during the whole of his terrible ordeal with the lords of the Admiralty, Andrew had never let her console him, as she consoled this man she barely knew. *And look what happened to you, Andy*, she thought, as she held Admiral Bright. *Maybe you should have done what this man is doing. Look what we have lost.*

Chapter Nine

'You must think me a very big fool,' the admiral said, his voice still muffled against her breast.

'I think nothing of the kind,' she said gently. Truth to tell, she had felt the calculus around her heart loosen a bit. 'I cannot imagine the burden you have carried through all those decades of war.'

He sat up, taking a handkerchief from his coat pocket. 'I'm an attractive specimen,' he murmured, not looking at her. 'Do I wipe my eyes or blow my nose?' He cursed unguardedly. 'Pardon me.' He pressed the cloth against his eyes, then blew his nose. 'He caught me broadside, Sophie. I had no idea who Lord Brimley was.'

He looked at her then, embarrassment colouring his cheeks. Without even pausing to think, she touched his face. So quick she barely felt it, he kissed her palm.

'Wasn't I the kind man to marry you to lift your burdens?' he said. 'Oh, the irony. I don't suppose you knew what you were getting into.'

'Did you?' she asked. *Does anyone?* she asked herself, feeling suddenly greener than the greenest bride.

They sat there in silence. 'Penny for your thoughts, Sophie,' he said finally. He stood up and pulled her to her feet, offering her his arm again as they turned towards their own manor.

She had no idea how to put into words what she was feeling, or if she even understood the emotions that tugged at her like a ship swinging on its anchor. 'I suppose you are thinking that life on land is complicated.'

'But what are *you* thinking?' he persisted.

'Precisely that,' she said, a little surprised at him. 'I don't know that I was even thinking about myself.'

'Thank you, then,' he replied. 'I doubt I deserve such attention.'

She was happy he seemed content to walk in silence. *I think I have learned something this morning,* she told herself as she matched her stride to his—not a hard matter, because they were much the same height. *Maybe I am learning that my troubles are not the only ones in the world.*

It was something to consider, and she wanted a moment alone to think about it. To her gratification, the admiral asked if she wouldn't mind spending the afternoon by herself, as he wanted to go down to the beach and think about things. 'Not at all,' she told him. 'Shall I ask Starkey to serve you luncheon on the beach?'

He nodded. 'Have him put it in a hamper. You don't mind?'

'I just said I didn't,' she assured him. 'Charles, if we are to rub along together, you need to take me at my word.'

'I suppose I must,' he agreed.

She ate her luncheon on the terrace, which Starkey had

swept clear, then went upstairs to count the sheets in Lord Hudley's linen closet—prosaic work that suited her mood. Thank goodness he had an ample supply was her first thought, then she blushed to think of all the activity on all the beds in the manor, at least once a year, when he held his orgies. No wonder he had sheets, and good ones, too. It was the same with pillowslips and towels. The old rascal practically ran a hotel for geriatric roués just like him.

The admiral hadn't returned by dinner. After a solitary meal in the breakfast room, she asked Starkey about it.

'He likes his solitude, ma'am, when he's troubled,' Starkey said.

She could tell by the look he gave her that Starkey considered her at fault for the admiral's mood. Let him think what he will, she decided, after an evening alone in the sitting room, where she made lists of projects for the house and tried to ignore the cupids overhead, with their amorous contortions.

To her bemusement, she did not sleep until she heard Bright's footsteps on the stairs. She sat up in bed, her arms around her knees, as she heard him approach her door, stand there a moment, then cross the hall to his own room. She lay down then, wondering if he had changed his mind about their arrangement. She knew he was embarrassed about his tears and doubted he had ever cried in the presence of anyone, much less a woman. 'Well, I cannot help that,' she murmured prosaically, as she composed herself for sleep.

She wondered if she would sleep, considering last night's adventure with the old gentleman from Northumberland. Hopefully, he was well on his way home. What was that he had called her—'his fair Cyprian'? She smiled to herself, pleased that for one night at least, she was not thinking of ruin or poverty, or where her next meal was coming from.

She woke in the morning to the sound of noise downstairs, and men talking and laughing as they hammered. She sat up and rubbed her eyes at the same moment the admiral tapped on her door.

'Come in, sir,' she said, wishing for a small moment that her nightgown was not so thin from repeated washings.

She shouldn't have worried. In his nightshirt and dressing gown, the admiral was as shabby as she was. It was an elaborate gown, though.

'My stars, did you find that in the court of the Emperor of Japan?' she asked, by way of greeting.

He carried a tea cup and saucer. She noticed he had not put on his hook yet, and his left sleeve hung over his wrist.

'You're close,' he said, as he nudged the door shut behind him and came to her bed. To her surprise, he told her to shift her legs and sat down. He handed her the cup. 'I was given this bit of silk and embroidery by the Emperor of China, whose name I cannot at the moment remember, but who had a fondness for the otter pelts I had brought him from a quick raid up the coast of New Albion. I have no idea what those Yanks call it now. But that was years ago, and it is scarcely fit for more than the dust bin.'

Amused, she sipped her tea. He watched her, a smile in his eyes. 'You look extraordinarily fine in the early morning,' he said. 'I didn't know your hair was so curly.'

'I usually have it whipped into submission by this time,' she replied.

'Well, that's a shame,' he told her. 'I rather like it this way.' He touched one of her curls, wrapping it around his finger. He didn't seem at all uncomfortable and she decided she liked it.

She wasn't sure why he had come into her room, because he seemed content to just sit on the bed while she drank her tea. She heard a thump from downstairs, grateful that it gave her something to ask him.

'Sir, *what* is going on down there?'

Her question seemed to remind him. 'Aye, madam wife, I did have a reason to come in here. Lord Brimley is not wasting a moment to help us. He has sent over an army of workers who are, as we speak, rigging up scaffolding in the sitting room, with the sole purpose of ridding us of randy cupids.' He leaned closer and again she breathed his bay rum. 'Mrs Bright, think how pleasant it will be to embroider in your sitting room and not worry about what those imps are doing overhead.'

She could tell his mood had lifted. 'You feel better,' she said.

He leaned even closer until his forehead touched hers. 'I do, madam. Thank you for allowing me solitude.'

'You only have to mention it and I will understand,' she said softly, since his face was so close to hers. 'That is our arrangement.'

Maybe an imp had escaped from the carnage in the sitting room below. For whatever reason, the admiral raised her chin and kissed her lips. 'I'm not very good at this, but I am grateful for your forbearance,' he told her, when his lips were still so close to hers.

On the contrary, he was quite good. In fact, she was disappointed that he did not kiss her again. *He's learned that somewhere in the world*, she thought, as she sat back, careful not to spill her tea into his lap, since he sat so close.

And there they sat, eyeing each other. Sally felt herself

relax under his gaze, which was benign. The imp must have still been in the room, because she found herself saying, 'I like it when you bring me tea in the morning.'

'I like it, too,' he said, his voice as soft as hers, almost as if he felt as shy. 'It could become a habit.' He dispelled the mood by flapping his empty sleeve at her and getting to his feet. 'If you are equal to the task, I thought we would abandon Chez Bright today and go to Plymouth. The under-steward that Lord Brimley sent is a paragon, and he so much as informed me in *such* a polite way, that I am a supernumerary.' He ruffled her hair, which made her laugh. 'So are you, madam. If we intend to cut a dash in the neighbourhood, we had better get ourselves some clothing that doesn't brand us as vagrants or felons.'

'I am certain you do not pay Starkey enough,' Sally told Bright as they settled back into a post chaise that the butler had arranged to convey them to Plymouth.

'You are most likely correct,' he replied. 'To show you the total measure of his devotion to me, he even enquired to find the most slap-up-to-the-mark modiste in Plymouth. His comrades in the fleet would never believe such a thing. Starkey is normally quite a Puritan.'

He hoped his wife would pink up at this news, and she did, to his pleasure. Amazing how a woman teetering on the other side of thirty could blush at the mention of a modiste, and still manage to maintain her countenance in a roomful of cupids doing things some people didn't even do behind bolted doors. He did not pretend to understand women. Looking at the pretty lady seated across from him, he thought it politic not to try. Better to let her surprise him with her wit, and most of all, her humanity. He was beginning to think the most impulsive gesture of his life was shaping into the best one.

The first thought on her mind, apparently miles ahead of new clothes, was to seek out a bookshop. 'I want to find something to entertain Mrs Brustein,' she explained, as he handed her down from the chaise. 'I intend to visit her as often as I can, and read to her.'

Even on the short few days of their acquaintance, he already knew it would be fruitless to pull out his timepiece and point out that they were already late to her modiste's appointment, but he tried. She gave him a kindly look, the type reserved for halfwits and small children, and darted into the bookshop. Knowing she had no money, he followed her in, standing patiently as she looked at one book, and then another.

He knew he had been attracted by her graceful ways, but his appreciation deepened as he admired the sparkle in her eyes. He wasn't entirely certain when the sparkle had taken up residence there, but it might have been only since early morning, when he had screwed up his courage and knocked on her door, bearing tea. His dealings with women had informed him early in his career about the world that few women looked passable at first light. Sophie Bright must be the exception, he decided. She was glorious, sitting there in bed in a nightgown too thin for company, if that was what he was. The outline of her breasts had moved him to kiss her, when he wanted to do so much more.

And here she was in a bookshop, poring over book after book until she stopped, turned to him in triumph and said, 'Aha!'

He took the little volume from her and glanced at the spine. 'Shakespeare and his sonnets for an old lady?'

'Most certainly,' his wife said. 'I will love them until I die, and surely I am not alone in this. Have you read them, sir?'

He wished she would call him Charles. 'Not in many

years,' he told her. 'I am not certain that Shakespeare wears well on a quarterdeck.'

She surprised him then, as tears came to her eyes, turning them into liquid pools. 'You have missed out on so many things, haven't you?' She had hit on something every man in the fleet knew, and probably few landsmen.

'Aye, madam wife, I have,' he said. He held up the book. 'You think it is not too late? I am not a hopeless specimen?'

She dabbed at her eyes, unable to say anything for a moment, as they stood together in the crowded bookshop.

He took her arm. 'Sophie, don't waste a tear on me over something we had no control over. I saw my duty and did it. So did everyone in the fleet.' He paused, thinking of Lord Brimley's young son, dead these many years and slipped into the Pacific Ocean somewhere off Valparaiso. 'Some gave everything. Blame the gods of war.'

She is studying me, he thought, as her arm came around his waist and she held him close. *I try to comfort her and she comforts me. Did a man ever strike a better bargain than the one I contracted with Sally Paul?* Bright handed back the book. He gave her a shilling and returned to the post chaise, unable to continue another moment in the bookshop and wondering if there was any place on land where he felt content.

Maybe he was not so discontent. He watched his wife through the window as she quickly paid the proprietor, shook her head against taking time to wrap the sonnets in brown paper and hurried back to the chaise.

'I'm sorry to delay you,' she said, after he helped her in. 'I don't *intend* to be a trial to a punctual man.'

He held out his hand for the book. 'Do you have a favourite sonnet?' He fanned the air with the book. 'Something not too heated for a nice old lady?'

To his delight, she left her seat on the opposite side of the chaise and sat next to him, turning the pages, her face so close to his that he could breathe in the delicate scent of her lavender face soap.

'This one,' she said. 'Perhaps Mr Brustein will want to read this one to her: "Devouring Time, blunt thou the lion's paws, and make the earth devour her own sweet brood..."' She shook her head. 'It's too sad.'

He brushed away her fingers and kept reading. 'Sophie, you're a goose. This is an old man remembering how fair his love once was, but that doesn't mean he's sad about the matter.' He kept reading aloud, thinking of the woman beside him, wondering how she would look in twenty years, even thirty years, if they were so lucky. *I believe she will look better and better as time passes*, he thought. 'Sophie, Mrs Brustein cannot argue with this: "Yet, do thy worst, old Time: despite thy wrong; My love shall in my verse ever live young."'

Charles looked at his new wife, the hasty bargain he made without much thought, beyond an overpowering desire to keep his sisters from meddling in his life. *Shakespeare could say it so well*, he told himself. *You will always be young, too.*

She looked at him in such an impish way that he felt the years fall away from him, too, much as from the sonneteer. 'There, now,' she said. 'Doesn't Shakespeare read better at forty-five than he did when you were ten and forced?'

She was teasing him; at the same time he was wondering if he had ever felt more in earnest. *I will frighten her to death*, he thought. *This is a marriage of convenience.* 'You know he does!' Charles handed back the book. 'You and Mrs Brustein can sniffle and cry and wallow over the verses, and I doubt a better day will be spent anywhere.'

Sophie tucked the book in her reticule. He thought she might return to her side of the chaise, but she remained beside him. 'Perhaps when we finish the sonnets, we will graduate to Byron. I will wear thick gloves, so my fingers do not scorch from the verse,' she teased. She nudged his shoulder. 'Thank you for buying this.'

'Anything, my dear wife, to further our connections in the neighbourhood,' he said. 'After years of riotous living coming from that house we laughingly call home now, we have a lot of repair work to do.'

As the chaise stopped in front of Madame Soigne's shop, he knew he had been saved from blurting out that he would prefer she read to him. *A man can dream*, he told himself, picturing his head in Sophie's lap, while she read to him. *A pity Shakespeare never wrote a sonnet about old admirals in love. No, well-seasoned admirals. I can't recall a time when I have felt less ancient.*

She hesitated in the doorway, hand on the doorknob, and looked back at him, which must have been his cue to join her and provide some husbandly support.

'Cold feet, madam wife? I expect you to spend lots of money. In fact, I am counting on it.'

Still she hung back. 'A few days ago, I didn't even have any thread to sew up a hole in my stockings.' She let go of the doorknob. 'You know, if I go to a fabric warehouse and buy a couple of lengths of muslin, I can sew my own dresses.'

Charles put her hand back on the doorknob. 'You don't need to! Don't get all Scottish on me.' He turned the knob and gave her a little boost inside, where Madame and her minions stood. From the look of them, they had nothing on their minds except the kind of service it was becoming increasingly obvious that his wife was not accustomed to. Sophie looked ready to burst into tears.

He took her about the waist with his hooked arm, which gave him ample opportunity to tug off her bonnet with his bona fide hand and plant a kiss on her temple. 'You can do this. Be a good girl and spend my money.'

He left her there, looking at him, her face pale. He turned to the modiste, who was eyeing Sophie with something close to disbelief. 'She's Scottish and doesn't like to spend a groat. Whatever she agrees to buy, triple it.'

'Charles!'

He liked the sound of that. He tipped his hat to her and left the shop.

Chapter Ten

W hen he returned, all measured for shirts and trousers and coats, Sally was waiting for him inside the shop, calmer now and drinking tea. She watched him through the window with Madame Soigne.

'I don't know how one man can appear so pleased when he knows I have been spending his money,' she commented.

The modiste looked through the window, where the admiral was getting out of the post chaise. 'How can you tell he is pleased?' she asked, squinting. 'He looks rather stern to me.'

'The way his eyes get small and kind of crinkle,' Sally said. 'The lines around his mouth get a little deeper.'

'If you say so,' Madame replied dubiously. She brightened. '*Bien*, you would know, would you not? He is your husband, and you have had years and years to study him.'

Good God, Sally thought, setting down the cup with a click. *I have known the man three days and she thinks we*

are an old married couple? This is a strange development.
'I...I suppose I have,' she stammered, not sure what else
to say.

The door opened. She felt a curious lift as his eyes got
smaller and he smiled at her. He nodded to the modiste.
'Did she spend lots and lots of my blunt, Madame?' he
asked.

'*Mais oui!* Just as you wished,' the modiste declared,
and ticked them off on her elegant long fingers. 'Morning
dresses, afternoon dresses, evening dresses—she would
only allow one ball gown—a cloak, a redingote, sleeping
gowns, a dressing gown...'

'When might these garments be ready?' He handed over
a wad of notes so large that Sally couldn't help a small
gasp.

Madame tittered and accepted the king's ransom gracefully. 'Oh, you seamen! I will put all my seamstresses to
work. Soon, Admiral, soon!'

Bright bowed. 'Madame Soigne, if you had been Napoleon's minister of war in the late disturbance, he would not
have lost.' He held out his hand to Sally. 'Come, my dear.
We now have to search for enough domestics to puff up
our consequence in the neighbourhood. Madame Soigne,
we bid you good day.'

There didn't seem to be any point in sitting across from
him, not when he held her arm and plopped her down
beside him. Besides, she had a confession. 'I had better
make a clean breast of it,' she told him, as the chaise pulled
away from the curb. 'Madame Soigne also sent for a milliner and a shoemaker.'

'I am relieved to hear it,' he remarked. 'I call that
efficiency.' He must have used her wry expression as an
excuse to keep his arm around her. 'You sound like a

tar on shore leave! Spend it all in one go and chance the consequences!'

'I call it a huge expenditure,' she lamented.

He refused to be anything but serene. 'Sophie dear, your duty is to rid me of sisters. That is no small task and it will require ammunition. You are dealing with ruthless hunters, who will stop at nothing. I consider you a total bargain.'

She looked at his face, noticed the crinkles around his eyes. 'You are quizzing me! I think you are shameless.'

He threw back his head and laughed. 'You think I exaggerate?'

'I know you do,' she said, trying not to smile. 'Were you this much trouble in the fleet?'

'This and more, but I achieved results,' he assured her. 'I do believe I will add to your duties, as well, my dear, since you feel I have done too much by clothing you in a style to suit my consequence. You're going to be charming the Brusteins with Shakespeare and helping slap my house into submission. Yes, you may find me something to do, while you're at it. Can you see me sitting on my thumbs this winter?'

'I cannot,' she agreed. 'I believe I will earn that wardrobe!'

He hugged her tighter, then released her. 'Laugh like that more often, Sophie. It becomes you.'

'I am not so certain I had much to laugh about,' she said frankly.

'Then maybe your fortunes have turned,' he said, equally frank.

Maybe they have, Sally decided, after luncheon at the Drake. She knew they had, when they came to the employment registry, and there sat the same pale governess she had shared the bench with only days ago. *I could still be sitting next to her*, she thought, giving the woman a smile.

Her smile turned thoughtful. She took her husband by the arm, which made him look at her with an expression that made her stomach feel deliciously warm. She walked him outside, grateful they were much the same height, so there was no need to tug on his sleeve like a child.

'Charles.' His name still sounded so strange on her lips, but she knew he enjoyed it. 'Charles, that lady is an out-of-work governess. She came with me on the mail coach from Bath, and see, she is still sitting here.'

'Times are hard,' he pointed out. 'After the tailor measured me—Lord, but he got personal with my parts—I walked down to the harbour and found any number of seamen begging, or leaning against buildings and trying not to beg. Peace is well enough, I suppose, but it certainly throws people out of employment. Do we *need* a governess? Is there something you are not telling me?'

Sally knew he was quizzing her, but she felt a wave of guilt pass over her, as she wished it was not too late to tell him her former name. He was teasing her, but his eyes were kind. *All I can do is go on*, she told herself.

'I know we have no need of a governess! When my clothing comes, I will need a dresser.' She leaned closer to him, not wanting to be overheard. 'May I at least ask her if she is interested in the position? I know how she feels, sitting there. I wonder if she is as hungry as I was.'

'Certainly you may ask her.' He walked a few steps with her, away from the registry. 'And you might as well know I hired several of those seamen on the docks to help Starkey do whatever it is he does so well; peel potatoes for Etienne, if he needs it; and assist my new steward in ridding the house—our home—of cupids *in flagrante*.' He patted her hand. 'I suppose we are both easy marks. Too bad I didn't know about this character flaw in you sooner.'

She leaned against his shoulder. 'Yes, Admiral! I suppose one of us should be surly and grim, to make this marriage a success.'

'Admiral, is it?' He winced elaborately, then grew serious. 'Sophie, there were months on end, maybe years, when I was grim. As for surly, you may ask any number of my subalterns. I hope those days are over. I know how much those men on the docks sacrificed for England. It gave me a real pleasure to hire them.'

She nodded. 'Then I suppose we are two fools. I will go ask her.'

'Suppose she cannot iron or make good pleats?' he asked, back to his light-hearted remarks.

'Then you will have to love your useful wife wrinkled,' she retorted, pinking up as she said it. 'I can show her how to iron,' she added honestly. 'I have never had a dresser.'

Her name was Amelia Thayn. After a long look at Sally, during which her eyes filled with tears, she nodded. 'Lady Bright, I am no expert with clothing. I am a governess.'

'I know that. I have never had a dresser before. I suggest that we will figure this out as we go along. And if you wish to keep looking for governess positions, while you are working for me, I have no objections.'

'You would *do* that?'

'Of course she would. My wife is kindness personified.'

Sally looked at the door, where her husband stood. *So are you*, she thought. 'It seems only logical,' she told Miss Thayn. 'I know you would rather be a governess, but these are hard times.'

They settled on a wage, and Sally left Miss Thayn there to collect her thoughts while she spoke with the employment agent about an upstairs maid, a downstairs maid, a maid of all work and a laundress. He promised to select the best he had and send them to her tomorrow. When she returned to the antechamber, the governess was ready to go.

'I owe a shilling to the landlady at the Mulberry Inn,' she said, keeping her voice low, as red spots burned in her cheeks. 'There is also the matter of...of several books I have pawned.'

At least you were not sleeping in churches, Sally thought, as they stood in the antechamber, as close to tears as her newest employee.

Admiral Bright came to her rescue. He handed several coins to Miss Thayn, who stumbled over her gratitude. 'Call this a bonus for coming to work in a den of iniquity! Settle up your affairs and come to the registry by nine of the clock tomorrow. This post chaise will conduct you and our other female workers to our house. You will be in charge.' He turned to Sally. 'My dearest, explain our home to this nice lady while I talk to the coachman.'

She did and was rewarded with a faint smile. 'The house is being painted, but it will require more paint in more rooms, I fear,' Sally concluded, as the admiral returned to them and helped them into the post chaise. 'Now we will take you to the...the Mulberry, you say?'

'I can walk there, I assure you,' Miss Thayn said.

'What, and not allow us to puff up our consequence?' Bright said. 'Really, Miss Thayn!'

Subdued into obedience by the admiral's natural air of command, which Sally knew she could never hope to alter, should she be given that task, Miss Thayn unbent enough to lean back in the chaise. She closed her eyes and gave a long sigh that sounded suspiciously like profound gratitude.

They deposited Miss Thayn at the Mulberry and listened to more profuse thanks. When they started east towards the coast, they passed a shabby inn rejoicing in the name of the Noble George. Sally took her husband's hand. 'Please stop here a moment.'

The admiral leaned out the window and spoke to the coachman. 'Now what, my dear?' he asked. 'It must be something clandestine. You're looking rosy again, Lady Bright.'

'Charles, you are the limit,' she said. 'When I was looking so hard for work myself, I came here to ask if they needed kitchen help.' She put her hands to her warm face. 'The landlord was a horrible man. He leered at me and told me if I wanted to work in his kitchen, he would turn out his little pots-and-pans girl and make room for me, if I wanted to supply other…services.'

'Bastard,' the admiral said mildly. 'I'm only being so polite because you really don't want to hear what I'm actually thinking. Shall I call him out and hit him with my hook? A few whacks and he would be in ribbons.'

'No! I want to hire that child to help Etienne. No telling what other demands that odious man has placed on her.'

'How old do you think she is?'

'Not above eight or nine.'

'Good God. I'll go in with you,' he said, his face dark.

He did, glowering at the landlord in probably much the same fashion he had cowed faulty officers, during his years as admiral. Sally felt considerable satisfaction to see how quickly the man leaped to Admiral Bright's mild enough suggestion that he produce the pots-and-pans girl immediately, if he knew what was good for him. As she waited, and the landlord hemmed and hawed, and looked everywhere but at the admiral, Sally reminded herself never to get on the ugly side of her husband.

When the girl came upstairs, grimy and terrified, she seemed to sense immediately who would help her, and slid behind Sally, who knelt beside her. The landlord tried to move forwards, but Charles Bright stepped in front of Sally and the scullery maid.

'That's far enough,' he said. His voice was no louder than ever, but filled with something in the tone that made the landlord retreat to the other side of the room.

Slowly, so as not to frighten the child, Sally put her hand on a skinny shoulder. 'I am Lady Bright and this is my husband, Admiral Sir Charles Bright.'

The scullery maid's mouth opened in a perfect O. She gulped.

'I have been hiring maids to work in my house. I need a scullery maid, and think you would suit perfectly.'

'M-m-me?' she stammered.

'Oh, yes. You might have to share a room with another maid in the servants' quarters. Would that be acceptable?'

'A room?' she asked, her voice soft.

'Yes, of course. Where do you sleep now?'

The little girl glanced at the landlord and moved closer to Sally. 'On the dirty clothes in the laundry,' she whispered.

Sally couldn't help the chill that ran through her spine. In another moment, Charles was beside her, his hand firmly on her shoulder.

'We'll do better than dirty clothes,' he said. 'What's your name?'

She shrugged, and scratched at her neck. 'General, they called me Twenty, because they thought I wouldn't live too long in the workhouse.'

Sally bowed her head and felt Charles's fingers go gentle against her neck.

'We'll find you a good name, Twenty,' he said. 'Will you come with us? Don't worry about him. Look at us.'

'I'll come,' she whispered.

'Excellent,' he said. 'Now, is there anything you want to fetch from your…from the laundry room? Lady Bright will go with you, if you'd like.'

'Nuffink,' was all Twenty said. She tugged at her over-large dress and patted it down with all the dignity she could muster. 'I'm ready now.'

'Very well, my dear,' Charles said, his voice faltering for only a split second. 'Go with this extra-fine lady to the chaise out front. I will have a few words with your former employer. Go on, my dear.' He glanced behind him at the landlord. 'I promise not to do anything I will regret.'

That worries me, Sally thought, *If you thrashed him, I doubt you would regret it.* She shepherded the scullery maid into the street, quickly boosting her into the chaise, where she looked around, her eyes wide.

'Cor, miss,' she whispered. 'I've never ridden in one of these!'

'We're going a few miles away to my husband's estate, where you will work for a French cook. He will treat you very well. So will we.' Sally could barely get the words out, as she watched tears slip down the child's face, leaving tracks through the grime.

She smelled abominably, but Sally hugged her and sat close to her. In a few minutes, her husband joined them. He sat opposite them.

'Twenty, I asked your former employer for your back wages. He was a little forgetful at first, but eventually he remembered that he owed you this. Hold out your hands.'

He poured a handful of pence in the astounded child's hands. They spilled through on to her dress, which she

stretched out to receive them. 'When we get home, I will
ask Etienne to find you a crock to keep them in.'

She nodded, too shy to speak, and edged closer to Sally,
who put her arm around the girl. Finally, it was too much,
and she burst into noisy tears. Disregarding her odour and
dirty clothes, Sally pulled her on to her lap, whispering
to her until she fell asleep. When she slept soundly, Sally
put her on the seat and rested the scullery maid's head in
her lap.

'That landlord told me she hadn't earned a penny
because she kept breaking things and stealing food,'
Charles said, his voice low. 'Perhaps Wilberforce should
look closer to home, if he wants to see the slave trade.' He
leaned forwards and tapped Sally's knee with his hook.
'You're quite a woman, Mrs B.'

She looked at him, shabby in old civilian clothes years
out of fashion because he had never been on land for most
of two decades. His hair could have used a barber's shears,
and he probably hadn't been standing close enough to his
razor this morning. There was steel in him, and a capability
that made her want to crawl into his lap and sob out every
misery she had been subjected to, like Twenty. All those
years at sea, spent protecting his homeland, seemed to be
reflected in his eyes.

'Thank you,' was all she said.

Starkey was aghast to see what they had brought home
with them, but Etienne didn't bat an eye. In no time, he
had water heating for a bath. When the water was ready,
and Twenty eyeing it with considerable fear, he appeared
with a simple dress.

'This was in a trunk in the room I am using,' he said.
'Here are some shears. Hold it up to her and cut it to size.
That will do for now.'

'Etienne, you're a wonder,' Sally said, as she took the bit of muslin and wondered which Fair Cyprian had worn it.

Twenty's protests died quickly enough, when she saw there was no rescue from a bath, followed by a pine tar block that barely foamed, but which smelled strong enough to drive away an army of lice. Her hair was already short. Trapping the towel-draped scullery maid between her knees, Sally trimmed and then combed her hair until it was free of animal companions.

Dressed in the hand-me-down, Twenty stood still for a sash cut from a tea towel, and then whirled in front of the room's tiny mirror. She stopped and staggered after too many revolutions, and flopped on the bed, giggling.

'I'll have something better made for you soon,' Sally told her.

'I couldna ask for more, miss,' she said, and it went right to Sally's heart. *I'm not sure I could, either,* she thought.

There were two small beds in the little room. While Sally made up one, over Starkey's protests that he could do it, Twenty sat at the table in the servants' hall and ate a bowl of soup, not stopping until she had drained it. Sally looked over to see Etienne struggling with his composure as he handed her a small roll, and followed it with two more. When Twenty finished, she yawned, moved the bowl aside and put her head on the table. In less than a minute, she slept. She woke up in terror and cried out when Starkey picked her up, but settled down when Sally took her in her arms and carried her into the little room. She sat beside the bed until Twenty slept.

'She doesn't have a name, Etienne,' Sally said, when she came into the servants' hall. 'She is your pots-and-pans girl. You should name her.'

'Vivienne, after my sister?' he said decisively. 'Vivienne was her age when she died. It is a good name.'

'Very well. You can tell her in the morning.'

She went upstairs slowly, tired in body, but more in mind. Etienne said he would bring supper soon, but she craved company more than soup or meat. She looked in the sitting room and up at the ceiling, which had been painted a sedate soft white.

'Starkey said it's only the first coat,' the admiral said from the sofa, where he sat with his shoes off and his feet out in front of him. 'You can tell them tomorrow what colour you would like.'

It was utterly prosaic, but she burst into tears anyway, and soon found herself burrowed in close to the admiral, his arm about her.

'I'm sorry,' she managed to gasp, before a fresh wave of tears made her shoulders shake.

'Oh, belay that,' he murmured. 'Is she going to be all right?'

She nodded, taking the handkerchief he held out with his hook. 'I don't know. Can we send for a physician tomorrow? When she was in the bath, I noticed her private parts… Oh, Charles, they're all inflamed. Do you think that horrible man…?' She couldn't say any more. He held her close.

'The physician will sort her out,' he said, his voice hard. 'Too bad I cannot have that man flogged around the fleet until the skin comes off his back in tatters.'

She shuddered. 'You've done that?'

'That and more, and for less offense, Sophie,' he said. He put his hand over her eyes, closing them. 'Don't think about it. The best thing that happened to Twenty was you.'

'Her name is Vivienne. Etienne named her.'

She sighed, happy to close her eyes behind his hand. He kissed the top of her head and cradled her against his chest.

'It's a tough world, my dear,' he said.

'Not here, not in this decrepit den of thieves,' she said softly. 'I'd like a very soft green in this room. Of course, that might require new furniture.'

She felt him chuckle, more than heard him.

They were sitting like that, close together, heads touching, when Starkey opened the door and cleared his throat.

'Sir, your sisters are here.' He paused, and closed his eyes against the horror of it all. 'They have brought Egyptian furniture.'

Charles groaned. 'Oh, Lord, there you go—new furniture.'

Chapter Eleven

Sally tried to sit up, but her husband had anchored her to him. She heard his intake of breath and looked at the door to see two ladies staring back, their mouths open, their eyes wide.

'Charles,' one of them wailed. 'What have you done? And without our permission!'

'My sisters,' the admiral said in a flat voice. He released Sally and got to his feet, holding out his hand for her. 'Sisters, my wife.'

The ladies in the doorway continued to stare. Finally, the younger one spoke and it was not a pleasant tone of voice.

'Charles William Edward Bright, What Have You Done?'

Dear me, she really does speak in capital letters, Sally thought. She glanced at her husband, who had turned bright red. 'Breathe, dear,' she murmured.

He cleared his throat. 'Fannie and Dora, I have somehow managed to find myself a wife without any assistance.'

Now what? she thought, eyeing the women. They were noticeably older than their little brother, and from the angry looks they darted at her, obviously considered themselves the last court of appeals for their little brother.

Charles tucked her hand in the crook of his arm and towed her to the door. 'Fannie and Dora, let me introduce Sophie Bright. We were married in Plymouth recently. Dearest, the one on the left is Fannie—more properly Mrs William Thorndyke—and the other one is Dora, more properly Lady Turnbooth. Their husbands have predeceased them, and they have ample time on their hands.'

'The better to provide our little brother with the guidance he requires on land,' Fannie said, not acknowledging Sally's curtsy.

'You have taught me well,' Charles said smoothly. 'I managed to find a wife on my own.'

'She's from Scotland!' Dora burst out. To Sally's chagrin, she buried her face in her handkerchief and the feathers on her bonnet quivered.

'Dora, it's not another planet,' her brother said, with just the merest hint of exasperation in his voice.

'Oats! Mildew!' Dora exclaimed, which made Charles's lips twitch, to Sally's amusement.

'I speak English,' Sally assured them. 'Won't you please have a seat? I will inform our chef of your arrival.'

'You needn't bother,' Fannie said in the brusque tone of someone used to commanding the field. 'I know how to handle French cooks. I will go down there and tell him what is what. I have done it before.'

Sally glanced at her husband. *This is one of those duties you have outlined*, she thought. *Let us see if I can earn my keep.* 'Mrs Thorndyke, that is my responsibility.'

Fannie didn't surrender without a fight. 'He is French! I can handle him.'

'So can I,' Sally said, grateful they could not see her heart jumping about in her breast. 'Do have a seat and visit with your brother.' She couldn't help herself. 'I know he has been expecting your company.'

Shame on her. Sally set her lips firmly together as Charles struggled manfully to turn his guffaw into a cough. 'Bad lungs from all that cold weather on the blockade,' he managed to say. She closed the door behind her, but not before he gave her a measuring look.

She leaned against the door for a moment. When she composed herself, she noticed a rough-looking man in the foyer. 'Yes?' she asked, wondering where he fit into the picture.

'I gots a wagonload of furniture,' he said, with no preliminaries. 'Nasty black dogs to sit on—Lord 'elp us—a statue of a bloke wearing a nappy. 'E walks funny, too, one leg in front of t'other.'

A pharaoh would have been right at home with our over-eager Penelope beside the front door, she thought, wishing Charles were there for this delicious interview. 'Just leave the dogs and statue in the wagon.'

The man revolved his battered hat in nervous hands. He eyed the sitting-room door with something close to terror. 'Them gentry morts will 'ave my 'ide if I don't unload.'

'And I will, if you do,' she said sweetly. 'What a dilemma.' She took a firm stance. 'This is my home.'

Looking at the delivery man, she was struck by the fact that it *was* her home, lascivious cupids and all. She considered the shabby man before her and felt her resolve slide away. *There cannot be much between this man and a workhouse.*

'Wait here.' She returned to the sitting room, and gestured to her husband, who was sitting between his sisters, both of whom were talking at the same time. He looked up, relieved, when she called his name and came into the hall, closing the door behind him.

'Your timing is exquisite. You are obviously my *deus ex machina*,' he told her.

'I continue to be an expensive one.' Sally explained to him about the delivery. 'If he doesn't deliver the Egyptian furniture, I doubt your sisters will compensate him for his efforts. I don't want that on my conscience, but I also do not want wooden jackals or pharaohs keeping either of us up at night or frightening the help.'

The admiral thought a moment. He looked at the delivery man, who continued to revolve his cap in his hands. 'Behind this manor is a stable. My man Starkey can show you. Unload the furniture there. What is your fee?'

The man named it and Charles paid him. 'That was simple enough, Sophie,' he said, after the man had left. 'Too bad I cannot unload my sisters there, too.' He eyed her. 'What is causing that wide-eyed stare, Sophie? Did I not pay him enough?'

She couldn't help the stare. She had never met anyone like him. 'Charles, you solved this problem in less than thirty seconds! I am stunned, that is all.'

'Quick decisions are a lifetime habit, my dear,' he told her, all serenity. 'It seems I made a quick one a few days ago.'

So he had. All she could do was look at him, her mouth open, until he gently reminded her to 'go belowdeck and alert my crew'.

She did as he asked, but not before he took her hand, bowed over it and kissed it. The door to the sitting room opened. He looked her in the eye and pulled her close to whisper in her ear, 'We are madly in love, or so I have told my sisters. Tell Etienne to bring up some soup, cold if he can manage it, and nothing else. It will offend his Gallic pride, but hopefully encourage my sisters to leave tomorrow.' He took the moment to kiss her cheek. 'Now. Back I go to the lion's den.'

Etienne was not a slow man; he understood precisely what Sally wanted. 'I will even put in too much salt and burn the bottom of the pan.' He sighed. 'I wouldn't commit such a desecration, if this were not a worthy cause, Lady Bright. There might even be some mouldy bread in the bin.'

She heard pans in the scullery and looked in to see Twenty—Vivienne—washing dishes. The child looked up and smiled. 'I'm not tired any more, mum.'

Sally felt tears prick her eyelids. *I think we have all wandered on to a good pasture*, she thought, as she nodded and returned upstairs, where Starkey waited to tell her he had prepared two rooms for her sisters-in-law. 'I moved your clothing and other items into the admiral's room, as well,' he told her, his face impassive.

'But...'

He easily overrode her. 'Admiral Bright commanded it. After all, you *are* newly married, and there is a pretence to maintain, isn't there?'

There was something in the dry way he spoke that told her volumes about his feelings. She felt her face grow hot, but she spoke calmly. 'Yes, there is, Starkey,' she said, keeping her voice steady even as her stomach churned from the arch look he gave her. 'We know this charade is to spare him his sisters, and so we shall.'

I do not have an ally there, she told herself as she entered the sitting room again. Two cold faces turned to glare at her, but there was the admiral, looking nothing but relieved.

'Sophie, dearest, I have been telling my sisters— our sisters now, eh?—that you and I have been faithful correspondents for several years, since the death of your husband in battle.'

Oh, my goodness, she thought. *We're creating a monster.*

'I wonder you did not say anything in your letters to us, brother,' Fannie told him, looking far from mollified. 'We could have visited...uh...Lady Bright in Bath.'

And then the admiral was looking at her, too, his eyebrows raised hopefully. She had no choice but to prevaricate. 'It was a matter of some delicacy,' Sally said finally. 'Surely you understand.'

Sceptical looks assured her they did not, but she had no idea what to say next, except, 'Etienne informs me that there is only soup. We will not be fully staffed until some time late tomorrow.' She held her hands tightly together, so they would not shake. 'We have arranged for you to sleep here tonight, and will wish you Godspeed tomorrow, when you leave.'

Mercifully, dinner was short. There was only so much attention to attach to leek soup, especially lukewarm soup with the flavor of burned pot competing with rancid butter. The hour in the sitting room seem stretched as taut as India rubber. It came to a merciful conclusion after one of Admiral Bright's more gory stories of sea battle, followed by shipwreck, starvation and imprisonment. 'And that, dear sisters, rounds out my career as a midshipman,' Bright told them as Fannie waved ammonia under Dora's nose until she sneezed. 'Unless you wish to hear about that regrettable instance of cannibalism.' Dora yanked the ammonia out of Fannie's hand and held it closer to her nose. 'No? Another day, then. Perhaps when you return in a month or two. At Christmas?'

What could they say?

* * *

Her head was pounding by the time the sisters closed the doors to their respective rooms, one of which had been hers. She only hoped Starkey had removed all trace of her presence. Admiral Bright seemed to take it all in his stride. He opened the door to his room wide.

'Starkey informs me there are no other beds in the place, Sophie.'

She glared at him. He staggered back as if she had shot him, which made Sally put her hand to her mouth to squelch her laughter. She let him tug her inside.

'I know, I know. It seems strange to me that the former owner could have had only three beds on this floor, considering how he used this property. Perhaps no one was particular. There *are* soft rugs in the empty rooms.'

Sally gasped. 'What *won't* you say?' she asked. 'Better I should ask, what did you say to them?'

'No more than you heard,' he told her. 'I didn't have time to fashion a great big whopper. Sit down, Sophie. I won't bite.' He patted the bed, where he sat.

She pulled up a chair from its place in front of the fireplace and sat there. 'So we have maintained a correspondence of some four or five years' duration.'

'Indeed we have. You were the soul of rectitude, and I was busy in the fleet. We scarcely set eyes on each other in all that time, but after a visit to Bath after Waterloo, one thing led to another, and here we are.'

'Do they really believe you?' she asked.

'I hope so.'

'You could have told them the truth. Maybe it would have been best.'

He began to unbutton his shirt. One button seemed to hang up in the fabric, so she sat beside him and undid it for him. He undid the cufflink on his handless arm, and held out the other arm so she could undo that cufflink.

'I considered it, but why should I embarrass someone who is doing me a favour? I remain convinced that once my sisters see I have managed to tie the knot without any more meddling from them, they will get bored and leave me—us—alone.'

'You know them better than I do,' she said doubtfully.

'I've been long years away from them, too,' he replied, as he pulled the shirt collar away from the harness and looked at her.

Without a word, she twisted the small metal tab that held it together.

'Help me off with my shirt, will you?' he asked, bunching up the fabric in the front.

She did as he asked. Holding the shirt, she watched as he shrugged out of the harness, exposing his maimed arm. He set the harness and its attached hook on the night stand by the bed. He held up his arm.

'You can see it was a clean amputation. The surgeon marvelled at how neatly that rope had separated me from what was obviously an accessory, since I seem to manage well enough without it.'

She looked at his arm, feeling the hairs on her neck raise, and then settle. 'Does it ever hurt?'

'It did when it happened. God, the pain. And then I swear I could feel my fingers. Wiggle them, even.' He smiled at her. 'It never hurts now.'

He went into his dressing room. She pulled the chair back to the fireplace and sat there. When he came out, he was in his nightshirt. He plopped down in the chair next to her, putting his bare feet on the ottoman. He took her hand, running his fingers lightly across her knuckles.

'I have put you in a bad spot. After all the nonsense, and

political manoeuvring—yes, even at sea, God help us—and constant vigilance, all I wanted when I came onshore was to be left alone, and my sisters wouldn't allow it.' He didn't even seem to be aware that he had raised her hand to his cheek. 'I think they meant well, but they will never understand that I just want to be left alone. I married you as a buffer, but that is hardly fair.'

She thought about what he was saying, even as he rested the back of her palm against his cheek. She felt the motion acutely, and the slow warmth spreading upward from her belly. He seemed unmindful of his action. *I know my place*, she reminded herself. A gentle resistance to his touch made him release her hand and look at her, apology in his eyes.

'What's the matter with me?' he asked suddenly. 'I am forty-five years old, long thought to be a sensible man, and I am telling lies—real prevarications—right and left. I don't understand myself right now.'

He leaped up from the chair, stalked into his dressing room again, and returned with his threadbare robe. He frowned, looking into the distance, as he tied an expert bow one-handed, then sat down again.

To lighten the moment, she looked at his robe. 'Please tell me you didn't order another robe from the tailor today,' she said. 'I rather like that shabby thing.'

'I didn't,' he told her. 'It never occurred to me.' He got up again and started to pace. 'Did you ever meet such an idiot?'

He seemed to be expecting an answer. She considered the question as he paced. 'You are forty-five and you have spent most of your life at sea…'

'…where life was much simpler,' he grumbled. 'I swear it was!'

'Let us consider this. Life at sea. Oh, yes, there was a

war on, wasn't there? It might have been difficult. You buy a house with cupids, just for the view.'

By now he was listening to her. He leaned against the fireplace, his eyes starting to disappear into a smile.

'Horrors! You marry a widow on woefully short notice.'

'Perhaps that was a smart idea,' he said, getting into the mood of her gentle teasing.

'The issue is still unresolved, sir.'

'And I am afraid of two domineering women. Sophie, I was an Admiral of the Fleet!' He began to pace again.

She looked at him then, studied his face as he stared back at her. She observed his grey hair, his prematurely lined face and the restless way he stalked from one small space to the other, the area defined by a crowded deck.

'I conclude that you never had a chance to be young, Admiral.'

He stopped and frowned, mouthed 'Admiral' to her amusement, walked another length and back, then sat down again. 'You could be right.' He started to hold her hand again, but thought better of it. 'It's a little late for a childhood now.' He almost smiled. 'You are stuck with rather a poor bargain, Sophie.'

'I beg to differ! You got rid of the Egyptian furniture. The cupids are fading.'

'Lord almighty! Dare we hope that my sisters will be gone tomorrow?'

He seemed more at peace now. His eyelids began to droop.

'I think we dare hope,' she said, keeping her voice soft. 'Go to bed, Admiral.'

He closed his eyes. 'Not unless you join me. I promise to keep my hand to myself.'

'I can sleep in this chair.'

'Nonsense. You're almost as tall as I am. It will take a master mechanic to straighten you out in the morning if you attempt it. You'll have your own room again, Sophie. Don't give me grief over this.'

She had no intention of arguing further, not with her own eyes closing. 'Very well. I will change in your dressing room and you will mind your manners.'

He was asleep when she came out of the dressing room, flat on his back with his maimed arm resting on his chest. *I don't mind this*, Sally thought, as she watched him a moment. She carefully pulled back the coverlet and slid between the sheets with a sigh. What a long day it had been.

She was careful not to move towards him, staying on her side of the bed and listening to his regular breathing. The homely sound of another human being eased her heart. She thought of all the days, weeks and months she had slept alone, worrying herself about money and shame until she woke as tired as she had been when she went to bed. This was different. True, the sisters were just down the hall. There were so many cupids left to paint over. Vivienne needed a physician. Other servants were coming.

'You're frowning.'

She gasped and turned her head, then closed her eyes as Charles Bright, her convenient husband, smoothed the lines between her eyes.

'Go to sleep, Sophie. Dream that we are both a little more intelligent in the morning.'

She rolled on to her side, away from him, trying to decide what was different. She listened to the admiral's even breathing again. *I am not worrying alone*, she told herself. *That is the difference.*

Chapter Twelve

Some time in the middle of the night, Charles Bright had a nightmare. He never shouted out in his sleep, but Starkey told him once that he muttered to himself and flailed about. He must have done both, but he didn't open his eyes. He started when a hand touched his back. As he lay there, surprised and disoriented, the hand began to gently massage his shoulder. He wanted to roll over, or say something, but he lay there quietly, enjoying the sensation of sharing his bed with a woman. It had been a long time. He couldn't remember when he had last spent an entire night in a woman's bed, and this was his wife. He smiled to himself and went back to sleep.

He woke at his usual time, but it was a better awakening than most. He gave all the credit to Sophie Bright, who had tucked herself in tight and draped her arm over his chest.

He knew she had begun the night with her back to him, and about as far away as she could get in the bed without tumbling off. He vaguely remembered the gentle feel of her hands on his back, when he had gone through his usual nightmare rigmarole. But here she was. He couldn't see her face, because her brown hair was spread all over his chest.

Her breasts were warm against his side. He wanted to run his hand down her arm, but he knew it would wake her up and probably alarm her. He could look, though, and it pained him that her arms were so slim. *Have you been living on air, lady?* he asked himself. He had learned, early in his association with his chef, not to burden him with over-attention, but it wouldn't hurt to go belowdeck soon and engage Etienne in a conspiracy to use more butter, milk and cheese and other such ingredients so dear to a French chef's palate.

It scarcely surprised him that he felt himself growing hard. A man would have to be made of sterner stuff than he was to resist what lay in his arms. What amused him was the fact that he couldn't remember a time in recent years when he had felt that way in the morning. But then, war and life had intervened, and he would blame them. Any romance he had enjoyed was most generally accomplished at night, and then followed by a return to the dock and a ferry out to his flagship. He hated to feel furtive out of what was a man's normal desire, but he had learned quickly enough that admirals were not supposed to have such passions; at least, if his captains were to be believed. It was a damned nuisance to be a good example.

During the worst of the crisis, after he reached flag rank, he had been continuously at sea for six years. He envied his dashing frigate captains, who could leave the fleet and return to land, now and then, for whatever extra-curricular activity they could sandwich in between naval assignments. The ocean was well and truly his home, and there were few women there.

But here was this pretty lady, his wife, and he had already assured her that this would be a marriage of convenience. *I am a dolt*, he thought, with a certain wry humour. *I've encouraged her to keep my sisters far distant. When they leave this morning, there's no excuse to keep her in my bed.*

Thoroughly dissatisfied with himself, Charles lay there feeling sour until his anatomy returned to its usual state of somnolence. Then he carefully edged himself out of Sophie's slack embrace. She turned her face up to him like a flower seeking sunshine, but did not open her eyes. She let out a soft sigh of satisfaction that went to his heart as almost nothing else could have. How ill used this lovely person had been, how trampled on. And why would any man married to her ever have even contemplated suicide, much less committed it? He couldn't fathom it.

After a wrestle in his dressing room about whether to garb for the day, or just pad down to the breakfast room for a cup of tea for Sophie, he put on his well-worn dressing gown and opted for bare feet. Perhaps his sisters weren't up yet. And if they were, too bad.

Fannie and Dora were already seated in the breakfast room, and looking none too pleased. He glanced at the side table, and hid his smile. Etienne Dupuis had exerted himself to one pitiful pot of porridge. He sniffed. His chef had burned it, too—excellent man. He took tea and joined his sisters.

Fannie wasted not a minute in telling him what she thought. 'Charles, your cook is more than usually pathetic!'

He sipped his tea. 'Fannie, give my chef a chance. He has no staff yet. You'll both be so much better off back in

London, until we get things sorted out here.' He engineered what he thought was an arch, knowing look. 'Besides, my dears, Sophie and I would like a little privacy. You understand, I am sure, having once been newly married yourselves.'

Dora blushed and nodded, but Fannie only set her lips in a tighter line, which reinforced his suspicion that the late Mr Thorndyke was no Romeo. 'I wish I could tell you that I believe your story about a long correspondence with… with…'

'My dear wife,' he supplied, feeling much the little brother.

'Your wife, but I am sceptical.'

Might as well bring out the big guns. Charles levelled a look at his older sister that he had spent a lifetime perfecting to use on wayward captains. 'Believe it, Frances,' he said, clipping off each word. 'I tried in many ways to tell you I have not been interested in any of the beauties you have thrown my way, and that I was entirely capable of finding a wife. If you fault me for not telling you about my…longstanding attachment to Sophie, I believe it is the right of every man to do those things for himself.'

He couldn't make it any plainer. Charles went to the sideboard and poured another cup of tea. 'I am going to take tea to my wife. All I ask is that you give us a few weeks of solitude.'

It pained him to hurt their feelings. He looked at his sisters, remembering how they had mothered him when all three of them were not so old, and their own mother had died. It had been a trying time, and these dear do-gooders had eased his childish heart.

'Give us a little time,' he said gently. 'When you come back in a while, there will be more servants, better food and hot water on demand. My dears, we're just not ready to entertain. It's as simple as that.'

Dora nodded, but glanced at Fran, who still looked stony. Dora opened her mouth to speak, but thought better of it, deferring, as always, to her old sister. Charles watched them for some sign of understanding, but found none in evidence, as he left the room.

At least the tea was still warm. He stood outside his own door a moment, wondering whether to knock, then tapped on the door with his wrist.

'Come in. You shouldn't have to stand on ceremony outside your own door!'

Oh, hell. He would have to put down the cup to turn the handle. 'I'm bringing you tea and I cannot open the door,' he said, embarrassed. 'Maybe it is true that many hands make light work. I'd settle for two, now and then.'

He heard light footsteps and the door opened on Sophie's bright face. 'Sorry. You intend to spoil me this morning, too?' she asked.

'Maybe I have started a tradition,' he told her, as she climbed back in bed. The outline of her hips against the much-washed flannel captured his eyes. Too bad she was so quick.

Sophie slid over far enough to allow room for him to sit, which flattered him. In fact, she patted the mattress and drew her legs up close to her chest. He sat down and handed her the tea, which she accepted with a smile that made his heart thud in his chest.

Sophie sipped and looked at him over the rim of the cup. 'I was hoping you would bring me tea.'

There were no blushes this time; they were just two people in a room with each other. What *had* happened last night? Had his nightmare, as unspectacular as it always was, given her yet another purpose in his life?

'I hope I didn't bother you with my restlessness last night.'

She shrugged. 'When I was younger and certainly more foolish, I read a very bad novel, where the hero thrashed and cried out and walked in his sleep, then ended up on the castle's parapet, ready to jump. All you did was mutter a little and try to sit up.' She rested her hand for the smallest moment on his wrist. 'Heavens knows you must have had more traumas than anything a female novelist could conjure. Those stories you told your sisters last night are probably only the mild ones, fit for ladies.'

'They are. I doubt even you are ready for the perils of masts falling in the midst of battle, or the sight of your gallant husband—still possessing both hands—swimming below the waterline in shark-infested waters to plug a sail into a hole. Sophie, mine was quite a career.'

She gave him that appraising look again, so totally turning all her attention to him that he felt unbelievably flattered.

'Very well, what?'

The moment he spoke, he realised something had happened in their relationship. He didn't think she was aware of it yet, but he was, acutely so. He suddenly felt at ease with this woman he barely knew, as though they were confederates. It was the most intimate moment of his life, and he wasn't even touching her. Her eyes were deep pools, and he felt completely at home, swimming in their depths. 'What?' he asked again.

'I know what will occupy your time,' she said, resting her chin on her updrawn knees and still mesmerising him with the intensity of her gaze. 'Your memoirs.'

He was not thinking of stuffy memoirs, not with her so close. 'Sophie, who on earth would read the blasted thing?'

She gave an exasperated sigh. 'Your men, anyone in England with blood in his veins. Me! I would read them. Oh, my goodness, I would.' She straightened her legs and took him by the arm. 'I will help you. You can dictate them to me.'

He relished her hold on him. 'Madam wife, you are all about in your head.'

He said it softly, because he was leaning closer to her. He kissed her and found her lips as soft as he thought they might be. She drew back slightly; he knew he had startled her. She only moved her hand from his arm to the side of his neck and returned his kiss.

In another moment, she had relaxed against the pillows and he was bending over her, pressing against her, their arms around each other, her hands splayed across his back. She sighed when the kiss ended, but continued to hold him close until someone knocked on the door and then opened it. She gasped in his ear.

Starkey stood there, shocked. For just a millisecond, his expression turned so dark and disapproving that Charles sucked in his breath. The look was gone as quickly as it came. Perhaps Charles had imagined it.

Starkey closed the door part way, averting his gaze. 'Beg your pardon, Admiral,' he said, his voice wooden. 'I usually help you with your harness about now.'

Her face crimson, Sophie sat up, her hands in her lap, her glorious lips tight together now. *What a position to be in*, Charles thought, angered at Starkey's blunder. 'You do usually help me,' he said, wishing he did not sound so brusque. 'Let that be one more job you need not worry about, unless I specifically ask. Knock and wait from now on, for God's sake.'

It came out hard and mean. *I can smooth it over later*, Charles thought, looking at Starkey's wounded expression as the door closed. He turned his attention to Sophie and blundered again.

'I didn't mean to do that,' he said, standing up, unwilling to look at her. He did take a little glance and saw the hurt in her eyes, as brief as Starkey's. 'But I also said this would be a marriage of convenience, did I not?' he asked, instantly angry with himself. Why had that come out so harsh?

'You did say that,' Sophie replied in a small voice. 'I'm sorry.'

'You have nothing to apologise for.' He got up and went to the door, except there was nowhere to go.

Sophie must have realised the same thing. He knew he had hurt her feelings, because she wouldn't look at him. 'I'll be dressed and out of your room in a moment,' she told him, her voice small.

She was as good as her word. He stared into the fireplace, wishing there was no one in his house except Sophie. The workmen were back in the rooms downstairs, moving around scaffolding and painting the stupid ceiling. Charles listened to other mechanics overhead in the attic, thumping for rotten boards and calling to each other. His sisters were on the prowl somewhere, ready to take umbrage the moment anyone offered any.

Sophie let herself out quietly. He heard the barest rustle of her skirt and looked around to see the back of her head as she closed the door.

'I am practically certifiable,' he declared to the door. He thought of the days he had sat at his desk at sea, considering thorny problems of cannon range, weather gauge, victuals going bad, water rationed, enemy close, crew sick—all the tasks he had to bend his mind to, every day of the war. The only thing on his mind right now was a woman, a subject almost foreign to a man so often at sea.

He had not imagined she had returned his kiss. In terms of days, she was a veritable stranger, but a lady about whom he had strong instincts. His quickness of mind had never failed him through decades of war. Charles took heart. *I made no mistake in the dining room of the Drake*, he thought. What he hadn't bargained on was how quickly she would touch his heart, body and mind.

'Sophie Bright. You're married to an idiot with one thing on his side—time. I believe I have the weather gauge, too. I cannot lose.'

He started to dress, then realised he needed to summon his testy servant and ask for help with the harness, since Sophie had fled the scene. He would ask Starkey's pardon and begin again.

I learned something this morning, he thought. He went to the bell pull, when he heard the front door close. It didn't precisely slam, but it closed loud enough. He looked out the window and there was his dear wife, walking down the weedy lane with some purpose in her stride. She had a book in her hand, but he was mostly interested in the way her skirt swayed from side to side.

'Ah, my dear, you are going to read to Rivka Brustein,' he told her retreating figure. 'A wise thing. Return when you are calm. My sisters will be gone, hopefully, and I will have thought this campaign through.'

Chapter Thirteen

Sophie slowed her steps as she approached the Brusteins' manor. Her face still felt hot from the embarrassment of Starkey seeing them like that. Or was it from the flush that flooded her chest after positively enjoying Admiral Bright's kiss? Andrew had been a slight man, frail, almost, especially in the last few months of his ordeal with Admiralty House. Clasping the admiral in her arms had been a new experience. He was a bigger man and she had found herself enjoying the weight of his upper body as he had begun to press down on her. It was a new sensation.

'Oh, Lord,' she whispered, putting her hands to her face. *Sally Bright, thank goodness you did not press up against him and sleep in his arms last night*, she thought. Considering their arrangement, so calmly worked out in that pew at St Andrew's Church, that would have been the outer limits of the role her husband had carefully outlined. True, she had patted him back to sleep, but anyone with half a brain would have done that.

She closed her eyes against the feeling that had taken such possession of her with that impulsive kiss. It had to be impulsive; surely he had no design to do such a thing. And why on earth did she kiss him back? Look where it led! All she had wanted to do then was undo that knot on his shabby robe and tug up his nightshirt.

She tried to consider the whole sequence rationally. It had been actually more than five years since she had been refreshed by a man. In the last year of his too-short life, Andrew had been too distracted to consider her a source of consolation. She didn't want to think about the admiral, because she felt herself growing warm in places where she had felt warm so little in recent years. Was it just that she wanted a man, or did she want *that* man?

Instinctively, she put her legs closer together until her knees touched, then managed a small laugh. 'You are such an idiot,' she reminded herself, keeping her voice low. *At least I did not throw myself on him last night*, Sophie thought, as she crossed the road and started down the much tidier lane to the Brustein manor. *That is a relief.*

The same cat was luxuriating in the same front window when she knocked. The housekeeper smiled to see her this time, though, and Jacob Brustein clapped his hands together like a child when she said she had come to read to Rivka Brustein.

'We were both hoping you were serious when you suggested that very thing,' he told her, as they walked upstairs. 'Your husband is elsewhere occupied?'

She told the old gentleman about Charles's sisters. 'They have wanted to manage him to the furthest degree, since he retired from the navy,' she said, as they went into Rivka's room. 'I believe he is trying to delicately manoeuvre them out of the house now.'

'And you thought it politic to be elsewhere,' Brustein said.

'They think I am a gross interloper,' she whispered.

'Relatives!' he replied. He touched his heart. 'Who would have them?' He came close to the bed and touched his wife's cheek. She opened her eyes. 'Rivka, my love. Look who has come to read to you!'

Jacob sat beside his wife a few minutes. He smiled when Rivka made a feeble shooing motion with her hand.

'This is for the ladies, Jacob! Find yourself something to do.'

With a wink at Sophie, he left the room quietly. Rivka turned her attention to Sophie. 'My dear girl. If you will leave the book here, I will make him read to me tonight, the old lover!' She folded her hands. 'But for now, you read.'

Sophie needed no more urging to begin with her favourites. When she finished those, she noticed that Rivka had closed her eyes, so she sat there silently, wondering whether to continue. After a long silence, Rivka spoke without opening her eyes. 'Do continue. Sometimes my eyelids are heavy, but I am listening.'

Sophie opened the little volume at random this time, and began reading. '"When my love swears that she is made of truth, I do believe her, though I know she lies."'

Sophie closed the book, her heart racing. *Good God, that is I*, she thought. She sniffed back tears, grateful that Rivka's eyes were closed.

She hadn't reckoned on the little lady in the bed, who opened her eyes and reached out her hand to capture Sophie's wrist. Her touch was as light as a bird's wing.

'Pitseleh, what on earth is the matter?'

There was no way Sophie could keep it in, not with such kindness in the old woman's voice. She let the story come out about her marriage of convenience, and how she had so nearly thrashed the whole thing that morning with what started as a simple kiss. She couldn't tell the whole, sorry tale, thinking it best to leave out Andrew's suicide. The admiral's marriage of convenience to a destitute widow was bad enough. 'Mrs Brustein, I am a failure at this marriage already and we are barely married!'

'Sophie! I may call you that, eh?'

Sophie nodded. 'Of course you may, Mrs Brustein. And if you have any advice…'

'My dear Sophie, I did not see my beloved Jacob's face until he raised my veil during our wedding. Was I terrified? Of this you may be certain. Did I learn to love him?' She wrinkled her nose, which made Sophie smile. 'We have four sons, two daughters—God bless them all—and he still sings to me at night if I ask him. Jacob has a lovely voice. Your admiral—is he a good man?'

'The very best,' Sophie replied, without hesitation. 'He could have done much better than me, I think.' She felt her face begin to flame. 'He…he made it quite clear from the outset that this was to be a marriage of convenience.'

Rivka managed an elaborate shrug. 'Minds can change, dearie.' She chuckled. 'Men like to think they do not need changing, so that must be our little secret.' Her tone became more reflective then, wistful even. 'We learned to love each other, and now I wish there were many more years ahead.'

'Surely there will be, Mrs Brustein.'

'You're a dear, but let us be realistic.' She touched Sophie's hand again, more emphatic this time. 'Do not waste time! We have so little of it.'

Those were good words. Sophie considered them as she walked home, teetered on the brink, then poured water on the whole matter by reminding herself that theirs was a marriage of convenience arranged by two rational people—one seeking a haven from poverty and the other eager to avoid meddling sisters. She would have to overlook the pleasant way Charles Bright smiled when he looked at her and forget about her admiration of someone who could make such swift decisions and not look back with regret. She knew it was the mark of a confident man, a leader. She had nothing to show for herself except a certain doggedness in times of crisis.

'Sophie, you can run his house and help him with his memoirs,' she said, employing that doggedness as she walked up the weedy lane. She stopped to look at the house when it came into view. Mechanics were crawling over the roof now, one and then another coming out of a hole near the chimney, looking for all the world like the four-and-twenty blackbirds baked in that dratted pie. As she stood there, she heard glass break. 'Bedlam,' she said.

Starkey met her in the foyer. 'The painters pushed a scaffold through the French doors. The sisters are no more,' he announced.

'Good God, did Charles shoot them?' she exclaimed.

'Really, ma'am,' he said, looking down his long nose at her, 'I should warn you that you have no allies there.'

'I believe that was patently obvious, Starkey.' *And I doubt I have an ally in you, either*, she thought. 'We can invite them back later, when the house is put back together again. Perhaps they will forgive me for being an encroaching mushroom and monopolising their brother.'

'If they will come,' he said ominously, bowed to her and stumped away on his wooden leg, still looking piratical and a little wounded now.

And you despise me because you think I am usurping your place with your master, she thought. *This was all supposed to be so simple, but it is not.*

Vastly discontented, she went in search of her husband. The painters in the drawing room looked at her with guilty expressions when she peered in. Yes, they had indeed sent a scaffold through the French doors. She sighed and moved on.

She found the admiral in the library, high up a ladder, throwing down books. Some of the small sculptures in the room were covered. The ones still exposed made her gasp.

'I tried to turn them around, but any direction is an eye-opener,' he said, as he pitched another book towards the centre of the room. He gestured to the bookshelves. 'I do believe that Lord Hudley bought every book the Vatican ever condemned.' He looked at her. 'Sophie, dear, should we just put a match to this whole place?'

She was tempted to tell him yes. She would have, except that he had just called her 'dear', even without any sisters around to bamboozle. She thought of a young and terrified Rivka, looking at an equally terrified Jacob when he raised her wedding veil.

She sat down. The sofa was comfortable and the fabric of excellent quality. 'No. This is a wonderful sofa. I like this sofa.'

He stared at her as though she had lost all reason.

'It suits me quite well, so you cannot burn down the house. Besides that, I can sit here and see the ocean, which is precisely why you bought this abomination in the first place. Really, Charles, you need to look past the...'

There was another crash from the sitting room.

'...little difficulties.'

'Sophie, you have lost your mind,' he said mildly, as he started down the ladder. 'Driven mad by my sisters, this house, who knows what?'

He sat beside her on the sofa; he even bounced a little, which made her turn away because she had to smile.

'It is a good sofa. Let's keep the house.'

They looked at each other then. Sophie thought she started first, but Charles was a hair-trigger second.

'I really should apologise—'

'Please overlook—'

They stopped. They looked at each other. *I don't care what you say*, she thought, her gaze not wavering. *You simply could not have been a terror to your men and an ogre in the fleet.*

He spoke first, his eyes on her. 'I propose that we overlook what happened this morning.' His eyes narrowed. 'I already recognise that sceptical expression of yours.'

'My thoughts precisely.'

Charles might have said he would overlook that early morning kiss, but then he put his arm around her. He gave her a quick squeeze, which she thought was possibly more brotherly than husbandly, but only by a tiny degree. 'Onward, madam.' He released her, but his arm still rested along the top of the sofa that neither of them, apparently, could do without. 'My sisters have gone. I have agreed to invite them for Christmas, or when the remodelling is done—whichever comes first. The physician is belowdeck with Vivienne.'

Sophie stood up quickly. 'I should be with her.'

'You should.' He took hold of her skirt and gave it a slight tug. 'No need to take the stairs two at a time, though. The servants also arrived. I believe Miss Thayn is sitting with her.'

'That *is* a relief!'

Truly, it was. When Sophie went to the servants' hall, her new dresser was sitting close to Vivienne. She watched them both for a small moment before they noticed her, pleased with Miss Thayn's attention to the young girl, who kept her eyes on the table. The physician was putting away some tools of his trade in his black bag. He looked up at Sophie.

'You must be Lady Bright.'

'Mrs Bright will do,' she replied, suddenly shy, with the other servants listening. She looked around the room, realising that she had never seen so many domestics in one place. *All this for two people*, she thought.

'Welcome to Admiral Bright's manor.' She wished she did not sound like a child trying to play the lady of the house. 'Things are a little rough right now, but we're glad you are here.' She looked for Starkey. 'You've already met Starkey, I am certain. Do believe me when I tell you he is totally in charge.'

She looked at each servant in turn, seeing nothing there but a desire to please. 'Starkey, they are yours.' She turned her attention to the physician. 'Sir, perhaps we could speak upstairs.'

He nodded, patted Vivienne on the head and followed her to the foyer. She apologised that there was no room in which to receive him. 'Sir, what can you tell me about my little scullery maid?'

The physician had a grandfatherly air to him, which Sophie imagined must have been good for business in the neighbourhood. It pained her to see his face grow solemn, then harden into an expression far from benign. 'Lady Bright, she has been interfered with.'

'Poor child,' Sophie murmured. 'I thought that was so.'

'Poor child, indeed,' he said.

'Is there anything…?'

'Just feed her well and treat her kindly. It will probably seem like a novel approach to the child. I expect she will thrive here.' He shook his head, serious. 'I cannot tell you what the final effect is. We may not know for years, but I am hopeful.'

He went to the door and opened it. 'There is no point in accusing the landlord. He would only deny it. We'll carry on and hope for the best. If you were hoping for some sort of redress, I am sorry to disappoint you, Lady Bright.'

It's no more than I ever expected of justice, she thought, remembering her husband's trial. 'I did not expect much,' she told him. 'I do appreciate your kind attention, though.'

He bowed himself out and left her standing in the foyer. She sat down and did nothing to stop the tears from coursing down her cheeks, not sure if she was crying for innocence cruelly used or her own discomfort with the law.

She felt a hand on her shoulder and started, looking up to see her husband, book in hand. He knelt beside her chair. 'Is it all too much, Sophie?' he asked.

How kind he was to ask. She dried her eyes and told him what the physician had said. 'He said there was no point in trying to get the landlord charged,' she told him, her voice muffled in the cloth square. She started to cry again.

Charles picked her up and sat in the chair with her in his lap. She thought about her resolve not to be a trial to the man, then turned her face into his coat and sobbed. His hand was gentle on her hair, stroking it. He said nothing, but she didn't need words. When she finished crying, she sat up and blew her nose. 'I cannot imagine that sort of terror,' she said, her face still muffled in his coat. 'Wondering if he would bother her this or that night, after a long day of overwork. There is no justice, is there?'

'Precious little, at times,' he said, his lips close to her ear. 'Thanks to you, though, those bad times are over for Vivienne.' He kissed the top of her head. 'I suppose I shouldn't do that, and it's one more thing to overlook, but I think you need a kiss on the head.'

She managed a watery chuckle. 'I suppose I did.' She looked at the book he held. 'Can that be the only book from Lord Hudley's library that is fit to read?'

'Precisely. I wanted to show it to you for that very reason.' He held it out from her. *'A History of the Roman Republic.* I suppose he bought it for the chapter on the rape of the Sabine women, but even that was a somewhat prosaic affair, or so I have read elsewhere. Imagine what a disappointment that was to the old roué.' He snapped the book shut. 'This, wife, is the foundation and cornerstone of our library to come. Start making a list of your favourite books. The statues and busts are on their way out, as we speak, so you can make your list in the library.'

'What about the books?'

'They are headed for the beach, where we will enjoy a monstrous bonfire tonight.' He shifted and she got off his lap. 'I am headed belowdeck to give a proper welcome aboard to our servants, and provide the usual rousing speech I gave to countless ne'er-do-wells in my command, officers included. You make your list and we will call it good.'

Sophie did as he said, sitting on the sofa she had declared so comfortable, a tablet in her lap.

She stopped for luncheon when it was brought to her, a fragrant, steaming consommé liberally dotted with croutons and accompanied by fresh fruit. Etienne was making up for his miserable breakfast—the kind guaranteed to drive away meddling sisters—and raising her spirits. The glazier came from Lord Brimley's estate next door, and soon the French doors were put to rights again. By the time the painters left the sitting room as the sun began to slant in the west, all had been restored. She took a few minutes to enjoy the simplicity of a ceiling covered with paint only, hiding a multitude of sinful cherubs. She sighed—only six or seven rooms to go.

Dinner was a ragout, served on the terrace, which had been swept clean by one of Starkey's new assistants. Eager to please, the 'tween-stairs maid—not much older than Vivienne—waited in the doorway as they ate, whisking away plates as soon as they finished.

Charles finally patted his stomach. 'Sophie, you must agree this place has some possibility now.'

She wiped her lips on a napkin and nodded to the child hovering close by. 'Do you think I could send Miss Thayn to the workhouse—?'

'Poor thing, what has she done? And so soon?' he interrupted.

'Wretch! I meant that she could go there to find us two more 'tween-stairs maids.'

Charles folded his arms and gave her his full attention. She was used to his searchlight expression now and merely smiled back, remembering other domestic conversations with Andrew, before their lives were ruined. *I could like this again*, she thought. *I really could.*

'I think Etienne will be happy to instruct one of them in culinary arts and Starkey can turn the other one over to the upstairs maid.'

'Would that be the domestic who was going through the linen closet with such determination? I kept moving when I passed the closet, because she looked ready to take an inventory of my clothing.'

'The very one,' Sophie said calmly. 'I have the distinct impression she does not suffer shabby genteels gladly. Only think how much our stock will rise when we are adequately clothed!'

He shuddered in mock terror. 'I am still amazed how complicated life on land is. And you think we need two more maids to help her terrorise us?'

'No, Charles. It will get two more orphans out of the workhouse.'

'That's important to you, isn't it?' he asked, after a long pause.

'More than you'll ever know.'

He took her hand and kissed it, then quickly set it back in her lap. 'Overlook that,' he told her.

'Certainly,' she said serenely.

As the shadows lengthened on the terrace, he didn't touch her again, but she was so mindful of his presence. She decided that was part of being an admiral. Consciously or unconsciously—probably the latter by now—he made his presence known by simply being there. What a reassurance he must have been to the fleet.

When it was nearly dark, one of Starkey's underlings torched the pile of books on the beach. 'Ah ha,' Charles said. He took her hand and pulled her up. 'Let's go watch the blaze up close. I like a good blaze, as long as it's not in my ship.'

He helped her down the wooden steps to the beach, and did not release her hand. 'Overlook that, too,' he said, as he led her closer to the bonfire. 'Sand is notoriously unstable.'

It was a stunning bonfire. Sophie looked back at the house to see the servants standing on the terrace, watching. Standing close to Miss Thayn, Vivienne was clapping her hands and jumping up and down, which made Sophie smile. She gestured with the hand that the admiral held. He turned around and smiled, too. 'It appears Vivienne has an ally in Miss Thayn. Do you reckon Miss T. knows anything about being a dresser?'

'I'm not certain that I care,' Sophie said. 'I am just glad she's employed.' She gestured again with the hand that the admiral wouldn't turn loose. 'And those men you hired.'

He put her hand close to his chest. 'I doubt they know a weed from a daffodil. Like you, I'm not certain I care, either. Oh, I should tell you this: that eager under-steward that Lord Brimley so kindly sent to us on approval—I believe his name is Crowder—has agreed to become my official steward.'

'And not Starkey?'

'He's my indoor man. I've given Crowder carte blanche to repair that little house that must have been a dower house and use it for his own. He even said he wouldn't mind some of the Egyptian furniture. He was careful to qualify.'

Sophie laughed and turned back to the bonfire. 'And here I thought you were going to add the jackals to the flames!'

He tucked her hand in the crook of his elbow now. 'Things have a way of working out, Sophie.'

He seated her on a convenient bench-sized piece of driftwood and joined Starkey by the wooden stairs for a discussion that appeared to require some gestures and conversation that his hold on her would have impeded. She owned to a feeling of discomfort, watching Starkey, who seemed to be arguing. *Perhaps I will have time to win Starkey over*, she thought. *It will be about the same time that pigs fly, I fear.*

But anything was possible. She turned her attention to the fire again, watching Lord Hudley's dirty books crackle and snap and float into the night sky like so many fiery dandelion puffs.

'Quite a sight, eh, missy?' she heard near her elbow.

'Where does ol' Double Hung want me to stow 'is bottles this year?'

She leaped to her feet and stared at a scruffy figure with an eyepatch and no more than one or two teeth in his mouth, which made spitting a wad of tobacco a convenient exercise. The missile whizzed past her shoulder and landed in the fire.

She knew better than to scream this time. 'H-hold that thought,' she said and started towards her husband, who was looking in her direction now. 'Charles, we have a visitor.'

'Like a moth to a flame, missy,' the man said, spitting the remainder of his wad into the bonfire. 'I'm a business-man! Be a good little piece o' muslin and summon your old squeeze. That's a good whore.'

Chapter Fourteen

Sophie ran to her husband and grabbed him around the waist. 'Overlook this!' she stammered and tried to burrow under his armpit.

'Sophie, I didn't know you cared,' the admiral teased, then looked where she pointed. 'What felon and miscreant is this? We seem to attract a motley crew.'

Keeping his arm around her, Charles walked closer to the bonfire again. 'Ahh,' he said finally, in a drawn-out exclamation that had equal elements of surprise and amusement in it. 'As I live and breathe, Leaky Tadwell! I thought you had been hanged years ago. You would have been, on my watch.'

Sophie tugged on her husband's arm. 'You *know* that man?'

'I would only admit it to my nearest and dearest,' he replied. 'Leaky Tadwell. Sophie, my love, let me present the most worthless seaman in any navy,' he said in a musing tone of voice. He looked beyond the fire to the water's edge. 'You have a cutter. Stolen from some ship, I don't doubt. To what do we owe this pleasure?'

The scruffy man bowed elaborately. 'Admiral Bright?'

'The very one. Probably the only one,' Charles said. He kissed the top of Sophie's head. 'Don't worry, wife. We're as safe as if we had good sense.'

Tadwell straightened up and knuckled his hand to his forehead, where he vigorously tugged the greasy bit of hair under a watch cap that looked old enough to have grown to his scalp.

'Who? Who? Who?' Sophie stammered.

'I married an owl,' the admiral replied, more to himself than Tadwell.

Safely corralled in Charles's arms—she didn't know how it happened, but he had both arms around her now, pressing her close—Sophie stared at the man by the fire. She watched his expression, which by now was registering more suspicion than surprise.

''Old on now, Admiral. Where is Lord Hudley?'

'He's extremely late, Leaky, for your information.'

The old vagabond yanked off his watch cap and wiped it across his face, unleashing the powerful fragrance of unwashed hair that made Sophie flinch. 'I'll say 'e is! I've been waiting 'ere since June 10th for the bonfire!' He squinted closer at Sophie. 'And what're you doing clutching a whore, Admiral? I thought you was the fleet's good example.'

Sophie gasped. He sounded so self-righteous that she forgot to be afraid. 'I am his wife, you grotty bag of sorry bones!'

'I think I love the way you roll your *r*'s,' her husband told her. 'Oh, say that again.'

'You are certifiable,' she declared.

'No, no, "grotty bag of sorry bones". Please, Sophie.'

She burst out laughing, which had the effect of making Tadwell back up this time, and look at them both suspiciously.

'Something ain't quite right,' he said. 'Where's ol' Double Hung?'

'I don't ever want to know how Hudley got that name,' Sophie murmured.

'Maybe that's the secret of his way with Fair Cyprians, two or three to a bed, and all that,' her husband said. 'Leaky, when I say "late", I mean dead. Spoon in the wall. Toes cocked up. I bought this misbegotten estate a few months ago.'

'I didn't know,' Tadwell said. 'Hmm.'

And there they stood, looking at each other. Sophie was the first to speak. 'Why are you here, and why is June 10th important to *you*?'

He made a grand gesture then with both arms stretched out that made Sophie want to gag again. He cast a hurt look at the admiral. 'After the navy turned me off without a character, I been smuggling the good stuff from France.'

'"Without a character"... You old rummy!' Charles exclaimed. 'Last I heard, you were flogged and stripped and left in Montevideo, hopefully to die.'

'Where a kindly old priest took me in. Got religion, I did.' Tadwell looked at Sophie, and his tone was a wheedling one. 'A man's got to earn a living, I says.'

She felt her husband's soundless chuckle, as he held her tight. 'Let me understand this, Mr Tadwell—' she said.

'Don't be formal. Leaky,' he interrupted.

'Leaky, then. You sneak French wine to the Devonshire coast and leave an order for Lord Hudley's annual bacchanal, when he lights a bonfire on the beach?'

He nodded to her and gave the admiral a squinty look. 'You're a bit sharper than yer old man, missy. That's it.

I must say, you outdid yourself this year. That's some blaze.'

'The party is over, and so is the war, Leaky,' Charles reminded him. 'You don't need to sneak it in, you old felon.'

Tadwell gathered what dignity he could. 'Maybe I like the spirit of the thing, Admiral!'

Charles shifted Sophie so he could look at her face. 'Wife, have you looked at the wine cellar here? Are we low?'

She felt her lips twitch. *If I look him in the eye I will fall down on the sand and laugh like a hyena*, she thought.

'Oh, dear, I think we must be quite low, if my love is unable to speak,' he said, with no more than a quiver in his voice. 'It's all right, dear. Don't trouble yourself over this. I'll ask this old boozer to leave us what he would have left Hudley. I'll even pay him, although I should alert the Sea Fencibles.'

'Not necessary, Admiral!' Tadwell exclaimed in such ringing tones that Sophie had to look around at him. 'Lord Hudley always paid me *before* delivery!'

'He obviously had more faith in you than anyone in the Royal Navy. I'm astounded.'

Tadwell grinned. Sophie shuddered at the bits of tobacco hanging to his few teeth. 'Tell me where you want it and I'll be gone as fast as green corn through a goose!'

Charles gestured over his shoulder. 'See that man there? The one with a peg leg? The one who is fifty times the sailor you could ever hope to be? That's Starkey and he will tell you where to put it.'

Tadwell nodded. 'Pleasure doing business wi' you, Admiral.' He sketched what could only charitably be called a bow. 'And Mrs Admiral, I didn't mean to call you a whore.'

Still in the safety of Charles's arms, Sophie watched the bottles nestled in straw end up stacked on the sand. Starkey marshalled his forces and they carried the wine indoors. Tadwell watched until the last bottle was gone, then tipped his watch cap to Sophie. In another minute, the smuggler worked the sails and the cutter vanished into the darkness.

The admiral watched, then turned back to the fading bonfire. 'It's a damned good thing we don't have to light another fire tomorrow night, Sophie. No telling who would show up on the beach.' He still held her hand, so he slapped the flat of his hook against his chest. 'I don't think I'm up to another visit from the Leaky Tadwells of the world.'

They walked slowly to the stairs and back on to the terrace, where the servants remained, Miss Thayn taking care of Vivienne.

'Lady Bright, do you need any help getting ready for bed?' Miss Thayn asked.

Sophie shook her head. 'Thayn, you and I will have to sit down tomorrow and discuss your duties. So far, my wardrobe doesn't amount to anything that can't be ignored with impunity! May I depend upon you to make sure that all the female domestics have places to sleep? When the attic rooms are repaired some will go there.'

'You may depend upon me, ma'am. Goodnight.'

There was a welcome brass can of hot water in her room, which made her sigh with pleasure. Everything had been replaced after Fannie vacated that morning, which only caused a small sigh, and then a personal scold as she reminded herself that her convenient marriage was getting all too comfortable. Still, after she put on her nightgown and carefully hung up her shabby dress, Sophie felt herself at surprisingly loose ends. She sat in the armchair by the fireplace, listening to the younger maids laughing and talking, going upstairs to their shabby rooms under the eaves. Charles said the workmen would be working in the attic tomorrow, repairing the roof and refurbishing the servants' quarters.

She couldn't help envying the girls their companionship, forged so quickly after only a day in the same household. She had seen them only briefly, but their small glances in her direction spoke volumes about their relief at employment. She knew the feeling precisely and it warmed her to provide security to at least a few, when so many were hurting. Sophie knew her husband felt the same way about hiring his few helpers from the docks.

She listened for Charles's footsteps on the stairs—funny how quickly she could recognise them. When she heard them, she knew he was accompanied by Starkey. The men spoke in low tones, but there was laughter, and she suddenly envied Starkey the comradeship, much as she knew he had envied her, earlier in the day.

'Charlie, you don't need me tonight to unharness you,' she said softly as she got up from the chair. She liked to kneel by her bed and pray—it was a habit from practically her babyhood, one encouraged by a Presbyterian mother. She knelt, but could think of nothing to say. She ended up just resting her head on the mattress, closing her eyes and then saying 'amen' after her knees started to ache.

Maybe there was something in the calmness of moonlight. Maybe there was a certain honesty that comes when even a plaguey house was still, and the mind had time to roam. After a few hours of fitful sleep, Sophie woke up. She sat up, realising she had forgotten to close the curtains. Moonlight streamed in and fell across her bed. She went to the window, leaned out and took a deep breath, then watched the light play across the ocean.

She took a coverlet from the end of the bed and made herself comfortable in the window seat, the better to watch the water. She thought through what she would say to Miss Thayn in the morning, and how she would let Starkey take the lead—it was his right—in managing household affairs. She never had more than two servants, anyway. She would do what Charles Bright asked of her—find him ways to keep busy, at least until he could decide whether or not life on land was to his choosing.

There was only one problem she foresaw. Sitting there in the moonlight, comfortable and well fed with no one around to question her, she knew she was falling in love with her convenient husband. She had felt the same way after she met Andrew Daviess, who had come down from the University of Edinburgh with her brother, Malcolm, who now lived in remote Bombay, courtesy of the East India Company.

Probably like most young women, if her mother was to be believed, Sophie had wondered if she would know when she was in love. She did, when she met Andrew. It was as though all her nerves hummed some new tune. Ordinary things looked better than usual. Ever practical, all she wanted to do was see his dear face again. He couldn't write to her; that would have been improper. All she could do was wait and see if he had felt anything in her presence. If she never saw him again, it would be silent suffering on her part. By some miracle, if he felt the same way, he would come back. He did.

Under the kindness of the moon, Sophie admitted to the same emotions now, even though she'd thought she would never feel that way again. Her life had felt over, after Andrew's funeral. And when Peter died, even as he had looked at her so trustingly to make him better, it was as though she had been handed a teaspoon to dig her own grave, minute by hour by day by week by month by year. She had been a woman with nothing to look forwards to.

Here she was, making plans again, all because a man sorely tried by his sisters had done a breathtakingly impulsive thing. She was determined to give Charles Bright no cause for regret, even if he never felt anything more for her than kindness. She wanted to analyse her feelings, wondering if they were more gratitude than love. To be sure, she was grateful, but was that all?

Tired finally, she got back into bed and slept soundly.

She didn't hear the maids making their way downstairs in the early hours, and she barely registered the arrival in her room of more hot water. The sun woke her finally, bright and hot. She lay on her back, contemplating the ceiling and filled with gratitude that Lord Hudley had felt no need to deck the ceilings upstairs with anything more complicated than plaster whorls.

Men with heavy shoes were tramping upstairs again. Soon they would be banging away at the roof, measuring and sawing. Charles was probably on the terrace, watching his outside army haul away the ashes from the book burning. She had noticed already how he liked to stand with his hands clasped behind him, as though he still trod a quarterdeck. And there would be Starkey, waiting for his orders. It was too much to hope that he would bring her tea again.

Then she heard him on the stairs and her heart started to beat faster. Maybe it was another worker, she told herself. Maybe it was even Miss Thayn, eager to find out her duties for the day. She held her breath, waiting for a knock, and let it out slowly when it came.

She was out of bed in a flash, opening the door. There he stood, smiling good morning. All she wanted to do was throw her arms around him and never let go. Instead, she held the door open, then closed it softly behind him, hurrying back to bed and making the coverlet straight.

He was already dressed. He set the cup and saucer on the nightstand and sat down on the bed, as he had for the last two mornings, watching her and saying nothing until she had sipped from the cup and pronounced it good.

'You're a sleepyhead this morning,' he said. 'The 'tween-stairs girl said you were still asleep when she brought in the hot water.' He ruffled her hair. 'Are you turning into a layabout?'

'I didn't sleep well,' she admitted.

'I didn't either,' he said, looking out the window.

'Worried about this work in progress you purchased?'

'Maybe that's it.' He sighed. 'Now the head builder says it would be wise to replace two of the chimneys.' He patted her leg, and she wondered if he was even aware of what he was doing. 'Watch your head when you come down the stairs. They're painting the ceiling in the main hallway now. Etienne wants to show you his menus for the week, and Miss Thayn is pacing up and down in the sitting room, ready to tackle whatever you have for her.'

Sophie held very still. His hand still rested on her ankle and she didn't want to move and remind him. She was so close to reaching out and caressing his face that she had to remind herself to breathe. 'Wh-what are we going to do with all these servants?'

'I don't know. Let's close up the house and ship out to Capri.'

'I think you're restless on land.'

'I know I am, Sophie dear. I'd give almost anything to walk a quarterdeck about now.'

So that was it. She moved her leg slightly and he remembered where his hand was. 'Excuse me. You can overlook that, can't you?'

She nodded. 'Maybe you shouldn't have retired.'

'It was time. Finished with that?' He hooked the cup handle neatly out of her grasp and set it back in its saucer. 'I had seen all the blood flowing from the scuppers, eaten all the mouldy bread and gelatinous water, and smelled all the bilge I ever wanted to. After twenty years of war, and a total of almost thirty-five years in the Royal Navy, I was sick to death of it.'

'Oh, my,' she said. 'But you still bought a manor that juts out into the water. I don't believe there is a room in this house without a sea view.'

'I made sure of that sea view from every window. I still love the ocean. I always will. Maybe I'm more full of contradictions than a tightly wound woman.'

She had to laugh at that. 'No you're not! You just need to figure out what to do with the rest of your life.'

'True.' He got off her bed and went to the window. He looked at her for a long while, then returned to sit beside her. He took her hand. 'Sophie, I never thought to survive the war. I doubt any man in the fleet did. Do you realise that we officers and men sleep in our coffins at sea? If I had died in action, they would have weighted me down with cannonballs, sewed me into my sleeping cot and chucked me over the side.' He put her hand to his cheek. 'Only Nelson was small enough to fit into a butt of brandy and return to land!' He smiled. 'We will agree he was a bit more of an icon, too.'

He looked at her hand, but did not let go of her. 'Well. Something works in a man's mind, when he sleeps in his own coffin and spends every livelong day in the tension of battle.'

'Every day?' she asked, keeping her voice soft, not

wanting to interrupt the flow of his thoughts. Andrew had never been one to open up with problems and she found herself deeply moved by this practical stranger. Except that he was no stranger. Maybe from the moment he sat down in that pew at St Andrew's, he was no stranger to her. 'Even during the slow times at sea?'

'Even then. We sent men up into the crosstrees to watch for foreign sails, but I don't know a commander worth his salt who was not always looking, too. Oh, God, wife, when you command a whole fleet, that vigilance is magnified exponentially. My mind is tired and I still pace. How can I forget?'

Sophie knew she would never question what she did then, if it was to be the only time or the first of many. *Rivka said I should think with my heart*, she told herself, as she gently extracted her hand from his and got up. She saw the disappointment in his eyes, but she knew it wouldn't last, not when she crossed to the door and turned the key in the lock.

She could hardly feel her bare feet on the carpet as she walked back to the bed, unbuttoned her nightgown and slowly dropped it. She could feel her face begin to flame, but she kept her eyes on his, noting how they took in her nudity. He began to breathe more quickly. She touched his head and moved close to him. He rested his cheek against her bare belly. She felt his eyelids close.

'There now,' she murmured. 'There now.' *I wish I weren't so thin*, she thought. *I wish a lot of things right now.*

After a long moment, he opened his eyes and looked up at her. His hand went to the buttons of his shirt and then to his harness. 'Help me out of this,' he ordered, his voice sounding almost rusty.

She did as he said, sitting beside him, helping to free

him of his shirt and then undoing the clasp at his neck, which held the harness together.

A modest woman, Sophie had never done this in broad daylight. As she helped Charles undo the buttons on his already bulging trousers, then climbed back into bed, she thought of all the times in the last year of his life she had wanted to comfort Andrew and he had rejected her. When her head was pillowed on the admiral's arm, and his fingers were gently tracing the outline of her breast, she didn't think about Andrew any more.

Chapter Fifteen

Charles had one rational thought, before instinct reigned. *Was I playing on her sympathies?* he asked himself, as he familiarised himself with his wife's body. Maybe he had worked on her kind heart. He needed what she obviously wanted to do; more than that, he wanted her.

'This is going to be a hard action to overlook,' he told her, his lips against her ear.

'Please.'

He could have resisted nearly anything except please, spoken so softly in his ear, but with an undercurrent of desire and demand that he didn't know women possessed. What an ignorant man he was! He had bedded women in many ports, some of low degree, especially when he was a young lieutenant, and others of more exalted pedigree, as he ascended in rank and power. They had all been willing—he was not a man to force an issue—but he couldn't recall one who had initiated lovemaking.

Sophie was different in all ways. As she began to stroke him, and murmur words more like music than words, he knew she wanted to soothe his agitation, and was ready to do it in time-honoured fashion, probably ever since the first man had gone to sea, suffered and whined to his wife on returning. At the same time, he sensed her own needs, a widow of five years with little outlet for her own passion. She knew precisely where to touch him; for one small moment, he envied her late husband for all his years with her. *I have come late to this party*, he thought, as he put her lips on her breast and felt her heart thundering against her ribcage. *Better late than never.*

He knew there should be niceties, but this was different. Even as he prepared to kiss his way around her breasts, Sophie was already trying to squirm under him. Fine, then. He was totally ready, barring any last-minute reservations on anyone's part.

When he entered her, Sophie let out a breath she must have been holding for months, so long it seemed to go on. Her arms and legs were tight around his body, her legs crossed high on his back as she moved in perfect rhythm with him. *Flexible*, he thought, as he held her close. He thought she might object to how tightly he held her, until she murmured 'so safe' in his ear, and he realised how terrifying her life had been for years. If a man covering her took away a few of her own demons, then he could hold her that way.

She had lashed herself to him, leaving him with a feeling of such relief, and he hadn't even climaxed yet. It was as though she was trying to exorcise years and years of war with her body. Considering the length of the war and its intensity, his mind told him this was an impossible task. But as she began to breathe deep and run gentle hands across his shoulders, he felt crusty layers of sorrow and terror, dished out in equal measure, begin to slough away.

He wasn't as gentle as she was, and he knew it, but his only qualm was for her fragility. She was too slim for his liking, and he hadn't even had time to begin a campaign with Etienne to pack a little more substance on to her frame. He tried to rise up on his elbows a time or two, but that only brought a tighter grip on his back. So be it, then. She wanted to bear his weight and he swallowed his qualms as he drove into her relentlessly and was rewarded with a moan she made no effort to stifle, as she tried to turn herself inside out in her climax.

A man of considerable patience, he bided his time until a second shudder shook her slender body, then he bowed over her for his own release, so sublime a surrender that he felt tears starting behind his eyelids. It was as though his wife had drained every ounce of weariness from him, taking it into herself and welcoming him with her own release.

She had not released him with her legs. He had no objection to kissing her hair at her perspiring temples, then her open mouth and then burying his face in the curls that tangled around her neck. She smelled faintly of talc, a scent he discovered he quite fancied.

'Sophie, Sophie,' he murmured. 'Kindly inform me if I am hurting you.'

She was too busy to answer him, continuing her movements, slower now, but no less imperative. He was diminishing, but made another effort, which was rewarded with a groan, and then complete relaxation of her legs, as though someone had tugged out all her bones, leaving her a soft pile. She opened her eyes and he was again smitten with the depth of them, as brown as good coffee. He kissed her again, tickling her tongue with his, which brought a low laugh to Sophie. She gently bit his lip and tried to shift her legs, which he took as a signal to move so she could draw a substantial breath.

Sophie settled herself next to him, still tucked close to his side, her cheek against his chest. After a moment, he felt tears on his chest. He raised up on his elbow and put his palm under her chin. 'Hey, none of that,' he said softly.

'I don't know what got into me,' she said finally.

'I did.'

He had hoped she would think that bit of ribaldry funny, but she put her face down into his chest again, so he could not see her eyes.

'What you must think of me,' she said. 'I've never done anything quite that forwards before.'

'I didn't think you had,' he told her, kissing the top of her head, 'and I'm the one who suggested a marriage of convenience. What must you think of *me*?'

She opened her mouth to speak, but a knock on the door closed it. Her eyes went wide and she sat up, grasping a sheet to cover her. 'Y-yes?' she said tentatively.

'It's Miss Thayn. The post chaise is here for me now. You'll need to tell me precisely what you want, Lady Bright.'

Mostly I want all of you servants to disappear, Charles thought.

'I'll be downstairs in just a minute, Thayn,' Sophie said.

'May I assist you in dressing?' she asked through the door.

'No! No!' Sophie said quickly. 'I mean…I'm quite capable. Just wait for me downstairs.'

She had to look at him then, and he saw the misery in his wife's eyes replace the pleasure in what he had done for her. She kept the sheet high, which would have seemed ludicrous to a cynic, which he was not. The gesture touched him and gave him the tiniest bit of insight into the character of women, this one in particular. Sophie Bright—he could think of her as no one but Sophie Bright now—was a modest woman. Just because he knew that she could burn like straw, she was still a modest woman.

Maybe that was the contradiction of women. He was a worldly enough man, but this sudden knowledge was a priceless glimpse into the depth of another person, one growing more important to him with each breath she took. War had put him in the grip of powerful emotion nearly all of his life. He thought he could imagine nothing more compelling. He looked at his wife, truly bone of his bone now. Even though he could see there was some rough weather ahead, he found himself nearly giddy with love, the most powerful emotion of all.

This was obviously not the time to divulge such a statement. She would not believe him, or think he was merely trying to placate her and soothe over what had been as shattering a release to her as to him. Truly, how it was possible to plunge into such intimacy in so short a time would have baffled him, too, as it obviously did her, except for one thing—he knew the full power of strong emotion. War had been his tutor. How much better was love, than war. He could tell her later.

'Sophie, be easy about this,' he said.

She sat still, probably listening for Miss Thayn's footsteps to recede. She couldn't meet his eyes. 'My late husband used to tell me that my abiding fault was an impulsive nature.'

Well, damn the man, Charles thought, feeling a real spark of anger at the wretch who had rendered Sophie's life a misery by one monumentally selfish act.

'Please believe me, I never thought beyond the moment I dropped my nightgown.' She put her hand to her face, still keeping that grip on the sheet. 'I shouldn't be so impulsive.'

Think carefully, he ordered himself. 'I know precisely why you did it, Sophie,' he said. 'You didn't think one moment beyond my comfort. Thank you for that. I needed what you gave me.' No need for her to know—and maybe she didn't even really know—how great had been her own need. 'I do feel better.' *By God*, he thought, *even a suit of armor would have felt release. Sophie is more powerful than she has any clue.*

She looked at him then, her face rosy. 'I think I need to know you better before I...' She faltered, unable to continue.

'Do that again?' he asked simply.

She nodded. 'Only a drooling fool could overlook it,' she told him.

He smiled then, pleased with even this tiny return of her good humour. 'Sophie, go get dressed. You already know I can button you up the back as good as Miss Thayn. And you'd better re-harness me before you go belowdeck.'

Respecting her modesty, Charles turned his back to her, giving her an easy escape to her dressing room in her nakedness. When the door closed quietly behind her, he rolled over and searched for his smallclothes and trousers.

He was buttoning his trousers when she opened the door, dressed but still flushed. 'I got all of them except two,' she said.

She came to the bed, and for one moment he hoped she would drop her clothes again. Instead, she turned around. He rested his handless arm against her back and pushed in the buttons with his fingers.

'Your turn,' she said. 'Now, where did I...?'

She got down on her knees and looked under the bed.

It was all he could do not to run his hand across her hips. 'My goodness, how did it get there?' she said, pulling out the harness.

She still had difficulty looking him in the eyes. She concentrated on putting the leather straps together and anchoring them with the clasp. He quickly slipped the hook and socket in place, second nature to him, and raised his arms so she could lower his shirt over them. The cufflinks went on quickly. As he watched her, she went to her dressing table and shook her head over the tangle of hair.

'Just run a brush through it and pull it back with a tie,' Charles suggested. 'In fact, if that was all you ever did with it, I'd be happy. You look good that way.'

She looked at him in the mirror. 'Men.' It said the world.

She went to the door, but he stopped her with a question, something he'd wanted to ask, maybe for years before he knew her. He almost felt shy asking.

'One thing, Sophie.' He held up his hook. 'Does it disgust you to look at my arm?'

She frowned at him, as if wondering how simple he was. 'Of course not, Charles. Makes you look distinguished. So does that grey on your temples.' She leaned her head against the door, giving him that solemn appraisal he felt inclined to enjoy, because it was so flattering. 'You'll always look like a hero.'

Then she was gone, hurrying down the stairs. Charles lay back in her bed, enjoying the fragrance she had left behind. The sheets were probably a disgrace. If he bundled them up carefully, the upstairs maid wouldn't be any wiser. He listened, heard no one stirring and quietly let himself out of Sophie's room and back into his own, across the hall.

Charles hadn't reckoned on Starkey being so silent, even

though he had known his body servant for years. Was that accusation in the man's eyes as he sat so primly on a straight-backed chair by the door? Good God, what had Starkey heard of the sexual tumult across the hall?

Not a word passed between them. Starkey gave him a cool, measuring look just skirting the boundaries of insolence. Starkey's gaze broke away first, so determined was Charles not to yield the quarterdeck to a servant.

Charles said only one thing. As he reflected on the matter later, only then did he realise it was most certainly the wrong thing.

'As you were, Starkey,' he said sharply.

Starkey left the room in total silence, head high and without a backwards glance.

Sophie remembered to watch her head in the corridor, which was now in the hands of the painting crew. She watched them a moment, until her heartbeat returned to normal and the high colour in her face subsided.

As she waited for calm, Sophie decided to rationalise the earlier event of the morning. Heaven knew the admiral seemed willing to do precisely that. She closed her eyes as she remembered Charles's body so heavy and comforting on hers, more welcome than rain to a parched land.

She squeezed her eyes even tighter shut, thinking of her abandonment in his arms, her disinclination to silence, her groans as he so effortlessly brought her to climax, not once, which at least toyed with marital decorum, but three times, which painted her as a wanton, almost.

She opened her eyes. Charles had in no way indicated any disgust at her behaviour. She knew she had refreshed him completely. The softening of his face when he left her body, and the way he had wordlessly encouraged her to nestle under his arm and rest her head on his chest, spoke of nothing but his own relief and great heartedness.

I tried to nurture and was nurtured in turn, she thought, as she smiled at the painters on their scaffolding and ducked into the sitting room, where Miss Thayn waited. *Charles is right; we should just leave it at that for now.*

Almost like a young bride, Sophie wondered only briefly if her own sexual ease showed. Surely not. There was no way Miss Thayn could see beyond what Sophie hoped was her calm demeanour. Still, Sophie knew, deep down in the core of her body, that she had never offered herself so eagerly, not even with Andrew, and been so amply rewarded.

After exchanging a few pleasantries with Miss Thayn, Sophie decided on a course of action that, if peculiar, seemed to suit them both.

'Thayn, I want you to go to the workhouse and acquire us two more orphaned girls. I believe we can find enough employment of a light nature to occupy them.'

'I am certain we can,' Miss Thayn agreed. She hesitated only a moment. 'Thank you for hiring me.'

'I could do no less,' Sophie replied. 'As you well know, I have sat on hard benches in employment registries.' She looked down, wondering how much more to say. 'I will explain more of this to you later.'

'Only if you feel inclined, ma'am,' Thayn told her. 'As for me, I am happy to help. I have worked so many years for the wealthy and seen little enough gratitude for what I do. Your home feels different.'

Home, is it? Sophie thought. *This sorry, ramshackle residence?* Home. That was food for thought.

'Thayn, think of the good we can do. If we find we cannot fill all their hours with work—and I suggest we

not try too hard to do that—I will depend upon you to fill
their time with lessons.'

Thayn nodded, her eyes bright with understanding.

Sophie laughed. 'It appears you will still be a governess
here. Do you mind if your pupils are society's dregs?'

There was no overlooking the affection on the governess's face. *I have found an ally and an altruist*, Sophie told
herself, pleased.

'Ma'am, think of the great good you can do.'

'We, Thayn, we,' Sophie amended. 'Let us go to the
bookroom. The admiral said he would leave a letter there
for you to present to the workhouse beadle and sufficient
funds to grease his palm, should he quibble.'

Tired, but triumphant, Thayn returned at the end of the
day with two urchins as thin of face as herself. Over tea on
the terrace, where Sophie had sat most of the afternoon,
watching Charles sitting on driftwood at the beach, his eyes
on the ocean, they compared notes. Thayn told Sophie she
had struck such a frugal bargain with the beadle, happy to
have two more mouths off his hands, that she had enough
of the admiral's money left to purchase several bolts of
cloth to make serviceable dresses and aprons for all the
domestics now in Admiral Bright's employ.

'I confess to being no dresser, ma'am, but I can sew,'
Thayn said, as she finished her tea. 'Your upstairs maid
informs me that she is adept with a needle, as well.'

'Have these little girls names?'

'One is Gladys, and the other I will call Minerva, after
my mother, if that is agreeable to you,' Thayn said. She
could not help herself then. 'Ma'am, what kind of a country
values children so ill as to not name the ones who might
not survive babyhood?'

'Ours, apparently,' Sophie murmured. She gazed at

the admiral on the beach, longing suddenly to go to him because he looked so lonely. 'Oh, I should tell you—the attic rooms are finished. May I put you in charge of assigning the female staff to wherever you think best?' She laughed, noting with a softness in her heart that the admiral turned around at the sound of her voice. 'Hopefully they will not mind ugly Egyptian furniture! The steward couldn't use it all.'

Miss Thayn joined in her laughter, but sobered quickly enough. 'Ma'am, I can imagine that it will far exceed a pallet on the floor.'

'It will,' Sophie agreed. 'And now, Thayn, perhaps I had better check out my other responsibility on the beach.'

Sophie felt her heart begin to hammer in her breast as she walked down the few steps to the beach. The men had cleared away all evidence of the bonfire, but there the admiral sat. He had paced the sand for a while, then adjourned to a prominent piece of driftwood. Her heart went out to him, a man misplaced on land, weary of the sea and not totally convinced either place was his choice now. *I must remind him of his memoirs*, she thought, *if we can overlook...other matters.*

He put his arm carefully around her waist. 'Sophie, I set the rules about this marriage of convenience, didn't I?'

'You did,' she agreed, wishing she did not sound so wary, wishing she had the courage to say what she was thinking, even as she marvelled at the speed with which she found herself in love. Could he ever understand that? Would he just think it was her gratitude, and not a love that was beginning to almost take her breath away? But she had to explain herself, even if it made her blush. 'I wanted to comfort you,' she said simply. 'It's a good way.'

'It worked,' he told her, sounding almost as shy as she felt.

'I know,' she replied, her voice soft. 'You've been so kind to me and that was my aim.' She took a deep breath, knowing she had never spoken so plainly to a man in her life. 'Let me say this: neither of us is inexperienced. I don't know about other women, but I comforted myself, too, by what I started.'

'Good for you,' he whispered.

I like that, she thought. 'I think I know your body now.'

'It's a basic one,' he agreed, half smiling. 'So is yours, but there's more to it than that, isn't there?'

'Yes, most certainly,' she replied, feeling more brave. 'I want to know your mind, too.' She hesitated.

'Go on,' he encouraged.

'If we don't know each other's minds, then how dare we proceed? The result would not be happy.'

He seemed to consider the matter, his arm still around her waist. 'I believe you are right.' He released his grip on her. 'Sophie, I know a lot about uncharted waters. We sail slowly, always sounding the depth.'

She thought she understood him, but saw a lee shore looming. *If he is to know my mind, I have to tell him my real name, and why I said nothing earlier*, she thought. *I have to. Would now be the time?*

She opened her mouth to speak, but the admiral was ahead of her.

'May I still bring you tea in the morning?' He asked it so gently that she hadn't the heart to express herself further.

'You know you may,' she said quietly.

'But just tea,' he said in haste, and the moment to confess was gone, because she had to smile and shake her head over their situation. He laughed and nudged her shoulder.

The branch creaked louder, then snapped, sending them both to the sand.

Sophie laughed, and felt disinclined to rise, especially since her husband was laughing, too. *How do these things happen?* Her head was pillowed on his chest again, but he did nothing more than hold her. The afternoon was warm. She breathed deep of the sea this time, finding it to her liking, where she thought it never would again.

'Sophie dear, what is my remedy for life on land?' he asked her finally, rising and helping her to her feet. He dusted sand off the back of her dress and she had only the slightest suspicion that his hand lingered overlong on her hips.

You're a sly one, husband, she thought, amused. 'We already covered that. Your memoirs, sir,' she reminded him. 'We will begin tomorrow.'

Again there was that half-smile, plus a look of faux-resignation. 'Very well, wife. After morning tea, it will be the bookroom. What danger can we run into in there?'

Chapter Sixteen

Sophie slept soundly and didn't wake up until her husband knocked on her door. She noticed with some suspicion that he wasn't wearing his hook. His eyes followed her gaze and he smiled beatifically.

'Wife, you are so suspicious,' he scolded, his voice mild as he handed her the cup and saucer, and let drop the hook and harness on the end of her bed. 'I'll have you know Starkey requested a few days' shore leave, which, he reminded me, is overdue. You'll have to help me with my ironworks for the next few mornings.'

First came the ritual they were accustomed to now. She slid over to make room for him and drank her tea. He leaned against her legs and even started to put his hand on her hip, but changed his mind. It was all she could do to keep a straight face.

'Wife, I have cleared the deck in the bookroom,' he announced as she sipped, his hand chastely in his lap, to her amusement. 'I have located paper, pen and pencil, whichever you prefer. I will endeavour to tell the whole truth and nothing but the truth, except, possibly, where shore leave is concerned. Can't have you thinking I am a total cad.'

'Wretch!' she said mildly, putting down the cup and drawing up her knees, so he had to straighten up. 'Your scandalous past is none of my business.'

'I suppose it is not,' he agreed. 'No scandal, dear. From Trafalgar to 1811, I was either milling about in the channel, or dragging my fleet into the Mediterranean, to see what mischief we could do to Boney's sailors.'

'You know you would do it all again in a minute, if called upon,' Sophie ventured, watching his face.

He surprised her. 'As to that, I wouldn't swear on a Bible. Land has its attractions.'

They looked into each other's eyes. Sophie felt herself growing warm again in that region south of her belly that had received such exercise only yesterday, and at about this time. She felt her delicate parts start to melt again as her brain suggested in no uncertain terms that she look away. With some reluctance, she focused her attention on the softly blowing curtain over her convenient husband's shoulder. *Good Lord, the man has broad shoulders*, she thought.

A knock on the door simplified her efforts to abide by whatever it was they had agreed to yesterday; she still wasn't sure.

'The timing in this house is wretched,' she was sure her husband muttered as he got to his feet and opened the door.

He turned his frown into an instant smile as he held the door open for one of the new workhouse girls, eyes wide and staring, who carried in a brass can of hot water.

'I…I…wasn't sure which door, your excellency,' she

whispered, nearly overcome with terror. 'I...I...tried t'em all.'

Sophie beckoned to the child. 'You did very well... Minerva? Gladys?'

'Minerva, mum,' the child whispered.

Charles took the brass can by its bale and lifted it from her grasp. 'That's a heavy assignment,' he said. 'Let's put it here on the floor by the wash basin. My madam is quite able to lift it when she needs it.' He winked at Minerva. 'My dear, a simple "Admiral" will suffice. I'm not as exalted as a bishop, and probably a tad more profane.'

Minerva only nodded and stared, then remembered to curtsy, as she backed towards the door. She paused and looked into the distance, as if trying to remember what came next. Her eyes lit up and she looked at Sophie again. 'Will there be anything else, mum?' she asked. 'Or you, your excel...excellent Admiral?'

'No, no, my dear,' Sophie replied, forcing down her laughter. 'You might tell Etienne that I will be down for breakfast in half an hour.'

It was the reply Minerva wanted, apparently. With relief in her eyes, she bobbed a curtsy and beat a hasty retreat. Charles closed the door and leaned against it, dipped his head and laughed softly. When he looked at her again, he wearing that dratted half-smile Sophie was finding so hard to resist. 'Maybe we should send the servants to Capri instead of us. The painting is nearly done in the hall now, and most of those naughty cherubs are now under paint. This house could actually be liveable, provided we don't get any more visits from the Leaky Tadwells of the world.'

He came back to her bed, took off his shirt and held out his harness. 'Buckle me up, my dear. No telling who will barge in next. I haven't heard from the Admiralty Lords in recent months, but they might be in the vicinity.'

She did as he asked, not even trying to hide her smile. When she finished, he kissed her cheek and put himself back into his shirt. She buttoned him without a word, wondering if he would peck her cheek again and disappointed when he did not. After tucking in his shirt tails, he went to the door.

'I'll be ready in the bookroom when you finish breakfast.'

'I won't be long,' she assured him, ready to fling back the coverlet, then deciding against it, because her nightgown had hiked up during the night.

'Take your time over breakfast, Sophie dear. I hope you won't think me a managing old husband, but I have encouraged Etienne to use a liberal hand with the butter and cream.' He scratched his head with his hook. 'It, uh, came to my attention about this time yesterday that you might want a little more padding in various venues. *Ciao, esposa*. Linger over breakfast.'

He was gone then, but not before she saw his grin. 'You, sir, are a complete rascal,' she murmured as she got out of bed and shook down her nightgown. *And you, Sophie, need to ask Minerva to bring you cold water with chunks of ice in it*, she scolded herself.

She had no difficulty lingering over breakfast, with buttery croissants and porridge with the clotted cream Devonshire was so renowned for, topped with raspberries. She was further encouraged by the folded note her husband had left by her place: 'If you don't try some of that cakey stuff with cheese on it, Etienne will go into a deep decline. Trust me: this is not something you want to witness. You should have seen him after the Battle of Basque Roads, when I had the temerity to tell him I was too busy for breakfast. Your loving and deeply concerned spouse, His Excellency, The Admiral Who Must Be Obeyed.'

You are going to bully me with kindness, Sophie thought, as she tucked into breakfast.

There was no putting off the bookroom, especially since it had been her suggestion as a means to keep the admiral occupied. Sophie reminded herself it was one of the conditions of their marriage—*not that anyone was precisely keeping the conditions*, she reminded herself, as she dabbed her lips and rose with what she hoped was resolution.

When she timidly opened the door, he stood by the window, rocking back and forth on his heels, as if impatient to begin. He turned around when he heard the door open and there was that half-smile again.

'I trust you did eat some of those...those...'

'Cheesy things?' she asked. 'They were delicious. Soon I will not be able to fit into those lovely clothes you have paid for.'

'Where are those, by the way?'

'Patience, patience,' she admonished as she looked at the desk. 'It takes time to sew dresses.'

She just stood there, unsure of where to sit. He indicated the desk. 'Sit yourself down, wife, and roll up your sleeves. I intend to do enough pacing about for both of us. Let me know if it makes you dizzy.' He rubbed his hands together. 'Where should I begin?'

She did as he said, squirming to make herself comfortable. In a moment he was kneeling by her chair and reaching under the seat to turn a screw.

'There now. That should allow your feet to touch the deck. Another turn?'

'One more.' His head was practically in her lap. For

some absurd reason that totally escaped her, she wanted to touch his hair. She thought of yesterday morning, when she had twined her fingers in his hair and felt her face go red. She told herself resolutely to admire his ears, think of anything but how pleasant had been that sensation, especially since her first climax had peaked when her hands were in his hair. *Heavens, Sophie, have a little temperance*, she scolded herself.

Thank goodness he stood up then. Trouble was, he didn't move from her side. And horrors, he put his hand on her shoulder, giving her neck a quick caress with his thumb. She couldn't help the small sigh that escaped her. Pray God he hadn't heard it. She had never felt so finely tuned to another person in her entire life.

'Where should I begin?' he asked softly.

Oh, gracious, keep your hand on my neck, she thought. *Start there.* 'Oh. Oh. I think at the beginning, don't you?' she managed to say.

'Do you have a sore throat?' he asked. 'You sound a little strangled.'

He moved his hand from her neck and she cleared her throat. 'It's just an early morning frog,' she said.

'Well, then. Get your pen ready. I was born in Bristol in 1771, youngest child and only son of a barrister...'

And so the morning went. Sophie felt herself relaxing as she concentrated on the page in front of her. The admiral had thoughtfully provided a number of pencils, which proved more rapid than dipping nib in ink, over and over.

After a short time, Sophie knew it would take some effort to achieve efficiency. She blamed herself. In his matter-of-fact way, what her husband told her held her spellbound. More than once he had to remind her to take his dictation.

He seemed to be swallowing his impatience as she struggled to write what he said, when all she wanted to do was ask questions. He must have realised it when she gasped as he told her his father had sent him to sea at age ten, then burst into tears.

'See here, wife, I know I told you earlier that I went to sea at ten,' he exclaimed, throwing up his hands and ceasing his contemplation of the fireplace. 'Come, come. You're such a watering pot over the mundane matters of my maritime career. Oh, hang it, Sophie! I know I have a handkerchief somewhere.'

He did, and he produced it, after taking her hand and plopping her down on his lap on the sofa, where she leaned against him and bawled. 'You're a silly widgeon,' he said a few minutes later, his tone much softer. 'It's always been that way in the navy. Sophie, you have the softest heart. How else is the navy going to train officers fit for command but to start them early? Sophie, Sophie.'

'You were just a baby,' she managed, when her tears had subsided and she was content to rest against his broad chest.

'Ten? My dear, don't tell a boy that!' His arms tightened around her. 'Mind the hook. It's on your port bow,' he cautioned, which made her chuckle in a watery way.

She sat up and blew her nose. 'Didn't your father want you to be a barrister?'

He brushed her hair from her eyes, anchoring it behind her ear. 'I had a better father than most, I think. He could see I spent all my time at the docks, watching the ships and begging for my own pinnace.' His eyes softened with the memory, and then he gently pulled her back against his chest. 'My mother cut up stiff, just like you are doing.' He kissed the top of her head. 'She cried, but she packed my first sea chest and sent me off to join the fleet heading for the American War.'

'The American War? You're not that old,' Sophie declared into his suit coat.

'Beg to differ, my dear. It was 1781, and I got in on the tail-end of the navy's humiliation by the French at Yorktown. Call it the Battle of the Capes. I spent it rushing notes from Captain Graves to his lieutenants on the gun decks.'

And dodging dead bodies and slipping on blood and gore, he thought. *I would never do that to a child of mine.* He held her out again and looked her in the eyes. 'Sophie, I've never been so frightened, but I also never wanted to be anywhere but on a quarterdeck for the rest of my life.' He put her off his lap. 'Now, sit at the desk and write that, will you?'

She did exactly that. Charles knew that if he held his convenient wife on his lap for many more minutes, he would end up locking the door, clearing off the desk and having his way with her in the bookroom, of all places. It took all his will to set her on her feet again and announce that he had some business elsewhere in the house.

After he had walked around the house, down to the beach and back, admired the painting in the last room on the main floor that needed it, he thought he could look in on her with complacency. She sat at the desk, tongue between her teeth, frowning at the paper as she wrote. Why would a woman look so attractive doing that? he asked himself. *Oh, hang it, Admiral*, he thought in disgust, *as far as you are concerned, Sophie Bright would look attractive scrubbing pots in the kitchen, up to her elbows in grease. You are a no-hoper.*

There were worse things, he decided, as he came into

the bookroom. To his relief, Sophie was her cheerful self again. She held out the paper with a flourish. 'I think I have captured the essence of your experience,' she told him as he came closer. 'Here. Read it.' She sat back in his chair, her lovely eyes on his face, confidence in every line of her posture. She was a far cry from the frightened woman sitting in the dining room of the Drake.

She was right. He read it over again, pleased at her distinctive way with words. He sat on a corner of his desk and put the page back in front of her. 'I couldn't have said it better, Sophie.'

He noted how she blushed at his kind words. *You are pleased by so little*, he thought. *Perhaps that is because you have had so little.*

She was still regarding him. She clasped her hands in front of her on the desk, reminding him forcefully of himself at sea and in command of a fleet.

'Speak, oh great one,' he teased, which made her laugh.

'This is how we should proceed, if you're agreeable,' she said, speaking so thoughtfully and without even the slightest idea how lovely she looked. 'You'll give me the bare bones of the tale and I will ask you questions. When we have finished, I will write your story the way I see it. You can change whatever you want, of course.'

He could see no reason why not to do it her way. 'I think you have hit upon an excellent division of labour, my dear! I will blather on about my naval career and you will do all the work. Perhaps I will show you some of my deadly dull memos to the fleet and you will see what a wise idea that is.'

'Lazy wretch,' she told him, which almost made his toes curl with pleasure.

'It's your idea, *cara mia*,' he said, holding up both arms.

* * *

They ate lunch on the terrace. Charles didn't want her out of his sight, no matter what he had said about observing the niceties and thinking about matters before rushing ahead. She simplified his afternoon by declaring her intent to visit across the lane with the Brusteins.

'Let me provide an escort,' he said.

She had no objections. She didn't mind when he offered his good arm, and she took it, taking her sweet time down their long driveway, where his yard crew attacked the weeds under the watchful eye of his steward.

'Crowder tells me that tomorrow there will be a gravel wagon here to eliminate the more egregious potholes,' he told Sophie. It was super-ordinary conversation, but it warmed him. He remembered his parents talking about fabric and ribbons for their daughters, or the price of good wool, when they sat together over breakfast, so many years ago. They were long in their graves, so he could only wonder if his father had enjoyed those mundane moments with his mother.

'I think you should ask Crowder about replacing that banister on the steps leading down to the beach,' she told him. Her arm was tucked close into him.

'I will do that,' he said. 'What would you think about bluebird boxes on the back lawn?'

Maybe it was the way he said it, but Sophie stopped and laughed. 'If only your men could hear you now,' she murmured. 'I would love bluebird boxes, your excellency.'

She was teasing him and fair game, so he ruffled her hair. The next thing he knew, she was in his arms. She gave him a quick hug, then released him, to his disappointment.

Overlook that, he almost said, but he didn't, because he knew they had gone beyond the silliness of that. As he ambled beside his wife, neither of them in a hurry, he suddenly knew that he would never be happy anywhere but where she was. There was so much he wanted to say, but that cautionary angel of his, the one that had kept him from many a lee shore, reminded him of his words from yesterday. *We will think this through*, he repeated. *We will be thoughtful, reasonable, mature adults. Maybe.*

With a rueful shake of his head, Jacob Brustein told them that Rivka was asleep. They sat with him in the sun-warmed parlour for tea, mainly listening, as the old financier admitted that his dear wife spent much of the time sleeping.

'She loves to see you, Sophie,' he said, holding out his cup for more tea. 'If you could visit in the mornings, I think you would find her more alert.'

'That is what I will do, then,' Sophie said as she poured. She smiled at Charles and he felt his own heart lift. 'The admiral is writing his memoirs. There is no reason why we cannot do that in the afternoons.'

'None at all,' he agreed.

Brustein beamed at him. 'Admiral! You are going to favour the world with your account of our late misfortunes as playthings of Napoleon?'

'Sophie thinks such a work will occupy me. I cannot see it being of much interest. I was no hero, just a persistent thorn in the Corsican's side—one of many.'

Brustein drank his tea, and then gazed with bright eyes at Sophie. 'Your children will appreciate the story, Admiral Bright. When they reach those trying years before adulthood, it will remind them that there was life in the old fossil, eh?'

The old fellow smiled at the modest way Sophie had looked away, her face rosy at his offhand mention of children. 'Sophie, too bad there are no adventures in the life of money lenders! My children have to love me just because. The admiral here has more going for him.'

Charles couldn't resist a sidelong look at his wife. She was a tender soul and he knew it. The idea of children took hold in his brain then, and he swallowed against the emotion. He had never thought to survive the war. There had been bitter moments when he was younger and gripped by the reality that Napoleon had the ordering his life, which left no room for a family. He was fated to be a sea-going machine, answerable only to Admiralty House, where wives were unofficially frowned upon because they tended to soften the hard edges needed to fight a world war.

In a short week, things had changed. He had no chart now to make a path for him through a matrimonial sea that he had blunted from the beginning. He might argue that he caught Sally Paul in a vulnerable moment. She had sensibly turned him down once. Only in her desperation had she agreed to a marriage of convenience. They had gone far beyond the limits, but as he sat in Jacob Brustein's parlour, on edge and uncertain, he began to grasp just how much he loved the woman beside him.

They could say what they wanted about thinking the matter through. He looked at Sophie, who had engaged the old man in conversation. Some day, perhaps he could tell her about the point of no return. It came on every voyage— that day when trouble came and a commander had to weigh the option of turning back or plunging forwards. Turning back often meant they could run out of victuals and water and die. Going ahead was an equally unknown quantity.

Sophie, my love, we have enjoyed each other's bodies and we cannot return to our convenient marriage, no matter what we might say to each other, he thought. *You are a naïve female, if you think this is possible. We have passed that point of no return. Our voyage is now in the hands of fate.*

He wished he felt more confident.

Chapter Seventeen

Whether she knew it or not—and how could she?—Rivka Brustein gently ruled their days now. It was a mild dictatorship. She was an old woman—a dying one—who took pleasure from having Sophie read to her. He had no objection. Sophie usually returned from those morning visits with a smile on her face.

'Charles, you should come with me and listen to Rivka talk about her childhood in what she calls the shtetl in Hamburg. Sometimes I think I could listen to people, take notes and write everyone's life story,' she told him in the bookroom, as he assumed his usual opening position at the fireplace.

'My dear, I haven't been on land long, but I do think confidences between the ladies are for their ears only! Besides, if you took notes on everyone, you wouldn't have time for me,' he added impulsively.

'Their stories would all come after yours,' she assured him. She smiled at him and he felt his heart melt. 'Now, where are we?'

Lord, who knows? he thought. *Ah, but you are speaking of my memoirs, are you not?* 'Let me see—we're at Camperdown, are we not? I was a lieutenant then, and back on the *Bedford*. Things looked bleak for a while, but only a while.' He grinned at her. 'I love to beat the Dutch!'

'Ah, yes,' she said. She looked up, her eyes bright. 'You don't like to be on the losing side.'

'I hardly ever was,' he replied. He thought a moment, embarrassed. 'That sounds so prideful.'

'It's the truth, though,' Sophie said, and finished a note to herself before looking up. 'You're not one to lie.'

He noticed how suddenly she became quiet then, turning even a little pale as she bit her lip.

'Sophie? Are you all right?'

She looked up quickly, the confusion on her face still there until she seemed to will it away. 'I am fine. Just had a thought. It's nothing. Pray continue. You were on the *Bedford* again at Camperdown.'

And so it went. After Charles spent a morning alone, chafing because Sophie was not there, they ate lunch on the terrace unless the weather was inclement—and it was a glorious summer in Devon—then adjourned to the bookroom. He narrated a portion of his life's work, usually while walking up and down in the room, while Sophie took notes and asked questions.

More than ever, he realised what a soft heart she had, which required that he stop now and then to sop up tears at his ill treatment from the French when he was captured once, or assuage her anguish when his ship went aground in foul weather. She didn't seem to take exception to the kiss he generally planted on her head or cheek after such trauma.

He discovered they could rub along pretty well, generally overlooking their previous, massive indiscretion, until

the morning she returned from the Brusteins to find her
dresses delivered. After she had expressed such remorse
when he had laid down what she considered such a large
sum of money at their initial purchase, Sophie hadn't mentioned the expected wardrobe. He wondered if she was a
little relieved at the non-appearance of the multitude of
dresses and other furbelows. Out of sight, out of mind,
perhaps.

But there they were, stacked in neat bandboxes and
pasteboard in the foyer where she could not fail to see
them. Charles was watching for her from a front window.
He had started doing that one morning when he had worked
quickly through whatever had to be done, and found himself out of sorts because Sophie Bright wasn't on the premises. He could think of nothing else that was making him
crabby—his stomach was full, his smallclothes didn't
pinch.

After that, he had begun to look for her return. He
observed how she usually idled down the driveway, which
was now neatly gravelled and weeded to a fare-thee-well,
stopping sometimes to talk to his steward, who was super-
vising the planting of bed upon bed of flowers. At other
times when no one was around, she stopped to blow her
nose and wipe her eyes. He knew he shouldn't feel light-
hearted at those moments, because they generally meant
that Rivka Brustein was having a bad morning. The fallout
from such sad tidings meant Sophie never objected when
he put his arm around her. When she put an arm around
him and leaned into his chest, his cup ran over.

He hadn't reckoned on what new clothes would mean
to a woman who had spent too many years living on the
fringe. He hadn't poked about among the clothes—no man
was that brave—but out of idle curiosity, he did lift the
lid on a bandbox to see what the ladies were wearing on

their heads these days. The bonnet that met his appreciative eyes was straw, with a green ribbon and bouncy little
green-dyed feathers that would look especially good on a
woman with brown hair and brown eyes. He applauded her
choice and congratulated himself for money well spent.

When he saw her dawdling towards the house close to
luncheon time, he couldn't resist opening the front door
and motioning her in. It flattered him to see her eyes light
up, especially since she had no idea what lay in store for
her. He flattered himself to think she was pleased to see
him.

'Your finery awaits you, madam wife,' he said as he
opened the door wider with a flourish.

She frowned, and he realised she had forgotten all about
the clothing from Madame Soigne's.

'Your dresses, Sophie,' he reminded her.

Her eyes wide, her hand to her mouth, she hurried past
him and went to her knees by the pasteboard boxes. With
his pocketknife, he slit the string and she opened the first
box, and then the next, her breath coming more rapidly.
With fingers that trembled now, she shook out a deep blue
dress—a shade not far from the Pacific in mid-ocean—and
held it up to her.

'Oh, Charles,' she breathed.

He had thought, tender soul that she was, that she
might burst into tears. She came close to him and turned
around. 'Unbutton me,' she ordered, her voice filled with
excitement.

He was happy to oblige, moving in close and taking an
appreciative breath of her sun-warmed hair, courtesy of a
particularly brilliant July day. 'Right here in the hall?' he
was foolish enough to ask, biting his tongue and suppress-
ing a groan when he realised what a ninny he was.

He could have cried when she turned around and laughed softly. 'Silly me,' she said.

He was about ready to clobber himself with an imaginary stick when she totally floored him by grabbing his hand and towing him after her into the sitting room. She closed the door. 'In here,' she said, her voice urgent, her eyes bright.

He did as she asked, releasing each wooden button on her shabby dress. Her chemise underneath was shabby, too. He stood close enough to see where she had sewn the lace back on, feeling some pride to know that probably included with the new clothing were chemises that needed no refurbishing. He wondered if she had succumbed to the new fashion of underdrawers, but knew he would never have the courage to ask, even if it was his business, which he suspected it wasn't.

The little vertebrae that delineated her spine still stood out in painful relief. He admired the pale brown freckles on her shoulders, remembering how they looked on her breasts, when they had been so intemperate last month.

Considering himself a paragon of virtue, given the degree of temptation he felt, Charles pulled the dress down so she could step out of it, her hand on his shoulder. She was fairly dancing about in her excitement, which made him think of her delight, more than of her body. She was like a child, which told him volumes about her skimping and sacrifice through some harrowing years.

He folded the old dress over the sofa back and turned around to see her enveloped in the new dress, her hands upraised. Without requiring direction, he tugged it down over her breasts until her face emerged. He didn't think he had ever seen her happier.

As if his thought communicated itself to her, she grew sober, or tried to. 'You must think I am a fearfully vain creature to get so excited about clothes,' she said, turning around so he could button her up.

'No, not really,' he said, entirely truthful. 'Any man standing between his madam and a new dress had better be wary.'

'You *do* think I am frivolous,' she said.

He could tell she was not fishing for denial because he already knew that was not something Sophie Bright indulged in. He pressed the hook against the fabric and began to button her. 'I think you have not had new clothes in a very long time.'

'I haven't,' she said, her voice as soft as a child's. She looked over her shoulder at him and he saw the tears in her eyes.

Charles kissed the corner of her eyes where the tears were forming, the saltiness making him acutely aware of how human she was and how she had suffered. She leaned her head against his shoulder and he knew that only an idiot certifiable in all of England's shires would not take her by the shoulders, turn her around and pull her close, her dress half-buttoned. His hand slipped in the convenient gap and rested on that pleasant junction where her hip met her waist. To his delight, her arms went around his neck. He was disappointed when she didn't kiss him, but she did something better, laying her cheek alongside his—they were much the same height—and breathing into his ear.

'You are a good, good man, Admiral Bright,' she whispered.

She pulled away then and turned around so he could continue buttoning her. He did, a smile on his face, then turned her around.

'You'll do, Mrs Bright,' he said, his voice gruff with emotion that seemed to be creeping into his life, now that he was landbound and the war over.

She went to the mirror over the fireplace, tugging the puffy sleeves into place, and straightening the collar. She turned around twice, looking down to admire the flounce like a little girl. His heart full, Charles could see her as a small child, doing precisely that. *Or a daughter of our own*, he thought, enchanted at the idea—one he had never entertained before—of a dark-haired child dipping and swooping in circles. It was heady stuff, and it pleased him as much as watching his wife.

'Another one?' he asked, not wanting to break the spell.

Eyes bright, she nodded. 'There was a pale yellow muslin. Just for summer. Can you find that?'

He could and did, marvelling at the softness of the fabric and how small it seemed in his hands. When he came back to the sitting room, closing the door again, she was all elbows, awkwardly trying to undo the buttons on the blue dress. Putting the yellow muslin over his shoulder, he took over the task until she had stripped down to her chemise again. He could see her dark nether hair through the washworn chemise, and the outline of her long legs backlit by the sun pouring in the window. While the sight aroused him, it also made him mindful of her innocent pleasure in new clothes and the trust that seemed to be developing between them.

'Arms up now,' he said as he lowered the simple frock over her head. 'These are tiny buttons. Is there a shortage of mother of pearl we don't know about and dressmakers are economising?'

'Charlie, it is à la mode,' she said.

Good Lord, his wife had given him a nickname. He smiled at her, thinking of the times his officers had called him 'Capital Charlie', but only—supposedly—out of his hearing. He had thought them silly; coming from his wife, it was endearing.

She reached behind her, touching his fingers as she tried to do up the buttons. For just a moment, she clasped his fingers in hers, then continued on to the buttons she could reach.

He completed the buttoning expedition, took her by the shoulders and moved her towards the mirror again. 'This is a keeper, Sophie,' he told her. 'I think primrose is your colour.'

She smiled at him in the mirror, made a little face just for him, then clasped her hands in front of her. 'I do like it. Madame Soigne is a miracle worker.'

'She had a lot of good material to work with, and I don't refer to fabric. Sophie, you're a beauty.'

She turned around, her hands still clasped, her face animated. He thought of a parched flower suddenly drenched in a spring rain. 'I've never been accused of that before.'

'Not even by your late husband?' He had to ask.

She shook her head.

'Well, then, he never saw you in yellow. Here. Turn around. Madame said something about a burgundy dress. I want to see that one.'

She could barely hold still for him as he unbuttoned her dress. As the tiny buttons fell away from the fabric, he found himself unable to resist kissing each small vertebra of her spine. She shivered, then made the smallest sound of satisfaction, something like a moan, but more of an exhalation of breath with a gentle sound attached to it.

When he encountered the chemise, he pulled it down, taking heart when Sophie pulled the unbuttoned dress from her shoulders and then unbuttoned her chemise in the front. It fell to her waist. Applauding his restraint, he concentrated on another kiss of her spine, then gave up all caution.

He gently reached around to knead her breast. For the first time in years, he yearned for two hands. She leaned back against him, the back of her head against his shoulder. It was easier than anything to kiss her neck, even as he lowered his hand to her belly and then further down.

Her breath coming more rapidly now, Sophie stepped out of the yellow dress. Fully aroused, he turned her around then, pressing her body into his. Her hands went to the buttons of his trousers as she tilted her pelvis forwards, ready to receive him standing up, as impatient as he was.

The door opened then. Looking over her shoulder as she made inarticulate sounds and released the last of his trouser buttons, he saw the horrified face of Starkey, who must have just returned from his leave of absence. Transfixed, Charles watched as his servant's eyes widened and then narrowed into tiny slits before he closed the door as quietly as he had opened it.

Mortified, Charles felt the breath leave his body as palpably as if Starkey had strode across the room, yanked Sophie aside and punched him in the guts. He leaped back and began fumbling at his buttons, even as Sophie tried to undo the string to his bulging smallclothes.

'No!' he said, and it came out with far more force than he intended. 'No, no,' he repeated, his voice much softer, even though he knew the damage was done.

He couldn't look her in the face, but he had no choice, not unless he wanted to turn away and humiliate her further. Her face was red and so were her breasts, which she was quickly covering now with trembling fingers. Not bothering to button her chemise, she snatched up her old dress. 'I'm so sorry,' she murmured, her voice barely audible. 'I thought you wanted... Oh, forgive me.'

As he stood there, struck dumb with what Starkey had witnessed and miserable that his own intemperance had put her in a place where he should be the one making apology, his wife buttoned her dress as quickly as she could with shaking fingers. She looked around for her shoes, which had come off at some point. With another inarticulate cry—this one of shame and not of pleasure—she gave up trying to find them. After a quick glance at his face and one more strangled, 'So sorry', she fled the room barefooted. She must have raced to the stairs, because he heard her pounding up them only moments later.

Nothing in his life had prepared him for a blunder as monumental as this one. He stood there in the middle of the sitting room, willing himself to calm. He looked down with shame, as his passion slid away as rapidly as it had come. When his hand was steady again, he buttoned his trousers. He didn't want to look in the mirror, not and see what horror the experience had probably etched on his face permanently. Trafalgar had turned his hair grey almost overnight; Basque Roads had aged him. He raised his eyes to the mirror, disgusted with himself.

Other than an unnatural pallor on his cheeks, he looked the same. Funny how the worse thing—humiliating the woman he was just about ready to love for ever—left no mark on him. He sat down, his legs unable to support him. Sophie was the injured one. He—they—had assured each other that time needed to pass to consider and reconsider this overnight marriage he had levied on her. He could not overlook that her eagerness to couple equalled his, but still, they needed to think it through. And then he had compounded the matter by his reaction to Starkey. No one could fault him for that; the last thing in the world he wanted was for his dearest girl to realise another had witnessed what was his alone to see.

'What do I do?' he asked himself, taking another look in the mirror.

He was momentarily distracted by the painters, rattling their buckets and laughing as they left the room across the hall where they had been working. He listened to them traipse down the hall, probably headed belowdeck for lunch. Good God, who could eat at a time like this?

It was simple what he had to do—talk to Starkey and then lie to Sophie. He had to lie; it would destroy her to know what the servant had seen. He looked in the mirror again and straightened his neckcloth. He had rebuttoned his fallfront trousers wrong, like a young boy in a hurry to get back to play after a call of nature. Vexed with himself, he did them up properly, took a deep breath, then another, and opened the door, Sophie's two beautiful dresses draped over his arm. He folded them neatly into the pasteboard box and looked up to see one of the housemaids watching them.

'Please get Minerva and Gladys to help you take these upstairs to Lady Bright,' he said.

She curtsied and he continued down the hall. As though it were hot to the touch, he stared for a long moment at the doorknob to the servants' quarters. With another deep breath, he opened it and went down the stairs as if mounting a flight of rude boards to a guillotine. What on earth could he say to Starkey, who had been his confederate in all his agonising over the The Mouse, and his determination to contract a tepid marriage of convenience? That narrowing of his servant's eyes had contained nothing but contempt. Who could blame him?

Well. I am the master here. I am the admiral, Charles told himself, as he descended the stairs at glacial speed. *He is my servant and he must bend to my will.*

He knew Starkey would be waiting for him in the servants' hall and he was not disappointed. When Charles opened the door, his longtime servant looked up with an unreadable expression on his face. Their eyes met and held. With a barely perceptible turn of his head, Charles indicated Starkey's room. The man rose at once and went to the door, holding it open for him.

There were two chairs in the small sitting room. They both sat down. Knowing it would be folly to avoid looking at his manservant, Charles stared him in the eyes.

'I wish you had not opened that door.'

Starkey was a long time in replying. 'Ayc, Admiral,' he said finally, 'and I must say I wish you had never contracted an alliance with someone you barely know.'

Charles glared at him, startled right down to his shoes at his servant's impudence. 'How dare you?' he demanded.

Starkey leaned forwards, greatly reducing the space between the two men. 'Admiral, I have known you for twenty years. These past six months, you have been going through considerable perturbation about your meddling sisters.' He put up his hand. 'Admiral, those are your very words.'

'Starkey...' he began, then stopped. It was true; Starkey had been in his confidence since the beginning of the whole business. He waved his hand. 'Go on. Tell me what you think.'

His servant sighed. 'When you settled on Miss Batchthorpe, you at least knew her brother well, and you paid her a respectable visit, spelling things out clearly.'

'I did.'

Starkey threw up his hands. 'And then...and then...you come back here and you're married to a complete stranger! And what do you tell me that very night, but that it is still a marriage of convenience. Admiral, I have eyes!'

Charles had nothing to say for a long moment. He leaned forwards, resting his elbows on his knees, so he would not have to look at Starkey, because he felt himself growing angry at the man's cheek, this man he had known far, far longer than Sophie Bright, who was probably sobbing her eyes out right now. Still, it would not do to anger his servant, particularly when he was so convinced he was right. He couldn't placate him; that would be a bigger folly. He would only explain himself once.

'Starkey, have you—' he stopped. Asking Starkey if he had ever been in love would only compound his weakness in the eyes of his servant. He was still the master '—have you ever had occasion to doubt my judgement?'

It was Starkey's turn to squirm a bit in his chair. 'No, sir,' he said finally.

Charles felt himself on slightly firmer ground. 'Even when you didn't understand what my whole intent was, in matters of the fleet?'

'No, sir, no, indeed! That was none of my—' He stopped. When he resumed, his voice had a dull tone. '—my business. Sir.'

'Neither is this,' Charles concluded quietly. He stood up. Starkey remained seated. Charles frowned at this small act of insubordination, but put it down to his servant's discomfort. 'We will say nothing more about it. You'll have to trust me to know what is my business alone, much as you would have trusted me with the ships and men in the fleet.'

Starkey leaped to his feet then, his hands balled into fists. 'Sir! Begging your pardon, but you don't know anything about her!'

Charles never thought he would have to dress down this man who had served him so faithfully through nearly an entire war, a man who had never given him cause for anger, so obedient had he always been. With all the force and power of his office, he glared at the man, stared him down and reduced him to nothing. 'As you were, Starkey. As you were! Don't *ever* forget again who you are.'

He turned on his heel and left the room. As he went up the stairs, his heart sore with abusing as faithful a man as any who had ever taken orders from him, Charles could not shake the feeling that he had committed a terrible wrong. *He's right, you know, no matter how you gloss it,* he forced himself to admit. *You really don't know her very well.*

Chapter Eighteen

It might have been a bright and glorious summer, but Sophie's hands were icy. Or maybe her face was so red hot from embarrassment that they seemed cold by comparison. She put her hands to her face and left them there, trying to warm them with her humiliation. Her eyes were dry; she was beyond tears, wondering how she could live in the same house with a man who had rejected all she really had to give him.

She squeezed her eyes shut, replaying in her mind what had happened in the sitting room. He had kissed her first, his lips on her spine, and then his hand on her breast, and more. Surely, after their first coupling when she had burned like tinder, he knew how he aroused her. And then when he turned her around and pulled her so tight against him, it was obvious they had worked each other into a high state.

She put her hands over her eyes, but she could not dismiss that mental picture of him so eager for her that he was ready to take her right there in the middle of the sitting room. She gasped as her traitor loins began to grow warm again, just thinking about it. There, at luncheon time, in the middle of the sitting room, she would have done anything he asked, because she loved him.

She loved him. She took her hands away from her face and placed them in her lap. Thank goodness she had not said those words to the admiral, especially not when his next gesture had been to thrust her away as though she was a drab from an alley in Plymouth, come to lure him next to a wall for a fast lay worth a brass coin. With some distaste, Andrew had told her about women like that in seaports. Sophie wrapped her arms around her body and shivered. *What must Charles think of me?* she asked herself.

Then why did he begin it? She had no answer to that.

She had huddled herself into a little ball on her bed, unwilling to move, when someone knocked on the door.

'Mum? Mum?'

It was the little girls. She opened the door to see them standing there with her lovely new clothes, the garments she never wanted to see again.

'Thank you, my dears,' she said with what she hoped passed for real gratitude. 'You may set those in my dressing room.'

They did as she asked; her heart heavy, she watched them through the open door. In spite of her distress, Sophie had to smile when Minerva opened one of the hatboxes and took the tiniest peek. The others gathered around for a look, too, and Gladys even jumped up and down.

'Lovely, aren't they?' she asked, as the little ones came into her bedchamber again. 'When you go downstairs, please ask Thayn to come up some time this afternoon and put them away.'

They bobbed three uneven curtsies, which made her

smile again. She had to ask. 'Vivienne, just what *is* Thayn doing downstairs?'

Vivienne came closer, her eyes bright. 'She's giving us lessons. Mum, did you know that Vienna is the capital of Austria?'

'I have heard that whispered about. What else is she doing?'

Vivienne glanced at her confederates. 'Monsieur Dupuis is teaching her how to cook!'

They giggled and Sophie had to smile again. 'I think there is more to this story!' she declared. 'Go ahead now. If Etienne can spare a moment, please tell him I would prefer to have luncheon in my room and not on the terrace.'

'I cannot face the admiral,' she whispered, as the door closed. 'Not as long as I live.'

She had seldom felt less like eating. She sat in the window seat, looking out at the ocean and wondering why on earth she had ever agreed to marry Charles Bright. She was a practical woman and the answer was quickly obvious. 'You were persuasive and I was desperate,' she told a pair of seagulls, squabbling on the terrace banister.

She wrapped her arms around herself. *I would be in the workhouse now, if it weren't for Charles Bright*, she reminded herself. It was true; despite the irregularity of the whole business, she was legally married to a man who had made certain requests in return for his protection. She was to keep his sisters at bay with her presence, or at least until they had resigned themselves and meddled no more. She had decided on her own to occupy the admiral with his memoirs. He had not asked her to become Lady Bountiful to the neighbours, or entertain a houseful of hopeful guests seeking a vacation on the Devonshire coast. He expected her to run his household and offer no particular impediments.

Sophie considered the matter in her rational way and decided she could manage the situation on one condition: the admiral had to remember what he had asked of her in St Andrew's Church, when she was at her worst.

She put her face down into her knees. *I still don't want to look him in the eyes for ten years at least*, she thought. *Maybe twenty.*

She raised her head and leaned back, thinking of Andrew. *Devil take the man! I had a comfortable husband once, who made no demands.* Still... She looked out at the ocean again. Andrew was tidy, meticulous in his duties, which involved columns and columns of figures and items. He was quiet, predictable and as ordinary as she was, until ruin faced him, and he could not exert himself to fight harder, even when he was completely in the right. *What's done is done*, she reminded herself. *I will do what is asked of me.*

A course of action, once decided upon, always put heart in her body, and it did so now, or at least until there was a metallic tap on her door. She felt her heart race again. If he had tapped on the door with his hook, that was because he carried something in his other hand. Oh, Lord, it was probably her luncheon. *If I do not open the door for him, there is no way he can get in*, she thought. It would be too hard to set down a tray one-handed without dropping it. She sat where she was and he rapped again.

'Sophie? I come bearing food and there is even a scone you can throw at me.'

Lord, what a hopeless man. I still don't want to see him. She sat where she was for a moment more, then the traitor better angel of her nature, as alluded to by St Matthew, gave her a prod. As the crow flies, the door was about fifteen miles from the window seat, but she traversed the distance and opened it.

'I was coming up anyway, and Etienne was using up all the help in the kitchen.'

He looked her in the eye and she had no choice but to return his gaze, not if she expected to continue living in his house. She was relieved to see no maddening half-smile on his face, but only real contrition, which brought the tears bubbling to the surface again. She sobbed out loud, put her hand to her mouth and retreated fifteen miles to the window seat again.

Charles set the tray down on the table between the chairs, steadying it with his hook. She glanced at him out of the corner of her eyes to see him pick up a scone and carry it to the window seat, where he offered it to her. 'Here. If Etienne were a terrible cook, it would be rock hard. It's damned fluffy, but you're welcome to throw it. Come on.'

She snatched the wretched biscuit from his hand and threw it at him. She missed, which made him laugh.

'That's all the chance you get, Sophie dear.' He reached in his pocket. 'Here's another handkerchief. Blow your nose, wipe your eyes and forgive me. You can do that in any order you prefer. Defer it, if you want, but I recommend a good snort.'

She glared at him and blew her nose. *Better get it over*, she thought. 'I thought you wanted me in the sitting room.'

'I did,' he replied with no hesitation, even though his face reddened. 'Sophie, didn't you hear those painters rattling down the hall with their buckets? I was fair terrified one of them would look in the room.'

She couldn't remember any noise from the painters. Of course, she hadn't been precisely listening by then, not with his over-eager carcass pressed so meaningfully against hers. Another moment or two, and she would have been down on the sofa in an activity not common in most sitting rooms.

'I...I don't recall any noise, but really, Admiral, perhaps we need to examine just what a marriage of convenience is.'

There. She had said it. She was almost afraid to look into his eyes. When she did, there was only a thoughtful expression.

'You're right, of course.' He scratched his head with his hook, which never failed to make her smile, even though she looked away this time, so he would not see it. 'I haven't been doing too well.'

Best be generous. 'I haven't either,' she said in a whisper. 'It just all seems rather sudden.'

'No argument there.' He sat down in the window seat, too.

'You don't know me very well.'

He frowned at her words, as though remembering something. 'No, I don't. To be fair, you don't know me, either.'

But I do, she thought. *You're kind and charming, and probably all the man I could ever want.*

The realisation startled her. *Sophie, are you the easiest trollop in England or does love sometimes work in odd ways?* she asked herself. 'What a wretched state of affairs this is!' she burst out. 'Please, sir, no memoirs this afternoon.'

She hadn't wanted to say that, because she knew it hurt him. She didn't know if she would have had the courage to face him so soon after such an embarrassing blunder, but there he was, trying to make amends.

'I'm sorry,' she said, her voice softer this time. 'I don't quite know what to do.'

He stood up then and patted her head. 'Never mind,

Sophie. I need to pay a visit to Lord Brimley this after-noon and thank him for his under-steward. Tomorrow, maybe?'

She nodded. 'And…and if Lord Brimley invites you to dine with him tonight, don't tell him no.'

She did hurt him then; she could see it in his eyes. He left the room without a backwards glance, closing the door firmly behind him.

They didn't resume the memoirs for a week. By the end of it, Sophie was hard pressed to remember a longer stretch of days. It was as though the astronomer royal had found an error in celestial accounting and chosen that week to even out the whole universe. Charles still brought her tea each morning, but he merely set it on her night table, spoke a few pleasantries that sounded rehearsed, then left it to her to drink alone.

She still spent her mornings with Rivka Brustein, going so far as to sob her heart out on her knees by the bed. The old woman's gentle hand on her head had been Sophie's balm in Gilead. She had not told Rivka what had brought about this gust of tears, and it hadn't mattered. 'Men are a separate species,' was Rivka's comment. 'It will pass. Look at me. Married forty years.'

Lunch on the terrace was better. There was always some-thing to comment on, considering that the repairs on their wretched house seemed to grow exponentially with every new revelation of real estate felonies and misdemeanors.

'There is a name for a house like this,' he told her over lunch on the terrace, at the end of that awful week. 'Money pit. I'm pouring pounds sterling down a rat hole.'

Sophie could commiserate. She felt like apologising for the leaky roof, the crumbling chimneys, the squeaks in the stairs and the way the water puddled in the laundry room—why must women apologise for everything?—but resisted the impulse. She hadn't bought the place.

'Tear it down and begin again,' she suggested.

'Where would we live?'

There was something in the way the sentence came out of his mouth that bathed her face like a gentle rain storm in summer. He was thinking of her, even as she was sulking.

'Under a downspout in the Barbican,' she said, which made him smile, and then laugh.

Impulsively, she picked up a scone and threw it at him, hitting him this time. He threw one back at her and missed, which made her laugh for the first time in what seemed like eons.

They took up the memoirs again that afternoon.

August was a strange month, spent anticipating Charles's knock on the door each morning. He had taken to sitting with her again while she sipped her tea. First he drew up a chair beside the bed, and then, towards the end of the month, she patted the space beside her on the bed and he sat there again, careful not to touch her.

He accompanied her a few times to the Brusteins' estate, even visiting Rivka, when Sophie told him over dinner that she particularly wished to hear his stories of the war. Sophie tried to buttress him against Rivka's growing frailty, but even her caution had not prepared him for the feeble woman who lay there, scarcely able to raise her hand when he came into the room.

'She has altered since we first visited,' was his comment as they left the house, arm in arm.

'I tried to prepare you,' Sophie said.

'It is hard to ever do that adequately, isn't it?' he replied. 'Jacob seemed to be holding up.'

Sophie nodded, but with no conviction. 'Charles, people just show their best face for company.'

'Do we do that?' he asked her.

She didn't reply. Of course they did. A week earlier, they had been visited by several of his former frigate captains from the Blue Fleet. Shy at first, but not concerned that any of them would know her, Sophie had made herself small about the place. By the evening meal, served on the terrace because the weather was still so fine, she was laughing at their stories and basking in her own glow when Charles insisted on reading portions of his memoir to them, and pointed her out as the real author.

'I just tell her a few old stories, and some home truths about life in the fleet, and she makes me look so good,' he declared. 'Every vain, peacocky admiral should have such an amanuensis.' He raised his wine glass to her. 'Wrong word, I suppose. She is the true author of my life.'

The way he said it made her blush, and then steal looks at him throughout dinner. *I am the author of your life?* she thought that night as she prepared for bed. He couldn't have really meant that. His own life had been so exciting, so vital to England's very life. What did she do but put his thoughts and words on paper? Still, she had difficulty getting to sleep that night, warm with his praise and wanting more.

All was going well belowstairs. Thayn had been quick to organise her beautiful clothes, putting her skill for precision and propriety to good use in the dressing room. Sophie could see that her heart was in the kitchen. At first she thought it was for her little pupils, for that is what Miss Thayn called them. The principal maid had proved to be an excellent choice and she willingly put Minerva and Gladys to work, teaching them how to work. Vivienne was reserved for Etienne, who delighted in teaching her his skills.

But it was obvious to anyone with eyes that Etienne's principal student was Miss Thayn herself. Even Charles noticed it. 'Sophie dear, I think my chef is in love,' he mentioned over dinner a few nights after the frigate captains had left.

'I am certain of it,' Sophie replied.

'Should I say anything? Do anything?'

'No, Charlie. Trust the French,' had been her calm reply, which made him shout with laughter and rub her head—she hadn't been able to cure him of that.

There was a fly in the ointment. To be truthful, Sophie might have been imagining the matter; perhaps she was too sensitive. It seemed to her that Starkey had given himself leave to turn a cold shoulder to her. Not that she minded; there were moments when he seemed to give her long, measuring stares that caused unease to grow within her.

Perhaps she was interfering with his role as overseer of the manor and its domestics. She screwed up her courage one morning to apologise to him, if she was assuming a role in the management of the household that stepped on his toes.

'No, Lady Bright, you are not encroaching,' he had replied. Something in his words made her gulp and wonder if he meant precisely the opposite.

'If I am, please let me know,' she had managed to say, even as she sensed his unspoken condemnation, 'I wouldn't for the world usurp your place here.'

'Wouldn't you?' he murmured. She felt her cheeks burn, because this wasn't the Starkey who had greeted her in May.

'Certainly not,' she said, relieved then when Charles called him away for some trifling service. The measuring look he gave her as he left made her blood run in chunks. She decided Starkey was not a servant to cross and tried to avoid him.

Sophie debated whether to mention the matter to Charles. After chewing it over in her mind, she chose not to. After all, master and servant had been in each other's company and confidence for years and years before she arrived so unexpectedly on the scene. She resolved to give Starkey no reason to feel any disgust.

As August turned to September, with its shorter days and hints of glorious autumn on the horizon, Sophie contented herself with the knowledge that she was well and truly in love with Charles Bright. Since their disastrous encounter in the sitting room, he had taken no liberties with her body, beyond touching her arm, or rubbing her head, which only made her laugh. She had begun to touch him, too, just a gentle hand on his arm. He made no mention of it, but she saw how his eyes seemed to grow warm when she touched him.

Maybe it was her idea, maybe it was his, but they had taken to walking along the shore after dinner. He told her more about his world-ranging career—some of the foolish things he had done as a young gentleman, or maybe as a midshipman, of the peal the sailing master had wrung over his head when he miscalculated sextant readings.

They often walked hand in hand as he told her of foreign ports and strange scenes she could only imagine. When she hesitantly began to tell him of her childhood in Dundrennan, he had kissed her hand and then tucked it closer to his body.

'You've never told me much about yourself, Sophie,' he said. 'I'd like to know more.'

It was on the tip of her tongue to tell him about Andrew Daviess, and his horrible falling out with the victualling board. Some part of her reasoned that she could probably keep it a secret for ever and he would be none the wiser. The other part of her, the part that was growing in love as each day passed, assured her that keeping such a secret from the man she adored was a betrayal.

The matter rested until the afternoon he embarked on another side of his career. They had sailed on all the seas by now, and were approaching the end of the endless war. He sat on the other side of the desk from her, his feet propped on the edge of it, leaning back in the chair. The first time Starkey had caught him doing that, the servant had sucked in his breath, then glared at her, as though she had led the admiral astray from his typical impeccable posture.

'Should I include some of my less unpleasant duties?' he asked.

She leaned forwards across the desk, laughing. 'Charlie, I haven't thought any of your life story has been as casual as that of a country squire! There is *worse*?'

'Yes, to my mind,' he replied. 'My duties occasionally included courts-martial, or other wicked dealings exposing the frailties of men who should have known better.'

She listened and took notes, asking a few questions, as he recalled some of the more colourful courts-martial. 'Some were repentant, others less so. Now and then a poor sod would protest his total innocence, even though all evidence weighed against him.'

He moved his feet from the desk and leaned towards her. 'I suppose I disliked them the most.'

'Care to add an example, or shall we move on?'

He was in a reminiscing mood. 'There was one case, rather a famous one. Perhaps you have heard of it. The superintendent of the royal victualling yard in Portsmouth was caught knowingly kegging up bad food to feed to unsuspecting seamen on long voyages.'

The pencil slipped from Sophie's fingers. She managed to stifle her gasp as she searched under the desk for it.

He stopped, his voice casual. 'Did you find the pesky devil? I shall ask Starkey to cut you some new pencils for tomorrow. Well, as I was saying, this was a truly egregious case. This fleet was heading to the Caribbean. The men on the three ships with the bad food dropped like flies. Nearly the entire squadron was devastated.' He peered at the bare sheet of paper in front of her. 'Am I going too fast?'

Numb, she shook her head. Her breath started to come in little gasps and she felt herself going light in the head. He looked closer at her, a frown on his face.

'My dear, you look as though you've had a bit of bad beef yourself!'

'It—it—it is nothing,' she managed to stammer. 'May—maybe the sun was little warm on the terrace.'

'It's raining,' he gently reminded her. 'We ate in the breakfast room.'

'Oh, yes.' She shook her head, trying to clear it, even though she knew there was nothing that would clear it ever again. *Good God, were you* there *at the trial?* She could barely think it. 'Yes, we did. Go on.'

She tried to pick up the pencil, but it fell from her fingers again. A smile on his face now, Charles picked it up and tucked it in her nerveless fingers. 'Sophie, you have such a soft heart! It was a bad business, though. So many men died, and in such agony, and all because a glorified clerk was greedy. I'll never forget the pleasure I had in looking

at…at…what was his name? Andrew…Andrew Daviess—
God damn his eyes—when the First Lord pronounced him
guilty, I think we all cheered. Certainly the spectators did.
But what do you know? The weasel hanged himself before
we could do the job!'

Chapter Nineteen

I've been pushing this dear lady too hard, Charles thought, as his sweet wife put her head down on the desk. Maybe the stories were too hard, but still, she had fared better when he described Trafalgar in all its blood and terrible human toll.

'I'm sorry, my dear. Did Etienne serve you a bad egg this morning?' He laid his hand on her head. 'Sophie, maybe you should go lie down. Here, let me help you up to your room.'

Wordlessly, she let him put his arm close around her, offering no objection when he kissed her cheek. For a heartbreaking moment, she clung to him, then bent forwards, as if her insides ached. 'Should I call a physician?' he asked, alarmed, as he helped her to her bed, put up her feet and started on her shoes.

'Oh, no,' she said. 'No, I'll be fine soon. Just let me alone for a while.'

He finished removing her shoes and did what she said, after sitting next to her a moment more. He put his hands to the buttons on her dress front, the pretty burgundy dress he most admired, even more than the primrose one, and began to undo them, until she stopped him by putting her hand over his.

'I can manage,' she said.

He stood up. He kissed his hook and blew in her general direction, which never failed to draw laughter from her. This time, she only gazed at him with bleak eyes, then closed them, as though the pain was too great.

'I'm sending Starkey for the physician,' he told her.

She sat up then. 'I don't need a doctor, Charles. Believe me, this will pass.'

He felt increasingly reluctant to leave the room. 'Sophie…'

'No, Charles,' she said. 'Not now. Please.'

He spent an uncomfortable afternoon and evening, dining by himself and disturbed by Starkey, who took the news of Sophie's illness with no interest. He seemed even to smirk. Surely Charles was mistaken. Starkey would never be so cruel. When he mentioned Sophie's sudden illness to Thayn, the dresser had assured him she would tend to his wife. When he saw her later, Thayn said Sophie was just tired. 'Admiral, I wouldn't worry.'

He did worry; he couldn't help himself.

After a restless night in which he paced his room and went across the hall several times to listen at Sophie's door, Charles took her tea to her, praying she would be better.

She was, to his vast relief, sitting up in bed with her usual smile. Well, close enough to her usual smile. There seemed to be a shadow in her face now; he could explain it no better than that. She made room for him on the bed, and had no objection when he told her they would end the bookroom sessions for a few days. Maybe a week, if she felt it was too much.

'Thank you, Charles,' she told him as she sipped her tea. 'I…I…oh, maybe I have been worried about Rivka. Maybe I should stay longer there and see if I can help dear Mr Brustein.'

'That's a capital idea, my dear.'

As they sat looking at each other, neither saying a word, he could not avoid seeing the sorrow that lingered in her eyes. Heaven knew Rivka meant a lot to her, a lady with no close family remaining. 'I think she needs you, my love,' he said, not realising the endearment had slipped out until her eyes widened.

'Which reminds me,' he began, reaching into the small pocket inside his coat, 'maybe this will brighten your day a little.'

The ring he had ordered earlier in the summer had arrived by yesterday's post, the one to replace the plain band he had decided was completely appropriate for The Mouse, but not really enough for Sophie Bright, the dearest star in his evening sky. He took the small pouch by his hook and opened it with his finger.

The ring slid on to the bed and lay there gleaming. Sophie gasped and put her hands to her face. She began to sob and he took a deep breath, unable to interpret these tears. Surely this wasn't making her more sad? Was it too much? Too garish? Good Lord, why was there not a manual for husbands?

'Sophie, tell me you like it,' he asked finally.

'It's beautiful,' she said, making no move to touch it. Perhaps it was his imagination, but she seemed to shift herself in the bed, as though to move out of the ring's orbit. 'The ring I have is perfectly suitable.'

She sounded so Scottish that he smiled. 'Maybe for The

Mouse, but not for you. You distinctly said you wanted diamonds and emeralds.'

'I was teasing you,' she said, even as she edged further away. 'You're such a kind man, Charles, but really, after all the expenses on this house, I just…can't.'

'You'll have to,' he told her, using his admiral's voice, maybe the one that had persuaded her in St Andrew's Church; heaven knew he had persuaded a generation of indecisive midshipmen. 'It's made just for you. Besides, at the risk of making you love me for my money alone, I can afford this bauble. Really, I can. Hold out your hand like a good girl.'

He gave her no choice, taking her hand—God Almighty, why did she tremble?—and resting it on his hook, while he gently removed the too-large ring she had wrapped thread around. She uttered an inarticulate sound when he put the diamond-and-emerald treasure on her finger. It fit perfectly.

'Made for your hand, Sophie, and none other. Thank you for being my wife. It's been quite a summer. Let us see what autumn and winter bring, eh?'

She made no objection when he put his arms around her and drew her close. Her arms tightened around his neck, one hand gentle on his hair. He drew away slightly and kissed her. She kissed him back with a fervour that ignited him.

He didn't take the trouble to remove his hook, getting up only to lock the door, and then returning to her side. She had removed her nightgown and lay there, watching him, her eyes roving over his body as though she was trying to memorise everything about him, from his grey hair to his stockinged feet. His trousers came off quickly enough—he and the hook were old friends—but she helped him with his smallclothes, then pulled him as close as she had that first time in June, enveloping him in the strength of her embrace. No part of her body was inaccessible to him as he explored her with his eyes, his hand, his lips.

Then it was her turn. He yearned to enter her, but she held him off long enough to render him practically spineless with her hands that could rove as slowly as his. And with twice the economy, he thought, with a smile that made her look at him so close that her eyes seemed crossed, and ask, 'What, Charlie?' He craved the gentle way she settled herself inside him finally.

'I love you, Sophie,' he spoke into her ear as she bent over him moments later, gasping in climax, her heart pounding so loud into his chest that it felt like another heart in his own body. Maybe this was what the Bible meant by bone of his bone, flesh of his flesh. There was a lot he hadn't understood before, stunted as his life had been by Napoleon, damn him to hell. He thought of the years he had been deprived of a woman's love, and then set it all aside as peace came into his heart for the last and final time. He gave her all he had and she accepted it with her whole body.

They lay peacefully together through much of the morning, making love again, then resting naked on top of the covers, hands together when they slept. Awakening, he toyed with her breasts and then settled his hand lower on her belly. She moved his hand lower and he knew what to do. He pleasured her all the ways he knew how, and they probably would have stayed in bed all day, except that Thayn finally dared to knock. Sophie rose up on his body. 'Yes?' she asked, still rocking her pelvis, holding his hand to her breast.

'Ma'am, Mr Brustein... He sent a servant...said you should come,' the dresser said from the other side of the door.

Sophie left his body far more quickly than she had entered it, running to the wash stand and washing herself in a hurry, her face set in a mask now, one that spoke of responsibility ignored. 'Oh, Charles, suppose she is worse,' she said, as she let him button her into his favourite burgundy.

'Then you will comfort her,' he said, kissing the back of her sweaty neck. 'Hand me your hairbrush.'

She sat still at her dressing table while he brushed her hair. She tied it quickly into a knot on the top of her head, something he liked especially. She showed him worried eyes in the mirror. All he could do was kiss her cheek and whisper in her ear, 'Sophie, no fears now.'

She shook her head. With a backwards look and a kiss blown in his direction, she hurried down the stairs. He never even heard the front door close. When he went to his own room and looked out the window, she was running down the lane, holding her dress high so she would not trip.

He bathed and dressed thoughtfully, grateful down to his toes that she had recovered from whatever malady had touched her so acutely yesterday. As he buttoned his vest, he decided that when they resumed his narrative, he could omit those sordid courtroom scenes. No need for the world to have cause to remember a scoundrel as full blown as Andrew Daviess.

The afternoon wore on, and then she returned, walking slowly, her head down. He ached for her already, because every line of her body drooped. When he leaned out of the open window and called her name, she looked up, scrubbed at her eyes, then started running towards him. Her arms opened when he swung wide the front door and took the steps in quick time, gathering her into his arms as she sobbed.

She felt almost light in his arms as he carried her into the sitting room, putting her on the sofa, then kneeling beside her. He held her while she cried, then later that night he held her again in his bed this time. She had started the night in her own room, but finished it in his. They had done nothing more than cling to each other, until she finally relaxed in slumber more exhausted than restful.

They made slow love in the morning light, dousing sorrows in their joy in each other. She seemed not to want to let him go. She made his heart complete and whole when she finally whispered in his ear, 'Charles, I love you. I have for so long. This has been the worst marriage of convenience in the history of the galaxy.'

He laughed and agreed, loving her with every fibre of his body, his mind and, most of all, his heart. If there was a luckier man in England, Charles knew he would never meet him.

Trust Madame Soigne to include a black dress among the lovely things his wife had ordered. As she dressed, Sophie told him, 'She said every lady should have a black dress. Oh, Charles, I didn't want to wear it so soon!'

Hand in hand, they walked down the long drive where now the leaves were falling, those that were not still clinging in all their orange-and-red glory to limbs ready to shake them free and prepare for winter. 'Another season is turning, Sophie,' he said. 'Do you know, it has been twenty years since I have seen falling leaves?'

She stopped and looked at him, tears in her lovely eyes. He knew in his heart they weren't tears for Rivka Brustein, but tears for him, because of all that he had missed. The knowledge humbled him and made him love her more.

She put her gloved hand to his cheek, caressing it, then continued her sedate walk beside him, as he hoped she would walk beside him for ever.

They paid their respects to the Brusteins. Rivka had already been buried in the family ground behind their estate, because there was no Jewish cemetery closer than London, and custom demanded speedy burial. David Brustein, Charles's man of business in the Plymouth office, had explained this in low tones. The old man's other sons were there, too, grouped around their father. Jacob accepted their condolences, then patted the seat beside him for Sophie. He took Charles by the hand.

'Thank you, Admiral, from the bottom of my heart, for loaning me your dear wife these past few months.'

'I couldn't have kept her away,' he said, seeking for a light touch. 'Not brave enough to try. So much for England's warriors, eh?'

The younger Brusteins smiled. The old man's voice grew stronger then, and he did not release Charles's hand. He half-rose from his seat, helped by his sons, the intensity in his eyes almost startling. 'Your neighbourhood visit to us last spring meant more to my dearest than you will ever know. All those years we waited, Rivka and I! Thank you. There is nothing I would not do for either of you. Please remember that.'

'We will,' Sophie said, when Charles found that he could not speak. 'Won't we, my dear?'

He nodded. Sophie tried to rise, but Jacob held her there. He looked at Charles.

'Admiral, may we borrow her a little longer? My daughters-in-law have begun to gather Rivka's clothing into bundles. Could she assist them?'

Charles looked at Sophie and she nodded. 'You may

have her as long as you need her today. I'll bid you good day, though.'

He touched Sophie's cheek, nodded to the others and left the house in mourning, black fabric draped everywhere and swathed around the door. He walked slowly back across the road and down his own lane, stopping when the house came in view. Sophie hadn't decided if she wanted the exterior stone painted, but she had readily agreed to the lemon trees on either side of the front door.

He looked again and frowned. There was a post chaise pulled up to the circle driveway. He could see some sort of lozenge on the door panel, but could not decipher it until he came closer. He stopped again when it became clear, curious now, wondering what business Admiralty House had with him. He assured the lords when he left London that he was not open to returning to the fleet.

Starkey met him at the door, a smug look on his face that caused Charles some disquiet. The man had changed in the few months since their encounter after the sitting-room event. He appeared monumentally self-satisfied about something; what, Charles had no idea.

'You're back from the funeral,' Starkey said, peering around him. 'And your…wife?'

I'll have to talk to him about impertinence, Charles thought. *Never thought I would.* 'Mr Brustein asked *Lady Bright* to stay behind and help.' He cleared his throat. 'Starkey, I believe you might still want to address me as Admiral, or sir, when you finish a sentence. Or perhaps I misheard you. Maybe that was it. Heaven knows I have been a few years before the guns.'

Starkey looked fuddled, which Charles found secretly pleasing. 'Aye, sir. Beg pardon, sir.'

'Who is here?'

'Sir Wilford Cratch, Admiral.'

Charles handed Starkey his hat and shrugged out of his overcoat. 'Wilford? He is still secretary to the First Lord, is he not?'

'Aye, sir. He's waiting for you in the sitting room.'

Hours later, Sophie walked home slowly, every bone in her body tired. Helping the younger Brusteins' wives pack Rivka's effects had worn out her mind even more. She fingered the paisley shawl that Jacob himself had put around her shoulders, telling her that Rivka told him to make sure she received it.

Sophie stopped in the long drive, looking up at the first stars, grateful beyond measure for the Brusteins' love, for Charles's love. He was probably watching for her now, ready to open the door and welcome her back into his arms. It wasn't going to be easy, but she knew she had to tell him about Andrew and try to explain why she had not said anything sooner. It couldn't wait now, not after she had confessed her love for him. He would understand.

The front of the house looked dark. She frowned and hurried faster, wondering why none of the servants had thought to light the lamps. She turned the handle on the door, but it would not open. She tried again, then knocked, her heart in her throat. She knocked again, alarmed, but heaved a small sigh when the door opened.

Starkey stood there. He did not move when she tried to enter. She stared at him, aghast at his insolence, but not reassured when he moved slightly aside, so she could barely edge past him. 'Starkey, where is my husband?' she asked, when he just stood there grinning at her.

He gestured with his head. 'In the bookroom. Knock hard.' He turned on his heel and left her in the empty hall.

Sophie took off her cloak slowly, leaving it on a chair

by the front door, which Starkey hadn't bothered to close. She removed her bonnet and set it there, too, great disquiet growing in her stomach. Where *was* everyone? Her footsteps seemed to thunder as she walked the length of the hall to the bookroom. She stood a moment to collect her jumbled thoughts, then opened the door.

Her husband looked at her, his expression blank. She stared in horror at what he was doing—ripping to pieces the memoir that she—they—had laboured at and laughed over all summer. The sound was so obscene that she put her hands to her ears.

'Close the door.'

Unnerved, she did as he said, then sat down in a chair closest to the door because her legs would not hold her. Eyes huge in her head, she watched him methodically rip the memoir to shreds, then rise and throw it in the fire with such force that she gasped.

Still he said nothing. He sat again at the desk and took a closely written sheet out of an envelope on his desk bearing the crest of the Royal Navy. She had seen the crest often enough in her home in Portsmouth with Andrew.

He pushed it towards her, as though he didn't even want to touch the paper when she did. 'I don't understand,' she began. 'What is wrong, Charles?'

'Read it.'

She picked up the sheet and sat down again. The light was not good, but she had no urge to move closer to the lamp by her husband. Sophie began to read. She felt the blood drain from her face, and then the words came at her in small chunks as though the admiral were hurling them at her. She dared only one look at him as she read, but that was enough; his expression was wintry.

There it was, spread out before her in totality: the polite introduction, the news that the First Lord wished to strenuously warn him about his wife, the former Sally Paul, who was in reality Sally Daviess, widow of as rank a criminal as ever served the navy. She could hardly breathe as she continued down the page, which listed all her late husband's crimes and misdemeanours and stated that his wife had disregarded the Admiralty's admonition that she inform them always of her whereabouts. Since they had never recovered any of the money Andrew Daviess had stolen, she must have secreted it somewhere.

She took a deep breath, and then another, her eyes beginning to smart as she read the final paragraph, warm in its approbation of John Starkey, who had taken it upon himself to ferret out this information and relay it to the First Lord. 'Your manservant has saved you from terrible shame and ruin. We trust you will compensate him accordingly. What you do with that woman is your responsibility.'

Not daring to look at her husband, Sophie set the letter back on the desk. She shivered.

'Have you nothing to say?'

She had never heard a colder voice, not even when listening through the doors during her husband's trial. Was this the same man who had told her he loved her, only that morning? She had deceived him and now her folly had come home to roost in terrible consequence.

She cleared her throat and tried to speak, but nothing came out. He slammed his fist on the desk and she jumped.

'Say something!'

She slowly raised her eyes to his, deriving tiny satisfaction that he looked away first, until it struck her that she had shamed him in front of his peers and his subordinates and he could not stand the sight of her. Her heart in her shoes, she realised it didn't matter what she said.

'What can I say?' she managed to tell him. 'You have

already condemned me. If I tell you there is more to this than you think, you won't believe me.'

She hung her head and rose to her feet, feeling older than dear Rivka, now dead, and wishing herself beside her in the coffin.

'How can there possibly be more?' he asked, his tone so full of scorn that she knew he did not expect an answer.

She had to try. 'There is. If you would let me—'

He slammed his hand on the desk again and she stopped, her heart in her mouth, so great was her terror.

'Get out.'

'Charles...'

She shrieked when he threw a paperweight at the door where it shattered, covering her with glass. She heard him shove back his chair, but she was out of the door then and running down the hall. Rivka's paisley shawl tore as she caught it on the newel post and she left it there, desperate to escape to her room, where she could at least turn the key in the lock.

She collapsed in a heap inside her door, reaching up to turn the key. She sat there huddled into a ball until she felt her breath return to normal. She listened for his footsteps, and slowly willed herself into calm as the upstairs hall remained silent.

Sophie crouched there, afraid to move, numb with Starkey's betrayal, mentally whipping herself because she had not been brave enough to reveal the whole story sooner. She had thought Charles would never know. She had not reckoned on a servant's jealousy.

When she felt strong enough to rise without falling down, she unbuttoned her dress, jerking away the two blasted buttons she could never reach. She took off the dress, holding it away from her so she would not get any more glass shards on her. She carefully shook her head over the wash basin, listening to the shards tinkle into the bowl. She dabbed at her face, grateful the glass had not penetrated her skin beyond a few places around her mouth.

She sat at her dressing table, taking the pins from her hair and then brushing it, stopping once to sob out loud, thinking of the moment only yesterday when Charles had brushed it for her. She grabbed the brush and dragged it through her hair ferociously until all the glass was gone, along with her anger.

What remained was sorrow of the acutest kind, a pain as deep as though someone had rammed a spike into her back, then twisted it up and down her spine. She sat there a long moment in her chemise, shivering and looking at her face, her expression desolate. *I loved that man*, she thought. *God help me, I must have loved him practically since our wedding. Now he thinks I am lower than dirt. I wish I had died with you, Peter and Andrew. We would still be a family.*

She went into her dressing room to get the dress she had been wearing when she sat so alone in the dining room at the Drake, a woman with no expectations. She put on the dress, then took it off again and removed her lovely chemise, standing there naked until she remembered where she had left her old chemise, the one she had patched and repatched. It felt almost like an old friend and she sighed. Her old dress went on again, and the patched stockings and shoes with a hole in the toe.

When she had dressed, she went to her writing table and took out several sheets of paper. She knew he would not listen to her. Perhaps he would read a letter, telling him that when they met and she introduced herself as Sally Paul, it was only what she had done for five years without a thought. If he had not proposed and she had not accepted, she would never have thought another thing about it, so acclimated she was to her maiden name again. It was an honest mistake. Her folly lay in saying nothing later.

She could explain that in a letter. There probably was no point in declaring how much she loved him, but she might anyway. He would likely destroy the letter without reading it. She could probably say whatever she wanted.

She began to write. It occupied her most of the night. And then she was gone.

Chapter Twenty

Charles remained an angry man for a long time, sitting in the bookroom and staring at the dent on the door where he had thrown the paperweight. He listened for any sounds from upstairs, but there were none, not even footsteps. He nearly rang for Thayn to check on her, but set his mind against it. *I am the wronged party*, he thought, in high dudgeon. *By God, I will not go snivelling above deck to determine her welfare.*

He stayed in the bookroom and seethed, when he wasn't fairly choked with the shame of having a visit from Sir Wilford Cratch—Cratch, the old man milliner!—who came only to sniff, judge and condemn, and who even went so far as to scold him—Charles Bright, a respected admiral of the fleet—for his unfortunate choice in females. Just the thought of this yanked Charles out of his chair to stalk around the bookroom.

As the hours passed, he began to regret the paperweight and his devilish aim. He meant to do nothing more than throw the blamed thing against the wall, but he had nearly hit her with it. No wonder she had nearly torn down the door in her desperation to escape from the bookroom.

Escape from him, more like. By midnight, Charles was up and pacing again, this time in shame for what he had done. Suppose he had actually struck her with the paperweight? The damned thing lay in thousands of pieces now. It would have fractured her skull. Just the thought of that brought him up short. He stood in front of the fireplace—cold long hours since—as some better portion of his brain reminded him—*sotto voce*, thank God—that this was a woman he had made love to with fierce abandon only that morning, and who had returned his love with equal fervency.

Come to think of it, nothing had prepared him for the depth of her love, if that's what it was. Considering how anger consumed him, this wasn't a notion he cared to entertain for any longer than it took to consider it. He resumed his restless pacing, but stopped again, dumbfounded by the blatant fact that only that morning, she had told him she loved him.

'And you threw a paperweight at her,' he said out loud, as the clock struck two. 'What were you thinking, idiot?'

He remained still. At no point since his last view of her terrified face had he heard a single noise from above. What if he had killed her? What if a shard of glass had entered her eye? Good God, she could be lying in a puddle of blood. She could be blind.

Charles opened the bookroom door and ran down the hall. He stopped at the stairwell, looking up into the darkness. He had heard the servant girls go upstairs to bed earlier, but there was no light in the hall. The whole house seemed to be on edge and silent, afraid of him. He sat down and removed his shoes, tiptoeing up the stairs to stop outside her door. Nothing. He listened, his ear close to the door panel, and thought he heard the faintest scratching. He couldn't tell what she was doing, but at least she wasn't dead. He went down the stairs again, stopping once when he stepped on glass fragments that went into his stockinged foot. He cursed and removed the glass, not even wanting to think about the paperweight.

The bookroom seemed so small. He went to the fireplace, staring down at the edges of the manuscript that he had ripped to pieces and thrown into the flames. Only tiny scraps remained. He picked up one charred corner, where only a few words were visible in her pleasing handwriting. *Why did I do that?* he asked himself. *All that work. All those hours she took my scattered ramblings and turned them into a fine document. We were nearly done.*

He sat down in his chair again and put his head down on his desk, pillowed in his hand. He had no intention of ever apologising—he was by far the wronged party, after all—but he could be generous enough to take a cup of tea to her in the morning. By God, that was more than most men would do, when so put upon, tried and wronged. *I'm doing that wretched woman a favour*, he thought. His eyes closed and he slept.

Charles woke after dawn, cross and creaky from sleeping in a chair. His discomfort was her fault, too. Since she had been doing the writing, he had adjusted the chair to her height. While close to his height, there was just enough difference to cause a backache of monumental proportions. *God's wounds, the trouble she has been to me*, he thought. *I'll fetch her tea this morning, but ever after, it's her responsibility. She knows where the breakfast room is.*

Breakfast was ready. He frowned at Etienne's usual excellent spread on the sideboard, especially the cheesy, cakey things that Sophie enjoyed so much. Maybe he would take her one of those, along with the tea. It wasn't a peace offering, mind you, no such thing, but she did like them. He had noticed yesterday morning when they lay twined together that her bones had more covering to them. Her face wasn't so thin any more, either, but more round and smooth, the way a goodly nourished woman's face should look. And it had never hurt that she was such a pretty thing, too.

He glanced at the mirror over the sideboard and frowned at his bloodshot eyes and whisker-shadowed face. That was bad enough, but he could almost see Sophie's terrified expression again, reflected in the breakfast-room mirror. He looked away, uncomfortable with the view.

He left the room, carrying Sophie's tea and breakfast, uneasy because the hall was still so silent. Usually he felt like he was tripping over servants, but no one was about. *They're afraid of me*, Charles thought. Well, he could probably hear Sophie out. She would apologise again, and he would be magnanimous; maybe even forgive her some day.

Charles knocked on the door, surprising himself by the eagerness he felt to hear her footsteps crossing her room and the door opening on her sunny face. He liked the untidy way her hair curled about her face. He could almost feel the glory of it when he buried his face in her neck and served her every bodily need, along with one or two of his own.

There were no footsteps. He knocked again, pensive this time, and willing to be understanding. She was going to make him set down the cup and saucer and turn the handle himself. Perhaps she deserved her irritation over his behaviour, no matter how well deserved his reprimand had been.

Still nothing. Balancing the cup and saucer, he slowly lowered them to the floor, then turned the doorknob. The room was empty, the bed not even slept in. The black dress she had worn to the Brusteins' lay in a circle on the floor, as if she had just stepped out of it. Maybe she was in her dressing room. He opened the door and took a long look before closing it and leaning against it. He glanced around the room. One of the little girls had brought the brass can of hot water. He went to it and touched it. Still hot. Where could Sophie be?

He went to the fireplace, still swept clean from yesterday morning's little fire. Head down, he was forced to remember that last night before she came home, and after Sir Wilford had left, he had ordered the upstairs maid not to lay a fire. *You're a spiteful bastard*, he thought, looking at the clean hearth.

When he sat down in the chair by the fireplace, he saw the sheets of paper on her writing desk. He leaped to his feet and sat at her desk, horrified to see both of her wedding rings resting on the folded sheets—the one good enough for The Mouse, and the other fit for the beloved wife of an admiral. Good thing he was sitting down; Charles felt all the air go out of his lungs.

She had written his name on the folded paper. As he stared in disbelief at it, he realised what had caused the scratching sound in the early morning hours. He picked up the letter, several pages thick. His hand shook as he opened it, to see her salutation, 'Dearest Charles'.

He couldn't continue looking at the words, and glanced at the wire wastebasket instead, overflowing with nearly blank sheets of paper. He fished them out; open-mouthed, he stared at all the salutations she had considered and discarded: Dear Charles, My Love, Dear Admiral Bright,

Dear Sir Charles. His eyes teared up at Dear Charlie. He swept the pile back into the wastebasket.

He sat a moment, working up his nerve, then took the letter back to the chair by the fireplace. He couldn't even get through the first paragraph without dabbing at his face. 'Dearest Charles,' she began, 'I apologise for wasting all of your good writing paper, but I wasn't certain how to start this. I suspect you won't even read it, but just throw it in the fire, so it hardly matters what I say. I should have thought of that before I wasted the paper.'

He put down the letter, scarcely able to breathe, then picked it up again. She began by begging his pardon, but urging him to understand that hers was an honest mistake. 'When you introduced yourself in the dining room, I naturally replied my name was Sally Paul, because I had been using my maiden name for five years. It would never have mattered, but you chose so impulsively to propose, and I so impulsively accepted, never thinking about the thorny business of my name, and the scandal attached to it, until the next morning. Fearing you would not understand, I went early to the vicar at St Andrew's and gave him my deceased husband's death certificate to record, ahead of our wedding. I should have said something then to you, but I felt the moment had passed when such a confession was appropriate. And truly, Charles, I did not want to go to the workhouse. That was to be my destination, had you not found me in the church that night.'

Me or the workhouse, Charles thought. *Dear Lord in heaven, she had no choice.* 'Oh, Sophie,' he whispered. He kept reading, even though each line of the missive seemed to grind into his flesh like the shards of the paperweight. 'For a while, I thought my deception would do no harm. You plainly spelled out that ours was to be a marriage of convenience, something to keep your meddling sisters at bay while you did whatever it was you were inclined to do. I am still not certain what that is. I did want to uphold my part, and reckoned that writing your memoirs would be useful. I wish you had not destroyed the manuscript. I put a lot of myself into it.'

Charles wasn't a man easily made ill. He had stood on plenty of bloody decks with bodies and parts of bodies around him and never blinked. This was different; this was worse, because his memoirs had become her labour of love. He might as well have ripped her heart from her body and thrown it on the flames. Setting down the letter, he barely made it to the washbasin before he vomited. He wiped his face and went to the door, closing and locking it, before returning to her desk.

His eyes wet, Charles continued, sobbing out loud at her sentence on the next sheet: 'The situation changed completely when I fell in love with you. I knew then that a true wife would not keep such a confidence from her husband. I can understand your anger. But please believe me, I meant you no harm.'

'You're kinder than I am, Sophie,' he muttered, when he could speak. 'I cannot condone my rage. It was shameful.'

Numb now, and practically forcing himself to breathe, Charles read on. Sophie had changed to the subject of her late husband. 'That man you so quickly dismissed as a glorified, greedy clerk and a weasel was never given a fair trial.'

Willing to be reasonable now, Charles read through her account of Andrew's felony—his suspicions that his supervisor, Edmund Sperling, brother of Lord Edborough, one of the Admiralty Lords, was raking money from the victualling department by countermanding Andrew's invoices for proper supplies and seeing that substandard food went into the kegs. 'Sperling pocketed the difference. He was well known to have gambling debts a-plenty. Andrew remembered daily visits to the victualling yard by Sperling's creditors.'

Charles set down the letter and rubbed his eyes. He could think of other chicanery from men who thought to line their pockets at the navy's expense, but this case went much higher than all of them. No wonder no one felt inclined to believe a lowly superintendent. He continued Sophie's letter, where she wrote of his despair, and his earnest effort to bring Sperling to account. 'My husband was too trusting, Charlie,' Sophie wrote. 'He took Sperling's own forged and altered notes and invoices to the man himself, thinking he would see the error of his ways and make it right. Sperling took the notes and invoices and they were never seen again. When accountants finally uncovered the scheme, after all those unfortunate men were dead of food poisoning, Sperling had no trouble casting all the blame on Andrew.'

Charles took the letter and went to the window, sitting down and leaning back against the little pillow Sophie had placed there, because this was one of her favourite places in their house. He opened the window, almost desperate for the comforting smell of the sea, even though the air was chilly. He took several deep breaths and returned to the letter. Sophie described the trial, which he remembered well. He sighed, thinking how troubled his wife had been the day he had brought up the matter for his memoirs, and his own rude remarks about her late husband. She was not allowed in the courtroom, but sat outside day after day, as her husband was excoriated, blamed, condemned and sentenced.

'He hanged himself in an outbuilding behind our home. One of our neighbours found him. The Admiralty was furious with him, so his body was taken and hanged again, then burned. Surely you remember this,' she wrote. 'I don't know where they dumped his ashes; they were never given to me.'

He did remember the sorry affair, and he remembered his anger that the coward Andrew Daviess had got off so easy. 'God help me, Sophie,' he murmured.

There was more to read, even though he was reading through a film of tears now. She said she truly had been deceptive, as far as Admiralty House was concerned, because they had charged her to keep them informed of her whereabouts. 'Since none of the money Andrew had supposedly stolen was ever recovered, they were convinced that I knew where it was, and would some day retrieve it. Charlie, would I have let my beloved son starve to death if I knew where *any* money was? Ignorant men. Changing my name kept them from hounding me. I would do it again, so I shan't apologise for that, too.'

You needn't apologise for anything, Charles thought. His arms felt too heavy to hold the letter, but little remained now to read. He continued, and broke his heart in the process: 'When you told me to get out, please be assured I left as fast as I could. I only took with me what I came with, so all your possessions remain in this house. Whatever you choose to believe, believe this: I love you with all my heart. I will never trouble you again, but please know that wherever you go in the world, there is one woman who will always love you. I suppose that is my cross to bear. Your dreadfully inconvenient wife, Sarah Sophia Paul Daviess Bright.'

An arrow pointed to a postscript on the back. He turned it over to read, 'Please, please do not dismiss any of the servants. I know you complain about tripping over them, but they have nowhere to go. My sins should not reflect upon them. S.B.'

He bowed his head over the letter, folding it even smaller because he could not bear to see her familiar handwriting. He had become so used to it, from all their days in the bookroom, when she patiently listened and questioned, then spent most of her evenings writing his story. It was all in ashes now, much like his marriage. Disgusted with himself, he looked in her dressing room again. All her beautiful clothes were hanging there in silent reprimand. He went to the burgundy dress, his favourite, and sniffed the fabric. It smelled like her. He stood beside it a long time.

Before he left the room, he went to the desk again. There was another sheet of paper there, folded like the letter, and with Sophie's familiar handwriting, but yellowed with age. He read her note: 'Before Andrew took all the incriminating documents to Sperling, I kept back this one—I suppose I was not as trusting as my husband. We showed it to a barrister, but he said it would have no value in a court of law, since the defendant's wife had procured it.'

He opened it, seeing the familiar invoice form from the victualling yard that had crossed his own desk thousands of times. What Sperling had done became perfectly obvious to him, but Sophie was right. No judge would ever allow the admission of such a document. Poor Sophie. Poor, naïve Andrew.

The letter and document in his hand, he went downstairs, then down the next flight to the servants' hall. Well, that explained where everyone was. From Minerva the youngest, to the two old tars he had rescued from the docks and employed in yard work, they sat there, silent and watching him. Starkey was at their head, looking so pleased with himself.

Charles drew himself up and minced not a single word. 'You all know what has happened. Lady Bright has left. I don't know where she has gone, but I need to know. If any of you have even the slightest clue, please tell me.'

He looked around, hopeful. His servants looked back, silent.

'Does anyone know? None of you saw her leave?'

Silence still. *That is Sophie*, he thought. *She made sure no one knew anything, so I could not turn my wrath on them.*

'Very well. Go about your duties, please. Starkey, I'd like a word with you. The beach.'

It was more than a word. It was many words, none of them spoken until his long-time servant had read Sophie's letter. Starkey tried to stop, but Charles thrust the letter back in his face. 'Read it, damn your eyes!' he shouted, not caring if the wind sent his words back to the house, where his staff was already frightened.

When he finished, Starkey tried to rise from the drift-wood stump, the same one Sophie had sat on when they made their way to the beach so many times that summer. Charles clamped his hook against his servant's shoulder, caring not the slightest when the man winced.

'What made you think to meddle in my affairs?' he asked, when he had regained some control. He lifted his hand and Starkey rubbed his shoulder.

'You didn't know anything about her, sir.'

Charles nodded. 'True. Tell me something, Starkey. Did you really think I needed your help with a wife?'

'No, sir.'

'Then explain yourself.'

Starkey was silent. Charles looked at him. 'Tell me what you did. All of it.'

Starkey looked down at his shoes.

'All of it!' Charles shouted.

Starkey couldn't speak fast enough then. Words tumbled out of him as he told Charles of visiting the vicar at St Andrew's Church, and seeing the parish record listing Andrew Daviess as Sophie's husband. 'I remembered him. I figured you were being diddled, sir. That's it! Honestly! I went to Admiralty House and they were glad to hear what I had to say.'

'Did you mention this matter to anyone else?'

Starkey hung his head even lower. 'Your sisters,' he muttered.

'Good God! What were you thinking?' Charles exclaimed.

'I told them what had happened and swore them to secrecy. I...I...knew the Admiralty was going to come down hard on Lady Bright.' He began to cry then. 'I told them...oh, God, I told them to be patient. That they would have their brother back again soon.'

Charles closed his eyes, speechless.

'I'm sorry, sir! I'm sorry!'

Charles took a moment to collect himself. 'Starkey, you have fed me a mean dinner, on top of the generous helping of remorse I can lay claim to, for my own actions. There is a strong possibility that Andrew Daviess is innocent. I remember Edmund Sperling. Lord Edborough had given him various positions at Admiralty House and none of them took. The man was hopeless. I intend to inquire into Sperling's business, Starkey, but first I must find my wife.'

Starkey nodded. 'I can go to Admiralty House and—'

'I think not,' Charles said. 'What you can do is clear out your rooms and get out of my sight. I'll give you your year's wages, but damned if I'll furnish you a character, since you have none.'

He said it kindly enough, but he meant every word. Starkey opened his mouth to protest, but Charles just shook his head. After another moment's reflection, he turned on his heel and made his way back to his house—full of servants, but more empty than a beggar's bowl.

Chapter Twenty-One

Charles wasted no time in sending out his yard staff to look for Sophie. They were resourceful seamen, down on their luck because peace has interfered, but they knew Plymouth as well as anyone. She hadn't been gone too long, and it was three miles to the Barbican, the seaport's centre.

'You know what she looks like,' he told them. 'Describe her. Ask around. She's probably going by the name of Sally Paul again.' *God knows she isn't using my name*, he thought.

He took his pride in his hands and walked next door to Lord Brimley's estate, unburdening himself to the old man, who was surprisingly sympathetic. He thought long and hard about stopping to see Jacob Brustein. Carriages were coming and going from the manor, but he decided against troubling him with news that a friend of his dear Rivka was gone from his life. He could tell Jacob later, when all the mourners had returned home.

The servants crept around quietly while Charles paced

the floor in the sitting room, choosing that room to worry in, because he had a clear view of the road. Maybe he was as naïve as Andrew, God rest his soul. He hoped to look up and see Sophie walking down the long drive, ready to return and give a second chance to a man who didn't deserve one.

By nightfall, he knew she wasn't coming. Starkey was gone, so he instructed his remaining yardman to build a bonfire on the beach. He sat there until Leaky Tadwell appeared, cheerful, interested, and ready to sell him more smuggled liquor.

'That's not it, Leaky. My wife is gone,' Charles said, almost surprising himself with his willingness to confide in a complete scoundrel.

'Scarpered off, did she?' Tadwell asked. Charles was surprised at the degree of sympathy in his voice. 'You probably do need more spirits. I can lay me mitts on a Fogale Milano that will make you disremember that you ever had a wife.'

'Leaky! No!' Charles sighed. 'I...I broke her heart and she left me.'

'Begging your pardon, Admiral, you have a lot to learn about gentry morts. She was a pretty thing.'

This was not going well, but Charles had no intention of scaring away a perfectly good source. 'Leaky, it's this way: you know everyone in Plymouth.'

'Devonport, too,' Tadwell added.

'Devonport, too. I want you to make discreet inquiries. Here. I've written a description of her. Just ask around. If anyone has seen her, let me know.'

Tadwell took the sheet and looked at it doubtfully. 'Can't read, Admiral. Otherwise, it's a great plan.'

Charles counted to ten and took back the sheet. 'I'll read

it to you. "Looking for a woman calling herself Sally Paul, or Sally Daviess". Can you remember that?'

Tadwell gave him a wounded look. 'Pray continue, Admiral. I ain't in me dotage.'

'Indeed not. She is nine or ten inches taller than you, Leaky. Her hair is brown and so are her eyes. She is of slim build, but not markedly so. She has the most wonderful Scottish accent.'

Tadwell nodded, and repeated what Charles told him. 'I remember all that, sir, from my earlier glimpse of her. But how else does she stand out? A lisp or a cackling laugh, like ol' Nosey?'

Charles shook his head. 'No, nothing like the grand duke. She's a quiet woman who will do nothing to draw attention to herself.'

Tadwell took off his greasy watch cap and scratched his hair. 'You're not making this easy, Admiral.'

'I know, Leaky. Do your best.'

So it went, the rest of that dismal autumn. He wrote to Dundrennan, and other Lowland cities and towns in Scotland, begging for news of such a woman. Nothing. The yard men returned empty-handed. Leaky Tadwell ranged the coastal towns, coming back with no news. When Charles thought to visit Jacob Brustein, the knocker was off the door. A note to David Brustein in Plymouth enquiring about Jacob's whereabouts informed him that his father had gone to visit a daughter in Brighton.

By Christmas, he could no longer fool himself. Sophie Bright was true to her word, Charles had to admit, even though it caused him unbearable anguish. She had said she would not trouble him again and she meant it. He spent one long evening in the bookroom, writing letters to Dora and Fannie, explaining the situation and begging to just let him alone.

His Christmas present to Miss Thayn was to offer her the title of housekeeper, which she accepted. Miss Thayn's present to him was to ask for two days off so she and Etienne could be married. He gave his consent most willingly, even though he could not overlook the envy he felt at another couple's happiness.

When the Dupuis returned from Plymouth, he gave Madame Dupuis the keys to his manor, keeping only the key to his wine cellar, which he took belowstairs, settling in for the month of January in a single-minded attempt to drink the shelves bare. He only glared at Etienne when his chef tried to coax him upstairs for meals, and was impervious to his new housekeeper's tears. He drank and wallowed, drank some more, grew shaggy and started to stink.

His rescue came from a wholly unexpected source, one he never could have imagined, which was why he probably paid attention.

The day had begun much like the ones preceding it. He woke up in the wine cellar, his mouth dry and his stomach sour. His head was lying in someone's lap, someone soft. For a small heartbreak of a moment, he thought it must be Sophie, come to save him from himself. When his vision cleared, he saw it was his sister, Dora, she who lived in Fannie's shadow and who had never in her life issued an opinion of her own.

'Dora?' he asked, hardly believing his eyes. *'Dora?'*

'The very same,' she replied, cradling his crusty head in her arms. 'Charles Bright, It's Time To Stop.'

Charles tried to smile at her, but his lips were cracked and starting to bleed. *There you go, speaking in capital letters*, he thought, remembering how he had described her to Sophie. He cried, uncertain whether they were a drunkard's tears, whether it tore his heart to think of his wife, or whether this was real relief that his sister had come to save his life.

He knew he was disgusting, but she held him close, crooning to him, wiping his tears with a lace handkerchief that smelled of lavender and other civilised things. He rested in her arms, thinking of how she and Fannie had looked after him when their mother died, he still a small lad, not even old enough to go to sea.

'Fannie?' he asked finally, hoping that one-word sentences could suffice, since he couldn't manage more.

'We Have Had A Falling Out,' she said, her voice as gentle as her fingers in his greasy hair. 'She thought you should suffer, especially after the way you treated us. I begged to differ. Politely, though, always politely.' She laughed, sitting on the floor in that cellar slimy with his vomit, holding him close. 'What a shock that was to her system! We parted and I came here. From the look of things, not a minute too soon. Charles, let me help you upstairs. We have some work to do.'

She could no more lift him out of the cellar than turn cartwheels down St James's Street, but a loud halloo brought the yard men running. They carried him to his bedroom, Dora right behind, admonishing them to have a care. He thought to protest when she stripped him naked and had the yard men help him into the tub, where she rolled up her sleeves and washed his hair first. She scrubbed away a month of filth from his body, scolding him all the while in her soft voice, the one that he used to think so irritating, but now was the sweetest sound he had heard in months.

All five feet of her, Dora cleaned him up, dried him off and popped him into a nightshirt. He was asleep before she tiptoed from the room.

He had slept around the clock and woke up ravenous. Dora shook her head at all his suggestions for the meal he wanted—a loin of beef the size of a dinner plate and a pound or two of potatoes—and spooned consommé down him instead, followed by toast and tea. After a day of this stringent regimen, she enlisted Minerva and Gladys to carry up the beef and potatoes. She watched every bite he took, looking at him over her knitting. The pleasant click of her needles soothed his battered heart. He slept again.

The room was empty when he woke up. One of the little maids must have brought hot water, because the familiar brass can stood on the washstand next to the basin. His hook was nowhere to be seen, but he didn't need it, anyway. What he needed was to see if he could stand up again.

Mission accomplished, after several tries, one of which sent him lurching towards his dressing room. He made a course correction that would have pleased his first sailing master, dead these many years, and managed to tip enough hot water into the basin to scrape away at his face.

It wasn't a good job. His month-long growth needed kinder attention than he could provide, but it would do. He patted on the bay rum, wincing when it collided with the little nicks he had administered in his pursuit of a smooth face again. Still, the effect was creditable. Now, where were his clothes?

Dora knocked and came into his room when he was sitting on his bed, contemplating his hook and harness, which someone had stashed in his dressing room. She was a quick learner. 'Now you're armed again,' she said when she snapped the last clasp into place.

He never knew her to make a joke before, and it warmed his heart. To show his gratitude, he even let her button his shirt.

She told him luncheon was being served in the breakfast room today, and allowed him to take her arm as he escorted her to the table. When he finished eating and folded his napkin, she cleared her throat.

'Charles, it is time you visited Admiralty House.'

'Dora, along with your other attributes, you are also a mind reader.'

Two nights later, Charles was installed in a handsome bedchamber at Dora's town house on a quiet side street near St James's Park.

'Stay as long as you like,' Dora told him, handing over a front-door key. 'My servants are as old as I am, and I wouldn't dream of keeping anyone up to await your return, should you choose to visit a Den of Dissipation.'

'I think I will confine my efforts to Admiralty House,' he said, pocketing the key. He sighed and looked out the window.

'I can come with you, if you like,' Dora said, her lip trembling.

You would fight tigers for me, sister, he thought, and it humbled him. He kissed her forehead. 'Dora, you've done everything I need. I couldn't ask for more. I'm in your debt for ever.'

He left the next morning while the other inmates still slept, and walked through St James's Park. Snow had fallen in the night, and the bare trees reminded him of Sophie's little book of sonnets, which she had left behind with everything else he had ever bought her. Until he went down to the cellar for a drink and never came up, he had been working his way through the sonnets.

"'Upon those boughs which shake against the cold, Bare ruin'd choirs, where late the sweet birds sang",' he murmured, looking at the small lake. He knew the sonnet by heart, but had no wish to continue. He did anyway, settling in his mind that he might never see Sophie Bright again. "'To love that well which thou must leave ere long".'

He continued east across the park to Horse Guards and Admiralty House, smiling to see it, thinking of all the times he had strode its halls, first as a lieutenant seeking a ship when none was to be had, on through the intense, gory years of his captaincy, and then the exalted state of his admiralty, when all doors opened to receive him. He was one of the anointed, one of the chosen, in the same league—well, no one was—with Horatio Nelson himself. What was it worth to him now? Less than dust.

By the time he approached the familiar entrance, London was open for business. He was dressed in his civilian clothes, but felt some small twinge of pride when he was recognised at once by the captains who waited for an audience, much as he had done. He revelled a moment in genuine happiness, greeting old friends and hearing new tales of a much slower peacetime navy, one not destined to shower down the honours and terrors of the long war. Charles smiled to himself to see young captains chafe at inaction. *Be careful what you wish for*, he thought.

His request to speak to the First Lord brought an immediate response. He scarcely had to wait a moment in the First Lord's office before he was bowing to Lord Biddle and then shaking his hand. Pleasantries were awkward; it was obvious that old Biddle knew very well what had transpired in Admiral Bright's private life. At least he kept his opinions to himself, dancing around them by asking about his manor and other approved subjects.

When the only safe topic left was the weather, Charles held up his hand. 'My lord, I have no desire to encroach upon your valuable time. May I ask, is Lord Edborough available? I have something particular to ask him.'

Biddle shook his head. 'Charles, you have missed him by mere months! He retired just before Christmas.'

'Where is he now?'

'You are in luck, actually. I saw him only yesterday at Lord Brattleton's crush in honour of his whey-faced daughter. Don't laugh; it was purgatory. I believe you will find him at his residence.' Biddle looked in a drawer and extracted a memo pad, scribbling on it. 'Here is his direction.'

'Thank you. Before I visit him, I would like to look at the transcripts of the trial of Andrew Daviess, supervisor of the Portsmouth victualling yard. It was in March of 1811, I believe.'

Lord Biddle sat a long moment, choosing not to meet Charles's glance.

'I am certain the transcripts are here, Lord Biddle,' Charles insisted, when the silence stretched on too long. 'I have every right to see them. I was there.'

'I cannot produce them.'

'I beg your pardon?'

'They no longer exist.'

'Oh.' His heart dropped to his ankles as Charles continued to regard the First Lord, whose face had turned quite red. 'They just disappeared? Took a powder? French leave?'

'Precisely.' The First Lord leaned forwards across his desk, his expression forced and hearty now. 'Charles, you know as well as any of us how the world works. There is no record of that trial.'

The glib words seemed to carom off every surface of Charles's brain. 'No record?' he repeated, not overly concerned that his voice was rising. 'I wasn't really there? I didn't testify? I heard no accusations hurled at whom I think—no, whom I know now—was an honest man? Nothing?'

They could probably hear him in the anteroom. He knew his voice could carry over a hurricane. But there was the First Lord, looking all disapproving now, prissy even, narrowing his eyes and probably wishing one of his favourite admirals to Hades. For the life of him, Charles could only think of what Dora would probably say at a moment like this.

'You should be ashamed of yourself, Lord Biddle. Good day.'

None of the officers waiting in the anteroom looked at him when Charles hurried from the building. He hailed a conveyance, one of many loitering about the government offices on as dreary a day as he had ever encountered.

The carriage couldn't go fast enough to suit him, but as he stood before Lord Edborough's elegant house, he knew his was a fool's errand. If Andrew Daviess had found no satisfaction, neither would he. Standing under the porch at Admiralty House, it had come home forcefully to him that the might of the Royal Navy extended far beyond the world's oceans. It had the power to ruin lives with total impunity. He could almost see poor Andrew Daviess attempting to make his puny claims against men who would crush him without remorse. The man had never had a chance.

Charles was shown into Lord Edborough's sitting room and spent nearly an hour waiting. He employed his time well, watching the rain run through a ruined downspout across the street, and looking at men and women hurrying down slick walkways. Mostly he thought of Sophie, wondering how she was, and whether she watched the rain fall, too.

'Admiral Bright! To what do I owe this great honour?'

He turned around to see Lord Edborough, a prosy man he had always liked well enough. More pleasantries followed, tedious in the extreme, now that he was bursting to talk. Unable to endure one more minute, he interrupted.

'My lord, I will be brief. Five years ago, the Royal Navy brought charges of graft, corruption and foul play against the supervisor of Portsmouth's victualling yard, a man named Andrew Daviess. I have reason to believe your brother was the guilty party.'

Lord Edborough was silent.

'You do have a brother, do you not?' Charles said, tried to the limit.

'I do, or I did,' Lord Edborough said finally. 'He has been dead these three years.'

Charles sat down without being invited to do so. 'Your brother ruined Andrew Daviess. His widow and small son were turned out to fend for themselves. The boy died and the woman was reduced to paupery.' He handed Lord Edborough the original forged and erased invoice that Sophie had kept back. 'This is potent evidence of his chicanery, but not enough to satisfy any court of law bent on covering up malfeasance. Take this, my lord. Tear it up. Burn it. It's the last bit of evidence against your foul brother, may he rot in hell. No court in the land will touch it. Your dirty secret is safe as houses. Good day.'

He made it to the door before Lord Edborough spoke. 'Admiral Bright, one moment.'

Charles turned around, not caring if he frightened the older man with the grimness of his expression. No need to worry, though. Lord Edborough's visage was more bleak.

Lord Edborough chose his words carefully. 'He was a weak one, was Edmund. Always in debt. None of us in the family approved of his actions.'

'Then he was guilty,' Charles said, his voice scarcely above a whisper.

Lord Edborough confirmed nothing. 'He was my brother, Charles, for good or ill.'

'But…'

'He was my brother,' the viscount repeated. 'If you attempt any action, I will come against you with all the force of the law.' He began to rip the invoice into tiny pieces, viscerally reminding Charles of Sophie's manuscript that he had shred in front of her horrified eyes. 'You have no proof. I will never tell a court of law what I have just revealed to you, Admiral Bright. Good day.'

Chapter Twenty-Two

Dora begged him to stay, but Charles was adamant.

'I have neglected my estate too long,' he told her as he slid the last clean shirt into his valise.

'Give me a few weeks, and I will send you an invitation to visit,' he told her after breakfast, as she stood outside with him. 'You'll be fair amazed at the transformation our—my—house had undergone. There is nary a naughty cupid in sight.'

On dreary days like today, he longed to stride a quarterdeck in some southern latitude.

Two nights in public houses had convinced him how weary he was of travel. On the third day, the coachman was willing to drive him right to his door, but the prospect of a house without Sophie in it trumped his weariness. Inventing some errand that could not be postponed, he asked to stop at the Drake for luncheon. He could complete his journey once he had eaten. No one paced back and forth in his sitting room, pining for a glimpse of him. His time was his own.

Apparently, his time was also the Drake's. He placed his order, but the waiter returned once and then twice, bearing the unwelcome news that the hotel had exchanged hands only a week ago, and things were not as they should be. Charles shrugged and went outside in the rain to advise his coachman to come inside, too, or find a better public house.

He sat down at his usual table again, unable to prevent his eyes from straying to that table to the front and left where he had first seen Sally Paul. It was foolish of him to think that his heart hurt, but it did. He rubbed his chest, resolving not to give the Drake his patronage any more.

A man sat in Sophie's spot, rattling through the newspaper, and casting angry glances at his timepiece. With a monumental oath, the man folded his paper, whacked the table with it, then left the dining room. An elderly lady taking tea nearby jumped in her seat and uttered a little shriek.

When no one came to straighten the table the irate man had deserted, Charles retrieved the newspaper. Making himself comfortable, he read the news, boring in the extreme, now that warships rode at anchor, or had been placed in ordinary. He finished the paper and refolded it, then unfolded it and turned to the back page, that section Sophie had been studying with such intent when he noticed her, and found he could not look away.

Notices were few; jobs were still scarce. He looked down the paper to the legal announcements, several of which had originated from Brustein and Carter's office three streets over. His eyes widened and he read them again.

On the face of it, there was nothing remotely interesting about a landowner searching for a lost relative, someone to whom he owed money. It was the writing that grabbed his attention and refused to let go, taking him back to the best moments last summer, when Sophie had laboured over his puny life story, infusing it with her own wit and skill. He read the announcement again; it was Sophie's writing.

He looked to the bottom of the announcement, with the initials D.B.—David Brustein, to be sure. Charles let out the breath he had been holding when he saw the lowercase s.b., following a slash. He stood up, unmindful of everything in the dining room. It couldn't be. He was imagining things. He read another similar announcement from D.B./s.b., and one more, this one S.B./s.b. Although the subject in all three announcements was pedestrian in the extreme, the words were not.

'You're still using my name,' he said out loud. He looked at the elderly lady with the tea and pointed at the announcement. 'She's still using my name!'

The woman glared at him and snapped her fingers to summon a waiter—probably to throw him out of the Drake—but he was already out the door, walking fast up the High Street, the newspaper still clutched in his hand. He passed several officers he had known for years. They hailed him; he ignored them. And then out of breath, he was standing before the modest door proclaiming Brustein and Carter.

He stood there a moment until he was breathing normally, then opened the door.

It was the same office he had always visited. In fact, he had stopped in before his trip to London, speaking as he always did to either David or Samuel Brustein, his men of business, now that Jacob had retired. He had chatted with David as he withdrew money, only last week.

Everything had changed now, even though it all remained the same: the dark panelling, the Turkish rug, the overstuffed chairs, the most junior clerk looking at him politely, waiting to honour whatever request he had.

'Admiral Bright? How may we help you today?'

He willed himself to remain calm as he stood in front of the clerk's desk. He indicated the announcements. The clerk looked at him, interest in his eyes. 'Yes?'

'Where is Sophie Bright?' he asked softly, when he wanted to rip the door to the interior offices off its hinges and run down the hallway, looking in all the cubicles this time, and not just David or Samuel's offices.

The clerk was silent. He adjusted his spectacles and stood up. 'Let me get Mr David Brustein.'

'I'm coming with you.'

'No, you're not,' the clerk replied crisply. 'Sir! Just wait here, please.'

I can be patient; I can be civil, Charles told himself as he said down, then stood up immediately, as David Brustein opened the door, straightening his neckcloth. He was a short man like his father and Charles towered over him.

'Mr Brustein, where is my wife?'

He said it softly; he knew he did. The last thing he wanted to do was terrify Sophie, if she was within hearing distance.

Brustein sat down on the edge of his clerk's desk, effectively blocking the interior door, even though it was patently obvious that Charles could toss him aside like a skittle. 'She's here,' he said. 'How did you find her?'

Charles sighed and closed his eyes. When he opened them, they were wet. And as he looked at the younger man, he saw Brustein's eyes welling up, too.

'Admiral? How did you find her?'

Wordlessly, Charles pointed to the announcements in the newspaper.

'I don't quite—'

'David, I would know Sophie's style of writing anywhere.' He tapped the initials. 'And there it is: s.b. for
Sophie Bright. Please. Let me talk to her.'

Brustein nodded just as the door opened and Samuel
came out, obviously curious to know what had taken his
brother to the reception room during the busiest part of the
day. The brothers spoke together in Yiddish, and Samuel
went back inside.

'He will ask Mrs Bright if she wishes to speak to you.'
David stood up then, no taller than ever, but exerting a
certain command. 'If she does not wish to speak to you,
you will have to go.'

'Aye, lad,' he replied.

He could be patient. His pride was gone, his faith in
the Royal Navy well nigh shattered after sifting through a
mountain of duplicity. As he waited, he knew that if Sophie
Bright would not see him, he would will the house to her
and take ship for South America. She would never want
for anything, and he would want for everything. But as the
Lord Admiral had so smugly exclaimed, that was how the
world worked.

The door opened. Charles's face fell to see Samuel,
and no one behind him. Was it to be Montevideo or Rio
de Janeiro? He didn't care.

'Admiral? Why don't you follow me?'

Dumbly, he turned towards the door leading to the
street. David Brustein stopped him, his hand on his arm.

'No, Admiral. Follow Samuel.'

Sophie was perched on a stool behind a tall desk, her
hands clasped in front of her, her face pale. With a gesture,
Samuel cleared the room of the other clerks at their desks.
Charles stood in the doorway, afraid to move one step
closer.

'I read one of the Brusteins' legal announcements. It sounded...' he gulped '...it sounded remarkably like your writing, Sophie.'

She watched his face, not wary, but solemn.

'Charles...are you well? You look thin. Surely Etienne is still in your employ. And Starkey, too, I suppose. Please tell me that Miss Thayn still—'

'Starkey is long gone,' he said, coming closer, but not too close. How beautiful she looked in the strong light coming through the double windows, the perfect setting for scribes. Her face had a gentle glow to it that he hadn't noticed before. He hadn't seen her in five months, come to think of it. 'I dismissed Starkey the day you left.'

She nodded.

'The others? I have to tell you, Miss Thayn is no more.'

'Charles! I was so hoping you would—'

'Steady as she goes, Sophie! She and Etienne decided to tie the knot. Miss *Thayn* is no more.'

She laughed at that. 'You wretch!' she scolded, and he had to gulp again and look away.

'The girls are fine, and Vivienne is planning to cook for me, so Etienne and Amelia can go away for a few weeks.' He hesitated, putting all his eggs in one fragile basket. 'You never decided on a good colour for the exterior.'

'Pale blue, I should think,' she said, getting off her stool and coming around the corner of the desk. 'It will look good against the lemon trees.'

He stared at her gently rounded belly, then dropped to his knees. She was in his arms in a moment, gathering him close as he pressed his face into her belly. Her hands rested on his head, and then she knelt, too, holding him close. 'You're too thin,' she said. 'Tell me you weren't sick!'

He could only shake his head and gather her closer. As

he did so, he felt the baby move, probably in protest at such close quarters in an already confined space.

'I never dreamed I would be a father,' he said many minutes later, when she had left off kissing him, and her hands were gentle on his back now. 'That was something so out of reach I never thought...'

'Think again, Charlie,' she told him, leaning on him to stand on her feet again. 'I believe it was that morning before we went to pay our respects to Jacob Brustein.' She tugged at his hand and he stood up, only to clasp her close, as their son or daughter protested with another high kick. Sophie laughed softly. 'Or it could have been the morning or two before that, or maybe...'

'We weren't much good at convenient marriages, were we, my darling?' Charles said.

She walked him to the door, opening it to see both Brusteins and the clerks waiting with an air of expectation. 'Gentlemen, I didn't mean to take you away from your accounts.'

David gestured to his own office. 'Go in there and talk,' he said. 'Sam and I will walk down to the Drake for tea.'

'The service is terrible there,' Charles said, before Sophie closed the door to David's office and pulled him into her lopsided embrace again. 'You'll wait for ever.'

He sat down, pulling her on to his lap. 'You walked to the Brusteins' that morning.'

Sophie nodded, resting against his chest. His hand went to her belly as though it belonged there. 'I didn't know where else to go, and Mr Brustein had said I could always depend on him. With all the carriages coming and going, I knew I'd get away.'

'I am so sorry,' he said, his voice betraying only a tiny portion of the anguish he felt.

She nestled closer, and her words were muffled in his

overcoat. 'For a long time, you were just one more person who had hurt me.'

'I know. What changed?'

She thought about it. She gave that small sigh with the little sound to it, and he realised how he had been craving to hear that again. 'Well, the baby, to be sure. I had no idea how you would feel about a child from my body, not after—'

'Sophie, don't even think it. I was cruel and you didn't deserve the way I treated you.'

He held her close until she stirred in his arms. 'I knew I would do anything to keep my baby safe. I'm not certain when it happened, but one morning I woke up and realised that if I never saw you again, mine would be a life not worth living.' She toyed with the button on his overcoat. 'But I had no way of knowing how you felt, so there the matter rested.'

'You left behind a persuasive letter, my love,' he told her. 'After I finished drinking all the liquor in the cellar, and after Dora dried me out and—'

'Dora? She Did What?'

He played with her curls that had come loose from her chignon. 'Sophie, you're speaking in capitals, just like Dora. It's true, and it can keep. More to the point, I went to Admiralty House and received the royal circumlocution. Would it surprise you to know that all records and transcripts from Andrew's trial have disappeared? Poof. Just like that.'

'Now we will never know.'

'Think again.' Cuddling her close, he told her about Lord Edborough's confession of sorts. 'He assured me I could never prove anything in a court of law, and he is right. Edmund Sperling is dead, though, if that is any consolation.' He sighed. 'A few months ago, when I was so proud and stupid, I wanted to see Sperling get his just deserts before a heavenly tribunal.'

'But not now?' she asked, her hands warm inside his overcoat now.

'No, my love. When I was younger, I wanted justice. Now that I am older, I yearn for mercy.'

He went back to his manor alone, but with a smile on his face. David and Samuel had both cut up stiff when he wanted to whisk his darling away from them that very hour. They reminded him that quarters were approaching, and they needed his gravid, beautiful wife for another week of work. 'She has made herself indispensable to us,' was David's last argument.

He could understand that completely. From the moment she gave him her startled consent to wed, Sarah Sophia Paul Daviess Bright had worked her own little magic on him. He thought about asking her what she was planning to do, if he hadn't found her, then decided he didn't care. Maybe some day she would tell him.

When he got home and made himself comfortable in his favourite chair in the sitting room—he still hated to go into the bookroom—he took out her little book of sonnets and turned to the twenty-ninth. For five months, he had never got beyond the first few lines about disgrace, and bootless cries, and troubling deaf heaven. Now his eyes roved lower. He smiled and mouthed the words, 'Haply I think on thee', then on to 'thy sweet love remembered', until he was content as never before, even if his dear one—dear ones—were still in Plymouth.

At any rate, they were until a carriage pulled up in front of his house. He put his finger in the book to save his place and looked out the window. 'Well, well,' he said. 'Sophie, you're so impulsive. Some day I will tell our children you proposed to me, because you just couldn't wait.'

He opened the door and stood there as the coachman helped her soft bulk from the vehicle. From now on that would be his office, and a good one it was, but he was content to watch her from the only slight distance that would ever separate them again.

The coachman unloaded her modest valise, climbed back aboard and tipped his hat to them both. She stood there, looking at him, her hand just naturally resting on her belly. She was obviously well acquainted with their child within. He had some catching up to do. He went down the steps and picked up her valise, then took her arm.

She stood there a moment, looking at the house. 'Yes, light blue. When will we have lemons? I would like one right now.'

Charles laughed and kissed her cheek. 'Decided not to stay and help the Brusteins?'

She carefully picked up his left arm and draped it around her shoulder, keeping his hook at a distance. 'I was miserable as soon as you left and they fired me.'

He shouted with laughter and gathered her close.

* * * * *

*Marrying the
Royal Marine*

CARLA KELLY

Prologue

*Stonehouse Royal Marine Barracks, Third Division,
Plymouth—May 1812*

Black leather stock in hand, Lieutenant Colonel Hugh
Philippe d'Anvers Junot, Royal Marine, stared into his
mirror and decided his father was right: he was lonely.

Maybe early symptoms were the little drawings that
deckled Hugh's memorandum tablet during endless meetings in the conference room at Marine Barracks. As
Colonel Commandant Lord Villiers covered item after
item in his stringent style, Hugh had started drawing a
little lady peeking around the edge of her bonnet. During
one particularly dull budget meeting, he drew a whole file
of them down the side of the page.

Hugh gazed more thoughtfully into the mirror, not
bothered by his reflection—he knew his height, posture,
curly brown hair, and nicely chiselled lips met the demands of any recruiting poster—but by the humbling
knowledge that his father still knew him best.

He had written to his father, describing his restlessness and his dissatisfaction with the perils of promotion. While flattering, the promotion had bumped him off a ship of the line and into an office. *I know I should appreciate this promotion*, he had written, *but, Da, I am out of sorts. I'm not sure what I want. I'm sour and discontented. Any advice would be appreciated. Your dutiful, if disgruntled, son.*

A week later, he had read Da's reply over breakfast. He read it once and laughed; he read it again and pushed back his chair, thoughtful. He sat there longer than he should have, touched that his father had probably hit on the matter: he was lonely.

Damn this war, he had thought then. The words were plainspoken as Da was plainspoken: *My dear son, I wrote a similar letter to your grandfather once, before I met your mother, God rest her soul. Son, can ye find a wife?*

'That takes more time than I have, Da,' he had said out loud, but Da was probably right. Lately, when he attended the Presbyterian church in Devonport, he found himself paying less attention to the sermon and more attention to husbands, wives, and children sitting in the pews around him. He found himself envying both the comfortable looks of the couples married longest, and the shy hand-holdings and smouldering glances of the newly married. He tried to imagine the pleasure of marrying and rearing children, and found that he could not. War had ruined him; perhaps Da wasn't aware of that.

It was food for thought this May morning, and he chewed on it as he took advantage of a welcome hiatus from a meeting—the Colonel Commandant's gout was dictating a start one hour later than usual—and took himself to Stonehouse Naval Hospital. He had heard the jetty bell clanging late last night, and knew there would be wounded Marines to visit.

The air was crisp and cool, but threatening summer when he arrived at Block Four, where his friend Owen Brackett worked his surgeon's magic on the quick and nearly dead. He found Owen on the second floor.

The surgeon turned to Hugh with a tired smile. 'Did the jetty bell wake you?'

Hugh nodded. 'Any Marines?'

'Aye. If you have a mind to visit, come with me.'

Hugh followed Brackett down the stairs into another ward. With an inward sigh, he noted screens around several beds.

'There was a cutter returning from Surgeon Brittle's satellite hospital in Oporto. The cutter was stopped at sea by a frigate with some nasty cases to transfer,' Owen said. 'Seems there was a landing attempted farther north along the Portuguese coast. Sit.'

He sat, never used to ghastly wounds, and put his hands on the man's remaining arm, which caused the Marine's eyes to flicker open.

'Meet Lieutenant Nigel Graves, First Division,' Brackett whispered before leaving.

'From Chatham?' Hugh asked, putting his lips close to the man's ear.

'Aye, sir. Serving on...*Relentless*.' It took ages for him to get out the words.

'A regular mauling?' he asked, his voice soft. 'Take your time, Lieutenant. We have all day.' He didn't; the Lieutenant didn't. It was a serviceable lie; both knew it.

Lieutenant Graves tried to sit up. Hugh slipped his arm under the young man's neck. 'What were you doing?'

'Trying to land at Vigo.'

'A one-ship operation?'

'Four ships, sir.' He sighed, his exasperation obvious. 'We didn't know each other! Who was in charge when the Major died?' He closed his eyes. 'It was a disaster, sir. We should have been better.'

Hugh could tell he wanted to say more, but Lieutenant Graves took that moment to die. Hugh gently lowered him to the cot. He was still sitting there when Owen Brackett returned, enquired about the time of death from him, and wrote it on the chart.

'A botched landing at Vigo,' Hugh said. 'Uncoordinated Marines working against each other, when all they wanted to do was fight! I've heard this before.'

'It makes you angry,' Owen said.

'Aye.' Hugh smoothed down the Lieutenant's hair. 'Each company on each vessel is a well-oiled machine, because we train them that way. Put one hundred of them on a ship of the line, and you have a fighting force. Try to coordinate twenty-five here or fifteen there from three or four frigates operating in tandem, and it can be a disaster.'

The surgeon nodded. 'All they want to do is their best. They're Marines, after all. We expect no less.'

Hugh thought about that as he took the footbridge back over the stream to the administration building of the Third Division. He was never late to anything, but he was late now.

The meeting was in the conference room on the first floor. He stopped outside the door, hand on knob, as a good idea settled around him and blew away the fug.

Why could someone not enquire of the Marines at war how they saw themselves being used in the Peninsula?

'You're late, Colonel Junot,' his Colonel Commandant snapped.

'Aye, my lord. I have no excuse.'

'Are those *stains* on your uniform sleeve?'

Everyone looked. Hugh saw no sympathy. 'Aye, my lord.'

Perhaps it was his gout; Lord Villiers was not in a forgiving mood. 'Well? Well?'

'I was holding a dying man and he had a head wound, my lord.'

His fellow Marine officers snapped to attention where they sat. It might have been a tennis match; they looked at the Commandant, as if on one swivel, then back at Hugh.

'Explain yourself, sir,' Lord Villiers said, his voice calmer.

'I visited Stonehouse, my lord.' He remained at attention. 'Colonel, I know you have an agenda, but I have an idea.'

Chapter One

Lord Villiers liked the idea and moved on it promptly. He unbent enough to tell Hugh, as he handed him his orders, 'This smacks of something I would have done at your age, given your dislike of the conference table.'

'I, sir?'

'Belay it, Colonel Junot! Don't bamboozle someone who, believe it or not, used to chafe to roam the world. Perhaps we owe the late Lieutenant Graves a debt unpayable. Now take the first frigate bound to Portugal before I change my mind.'

Hugh did precisely that. With his dunnage stowed on the *Perseverance* and his berth assigned—an evil-smelling cabin off the wardroom—Hugh had dinner with Surgeon Brackett on his last night in port. Owen gave him a letter for Philemon Brittle, chief surgeon at the Oporto satellite hospital, and passed on a little gossip.

'It's just a rumour, mind, but Phil seems to have engineered a billet for his sister-in-law, a Miss Brandon, at his hospital. He's a clever man, but I'm agog to know how he managed it, if the scuttlebutt is true,' Brackett said. 'Perhaps she is sailing on the *Perseverance*.'

'Actually, she is,' Hugh said, accepting tea from Amanda Brackett. 'I've already seen her.'

'She has two beautiful sisters, one of whom took leave of her senses and married Phil Brittle. Perhaps your voyage will be more interesting than usual,' the surgeon teased.

Hugh sipped his tea. 'Spectacles.'

'You're a shallow man,' Amanda Brackett said, her voice crisp.

Hugh winced elaborately and Owen laughed. 'Skewered! Mandy, I won't have a friend left in the entire fleet if you abuse our guests so. Oh. Wait. He's a Royal Marine. They don't count.'

Hugh joined in their laughter, at ease with their camaraderie enough to unbend. 'I'll have you know I took a good look at her remarkable blue eyes, and, oh, that auburn hair.'

'All the sisters have it,' Amanda said. 'More ragout?'

'No, thank you, although I am fully aware it is the best thing I will taste until I fetch the Portuguese coast in a week or so.' He set down his cup. 'Miss Brandon is too young to tempt me, Amanda. I doubt she is a day over eighteen.'

'And you are antiquated at thirty-seven?'

'I am. Besides that, what female in her right mind, whatever her age, would make a Marine the object of her affection?'

'You have me there, Colonel,' Amanda said promptly, which made Owen laugh.

She did have him, too, Hugh reflected wryly, as he walked from Stonehouse, across the footbridge, and back to the barrack for a final night on shore. *Perhaps I am shallow*, he considered, as he lay in bed later. Amanda

Brackett was right; he was vain and shallow. Maybe daft, too. He lay awake worrying more about his assignment, putting Miss Brandon far from his mind.

Hugh joined the *Perseverance* at first light, the side boys lined up and the bosun's mate piping him aboard. His face set in that no-nonsense look every Marine cultivated, and which he had perfected, he scanned the rank of Marines on board. He noted their awed recognition of his person, but after last night's conversation, he felt embarrassed.

He chatted with Captain Adney for only a brief minute, knowing well that the man was too busy for conversation. Out of the corner of his eye, he noticed Miss Brandon standing quietly by the binnacle, her hands clasped neatly in front of her, the picture of rectitude, or at the very least, someone just removed from the schoolroom herself. Amanda Brackett had said as much last night. She was a green girl.

He had to admit there was something more about Miss Brandon, evidenced by the two Midshipmen and Lieutenant grouped about her, appearing to hang on her every word. She had inclined her head to one side and was paying close attention to the Lieutenant. Hugh smiled. He could practically see the man's blush from here on the quarterdeck.

Miss Brandon, you are obviously a good listener, he thought. *Perhaps that compensates for spectacles.* The moment the thought swirled in his brain, he felt small again. *What a snob I am*, he concluded, turning his attention again to Captain Adney.

'…passage of some five days, Colonel, if we're lucky,' he was saying. 'Is it Oporto or Lisbon for you?'

It scarcely mattered, considering his *carte blanche* to wander the coastline on his fact-finding mission. Perhaps he should start at Lisbon. 'Oporto,' he said. He knew he had a letter for Surgeon Brittle, Miss Brandon's brother-in-law, but he also knew he could just give it to her and make his way to Lisbon, avoiding Oporto altogether. 'Oporto,' he repeated, not sure why.

'Very well, sir,' Captain Adney told him. 'And now, Colonel, I am to take us out of harbour with the tide. Excuse me, please.'

Hugh inclined his head and the Captain moved towards his helmsman, standing ready at the wheel. Hugh watched with amusement as the flock around Miss Brandon moved away quickly, now that their Captain was on the loose and prepared to work them.

Hardly knowing why, Hugh joined her. He congratulated himself on thinking up a reason to introduce himself. He doffed his hat and bowed. 'Miss Brandon? Pray forgive my rag manners in introducing myself. I am Lieutenant Colonel Hugh Junot, and I have some business you might discharge for me.'

She smiled at him, and he understood instantly why the Lieutenant and Midshipmen had been attracted to her like iron filings to a magnet. She had a direct gaze that seemed to block out everything around her and focus solely on the object of her interest. He felt amazingly flattered, even though she was doing nothing more than giving him her attention. There was nothing coy, arch or even flirtatious about her expression. She was so completely *present*. He couldn't describe it any better.

She dropped him a deep curtsy. Considering that it

was high summer and she wore no cloak, this gave him ample opportunity to admire her handsome bosom.

'Yes, Colonel, I am Miss Brandon.'

As he put on his hat again, her eyes followed it up and she did take a little breath, as though she was not used to her present company. He knew she must be familiar enough with the Royal Navy, considering her relationship to a captain and a surgeon, but he did not think his splendid uniform was ringing any bells.

'I am a Marine, Miss Brandon,' he said.

'And I am a hopeless landlubber, Colonel,' she replied with a smile. 'I should have known that. What can I do for you?'

What a polite question, he thought. *It is almost as if I were infirm. She is looking at me as though I have a foot in the grave, no teeth, and more years than her brothers-in-law combined. What an ass I am.*

Feeling his age—at least every scar on his body had not started to ache simultaneously—he nodded to her. 'Miss Brandon, I have been charged by Surgeon Owen Brackett to take a letter to your brother-in-law in Oporto. I suppose that is why I sought to introduce myself, rather than wait for someone else—who, I do not know—to perform that office.'

That is marvellously lame, he thought sourly, thinking of the gawking Midshipmen who had so recently claimed her attention, and mentally adding himself to their number.

The deferential look left her face. 'Taking a letter to my brother-in-law is a pleasant assignment, sir. I am headed to the same place. Do you know Surgeon Brittle?'

'Not yet.'

'If you are too busy to discharge your duty, I can certainly relieve you of the letter, Colonel,' she told him.

'I am going there, too.'

He could think of nothing more to say, but she didn't seem awkwardly waiting for conversation. Instead, she turned her back against the rail to watch the foretopmen in the rigging, preparing to spill down the sails and begin their voyage. It was a sight he always enjoyed, too, so he stood beside her in silence and watched. Although he had scarce acquaintance with the lady beside him, he felt no urge to blather on, in the way that newly introduced people often do.

The *Perseverance* began to move, and he felt his heart lift, so glad he was to be at sea again and not sitting in a conference room. He would range the coast, watch his Marines in action, interview them, and possibly formulate a way to increase their utility. With any luck, he could stretch his assignment through the summer and into autumn.

'I have never sailed before,' Miss Brandon said.

'You'll get your sea legs,' he assured her, his eyes on the men balancing against the yardarms. He hoped it wasn't improper to mention legs to a lady, even the sea kind.

In a few more minutes, she went belowdeck. He watched Marines working the capstan with the sailors, and others already standing sentry by the water butt and the helm. He nodded to the Sergeant of Marines, who snapped to attention, and introduced himself as the senior non-commissioned officer on board. A thirty-six-gun frigate had no commissioned officer. Hugh explained his mission and told the man to carry on.

He stayed on deck until the *Perseverance* tacked out

of Plymouth Sound and into the high rollers of the Channel itself. He observed the greasy swell of the current and knew they were in for some rough water. No matter— he was never seasick.

He went belowdeck and into his cabin, a typical knocked-together affair made of framed canvas, which was taken down when the gundeck cleared for action. His sleeping cot, hung directly over the cannon, was already swaying to the rhythm of the Atlantic Ocean. He timed the swell and rolled into the cot for a nap.

Because Miss Brandon had admitted this was her first sea voyage, Hugh was not surprised when she did not appear for dinner in the wardroom. Captain Adney had the good sense to give her the cabin with actual walls, one that probably should have gone to a Lieutenant Colonel of Marines, had a woman not been voyaging. The Sergeant had posted a sentry outside her door, which was as it should be. There were no flies growing on this little Marine detachment, and so he would note in his journal.

There was no shortage of conversation around the wardroom table. The frigate's officers let him into their conversation and seemed interested in his plan. Used to the sea, they kept protective hands around their plates and expertly trapped dishes sent sliding by the ship's increasingly violent motion. When the table was cleared and the steward brought out a bottle, Hugh frowned to hear the sound of vomiting from Miss Brandon's cabin.

The surgeon sighed and reached for the sherry as it started to slide. 'Too bad there is no remedy for *mal de mer*,' he said. 'She'll be glad to make land in a week.'

They chuckled, offered the usual toasts, hashed over

the war, and departed for their own duties. Hugh sat a while longer at the table, tempted to knock on Miss Brandon's door and at least make sure she had a basin to vomit in.

She didn't come out at all the next day, either. *Poor thing*, Hugh thought, as he made his rounds of the Marine Privates and Corporals, trying to question them about their duties, taking notes, and wondering how to make Marines naturally wary of high command understand that all he wanted was to learn from them. Maybe the notion was too radical.

Later that night he was lying in his violently swinging sleeping cot, stewing over his plans, when someone knocked on the frame of his canvas wall.

'Colonel, Private Leonard, sir.'

Hugh got up in one motion, alert. Leonard was the sentry outside Miss Brandon's door. He had no business even crossing the wardroom, not when he was on duty. *Your Sergeant will hear from me, Private*, he thought, as he yanked open his door.

'How dare you abandon your post!' he snapped.

If he thought to intimidate Private Leonard, he was mistaken. The man seemed intent on a more important matter than the potential threat of the lash.

'Colonel Junot, it's Miss Brandon. I've stood sentinel outside her door for nearly four hours now, and I'm worried.' The Private braced himself against the next roll and wiggle as the *Perseverance* rose, then plunged into the trough of a towering wave. 'She was puking and bawling, and now she's too quiet. I didn't think I should wait to speak until the watch relieved me, sir.'

Here's one Marine who thinks on his feet, Hugh thought, as he reached for his uniform jacket. 'You acted wisely. Return to your post, Private,' he said, his voice normal.

He had his misgivings as he crossed the wardroom and knocked on her door. Too bad there was not another female on board. He knocked again. No answer. He looked at Private Leonard. 'I go in, don't I?' he murmured, feeling suddenly shy and not afraid to admit it. There may have been a great gulf between a Lieutenant Colonel and a Private, but they were both men.

'I think so, sir,' the Private said. 'Do you have a lamp?'

'Go get mine.'

He opened the door and was assailed by the stench of vomit. 'Miss Brandon?' he called.

No answer. Alarmed now, he was by her sleeping cot in two steps. He could barely see her in the gloom. He touched her shoulder and his hand came away damp. He shook her more vigorously and was rewarded with a slight moan.

No one dies of seasickness, he reminded himself. 'Miss Brandon?' he asked again. 'Can you hear me?'

Private Leonard returned with his lantern, holding it above them in the tiny cabin. The light fell on as pitiful a specimen of womanhood as he had ever seen. Gone was the moderately attractive, composed young lady of two days ago. In her place was a creature so exhausted with vomiting that she could barely raise her hands to cover her eyes against the feeble glow of the lantern.

'I should have approached you sooner, sir,' Private Leonard said, his voice full of remorse.

'How were you to know?' he asked. 'We officers

should have wondered what was going on when she didn't come out for meals. Private, go find the surgeon. I am relieving you at post.'

'Aye, aye, Colonel.'

Uncertain what to do, Hugh hung the lantern from the deck beam and gently moved Miss Brandon's matted hair from her face, which was dry and caked. She didn't open her eyes, but ran her tongue over cracked lips. 'You're completely parched,' he said. 'Dryer than a bone. My goodness, Miss Brandon.'

She started to cry then, except she was too dehydrated for tears. Out of his element, he didn't know how to comfort her. Was she in pain? He wished there was a porthole he could open to let in some bracing sea air and banish the odour. Poor Miss Brandon was probably suffering the worst kind of mortification to be so discovered by a man she barely knew. If there was a better example of helplessness, he had never encountered it.

Private Leonard returned. Hugh looked behind him, but there was no surgeon.

'Sir, the surgeon and his mate are both tending to a foretopman who fell from the rigging.' Private Leonard made a face. 'He reminded me that no one dies of seasickness and recommended we get some water and vinegar so she can clean herself up.'

'Private, she can't clean a fingernail in her condition,' he said. He stood there a moment, looking down at Miss Brandon, then at the Private. 'Go get a quart or two of vinegar from Cook and a gallon of fresh water. If anyone gives you any grief, tell them they don't want to know how bad it will be if I have to come up and do it myself!'

The Private stood even straighter. 'Aye, aye, sir. Should I get some cloths, too?'

'As many as you can gather. Good thinking.'

He closed the door behind the Private, who pounded up the companionway, obviously glad to have a purpose. He found a stool and pulled it close to the sleeping cot, which was swaying to the ship's roll. He tried to keep his tone conversational, knowing that nothing he was going to do in the next hour would be pleasing to a modest lady. 'Miss Brandon, the surgeon cannot come, but he has declared that no one dies of seasickness. You will not be the first, and certainly not on my watch.'

'I. Would. Rather. Die.'

At least she was alert. 'It's not allowed in the Royal Navy, my dear,' he told her kindly. 'When Private Leonard returns, I am going to tidy you, find you another nightgown, and put you in my sleeping cot, so I can swab down this one.'

She started to cry in earnest then, which was a sorry sight, since there were no tears. 'Leave me alone,' she pleaded.

'I can't leave you alone. I would do anything to spare you embarrassment, Miss Brandon, but you must be tended to.'

'The surgeon?'

'Busy. My dear, you'll just have to trust me, because there is no one else.'

She hadn't opened her eyes in their whole exchange, and it touched him to think how embarrassed she must be. She was obviously well educated and gently reared, and this was probably the first time in her whole life she had ever been alone with a man who wasn't a relative. He wasn't sure what to do, but he put his hand against her soiled cheek and held it there until she stopped her dry sobbing.

Private Leonard returned with the vinegar and water. He had tucked clean rags under his arm, and removed them when he set down the bucket. 'I'll get some sea water, too, Colonel,' he said. 'That fresh water isn't going to go far, and you can swab her down with salt water.'

'Do it, Private. When you return, close the door and resume your sentry duty. If there are two of us trying to help Miss Brandon, it'll be too much for her.'

He could see that Private Leonard was relieved by that order. He came back soon with two buckets of sea water; God knows there was plenty of it to spare on a frigate in a squall. Private Leonard closed the door quietly.

Miss Brandon tried to sit up and failed. 'If you leave the water, I can do this myself,' she managed to say.

'Begging your pardon, Miss Brandon, but I don't think you even have the strength to scratch your nose right now,' he told her. 'I am so sorry that no one knew the extent of your extremity, or believe me, it would not have come to this.'

She opened her eyes then, and he saw all the shame, embarrassment, and humility in the world reflecting from them. All she could do was shake her head slowly and put up her hands to cover her chest.

It was such a defensive gesture that his heart went out to her. She was soiled and smelly and more wretched that the worst drab in the foulest slum in the rankest seaport he had ever visited. The last thing he wanted to do was violate her dignity, which was all she had remaining. He rested his hands gently on hers. 'Whatever I do for you,

I do out of utter necessity, Miss Brandon. I can do no less because I never back down from a crisis.' He smiled at her. 'My, that sounds top-lofty, but it is true. Take a leap of faith, Miss Brandon; trust me to be kind.'

She was silent a long while, her hands still held stubbornly in front of her. 'I have no choice, have I?' she said finally.

'No, you don't. Take that leap, Miss Brandon. I won't fail you.'

Chapter Two

Miss Brandon didn't say anything, but her hands relaxed. Hugh did nothing for a moment, because he didn't know where to begin. He looked closer in the dim light. She was wearing a nightgown, which chastely covered most of her, so his task was not as uncomfortable yet as it was going to get. He opened the door.

'Private, go in my cabin. Bring my shaving basin, plus the silver cup next to it.'

He was back in a moment with the items. Hugh put his hand behind Miss Brandon's back and carefully raised her upright. He dipped the cup in the fresh water Private Leonard had brought, and put it to her lips.

'It will only make me vomit,' she protested weakly.

'Just swirl it around in your mouth, lean over the edge of the cot and spit it out.'

'On the *floor*?' she asked, aghast.

'Yes, ma'am. The deck—the floor—has suffered some ill usage. I'll never tell.'

She sighed. He held the cup to her parched lips and she

took a small sip, doing what he said and spitting on the deck.

'Try another sip and swallow it this time.'

She started to protest, but gamely squared her shoulders and did as he said. 'My throat is on fire,' she said, her voice a croak.

'I imagine it is raw, indeed, Miss Brandon, considering the ill treatment it has suffered for nearly two days.' It smote him again how careless they had all been not to check on her. 'Try another sip. Just a small one.'

She did, then shook her head at more. They both waited, but she kept it down.

'I'm encouraged. Just sit here,' he told her. 'I'm going to mix some vinegar in this little bit of fresh water and wipe your face and neck. I'll see what can be done with your hair.'

Silent, she let him do what he wanted, turning her head obediently so he could swab around her eyes and nostrils. 'Soon I'll have you smelling like a pickle, Miss Brandon,' he joked, trying to lighten the mood. She did not indicate any amusement, which hardly surprised him. When her face was as clean as he could manage, he added more vinegar to the bucket of sea water and wiped her neck and ears.

Her hair took much longer, as he pulled a few strands at a time through the vinegar-soaked cloth between his fingers, working as quickly and gently as he could. He had to stop for a while when the ship began to labour up and down steeper troughs, as the storm intensified. She moaned with the motion, so he braced the sleeping cot with his body so it would not swing. As he watched her face, it suddenly occurred to him that part of her problem was fear.

'Miss Brandon, I assure you that as bad as this seems, we're not going to sink,' he said. He spoke loud enough to be heard above the creaking and groaning he knew were normal ship noises in a storm. 'Ships are noisy. The sea is rough, I will grant you, but that is life in the Channel.'

She said nothing, but turned her face into his shoulder. Hugh kept his arms tight around her, crooning nothing that made any sense, but which seemed to calm her. He held her close as she clung to him, terrified.

When the waves seemed to subside, he released her and went back to cleaning her long hair. When he felt reasonably satisfied, he knew he could not avoid the next step. 'Miss Brandon, do you have another nightgown in your luggage?'

She nodded, and started to cry again.

'I'd happily turn my back and let you manage this next part by yourself, my dear, but I don't think you're up to it. You can't stay in this nightgown.'

After another long silence during which he made no attempt to rush her, her hands went to the buttons on her gown. She tried to undo them, but finally shook her head. Without a word, he undid her buttons. 'Where's another nightgown?' he asked quietly.

She told him and he found it, fragrant with lavender, in her trunk. Taking a deep breath, Hugh pulled back the sheet. Her hand went to his wrist, so he did nothing more until she relaxed her grip.

'I'm going to roll up your nightgown, so we can best keep the soiled part away from your face and hair when I pull it over your head. Miss Brandon, I regret the mortification I know I am causing you,' he said.

She was sobbing in good earnest now, and the parched sound pained him more than she possibly could have realised. Not only was he trampling on her female delicacy now, but jumping up and down on it.

'No fears, Miss Brandon, no fears,' he said quietly, trying to find a balance between sympathy and command.

Maybe she finally realised he was an ally. He wasn't sure he would have been as brave as she was, considering her total helplessness to take care of herself. Feeling as stupid and callow as the merest youth, he couldn't think of a thing to say except, 'I mean you no harm. Not ever.'

He wondered why he said that, but his words, spoken quietly but firmly, seemed to give Miss Brandon the confirmation she needed of his utter sincerity. She stopped sobbing, but rested her head against him, not so much because she was tired now, but because she needed his reassurance. He could have been wrong, but that was what the moment felt like, and he wasn't one to quibble.

Without any talk, he continued rolling up her nightgown as she raised her arms. His fingers brushed against her bare breast, but they were both beyond embarrassment. Even though the night was warm, she shivered a little. He quickly popped her into the clean nightgown, pulling it down to her ankles, then helped her lie back. She sighed with relief and closed her eyes.

The winds picked up and the ship began another series of torturous swoops through the waves. He braced the cot against his hip and kept his arms tight around Miss Brandon as she clung to him and shivered.

'I don't know how you do this,' she said finally, when the winds subsided.

'It comes with the job,' he replied and chuckled.

'Are you never seasick?'

'No.'

'Are you lying?'

He wasn't, but he wanted her to laugh. 'Yes.' He knew nothing in the rest of his life would ever put him at ease more than the slight sound of her laugh, muffled against his chest.

Since his arms were around her, he picked her up. She stiffened. 'I'm going to carry you across the wardroom to my pathetic cabin, and put you in my cot. You're going to promise me you won't be sick in it, and you're going to go to sleep. I'll come back in here and clean up everything.'

'A Lieutenant Colonel in the Royal Marines,' she murmured, and Hugh could hear the embarrassment in her voice again.

'I can't help that,' he told her, and was rewarded with another chuckle. 'I've swabbed a deck or two in my earlier days.' He wasn't going to tell her how unpleasant that had been, cleaning up a gun deck after a battle. Nothing in her cabin could ever compare with that, but he wasn't going to enlighten her further.

He was prepared to stay with her in his cabin until she felt easy, but she went to sleep almost before he finished tucking his blanket around her. He looked down at her, smelling of vinegar now, but as tidy as he could make her, in his clumsy way. He looked closer. There was something missing. He gave her a slight shake.

'Miss Brandon, where are your spectacles?'

She opened her eyes, and he saw nothing but remorse. 'I…I fear they landed in that basin by the cot, when I vomited.'

She started to laugh then, which must have hurt because her hand went to her throat. 'Don't look so stunned, Colonel,' she told him. 'I am quizzing you. They're in my trunk, next to my hair brush.'

He grinned at her, relieved that she could make a joke. 'I'll get you for that.'

'You and who…?' she began, then drifted to sleep.

He stood there another long moment, watching her sleep, dumbfounded by her resiliency, and not totally sure what had just happened. 'I'd have looked for them in that foul basin, I hope you know,' he whispered, then left his cabin.

He spent the next hour cleaning Miss Brandon's cabin. Before Private Leonard went off duty and was replaced by another sentry, he swore him to utter secrecy on what had passed this evening.

'Sir, I would never say anything,' the Private assured him. 'She's a brave little trooper, isn't she?'

Hugh would have spent the night in her cot, except that it was wet with vinegar and he didn't relish the notion. He could put his greatcoat on the floor in his cabin and not disturb Miss Brandon at all. He put her nightgown to soak in the bucket with sea water, and poured in the remaining vinegar. He found his way to the orlop deck, where the surgeon, eyes bleary, was staring at a forefinger avulsion that gave Hugh the shivers.

'He caught it on a pump, if you can imagine,' the surgeon murmured. He patted the seaman who belonged to the finger. 'Steady, lad, steady. It looks worse than it is, as most things do.'

While the seaman stared at his own finger, Hugh took

the surgeon aside and explained what had happened to Miss Brandon.

'Poor little lady,' the surgeon said. 'I hope you were gentle with her, Colonel.'

'I did my best.'

The surgeon shook his head. 'Only two days out, and already this voyage is more than she bargained for, I'm certain. All's well that ends. Give her some porridge tomorrow morning and a ship's biscuit, along with fortified wine, and all the water she will drink. That should take care of the dehydration.'

Hugh walked thoughtfully back to his deck, after looking in on the unconscious foretopman, with the surgeon's mate sitting beside him. A howl from the orlop told him the surgeon had taken care of the avulsion. *Give me Miss Brandon and her troublesome seasickness any day*, he thought with a shudder.

Counting on his rank to mean something to one of the captain's young gentlemen, he asked for and received a blanket and returned to his cabin. He looked down at her, asleep in his gently swaying cot. *Poor little you. The surgeon was right; you didn't bargain on this*, he thought.

Surprisingly content with his lot, Hugh spread his overcoat and pulled the blanket over him. He woke up once in the night to check on her, but she was breathing deeply, with a small sigh on the exhalation of breath that he found childlike and endearing. Feeling charitable, he smiled down at her, and returned to his rest on the deck.

A fierce and nagging thirst woke Polly at sunrise, rather than the noise of a ship that she had feared last night would sink at any minute. She stared at the deck beams overhead, wondering where she was, then closed her eyes in total mortification when she remembered. *Maybe if I keep my eyes closed, the entire world will move back four days. I will remain in Torquay with my sister Nana and none of what I know happened will have taken place*, she told herself.

No such luck. She smelled of vinegar because she had been doused in it, then pulled from her nightgown and—horror of horrors—been set right by a Royal Marine of mature years who would probably rather have eaten ground glass than done any of the duties her care had required.

If she could not forget what had happened, perhaps Lieutenant Colonel Junot had transferred during the night to another vessel, one sailing to Australia. Failing that, hopefully he had suffered amnesia and remembered nothing past his tenth birthday. No such luck. She could hear someone snoring softly, so she rose up carefully on her elbow and peered over the edge of the sleeping cot.

There lay her saviour, a mature man—not a Midshipman—with curly dark hair going a bit grey at the temples, a straight nose, and chiselled lips that had caught her attention a few days ago, when she was still a reasonable being. He lay on his back and looked surprisingly comfortable, as though he had slept in worse places. He had removed his shoes, unbuttoned his dark trousers, and unhooked his uniform tunic, so a wildly informal checked shirt showed through. The gilt gorget was still clasped around his neck, which made her smile in spite of her mortification, because he looked incongruously authoritative.

He opened his eyes suddenly and he smiled at her,

because she must have looked even funnier, peering at him over the edge of the sleeping cot like a child in a strange house.

'Good morning, Miss Brandon. See? You're alive.'

If he had meant to put her at her ease, he had succeeded, even as he lay there all stretched out. He yawned, then sat up, his blanket around him again.

'Would you like some water?' he asked.

She nodded, then carefully sat up, which only made her lie down again, because the room was revolving.

He was on his feet in an instant, turning his back to her to button his trousers, then stretching his arm up to grasp the deck beam as he assessed her. 'Dizzy?'

She nodded, and wished she hadn't. 'Now the ship is spinning,' she groaned.

'It will stop.' He brought her a drink in a battered silver cup that looked as if it had been through a campaign or two. His free arm went behind her back and gently lifted her up just enough to pour some water down her sorely tried throat. 'Being as dried out as you are plays merry hell with body humours, Miss Brandon. You need to eat something.'

'Never again,' she told him firmly. 'I have sworn off food for ever.'

'Take a chance,' he teased. 'You might be surprised how gratifying it is to swallow food, rather than wear it. Another sip now. That's a good girl. Let me lay you down again.'

After he did so, he tucked the blanket up to her chin again. 'You'll do, Brandon,' he told her in a gruff voice, and she knew that not a kinder man inhabited the entire universe, no matter if he was a Marine and fearsome. 'Go back to sleep.'

She closed her eyes dutifully, certain she wouldn't sleep because she was so embarrassed, except that the Colonel yawned loudly. She opened her eyes at such rag manners, then watched as he stretched and slapped the deck beam overhead, exclaiming, 'I love a sea voyage, Brandon. Don't you?' which made her giggle and decide that perhaps she would live, after all.

When she woke again, it was full light and the Colonel was gone. She sat up more cautiously this time, pleased when the ship did not spin. She wasn't sure what to do, especially without her spectacles, except that there they were in their little case, next to the pillow. *What a nice man*, she thought, as she put them on.

She looked around. He had also brought over her robe, which she had originally hung on a peg in her cabin. *I think he wants me gone from his cabin*, she told herself, and heaven knew, who could blame him?

As for that, he didn't. Colonel Junot had left a folded note next to her robe on the end of the cot, with 'Brandon' scrawled on it. She couldn't help but smile at that, wondering why on earth he had decided to call her Brandon. All she could assume was that after the intimacy they had been through together, he thought Miss Brandon too formal, but Polly too liberal. Whatever the reason, she decided she liked it. She could never call him anything but Colonel, of course.

She read the note to herself: *Brandon, a loblolly boy is scrubbing down your cabin and will light sulphur in it. The stench will be wicked for a while, so I moved your trunk into the wardroom. Captain Adney's steward will bring you porridge and fortified wine, which the surgeon insisted on.*

He signed it 'Junot', which surprised her. When he introduced himself, he had pronounced his name 'Junnit', but this was obviously a French name. That was even stranger, because he had as rich a Lowland Scottish accent as she had ever heard. 'Colonel, Brandon thinks you are a man of vast contradictions,' she murmured.

She climbed carefully from the sleeping cot, grateful the cannon was there to clutch when the ship shivered and yawed. *I will never develop sea legs*, she told herself. *I will have to become a citizen of Portugal and never cross the Channel again.* When she could stand, she pulled on her robe and climbed back into the sleeping cot, surprised at her exhaustion from so little effort. She doubled the pillow so she could at least see over the edge of the sleeping cot, and abandoned herself to the swaying of the cot, which was gentler this morning.

She noticed the Colonel's luggage, a wooden military trunk with his name stenciled on the side: Hugh Philippe d'Anvers Junot. 'And you sound like a Scot,' she murmured. 'I must know more.'

Trouble was, knowing more meant engaging in casual conversation with a dignified officer of the King's Royal Marines, one who had taken care of her so intimately last night. He had shown incredible aplomb in an assignment that would have made even a saint look askance. No. The *Perseverance* might have been a sixth-rate and one of the smaller of its class, but for the remainder of the voyage—and it couldn't end too soon—she would find a way to avoid bothering Colonel Junot with her presence.

In only a matter of days, they would hail Oporto, and the Colonel would discharge his last duty to her family by handing her brother-in-law a letter from his former chief surgeon. Then, if the Lord Almighty was only half so generous as both Old and New Testaments trumpeted, the man would never have to see her again. She decided it wasn't too much to hope for, considering the probabilities.

So much for resolve. Someone knocked on the flimsy-framed door. She held her breath, hoping for the loblolly boy.

'Brandon? Call me a Greek bearing gifts.'

Not by the way you roll your r's, she thought, wondering if Marines were gluttons for punishment. She cleared her throat, wincing. 'Yes, Colonel?'

He opened the door, carrying a tray. 'As principal idler on this voyage, I volunteered to bring you food, which I insist you eat.'

If he was so determined to put a good face on all this, Polly decided she could do no less. 'I told you I have sworn off food for the remainder of my life, sir.'

'And I have chosen to ignore you,' he replied serenely. 'See here. I even brought along a basin, which I will put in my sleeping cot by your feet, should you take exception to porridge and ship's biscuit. Sit up like the good girl I know you are.'

She did as he said. As congenial as he sounded, there was something of an edge in his imperatives. This was something she had already noticed about her brother-in-law Oliver, so she could only assume it had to do with command. 'Aye, sir,' she said, sitting up.

He set the tray on her lap. To her dismay, he pulled up a stool to sit beside the cot.

'I promise to eat,' she told him, picking up the spoon to illustrate her good faith, if not her appetite. 'You needn't watch me.'

He just couldn't take a hint. 'I truly am a supernumerary on this voyage, and have no pressing tasks. The Midshipmen, under the tender care of the sailing master, are trying to plot courses. I already know how to do that. The surgeon is pulling a tooth, and I have no desire to learn. The Captain is strolling his deck with a properly detached air. The foretopmen are high overhead and I wouldn't help them even if I could. Brandon, you are stuck with me.'

It was obviously time to level with the Lieutenant Colonel, if only for his own good. She set down the spoon. 'Colonel Junot, last night you had to take care of me in ways so personal that I must have offended every sensibility you possess.' Her face was flaming, but she progressed doggedly, unable to look at the man whose bed she had usurped, and whose cabin she occupied. 'I have never been in a situation like this, and doubt you have either.'

'True, that,' he agreed. 'Pick up the spoon, Brandon, lively now.'

She did what he commanded. 'Sir, I am trying to spare you any more dealings with me for the duration of this voyage.'

His brown eyes reminded her of a spaniel given a smack by its owner for soiling a carpet. 'Brandon! Have I offended you?'

She didn't expect that. 'Well, n…no, of course not,' she stammered. 'I owe you a debt I can never repay, but—'

'Take a bite.'

She did, and then another. It stayed down, and she realised how ravenous she was. She ate without speaking, daring a glance at the Colonel once to see a pleased expression on his handsome face. When she finished, he moved

aside the bowl and pointed to the ship's biscuit, which she
picked up.

'Tell me something, Brandon,' he said finally, as she
chewed, then reached for the wine he held out to her. 'If
I were ever in a desperate situation and needed your help,
would you give it to me?'

'Certainly I would,' she said.

'Then why can't you see that last night was no different?'

He had her there. 'I have never met anyone like you,
Colonel,' she told him frankly.

He didn't say anything for a long moment. She took
another sip of the wine, then dipped the dry biscuit in it,
which made him smile.

'Look at it this way, Brandon. You have a friend.'

What could she say to that? If the man was going to
refuse all of her attempts to make herself invisible for the
remainder of the voyage, she couldn't be little about it.

'So do you, Colonel Junot.'

Chapter Three

'Excellent!' he declared. 'If you're up to it, I recommend you dress and go on deck. The surgeon found quite a comfortable canvas chair—I tried it out—and moved it to the quarterdeck. Believe it or not, it's easier to face an enemy, which, in your case, is the ocean. We can't have that, Brandon. Fearing the ocean is scarcely patriotic, considering that we are an island nation.'

'I believe you are right, Colonel,' she said, amused.

He lifted her out of the sleeping cot, set her on her bare feet, and walked next to her, his hand warm on the small of her back to steady her, across the short space between his door and the door to her cabin. She could smell sulphur fumes behind the door, and was glad he had moved her trunk into the wardroom.

She shook her head when he offered further assistance, even though she did have trouble standing upright.

'You'll learn,' he assured her, then bowed and went up the companionway.

She took what clothing she needed from her trunk, pausing a time or two to steady herself against the ship's movement. She hadn't even crossed the small space back to Colonel Junot's cabin when a Marine sentry came down the companionway, the same Marine who had stood sentinel last night.

'I want to thank you, Private, for alerting the Colonel to my predicament last night,' she told him.

'My job, ma'am,' he replied simply, but she could tell he was pleased.

That was easy, Polly thought, as she went into the cabin and dressed. Her hair was still a hopeless mess, but at least it smelled strongly of nothing worse than vinegar. 'My kingdom for enough fresh water to wash this tangle,' she murmured.

She cautiously made her way up the companionway to the deck, where she stood and watched the activity around her. No part of England is far from the sea, but she had spent most of her eighteen years in Bath, so she felt herself in an alien world. It was not without its fascination, she decided, as she watched the Sergeant drilling his few Marines in a small space. Close to the bow, the sailing master was schooling the Midshipmen, who awkwardly tried to shoot the sun with sextants. Seamen scrubbed the deck with flat stones the size of prayer books, while others sat cross-legged with sails in their laps, mending tears with large needles. It looked endlessly complex and disorganised, but as she watched she began to see the orderly disorder of life at sea.

She looked towards the quarterdeck again and Captain Adney nodded to her and lifted his hat, indicating she should join him.

'Let me apologise for myself and all my fellow officers for neglecting you,' he said. 'Until Colonel Junot told us what was going on, we had no idea.'

Hopefully, he didn't tell you everything, Polly thought, even though she knew her secrets would always be safe with the Colonel. 'I am feeling much better,' she said.

'Excellent!' Captain Adney obviously had no desire to prod about in the workings of females, so there ended his commentary. He indicated the deck chair Colonel Junot had spoken of. Clasping his hands behind his back, he left her to it, resuming his perusal of the ocean.

Polly smiled to herself, amused by the workings of males. She looked at the chair, noting the chocks placed by the legs so the contraption would not suddenly slide across the quarterdeck. She tried not to hurl herself across the deck, wishing she understood how to ambulate on a slanted plane that would right itself and then slant the other way.

'Brandon, let me suggest that, when you stand, you put one foot behind the other and probably a bit farther apart than you are used to.'

She looked over her shoulder to see Colonel Junot on the steps to the quarterdeck. He came closer and demonstrated. She imitated him.

'Much better. When you walk, this is no time for mincing steps.' He smiled at her halting effort. 'It takes practice. Try out the chair.'

She let him hand her into it, and she couldn't help a sigh of pleasure. Amazing that canvas could feel so comfortable. *I could like this*, she thought, and smiled at the Colonel.

He smiled in turn, then went back down the steps to the main deck, where the Sergeant stood at attention now with his complement of Marines. A word from Colonel Junot and they relaxed, but not by much. In another minute the Sergeant had dismissed them and he sat with Colonel Junot on a hatch.

Polly watched them both, impressed by their immaculate posture, which lent both men an ever-ready aspect, as though they could spring into action at a moment's notice. *I suppose you can,* she told herself, thinking through all of the Lieutenant Colonel's quick decisions last night. He had not hesitated once in caring for her, no matter how difficult it must have been. And he seemed to take it all in stride. 'You were my ever-present help in trouble,' she murmured.

She gave her attention to the Colonel again, after making sure the brim of her bonnet was turned down and they wouldn't know of her observation. While Colonel Junot was obviously a Scot, he did look French. She realised with a surprise that she wanted to know more about him.

Why? she asked herself. Knowing more about Lieutenant Colonel Hugh Junot would serve no useful purpose, beyond pointing her out as a flirt, something she knew she was not. 'Bother it,' she muttered softly.

She had convinced herself that the best thing she could do for the remainder of this voyage was to follow her original plan and have as little to do with the Marine as possible. Once he was busy with whatever it was that had taken him on this voyage, she would be ignored, which suited her down to the ground. She had never sought the centre of the stage.

Come to think of it, why was Colonel Junot on this voyage? *Bother it,* she told herself again. *I would like to ask him.*

She knew better. Through Nana, she knew these men sailed with specific orders that were certainly none of her business, no matter how great her curiosity. 'Bother it,' she muttered again, and closed her eyes.

She slept, thanks to the gentle swaying of the canvas seat, comforting after the peaks and troughs of last night's squall. When she woke, her glasses rested in her lap. Lieutenant Colonel Junot stood next to her chair, his eyes scanning the water. She was struck all over again with his elegance. Compared to naval officers in their plain dark undress coats, the Marines were gaudy tropical birds. He had not an ounce of superfluous flesh, which made him different from the men she noticed in Bath, who were comfortably padded in the custom of the age.

I am among the elite, she told herself, as she put on her spectacles, bending the wires around her ears again.

Her small motions must have caught Colonel Junot's eye because he looked her way and gave her a slight bow, then came closer.

'How are you feeling?' he asked.

'I am better today,' she said simply. 'Perhaps this means I will not have to seek Portuguese citizenship and remain on the Iberian Peninsula for ever.'

He laughed and looked around for something to sit on, which gratified her further. He didn't seem to mind her company. He found a keg and pulled that beside her chair.

He looked at her a moment before he spoke, perhaps wondering if he should. He cleared his throat. 'I suppose you will think me a case-hardened meddler, Brandon, but I have to know—how on earth did you receive permission to travel into a war zone?'

She was surprised that he was curious about her. She leaned towards him. 'Haven't you heard? I am to be a spy.'

'I had no idea, Brandon. I will tell only my dozen closest friends.'

It was her turn to smile and brush aside the crack-brained notion that the Colonel was flirting with her. Now it was his turn for disappointment, because she couldn't think of a witty reply. Better have with the truth.

'I don't know how I got permission, Colonel,' she told him. 'I wrote to my sister, Laura Brittle, whose husband, Philemon, is chief surgeon at a satellite hospital in Oporto.'

'I have heard of him. Who hasn't? That little hospital in Oporto has saved many a seaman and Marine in just the brief time it has been in operation.'

She blushed, this time with pleasure that he should speak so well of her brother-in-law. 'I wrote to Laura and told her I wanted to be of use.'

'I've also heard good things about Mrs Brittle.'

'She's incredible.'

'Aye. And your other sister?'

'Nana loves her husband and sends him back to sea without a tear…at least until he is out of sight,' she said frankly. There wasn't any point in being too coy around a man who, in the short space of twenty-four hours, knew her more intimately than any man alive.

He wasn't embarrassed by her comment. 'Then he is a lucky man.'

'He knows it, too.'

She realised their heads were close together like conspirators, so she drew back slightly. 'Colonel Junot, I thought I could help out in the hospital. Laura said they have many men who would like to have someone write letters for them, or read to them. I could never do what she does, but I could help.' She shook her head, realising how puny her possible contribution must sound. 'It isn't much, but…'

'…a letter means the world to someone wanting to communicate with his loved ones, Brandon. Don't sell yourself short,' he said, finishing her thought and adding his comment. 'Still, I don't understand how a surgeon and his wife could pull such strings. Are you all, by chance, related to King George himself?'

'Oh, no! I have a theory,' she said. 'Tell me what you think. I'll have to show you the letter from the Navy Board, addressed to Brandon Polly, which I received whilst I was visiting Nana. Do you think… Is it possible that Laura or Philemon transposed my name on purpose? Polly Brandon would never do, but Brandon Polly would cause not a stir.'

He thought a minute. 'What is more likely is at one point in the correspondence there may have been a comma between the two names. Orders or requests are often issued that way.'

He looked at her, and seemed to know what she was thinking. 'There now. You've answered *my* question, which surely must entitle you to one of your own. Go ahead and ask what everyone wants to know. How does someone who sounds like a Scot look like a Frenchman, and with a Froggy name, too?'

'I *am* curious,' she admitted.

'Simple. A long-ago Philippe Junot—he had a title, so I'm told—came to Scotland from France as part of the entourage of Mary of Scotland. No one precisely knows how it happened, but he managed to avoid the turmoil surrounding her and blended into the foggy, damp woodwork of Scotland near Dundrennan. He lost his title, but acquired considerable land near Kirkcudbright.'

'My goodness.'

'My goodness, indeed. The Junots are a prolific breed, and each generation traditionally rejoices in a Philippe. My father is still well and hearty, but some day I will head the family.'

'You chose to serve King and country?' Polly asked, fascinated.

'I did. Granted, Kirkcudbright is a pretty fishing village, but it is slow and I liked the uniform.' He held up his hand. 'Don't laugh, Brandon. People have been known to join for stranger reasons.'

'I cannot believe you!' she protested.

'Then don't,' he replied serenely. 'I love the sea, but I require land now and then, and an enemy to grapple with up close. That's my life.'

'What…what does your wife say to all this?' she asked. *That is hardly subtle*, she berated herself. *He will think I am an idiot or a flirt, when I am neither.*

'I wouldn't know, since I don't have one of those luxuries. I ask you, Brandon—why would a sensible woman—someone like yourself—marry a Marine?'

He had neatly lofted the ball of confusion back in her court. 'I can't imagine, either,' she said without thinking, which made him laugh, then calmly bid her good day.

I've offended him, Polly thought with remorse. She watched him go, then reasonably asked herself why his good opinion mattered.

Captain Adney's steward kindly brought her bread and cheese for lunch. She went below later, and found that her trunk and other baggage had been returned to her cabin. The sentry had moved from the Lieutenant Colonel's door to her own, as though nothing had happened.

When she went topside again, the Captain told her the afternoon would be spent in gunnery practice, and that she might be more comfortable belowdeck in her own cabin, one of the few not dismantled, so the guns could be fired. 'It is your choice, but mind you, it's noisy up here,' he warned, then shrugged. 'Or down there, for that matter.'

She chose to remain on deck. The chair had been moved closer to the wheel—'Out of any stray missile range,' the captain told her.

He didn't exaggerate; the first blast nearly lifted her out of the chair. She covered her ears with her hands, wishing herself anywhere but at sea, until her own curiosity—Miss Pym called it an admirable trait, if not taken to extremes—piqued her interest. Cringing in the chair, trying to make herself small with each cannonade, she watched as each man performed his task.

Someone tapped her shoulder. She looked around to see Colonel Junot holding out some cotton wadding and pointing to his ears. She took the wadding from him and stuffed it in her ears, observing that he seemed as usual, and not in any way offended by her earlier comment. *Perhaps I make mountains out of molehills*, she told herself, as he returned to the main deck, watching the crews there as she watched them from the quarterdeck.

His eyes were on the Marines. Some of them served the guns alongside the naval gunners, and others lined the railing, muskets at the ready, their Sergeant standing behind them, walking up and down. A few Marines had ventured aloft to the crosstrees with their weapons.

Through it all, Colonel Junot observed, and took occasional notes.

It was all a far cry from Bath, and she knew how out of place she was. *I wonder if I really can be useful in Oporto*, she thought. Nana had wanted her to stay in Torquay. What had she done of any value on this voyage yet, except make a cake of herself with seasickness? She wondered why Colonel Junot thought her worth the time of day.

It was still on her mind as she prepared for dinner that evening. Only three more days, she thought, as she reached around to button her last button.

When she ventured into the wardroom, Colonel Junot came up behind her and without a word, buttoned the one in the centre of her back she never could reach. The other men were already busy at dinner; no one had noticed. *I can't even dress myself*, she thought, flogging her already-battered esteem.

Polly had little to say over dinner. For all she paid attention, she could have been shovelling clinkers into her mouth, and washing them down with bathwater. All she could think of was how ill equipped she was to leave England. Probably she should never have even left Bath, uncomfortable as Miss Pym had made her, especially after she had turned down Pym's invitation to stay and teach the youngest class. At least at the Female Academy, she knew precisely where she stood, in the order of things.

Bless his heart, Colonel Junot tried to engage her in conversation, but she murmured only monosyllables. Before the endless meal was over, even he had given up, directing his attention to war talk, and then ship talk. She was as out of place as a Quaker at a gaming table.

Polly had never felt quite this gauche before, almost as though her spectacles were ten times too large for her face, with every freckle—real and imagined—standing out in high relief. And there sat the Lieutenant Colonel next to her, an officer with handsome features, distinguished hair going grey. He was quite the best-looking man she had ever seen, and what had he seen of her except someone who needed to be cleaned up, held over a basin, or buttoned up the back? She burned at her own failings, compared to Colonel Junot's elegant worldliness, and longed to leave the table as soon as she could decently do so.

The dinner ended after a round of toasts to the ship, the men, and the King. She was free to go. She stood, and all the men stood out of deference, even though she knew in her heart of hearts that she was the weakest link at the table.

Polly was only two or three steps from her door, but there was the Colonel, bowing and offering his arm, as he suggested a turn around the deck. She didn't know how to say no, or even why she wanted to, so she took his arm.

The wind blew steadily from the west, making it the fair wind to Spain her brother-in-law Oliver had mentioned during his last visit to Torquay. Polly breathed deep, half-imagining she could smell the orange blossoms in Nana's garden, while she wished herself there.

Colonel Junot walked her around the deck, commenting on the workings of the ship, pointing out the phosphorescence in the water, which he didn't understand, but which intrigued him. She could tell how much he loved the sea, and she felt her shyness begin to recede. He still seemed to be taking care of her, as though someone had given him that role when he first saw her on deck in Plymouth. She knew no one had, which made her feel protected. It was not a feeling she was accustomed to; probably none of Lord Ratliffe's daughters was.

'This voyage has been a real trial for you, Miss Brandon,' he said finally.

She wished he had continued calling her simply Brandon. He steadied her as they went down the more narrow companionway, and into the wardroom again, which this time was full of Marines.

All twenty of the frigate's small complement of Marines had assembled, each carrying a flask. Private Leonard had borrowed a medium-sized pot from the galley, which he set by her door. He saluted the Lieutenant Colonel and stepped forwards, eyes ahead.

'Colonel Junot, if we may take the liberty…'

'By all means, Private.'

The Private looked at her then, flushed, and glanced away, addressing his remarks to someone imaginary over her shoulder. 'Miss Brandon, there's nothing pleasant about vinegar. We decided you should have an opportunity to wash your hair with fresh water. With the Lieutenant Colonel's permission, we decided to give you our daily ration, and we will not take no for an answer.'

He said it practically in one breath, then stepped back. As she watched, tears in her eyes, each Marine poured his drinking water for the day into the pot. When they finished, Colonel Junot went to his cabin and brought out his own flask, adding it to the water in the pot.

'You'll be thirsty,' she protested feebly, when everyone finished and stood at attention.

'Just for a day, ma'am,' the Sergeant of the guard said. 'We've been thirsty before.'

He turned around smartly on his heel, and with a command, the Marines marched back to their posts, or to their quarters between the officers' berths and the crew. Private Leonard remained at his post outside her door, eyes ahead again, every inch the professional.

'Open your door, Brandon, and we'll get the pot inside,' Colonel Junot said.

She did as he directed, standing back as Lieutenant Colonel and Private lifted in the pot, careful not to splash out a drop of the precious fresh water. She had never received a kinder gift from anyone in her life.

The Private went back to his post, but Colonel Junot stood in her room, a smile playing around his expressive lips.

'Colonel, I could have waited until we reached port. They didn't need to do that,' she said.

'It was entirely their idea, Brandon,' he replied, going to her door. 'They only asked that I distract you on deck long enough for them to assemble. Look at it this way: if you ever decide to take over the world, you have a squad of Marines who would follow you anywhere.'

'Why, Colonel?' she asked.

It was his turn to look nonplussed. He was silent a long moment, as if wondering what he should say to such a question. 'Possibly just because you are Brandon Polly, or Polly Brandon. Sometimes there is no reason.'

'No one ever did anything so nice for me before,' she said, wincing inwardly because she didn't want to sound pathetic. It was true, though.

'No? Not even your sisters?'

She could tell he was teasing her now, but there was still that air of protection about him, as though she had become his assignment for the voyage. 'My sisters are different,' she told him, feeling her face grow rosier. 'They are supposed to be kind.'

He laughed at that. 'So is mine,' he confided.

She didn't mean to look sceptical, but the Colonel seemed to be sensitive to her expression. 'Here's how I see it, Brandon—you've made a tedious voyage more than usually interesting.'

She couldn't imagine that tending a female through seasickness qualified as interesting, but she wasn't about to mention it. She knew she should just curtsy and wish him goodnight. She would have, if some imp hadn't leaped on to her shoulder, and prodded her. 'I...I...most particularly like it when you call me Brandon,' she said, her voice low. 'Some of the other students at Miss Pym's had nicknames. I never did.' She stopped in confusion. 'You must think I am an idiot.'

'Never crossed my mind, Brandon.'

She held her breath as he lightly touched her cheek.

'Goodnight, now,' he told her. 'If you need help with your hair tomorrow, I'm just across the wardroom.'

Chapter Four

Hugh couldn't say he had any power to encourage the wind and waves, but he considered it a boon from kind providence that Polly Brandon did need his help in the morning to kneel at the pot and wash her hair, while the deck slanted. They decided that his firm knee in her back would anchor her to the pot, and she had no objection when he lathered her hair, and rinsed it using a small pitcher.

The entire operation involved another pot and pitcher, which led him to comment that between pots and pitchers, women were a great lot of trouble. If she hadn't looked back at him then with such a glower, her hair wet and soapy, he could have withstood nearly anything. He had no idea a woman could look so endearing with soap in her hair. She wasn't wearing her spectacles, of course, which meant she held her eyes open wider than usual, perhaps seeking more depth and more clarity. The effect jolted him a little, because her nearsighted gaze was so intense, her eyes so blue. The shade reminded him of a spot of deep water near Crete where he had gazed long and hard when he was a younger man.

When not coated in vinegar, her auburn hair was glossy. Hugh was half-tempted to volunteer to comb the tangles from her hair, but he had the good sense to strangle that idea at birth. To his surprise, he was finding her uniquely attractive.

Even after two decades of war, he knew enough about women, having bedded them in all seaports when occasion permitted, no different from his navy brethren. By common wardroom consent after one memorable voyage through half the world, he and his fellows agreed that the most beautiful women lived on the Greek isles. He knew at least that *he* had never seen a flat-chested female there. So it went; he was a man of experience.

But here was Brandon—why on earth had he started calling her such a hooligan name?—who, even on her best day, could only stand in the shadow of the earth's loveliest ladies. It was all he could do to keep his hands off her, and he had seen her at her absolute worst. No woman could have been more hopeless than Polly Brandon of two days ago, but here he was, wanting to devise all manner of subterfuges to keep her talking to him. It was a mystery; he had no clue what had happened in so short a time.

He sat down at the wardroom table, hoping to keep her there with him while he thought of something clever to say. To his dismay, she went into her cabin, but came out a moment later with her comb. She was getting more surefooted by the hour, timing her stride to the roll of the ship, but she did plop unceremoniously on to the bench and laughed at herself.

She fixed him with that penetrating gaze he was coming to know. 'You have my permission to laugh when I am no more graceful at sea than a new puppy would be.'

'I daren't,' he said. 'Suppose some day you find me in desperate shape—say, for example, at Almack's? I would hope you would be charitable, so I will be the same.'

'Coward,' she teased. She unwound the towel, shook her head, and began to comb her hair. She seemed to be waiting for him to say something, but when he didn't, she took the initiative. 'Three days at sea and my manners have taken French leave, Colonel. Miss Pym always did say I was too nosy by half, but what are *you* doing here?'

Admiring you, he thought. That would never do; perhaps honesty deserved its moment in the sun. 'I shipped out to the Peninsula because I could not stand one more moment of conference meetings in Plymouth.'

'You're quizzing me,' she said with a laugh.

'Well, no, I am not,' he contradicted. 'I probably should have turned down my promotion from Major to Lieutenant Colonel, but one doesn't do that.'

'No harm in ambition,' she told him, trying to sound sage, and blithely unaware how charming was her naïveté.

'True,' he agreed. 'Trouble is, a step up means different duties at Division Three. Now I am chained to a desk and report for meetings, where I sit and draw little figures and yawn inside my mouth, so my tonsils won't be seen.'

She laughed and touched his sleeve. Just one quick touch, but it made him pleasantly warm. 'Colonel, I used to do the same thing in theology class, where God was so cruel as to make time stand still.'

'Exactly.' *Well, aren't you the charming rogue*, he thought. *No vicar for a husband for you, I should think.* 'As with most things, there is more to it than that. I went to Stonehouse Hospital to visit the newest arrived Marines invalided there. One of them died in my arms, after wishing there was something more he and his fellow Marines could do to end this stalemate with Boney. I chose not to let his sacrifice be for naught.'

Polly nodded, her face serious. He continued, 'I asked permission of the Colonel Commandant to conduct impromptu visits to various ships off the Peninsula, and in Lisbon where a Marine brigade is based. I want to find out how the men feel about what they do, and if, indeed, we Marines could do more. Brandon, these are men with vast experience, who surely have ideas! I have *carte blanche* to stay as long as I wish, and then compile a report. That is why I am here.'

She looked down at her hands, then up at him over her spectacles. 'We are both running away, aren't we, Colonel Junot? I could have stayed in Bath and taught the younger pupils at my school, or at least stayed in Torquay and helped my sister Nana, who is increasing again.'

'But you want to see the wider world, even such a tattered one as this is proving to be, with its everlasting war?'

She frowned, and he could tell she had considered the matter. 'I think we know I don't belong here. Maybe I should have stayed in Torquay.'

Then I never would have met you, he realised. It was such a disquieting thought that he wanted to dismiss it. He chose a light tone, because that was all he could do, and even then, it was wrong to his ears. 'If it's any comfort, I felt the same way at my first deployment in service of King and country.'

'When was that? Where did you go?' she asked, her interest obvious.

What could he say but the truth, even though he knew

it would age him enormously in her eyes. 'It was 1790 and I was bound for India.'

'Heavens. I had not even been born,' she told him, confirming his fear.

Get it over with, Hugh, he told himself sourly. 'I was fifteen and a mere Lieutenant.'

She surprised him then, as she had been surprising him for the three days he had known her. 'Heavens,' she said again, and he cringed inwardly. 'Colonel, I cannot imagine how fascinating India must have been. Did you see elephants? Tigers? Are the women as beautiful as pictures I have seen?'

She didn't say a word about his age, but calmly continued combing her hair, her mind only on India, as far as he could tell. He felt himself relax. 'Do you want to hear about India?'

'Oh, my, yes, I do,' she said, her eyes bright. 'Colonel, I have never been anywhere!'

'Very well,' he began, eager to keep her there. 'We landed in Bombay during the monsoon.'

'You were seasick,' she said.

'I told you I have never been seasick,' he replied, 'and I meant it.'

'Very well. Since I was not there, I shall have to believe you.' She put her comb down and clasped her hands together. 'Tell me everything you can remember.'

If some celestial scamp in the universe—an all-purpose genie would do—had suddenly whisked away all the clocks and banished time to outer darkness, Polly knew she would be content to listen for ever to Colonel Junot. While her hair dried, she and the sentry who joined them at the Colonel's suggestion heard of tiger hunts, an amphibious storming of a rajah's palace in Bombay, and of the rise of Lord Wellington, the 'Sepoy General'. India was followed by Ceylon and then Canada, as Colonel Junot took them through his Marine career.

It became quickly obvious to Polly that he loved what he did, because she heard it in his voice. She saw it in the way he leaned forwards until she felt like a co-conspirator in a grand undertaking. His storytelling had her almost feeling decks awash and seeing rank on rank of charging elephants and screaming Indians, as he told them so matter of factly about what he did to support himself. He was capability itself.

Through years of indoctrination, Miss Pym had pounded into her head how rude it was to stare at anyone, especially a man, but the Colonel was hard to resist. A natural-born storyteller, he became quite animated when he spoke of his adventures, which only brightened his brown eyes and gave more colour to his somewhat sallow cheeks—he had obviously spent too much time the past winter sitting at conference tables. She was having a hard time deciding if his finest feature was his magnificent posture and bearing, or his handsome lips, which had to be a throwback to his French ancestry.

Colonel Junot was different, she knew, if for no other reason than that he found her interesting. As she listened to him, injecting questions that he answered with good humor, Polly discovered she was already steeling herself against the time he would bow and say goodbye.

'And that is my career, Private Leonard,' Colonel Junot concluded, looking at them both. 'Private, as you were.

Brandon, excuse me please.' He rose, bowed to her, and went his stately way up the companionway.

'I live such an ordinary life,' Polly murmured, watching him go.

She went on deck at the end of the forenoon watch, pleased to notice the chair she had sat in yesterday had been relocated to its original place, which probably meant there would be no gunnery practice today. She had brought a book topside with her, something improving that Miss Pym had recommended. She decided quickly that a treatise on self-control was a hard slog on a ship's deck where so much of interest was going on. She was happy enough to merely close it, when what she really wanted to do was toss it into the Atlantic. Maybe that wasn't such a shabby idea. Book in hand, she went to the ship's railing.

'Brandon, I hope you are not considering suicide.'

She looked around to see Colonel Junot. 'No, sir. This book is a dead bore and I am about to put it out of its misery.'

He took the book from her hand, opened it, rolled his eyes, then closed it. 'Allow me,' he said, and impulsively flung the thing far into the ocean. 'I hope you were serious.'

'Never more so,' she told him firmly. 'It was a gift from my aunt, who was headmistress at the female academy I attended in Bath, and—'

'I should apologise then for deep-sixing it,' he said, interrupting her.

'Oh, no. Don't you have any relatives who annoy you?'

He thought a moment, then he laughed. 'Who doesn't!'

Walking with more assurance back to her chair, she

seated herself, giving the Colonel every opportunity to nod to her and continue on his way. To her delight, he pulled up yesterday's keg and sat beside her.

'Brandon, give me some advice.'

'Me?' she asked, amazed.

'Yes, you,' he replied patiently. 'Under ordinary circumstances, you appear quite sensible.'

'Thank you, sir,' she teased, and put a hand to her forehead like a seaman.

'I have told you what my aim is on my fact-finding mission.' He must have caught the look in her eye, because he wagged a finger at her. 'Don't you even presume to call it "taking French leave from the conference table".'

'I would never, sir,' she said solemnly, which made him look at her suspiciously.

'Seriously, Brandon, how can I approach Marines?'

She looked at him in surprise. 'Colonel, you would know far better than I!'

'I don't. On this ship, for example—which for our purposes we will call "Any Frigate in the Fleet"—I communicated my wishes to the Sergeant, and he passed them to his men. Everyone is stiff and formal, and I can almost see their brains running, trying to work out what it is I *really* want to know.'

Polly thought about what he had said, but not for long, because it seemed so simple. 'Can you not just sit with them as you are sitting casually with me? Tell them what you told me about the dying Lieutenant, and what it is you wish to do. Look them in the eye, the way you look me in the eye—you know, kindly—and tell them you need their help. Why need you be formal?'

He watched her face closely, and she could only hope he had not noticed her odd little epiphany. 'You *are* kind, you know,' she said softly.

'Thank you, Brandon, but no one can get beyond my rank to just talk to me. There is a larger issue here, one I had not thought of: this may be the first time in the history of the Marines that an officer has actually asked an enlisted man what he *thinks*.'

'That is a sad reflection,' she said, after some consideration. 'Everyone has good ideas now and then.'

'We never ask.'

He was looking far too serious, as though his good idea in Plymouth was already on the rocks. She put her hand on his arm, and he glanced at her in surprise. *Just two days, and then you are gone*, she thought. 'I told you, you are kind. Don't give up yet. You'll find a way to talk to the men.' She took her hand away and looked down, shy again. 'When I was so desperate, you found a way to put me at ease.'

'That was simplicity itself. You needed help.'

'So did the Lieutenant who died in your arms, Colonel,' she told him, finding it strange that she had to explain his own character to him, wondering why people didn't see themselves as they were. 'Just be that kind man and you will find out everything you want to know.'

She stopped, acutely aware she was offering advice to a Lieutenant Colonel of Marines, who, under ordinary circumstances, would never have even looked at her. 'Well, that's what I think,' she concluded, feeling as awkward as a calf on ice.

He nodded and stood up, and Polly knew she had not helped at all. He put his hands behind his back, impeccable. 'I just go and sit on that hatch and call over the Marines and speak to them as I speak to you, Brandon?'

'You could take off that shiny plaque on your neck and unbutton your uniform jacket,' she suggested, then could not resist. 'Let them see you have on a checked shirt underneath.'

His smile was appreciative as he fingered the gorget against his throat. 'I must remain in uniform, Brandon, and the gorget stays. I will try what you say.' He did not disguise the doubt in his voice.

She clasped her hands together, unwilling to let him go, even if it was only to the main deck. 'Colonel, you could practise right here. Ask me questions. I could do the same to you.'

'Why not?' He contemplated her for a moment, and she suddenly wished she was thinner, that her hair was not so wind-blown, and that her glasses would disappear. He was looking her right in the eyes, though, so maybe he didn't notice.

He flexed his fingers and cleared his throat. 'Private Brandon, as you were, please! Let me set you at ease. I'm here to ask questions of you that will never be repeated to your superior. I will not even name you in my report.' He looked at her, his eyes sceptical. 'What do you think so far?'

'You could smile,' she suggested.

'Too artificial,' he replied, shaking his head. 'That would terrify them because officers never smile.'

'I don't understand men,' Polly said suddenly.

'You weren't meant to,' he told her gently, which made her laugh. 'All right. All right. Private Brandon, tell me something about yourself. Why did you join the Royal

Marines? I'm curious.' He peered at her. 'Just tell me something about yourself, Brandon, something that I don't know.'

She thought a moment, and realised with a sudden jolt that she had reached that place where Nana had once told her she would one day arrive. '"Polly, dear, you must never deceive a man about your origins,"' Nana had told her only a week ago.

'My father was William Stokes, Lord Ratliffe of Admiralty House,' she said. 'I am one of his three illegitimate daughters, Colonel.'

To her relief, he did not seem repulsed. 'That accounts for all the years in boarding school in Bath, I suppose. Tell me more, Brandon. What do you like to do?'

'After that, you really want to know *more*?' she asked in surprise.

'Indeed, I do, Private Brandon,' he said simply. 'Remember—I'm supposed to extract answers from you and keep you at your case. I am interested.'

'Our father tried to sell my older sisters to the highest bidder, to pay off his debts,' she went on.

'What a bad man,' the Colonel said. 'Is he the Admiralty official who died in a Spanish prison and is thought by some to be a hero?'

'He died in Plymouth, and, yes, some think him a hero,' she said, her voice barely audible.

He amazed her by putting his hand under her chin and raising it a little, so he could look her in the eyes. 'You managed to avoid all this? How?'

Don't you have eyes in your head? she wanted to retort. 'Come now, Colonel,' she said. 'I am no beauty. My father chose to ignore me.'

For some reason, her bald statement seemed to embarrass the Colonel, whose face turned red. 'Shallow, shallow man,' he murmured, when he had recovered himself. 'He never really took a good look at you, did he?'

Startled, she shook her head. 'He demanded miniatures of my sisters, but not of me.'

'Thank God, Brandon,' the Colonel whispered, his eyes still not leaving her face. He gazed at her for a long moment, and then seemed to recall what he was doing. He sat back and regarded her speculatively. 'I think I can do those interviews now,' he said. 'If I show a genuine interest in what these enlisted men are telling me, look them in the eyes and wait, I might have success. Is that it?'

'I think it is,' she replied, relieved that he had changed the subject, and a little surprised at how much information she had given him with so little encouragement. 'You're actually rather good at interviewing, I think.' Then she couldn't help herself. 'Only don't chuck them under the chin.'

He laughed and held up his hands in a surrender gesture. 'Too right, Brandon! Wait. You never told me what *you* like to do, only about your dreadful father. There's more to you than him.'

She had never thought of it that way before. 'I like to plant things. Before I left Torquay, I helped my brother-in-law's mother plant a row of Johnny Jump-Ups in pots. We…we were going to do snapdragons next, but the letter came and I went to Plymouth. It's not very interesting,' she said in apology.

'You'd like Kirkcudbright, the village where I grew up,' he said. 'Everyone has flowers in their front yard. It smells like heaven, around July. And it *is* interesting.'

The Colonel put his hand on her cheek then, as he

had the other evening. 'Don't ever sell yourself short, Brandon,' he said quietly. 'Incidentally, I like to carve small boats.'

He bowed and left the quarterdeck for the waist of the frigate, where the guns were tied down fast. She watched as he spoke to the Sergeant of the guard, then sat down on the hatch.

'That's the way,' Polly murmured quietly, her heart still beating too fast. 'Surely they won't remain standing if you are seated.'

Trying not to appear overly interested, she watched as the Marines not on duty approached Colonel Junot. He gestured to them, and in a few minutes, they were seated around him.

'Talk to him,' she whispered. 'Just talk to him. He's nothing but kind. All it takes is one of you to speak.'

One of the Privates squatting on the edge of the gathering raised his hand. Colonel Junot answered him, and everyone laughed, even the man who asked the question. Then others joined in, talking to the Colonel, to each other, and even calling over some sailors.

You just have to be yourself, she thought, imagining Colonel Junot's capable hands carving little boats for children. *Just be the man who was so kind to me.*

Chapter Five

Maybe it was the wistful way Polly Brandon had spoken of snapdragons. As Hugh had tried out his interviewing skills on a squad of obliging Marines, he'd found his mind wandering to the lady in the canvas chair.

He could be thankful he was aboard one of his Majesty's typical warships, which did not believe in mirrors on the bulkheads. He had enough trouble frowning into his shaving mirror the next morning and seeing nothing but grey hair starting to attack his temples. As he stared in total dissatisfaction, a brave better angel of his nature did attempt to remind him of his own words to Brandon a day ago, when he so sagely advised her not to sell herself short. The angel shrugged and gave up when he chose not to admit he was doing exactly the same thing to himself.

'I am too old,' he told his reflection in the shaving mirror as he scraped at his chin, which only made him wince—not because the razor was dull, but because none of those obstacles loomed any higher than the molehills they were to him. All he could think of was his August 9, 1775 birth date in the family Bible back home.

When his face was scraped sufficiently free of whiskers, he sat naked on the cold cannon in his cabin, glumly willing himself to be as practical as he ordinarily was. He reminded himself he was on duty, in the service of his King, headed into the war, and destined to be busy. Another day or two would pass and he would never see Polly Brandon again. For his peace of mind, it couldn't come too soon. Hugh did know one thing —what ailed him had a cure, and it was probably to continually remind himself that he was too old for the bewitching Polly Brandon.

Two days later, he could have made his resolve less problematic if he hadn't been pacing on deck in the early hours, dissatisfied with himself. If he had a brain in his head, he would skulk somewhere on the ship when it docked in Oporto. Brandon would go ashore, and he would never see her again. He could go on to Lisbon.

That was his plan, anyway—a poor one, but serviceable enough. Trouble was, the view of Oporto took his breath away, and he was down the companionway in a matter of minutes, knocking on her door to tell her to step lively and come on deck for a look.

Why did you do that? he scolded himself, as he returned topside. His only hope was that she would look unappetising as she came on deck, maybe rubbing her eyes, or looking cross and out of sorts the way some women did, when yanked from slumber. If that was the case, he might have an easier time dismissing her. He could go about his business and forget this little wrinkle in his life's plan, if he even had a plan.

No luck. She came on deck quickly, a shawl draped

over her arm. He smiled to see that she still couldn't quite reach that centre button in back. *I won't touch it*, he thought. Her face was rosy from slumber, her eyes bright and expectant. She merely glanced at him, then cast her whole attention on the beautiful harbour that was Oporto. She had wound her long hair into a ridiculous topknot and skewered it with what looked like a pencil. She looked entirely makeshift, but instead of disgusting him, he wanted to plant a whacking great kiss on her forehead and see where it led. *Lord, I am hopeless*, he thought in disgust.

She was too excited to even say good morning, but tugged on his arm. 'Where is the hospital?' she demanded.

He pointed to the southern bank. 'Over there, in that area called Vila Nova de Gaia. Turn round.'

She did as he demanded, and he buttoned up the centre button. 'You need longer arms,' he commented, but she was not paying attention to him.

'I have never seen anything so magnificent,' she said in awe. 'Perhaps it was worth all that seasickness. Have you been here before?'

'Years ago, Brandon. I think I was your age.' He chuckled. 'For what it's worth, my reaction was much like yours.' *There, Miss Brandon, that should remind you what a geriatric I am*, he thought grimly.

If she heard him, she didn't seem to mind. Brandon watched as a cutter swooped from the southern shore to the side of the *Perseverance* and backed its sails, then watched as the flag Lieutenant ran up a series of pennants. 'What's he doing?' she asked.

'Giving the cutter a message. Our surgeon told me the hospital sends out this cutter at every approach of the fleet, to enquire of the wounded. Ask the flag Lieutenant what message he is sending.'

Surefooted now, Polly hurried to the Lieutenant. 'He is signalling "Wounded man on board. Prompt attention." He said the cutter will take the message to the hospital wharf and there will be a surgeon's mate with a stretcher there when we dock,' she told him in one breath as she hurried back to his side.

'It appears that your brother-in-law doesn't miss a trick,' Hugh said. 'I'm impressed.'

Polly nodded, her eyes on the shore again. 'I asked the Lieutenant if he could also signal "Brandon on board", and he said he would.' She leaned against him for one brief moment, or maybe she just lost her footing. 'I have not seen Laura in nearly two years.'

The winds were fair into Oporto. As the harbour came nearer, she hurried below to finish dressing. When she came back, she was as neat as a pin. He stood close to her when they approached the mouth of the mighty river, knowing there would be a series of pitches and yaws that might discomfort her, as the Douro met the Atlantic. Besides, it gave him plenty of excuse to grip her around the waist to prevent her losing her footing. He couldn't deny he was touched by how completely she trusted him to hold her.

'I may never get used to the sea,' she confessed, as he braced her.

'It isn't given to everyone to relish going down to the sea in small boats, despite what the psalm says.'

'No argument there,' she agreed cheerfully. 'The less business I have in great waters, the better.'

It wouldn't hurt to ask. 'Of you three sisters, are you

to be the only one who avoids the navy?' *What about Marines?* he wanted to ask.

She wasn't listening to him, but was back at the railing, intent on the shoreline, her mind and heart on her sister, he was certain. He tipped his hat to her and went belowdeck to find the letter Surgeon Brackett wanted him to deliver to Philemon Brittle. Better to just hand it to Brandon and let her do the honors. The voyage was over, after all.

He couldn't bring himself to hand it to her, not there at the railing, or after the gangplank came down on the wharf, and certainly not when Polly had thrown herself into the arms of a tall, beautiful woman with auburn hair.

It was a brief embrace. The woman—she must be Laura Brittle—quickly turned her attention to the foretopman on the stretcher, as her husband planted a quick kiss on Polly's cheek, shook hands with the *Perseverance*'s surgeon, and engaged him in conversation.

'Are you planning to stay in Oporto, Colonel Junot?' Captain Adney asked.

'Perhaps,' he temporised.

'We'll be at the navy wharf today and then sailing the day after, if winds and tide are willing.'

'Very well, sir. I'll sail with you.' He couldn't very well say anything else. He stood at the railing, uncertain, wanting to go down the gangplank and introduce himself, and suddenly shy. He looked at Polly for a clue, and she beckoned him.

That was easy. In another moment he was smiling inwardly at Polly's shy introduction, and bowing to Mrs Philemon Brittle, who truly was as beautiful as her younger sister had declared. Philemon Brittle held out his hand and he gave it a shake, impressed with the strength of the surgeon's grasp.

'Do join us for luncheon, Colonel, unless you have urgent business that takes you elsewhere,' Mrs Brittle said.

'Since the King of Portugal is probably taking his ease on a beach in Brazil, and Boney is on his way to Russia, if reports are accurate, I am at a momentary loss for luncheon engagements,' he joked, which made her smile and show off the dimple he recognised in Polly's cheek, too.

'Very well, sir. If Marshal Soult should show his brazen face here again, we'll release you before the sorbet. Come, Polly. Colonel?'

He walked up the hill from the wharf with a sister on either side of him. He looked from one to the other, which made Polly stop.

'Laura, this is droll! Colonel Junot is comparing us!'

So much for my peace of mind, Hugh thought, surprisingly unembarrassed, since he had made an obvious discovery that was probably clear to everyone except Polly herself. 'You have me, Brandon. Anyone with two eyes can see that you and Mrs Brittle are sisters.'

'I have told her that many times,' Mrs Brittle said. 'Perhaps she will choose to believe me some day. Thank you, Colonel Junot!' She paused then, and her eyes narrowed slightly. 'Brandon? Apparently you have either chosen a nickname for Polly, or you are on to our own effort to get my sister to Portugal.'

'You *were* right, Colonel!' Polly exclaimed. 'Laura, I don't know why he calls me that, but we did wonder if perhaps some correspondence came from Portugal requesting a Brandon Polly for service.'

'It was the feeblest attempt,' Mrs Brittle said as they resumed walking again. 'Philemon hoped some over-worked clerk at the Navy Board would apparently do what he did. Perhaps I shall call you Brandon, too, my love. Welcome to hard service in the navy.'

If Polly had a rejoinder ready, it went unnoticed when an orderly at the top of the hill called for Mrs Brittle. Alert, Laura put her finger to her lips and listened.

'Ward C, mum! Lively now!'

Without a word of explanation, Mrs Brittle hiked up her skirts to reveal shapely legs and ran up the hill, for-getting her company completely, it seemed. She stopped halfway up and looked back, but Hugh just waved her on. He took Polly's arm, content to walk the rest of the way with her.

'I gather all the rumours are true, Brandon. Wouldn't it be nice some day if your gifted sister could be recog-nised for what she is doing here?'

'I doubt it would concern her,' Polly replied, and he could hear the pride in her voice. 'She would probably just laugh, and say the war is harder on wives like Nana, who wait. It must be so hard to be apart from one's love.'

Maybe I am about to find out, Hugh thought to himself. *Or maybe I am just an idiot.*

They arrived at the convent and were greeted immedi-ately by a nun, who directed them to the dining room. The table was already set; from the looks of things, the Brittles had left their meal when the *Perseverance* docked. Hugh pulled out a chair for Polly, taking a deep breath of her sun-warmed hair as he did so, remembering how he had helped her wash it.

They were just beginning what looked like empanadas

when Mrs Brittle came into the room, hand in hand with a youngster whose hair was the same shade as his mother and aunt's. She knelt gracefully and kissed his cheek. 'Danny, that's your aunt Polly Brandon.' She repeated it in Portuguese. 'His Portuguese is better than mine,' Mrs Brittle explained.

'Laura, he looks like you,' Polly said.

'The hair, anyway,' Laura said as she sat him down on a chair with a medical book as a booster. 'He has his father's eyes and general capable demeanour.'

'Does he run with the herd?' Hugh asked, gesturing towards the courtyard, which he saw through the open door. Other children about Danny's age played there.

'Indeed, he does, which frees me for hospital work,' Laura said.

Polly looked where he looked. 'Goodness, are you running an orphanage, too?'

'No, my love,' Mrs Brittle said. She hesitated, glancing at Hugh, and he understood immediately whose children they were, considering Oporto's sad history with the French invaders.

She reached across her corner of the table and touched Polly's hand. 'When the French came here in '08, they brutalised the young women they did not murder. These children are one result of that misery.'

'Oh,' Polly said, her voice small. 'Where are their mothers?'

Hugh watched Polly's expressive face. *You are so young, so naïve*, he thought. *Let us hope this is the worst face of war you see.*

'Oporto is a sad town, my love,' Mrs Brittle said. She cupped her hand gently against her son's cheek as he ate his empanada. 'We have tried to make life as good as we can for these unfortunates.' She looked at Polly. 'Dearest, this is why we want you here.'

'I don't understand,' Polly said. 'I thought I was to help in the wards.'

'We want you to teach English to the young mothers—some are here—and to the nuns. I haven't time, and they would be so much more useful here. Perhaps, in time, they will find work with the English port merchants, when they return from Lisbon and London.'

'I can teach them,' Polly said. Her eyes on the children, she rose and went to the door, where she could see the children playing. 'Seems a strange way to fight Boney.'

'Not at all,' Mrs Brittle said. She held a cup to Danny's lips and he drank in large gulps. 'Slow down, little one. You'll be back there soon enough.' She looked apologetically at Hugh. 'Colonel, you will find us a strange household. My husband sends his regrets, but ward walking always trumps food. Perhaps he'll wander through tonight for our evening meal, which I trust you will share with us.'

He didn't hesitate. 'With pleasure.'

'In fact, Colonel Junot, you may stay the night here, unless you prefer a smelly frigate.'

'I can do that, too,' he replied, glad for the invitation.

He looked at Polly, but her eyes were on the courtyard. As he watched her, she rose quietly and held out her hand to her nephew, who took it without hesitation and led her from the room in such a forthright manner that he smiled.

'Now there's a lad who has things under control.'

'I told you he was like his father,' Mrs Brittle said, her voice soft with love as she watched her sister and son.

He thought he should make his excuses and leave then. This was a busy woman. He made to rise, but she raised her hand to stop him, then poured him another glass of port. 'As onerous as work is here, we cannot fault the wine, Colonel.'

He drank, pleased to agree with her. His eyes went again to Polly, who was sitting on the grass now, with children around her. He watched as two women about her age came closer, hesitated, and moved closer. 'She's a bit of a magnet,' he murmured, more to himself than Mrs Brittle. 'I noticed that on the ship, too.' He chuckled, then stopped, because Mrs Brittle was giving him that thoughtful stare again.

'I think there were two Lieutenants who would have followed her to the ends of the earth,' he continued, speaking too fast. *Maybe one Lieutenant Colonel*, he thought, glad Mrs Brittle could not read his mind.

'She would only stare at you if you suggested such a thing.'

'I know, Mrs Brittle. She seems to think she is a duckling among swans.'

Mrs Brittle poured herself another glass. 'Thank you for being such a gallant escort, Colonel. I was hoping there would be someone mature like you on board, to shepherd her safely.'

Ouch, he thought, mentally counting every grey hair at his temples. 'You can always count on the Marines, Mrs Brittle.'

Lord, but that sounded feeble, he scolded himself as he said goodbye to Mrs Brittle and walked back to the dock down the well-travelled path, where he planned to retrieve a small duffel of his own and arrange for Polly's luggage to be sent up the hill. The Sergeant of Marines had released his men to shore, where he drilled them. Hugh watched in appreciation and some pride at their neat rank and file. 'We are so few in this war,' he murmured, and thought of Lieutenant Graves breathing his last in his arms. 'I have work to do.'

From the startled look on Laura's face, Polly knew she should have disguised her disappointment that Colonel Junot had left the hospital. 'I…I only wish he had said goodbye, but I suppose duty called,' she said. *And, oh, can I change a subject*, she thought. 'Laura, the young women are so shy. I declare they are like deer.'

Laura removed the medical book from Danny's chair and patted it. Polly sat down. 'You must treat them so gently. They have been through a terrible experience at the hands of the French.' She sighed. 'It is one I can appreciate more than most, perhaps. They were wretchedly ill used, and feel the world's censure.'

'You…you said some of the women returned to their villages and left their babies here?'

'They did, and I call it no foul. Everyone deals differently with violation of such a magnitude. I can assure you the mothers who remained love their little ones, who are surely not to blame for their entry into the world.' She took Polly's hand in hers. 'My dear, you and I know the inside of an orphanage. Only Nana had a home in her early years.' She looked Polly in the eye. 'Is it wrong of me to have thrust you into this?'

Polly shook her head. 'No, a thousand times, Laura. I trust this is one foundling home where the little ones are touched and loved.'

'You know it is,' her sister said firmly, then looked down as her cheeks flamed. 'Other than Nana's embrace when we met in Torquay, my beloved Philemon was the first person who ever hugged me, and I was twenty-seven.'

Polly moved her chair closer and they sat hand in hand until an orderly ran down the hall, calling for Mrs Brittle.

'Duty calls,' Laura said, but Polly heard no regret in her voice.

She stood up, but Polly did not release her hand. 'Tell me you don't mind all this hard work, sister,' she said, tugging on her hand, 'or the fact that you receive no recognition for it.'

Laura let go of Polly's hand gently. 'I only have to look into the eyes of the men I save, or into my husband's eyes, to receive all the reward I need, this side of heaven, my love. You'll understand some day.'

'That's what Nana says, too,' Polly grumbled. 'Some day. Some day.'

Laura laughed. 'Don't be so impatient to grow up! Go back to the courtyard and make some more friends.' She kissed the top of Polly's head. 'And if Danny gets stubborn and won't share, encourage him to do so. Mama says.'

She spent a pleasant afternoon in the courtyard, trying to imagine what Oporto must have been like when the French controlled it and the Portuguese suffered so greatly. She counted ten little ones, all about two years of age, like her nephew. Two of them decided to nap on cots in the shade of a mimosa tree, and three young women watched over them all.

One of the women, Paola, could speak some English, but Polly found herself mostly smiling and wishing she knew more of the language. She did learn a handclapping game in Portuguese, where even Danny corrected her pronunciation. She decided the whole afternoon was a lesson in humility for Miss Pym's star pupil and spent her time more profitably, sitting cross-legged in the grass and folding bits of paper into hopping frogs, a skill she had learned from Nana.

The whole time, Paola sat close to her in the grass, with several children in her lap. 'I am determined to learn Portuguese,' Polly told her, and smiled back when the young girl smiled at her.

The smile left Paola's face when she heard footsteps and looked over her shoulder. Polly watched her freeze and seem to shrink inside her own skin.

She looked around, wondering what could be the trouble. Colonel Junot stood in the open doorway to the courtyard, watching them, a smile on his face. Polly carefully put her arm around Paola, who had moved her legs to the side as though she wanted to leap to her feet. 'No, no,' Polly whispered. 'He is a friend. *Amigo?*'

Paola froze where she was, scarcely breathing. Imagine that much fear, Polly thought. She tightened her grip on the young girl. 'Colonel Junot, if you don't mind, you're frightening this girl,' she said softly.

He stared at her in disbelief at first, and then he sighed and turned away. She heard his footsteps recede down the corridor. *Please don't leave before you say goodbye*, she thought in sudden anguish.

Chapter Six

To Polly's infinite relief, Colonel Junot joined them for dinner. 'I was afraid you had come to the courtyard to say goodbye to me,' she told him.

'Oh, no, Brandon,' he assured her. 'Your sister kindly invited me to eat here and then stay the night. I have been quartered in a chaste cell formerly inhabited by someone—perhaps her name was Sister Quite Prudent—who obviously had God's ear. It can only do me good.'

I'm going to miss your wit, she thought suddenly. *What a short acquaintance this has been.*

Dinner was sheer delight, with young Daniel Brittle sitting on the medical books again, and Philemon actually free to join them. 'What do you think of our society?'

'I like it, Surgeon Brittle,' Hugh said. 'You run a ship-shape operation with good results.' He lowered his voice. 'I'm afraid I frightened one of the young women in the courtyard this afternoon. I suppose one uniform is pretty much the same as another to them.'

'Alas, yes,' Laura chimed in. 'No one wears a uniform here, and our Marine sentries don't go in the courtyard.'

While the Brittles listened, Hugh explained his purpose in coming to Portugal. 'Surgeon Brittle, I would consider it a special favour if you or your excellent wife would show me around the hospital tomorrow. I'd like to reassure myself that your protection is adequate.'

'We can do that.' Philemon leaned back in his chair and glanced at Laura. 'Danny appears to be drooping, Laura. Colonel Junot and I can entertain ourselves with Oporto's major export, if you and Polly want to see him to bed.'

The little boy went with no protest, happy enough for his mother to tuck him in bed, sing a lullaby in Portuguese, and watch until he slept, his arm around a doll made of surgical towels.

'You look a little weary yourself, sister,' Laura said. 'I can't think of a lullaby for your age, but you can tell me about the voyage, and how our sister does.'

Polly decided bliss was a flannel nightgown, two pillows behind her head, and sharing family stories with her sister, a luxury of such magnitude she never could have imagined it only three years ago. She described Rachel at three, and Nana's quiet competence, as counterpoint to the tremendous strain she lived under, and the next expectation, due in September.

Laura listened, adding her own commentary. During a lull, she cleared her throat, then sat up a little higher in the bed. 'Polly, I don't want to pry... Oh, yes, I do! It seems to me that Colonel Junot—heavens, he sounds more Scottish than Macbeth—is your champion.'

Polly stared at her, eyes wide. 'Champion?' she repeated. 'I can't imagine.'

Laura levelled her with a glance, probably one she practised on Danny. 'Confess,' she said.

There obviously wasn't any point in trying to keep the events of the voyage a secret. 'Several centuries back, his ancestors came to Scotland from France with Mary of Scotland. That's why he is "Junnit" now, and—' Polly stopped, and looked at Laura for reassurance. 'As for champion—sister, I don't think I would have survived the voyage without him.'

As Laura listened, only interjecting a faint 'Oh, my', or 'Gracious', as thc tale became more fraught, Polly described the whole voyage, leaving nothing out. 'When… when I was feeling better, I honestly tried to avoid him, so he wouldn't have to be reminded of the embarrassing circumstances I had placed him under, but he was just so matter of fact! You would have thought he had done nothing more than…than pull a splinter out of my finger. I tried to be mortified, but he never let me.'

Even Laura, who had probably seen everything by now, stared at her. 'Polly, Colonel Junot may be as rare a man as I have ever heard of! We all owe him a debt.' She thought a moment, choosing her words like ripe strawberries in a summer market. 'That is all you owe him, though.'

Polly watched her sister, unable to overlook the worry in her eyes. She decided to put her at ease. 'Sister, he is much too grand and important to pay me any attention, beyond that which I have described to you.'

She did not expect to feel any pain at that bald announcement, but she did. 'He's a man of some distinction, Laura. Men like that don't…' She couldn't say it. 'Well, they don't.'

'You don't think he's too old for you?'

Surprised, Polly sat up. 'I…I never thought of him that

way.' She swallowed, suddenly wanting this conversation to end, because she felt unwanted tears teasing her eyelids. 'Age never entered in. Heavens, sister, he is a Colonel of Marines! I doubt he will even remember my name next week.'

'Are you so certain?' Laura asked. Suddenly the air hung heavy between them.

It was as if they both decided to change the subject at the same time, and spoke next of inconsequentials. Gradually Laura said less and less. Soon her head drooped on Polly's shoulder and she slept. Polly made herself comfortable, knowing that Philemon would eventually come in search of his wife. Finally, she heard Colonel Junot's firm footsteps receding down the long corridor. Philemon knocked softly on the door, then opened it.

Polly put a finger to her lips, and he smiled to see his wife asleep. Walking quietly to the bed, he picked her up, winked at Polly, and mouthed 'goodnight'. He looked down at his sleeping wife, then at Polly. 'You're just what this doctor ordered,' he whispered, then grinned. 'And you brought along your own Marine for protection.'

'He's not *my* Marine,' she whispered back. Philemon left the room as quietly as he had entered it. Polly frowned at the ceiling. 'What is wrong with my relatives?' she asked out loud.

Hugh's peers back in Plymouth would never believe him if he told them he spent the night in a nun's bed. He woke early, as usual, but felt disinclined to move. Miracle of miracles he hadn't roused earlier, considering the amount of port he had drunk last night, which also accounted for the slight buzz in his brain.

Part of the pleasure Hugh felt was his convivial evening with Philemon Brittle, a remarkable man, if ever there was one. He had handed over the letter from their mutual friend, Owen Brackett, which Brittle read right then, after apologies to his guest.

In the manner of men engaged in years of warfare, they had spent the next half-hour refighting naval battles, discovered they had both served at the Battle of the Nile and Trafalgar, and had decided—Brittle, anyway—each was deserving of confidences.

'Polly's a sight for Laura's sore eyes,' Brittle had said, as they finished one bottle and popped the cork on another. 'She works so hard, and misses her sisters so much.' He poured another measure. 'I hope it is not a felony to bamboozle the Navy Board, but we thought it worth a try to get Brandon Polly here.'

'I've been calling her Brandon,' Hugh confessed. 'I suppose that is rag manners, but it was one way to take her mind off as wicked a case of the pukes as I have ever seen.' He laughed. 'She told me she was determined to take up residence in Portugal and never attempt the ocean again.'

They had sailed into more prosaic conversational waters then, concluding only when the surgeon stoppered the bottle of port, telling Hugh it was time he went in search of his wife.

He had found her in Polly's room. Hugh had continued down the hall, but stood in the shadows and watched as, a few moments later, Brittle came out carrying his sleeping wife. He knew he was a voyeur, but Hugh had not looked away when she woke and her arms went around Brittle's neck and she kissed him.

Well, Surgeon Brittle, I shall have to report to Owen Brackett that you are enjoying a better war than most, Hugh had thought, as he went into his virginal cell and closed the door quietly. His dreams had been livelier than usual that night.

Preparing for the day was no more bare bones than usual. His only misgiving came as he dressed, wearing the black-and-white checked shirt that Polly seemed to have taken a shine to. He tucked the long tails into his navy blue trousers, and stood there a long minute, holding the gorget he had worn around his neck for years. Habit prevailed. He hooked it around his neck, but tucked it inside his shirt because he was out of uniform. Feeling decidedly naked without his uniform coat, he settled for a nondescript waistcoat he usually kept in his duffle as an antidote to cold mornings. *I must look like a brigand*, he thought, then reminded himself that vanity in a Lieutenant Colonel of Marines was out of place.

He retraced his steps to the dining room, hoping to see Polly Brandon. He was disappointed; Laura Brittle sat alone at the table, sipping tea. He hesitated to enter, but she had heard his footsteps.

'Do join me, Colonel Junot,' she called. When he came in the room, she indicated the food on the sideboard. 'Philemon is already ward walking, Danny is in the courtyard, with my sister.'

Porridge, cream, and yesterday's empanadas seemed to be the menu. He filled his plate and joined her as she poured him tea. He wasn't inclined to converse much over meals— maybe this was a consequence of the urgent nature of his wartime life—and she seemed to sense that. When he finished, he sat back. Something slightly militant in her eyes told him she did not suffer fools gladly, or, apparently, Colonels.

'Colonel, as much as you would probably rather not mention it, I must thank you for your unparalleled kindness to my sister on the voyage. She told me how you helped her.'

'It truly was nothing,' he assured her. *That is safe enough*, he thought, daring to relax. 'I only feel sorry it was necessary for a young lady to have to pawn her dignity so completely.' He laughed softly. 'She ain't much of a sailor, but she is a trooper.'

They laughed together. He watched Mrs Brittle's expressive face, seeing so much of Polly in her that it surprised him. Physically they were different—Laura tall and slim, and Polly shorter and probably destined to a life of decisions between one cream bun or two—but he could not overlook the matching dimples and lovely hair.

Then it came; he could see it in her eyes and the way she set her lips in a firm line. He braced himself.

'What do you know of us sisters?' she asked.

He shrugged, not sure of himself, but too stubborn to roll over and play dead. 'I have heard things,' he said simply. 'In fact, she told me about her father.'

He had startled her, but she recovered quickly. 'It's true. We have all decided never to gild a lily, Colonel. Still, I have to wonder why she said so much.'

Hugh said nothing, unwilling to pave her way. He poured himself more tea, then gave Mrs Brittle his full attention. He wondered for only a short moment what her game was, because he realised how transparent he must be to an observant woman who was a great protector of her sisters. 'Say on, madam,' he murmured, bracing himself.

'Nana was able to get away to safety in Plymouth with her grandmother. I had no one's support, so my first marriage lined our father's pockets and fair ruined me. Polly was never a victim because our father never could see past her spectacles. For that, Nana and I are profoundly grateful. Polly sees it differently, I think.'

Chastened, Hugh allowed his gaze to wander. *I was one of those shallow ones, at first, but you'll never hear that from me*, he thought.

What she was telling him became clear. He knew superior intellect had no role in his sudden wisdom because he knew himself well enough. 'Which is worse, Mrs Brittle—to be in peril because of beauty, or ignored because of perceived lack of it?'

'*Touché*, Colonel,' she said, impressed. 'Polly feels like a wren among birds of paradise, although nothing could be further from the truth. But *you* have noticed.'

He looked at her, his heart sinking because he knew she had taken his measure, no matter how well he had thought to hide it. 'You have me, Mrs Brittle. I'll admit that I have become an admirer of your sister. It only took a short voyage.'

'I thought as much,' she replied, her tone in no way calculated to embarrass. 'I have to ask—are you even aware that you have a proprietary air around her?'

It was his turn for surprise. 'No!'

'You do,' she said, giving considerable weight to two words.

He thought a long moment before he spoke, knowing that what he said would end any further connection. 'I'm certain she has no notion of my regard, beyond any consideration of a gentleman towards a female travelling alone. I helped her. That was enough, as far as she is concerned. How could I possibly mean anything to her on such short notice, and in such a circumstance?'

'I trust you are right,' Laura said.

He could hear the finality in her voice. 'I am right, madam. I…I have no plans to pursue the matter, so rest assured.' He made himself smile. 'Nothing like a good war to put the screws on an actual life, eh?'

He should never have said that, because it broke his heart, even as he knew he had ample cause to dislike Laura Brittle.

Not willing just then to stay another moment in Mrs Brittle's company, he stood up. 'Enough said,' he told her, with what he thought was an admirable bit of forbearance. 'I'll only be here the rest of the day, then off to Lisbon on tomorrow's tide.'

It pleased him a little to see her suddenly unsure, as though she regretted her interference in Polly Brandon's life. Maybe she could tolerate his plain speaking, since she was so eager to dish out her own. He took a deep breath. 'You and Mrs Worthy still see Brandon as a child, don't you?'

'She is,' was Laura Brittle's firm reply.

'Take another look,' he said quietly, then bowed and left the room.

Philemon had told Hugh last night where the principal ward was located. He reminded himself that his sole purpose in Oporto was to further his interviews with the Marines serving in small detachments. He would have got off scot-free if he hadn't glanced into the courtyard as he strode so purposefully away, ready to chew nails.

He slowed down; he stopped, making sure he was in the shadow of a colonnade. There she sat on the grass, cross-legged but decorous—Brandon Polly on the Navy Boards rolls, and Brandon for ever in his heart. He knew it now; Laura Brittle had succeeded in convincing him of the matter, even as she pulled the rug out from under him.

Brandon was dressed in something light and her hair was again atop her head in that silly way she had of twisting it there with a pencil or skewer. She had already attracted her nephew to one leg, and a darker-skinned youngster of roughly the same age—some Frenchman's memento— was ready to plop himself down on the other. Her arms were full and her face so pretty in that way of women with children.

How bitter this was. Polly Brandon was precisely the woman he wanted to mother his own children, children destined never to be born because the timing was off, and Napoleon, that bastard, insisted on hogging everyone's attention and effort. *Brandon, you are the wife I will never have*, he thought. *At least there is no crime in remembering you.*

He moved quietly from the shadow and continued his way down the corridor to the convent's chapel, which had been appropriated as the major ward. Philemon had told him that since the French has desecrated it, the Catholic hierarchy in Portugal had been willing enough, and marvellously patriotic, to turn over the use of major portions of the convent to the Royal Navy as a satellite hospital.

He walked into the ward, looking for Philemon Brittle, and found him in a former lady chapel, seated at a desk, poring over a sheaf of papers.

Brittle smiled to see him and indicated a chair. 'Feel

free to talk to my Marine guards,' he said. 'I have them posted in here, as you can see, and by my apothecary, and at each entrance.'

It seemed so few to Hugh. 'Do you feel secure enough which such a small detail?'

The surgeon shrugged. 'I confess I do not think about the matter over much. We're close to the navy wharf for safety—you were there yesterday—and this side of the Douro River is under control. We never cross the river to Oporto proper without an escort, though, mainly because none of your Marines has any faith in the British army's ability to keep the Frogs away.'

They both laughed, as only a navy surgeon and a Marine could who were well acquainted with service jealousies. 'I suppose we're a pack of fools, Colonel,' Philemon admitted. 'There's been no indication of French in the vicinity, but it's lively enough this summer, with Beau Wellesley on the prowl east of us, and Soult and Marmont playing their cat-and-mouse games.'

'And here all is peaceful.'

'For now. My own sources suggest battle soon, although the fleet itself seems quiet.' Philemon leaned back in his chair. 'You'd be amazed how this chapel can fill up with army wounded. They've taken to shipping us their worst cases, even though this was never intended as an army hospital. The advantage is we can get them off the Peninsula sooner, so it works out. I leave it to the Admiralty and Horse Guards to squabble, and let us alone to heal whom we can.'

Philomen peered closer at Hugh. 'But you are not concerned about that, are you?' He paused, but only briefly. 'Did my wife give you what-for over Polly?'

'She said my proprietary air was too obvious, and perhaps I should turn my attention elsewhere, since Polly is so young,' Hugh admitted, miserable and hoping it did not show. 'I assured her I would be gone soon enough and not likely to return. I admit I was not as nice to Mrs Brittle as I should have been. She still sees Brandon as a child.'

Out of the corner of his eye, Hugh could see a nun standing in the doorway. Philemon nodded to the woman, then rose. 'Duty calls. Don't look so glum, Colonel Junot! If it's any consolation, Laura and I don't see eye to eye on some matters. Oliver Worthy and I can both testify to the value of persistence, where the daughters of the late and unlamented Lord Ratliffe are concerned. Good day, now. Feel free to roam the place and question whomsoever you will.'

Hugh did, visiting first two Marines in hospital, and then making his rounds of the building, explaining himself and then questioning. The result was more food for thought, and the satisfaction of knowing he was improving in his offhand interrogations. His pleasure in whatever good he might be doing gave way to a gnawing feeling that he wanted to at least glimpse Polly Brandon again, before he made his way back to the navy wharf and his duty.

He passed through the corridor again, and this time was rewarded. There she was now, her hair more decorous, and her admirers grown to include more children and young mothers, some of whom looked no older than his nieces living so peacefully in Scotland on his land. He had heard stories of the French in Oporto, and the terrible prices exacted so often by conquerors.

He hoped he would not frighten anyone, but he had to

say goodbye to Polly Brandon. There were a few startled glances in his direction as he crossed the courtyard, but no one scarpered away. To his gratification, Polly rose to meet him, a smile on her face.

They met in the centre of the courtyard, and the sun was warm on his back. The scent of orange blossoms was all around, and the peppery odour of roses, fragrances he knew he would always associate with Polly Brandon, even if he never saw her again, which seemed likely, considering her sister's vigilance.

'I approve the shirt,' she told him with no preliminaries.

'I'll pass your encomium on to the Navy Board's chief commissary, who is probably some poor overworked functionary behind a tall desk,' he teased back.

How could he have ever though her plain? Were all men, when faced with spectacles, as stupid as he was? If anything, the spectacles gave her an impish look, especially since they always seemed to be perched a little low on her nose.

He couldn't help himself. He pushed up her glasses. 'You could probably tighten the little screws in the corner.'

Her cheeks grew quite pink then, and he liked the overall effect almost well enough to kiss her, except it had been ages since he had kissed a woman, and he probably wasn't all that good any more, if he ever had been.

Why couldn't he just say goodbye? Just a word and bow and off he would go, back to war. All he could do was stand there, filled with so much regret he wanted to drop to his knees in utter misery.

'You're leaving,' she said quietly.

'Time and tide, Brandon,' he told her. 'I want to talk to the Marines at the wharf, and get on board the *Perseverance*.' Unable to look into her eyes, he looked at the young women watching them. 'You are making friends. Are they to be your pupils?'

'They are,' she said, 'and any of the sisters who care to join us.' She frowned. 'It isn't much of a way to fight Boney, though, is it? Not like my sisters.'

'Be your own person, Brandon,' he said, not meaning to sound like a Colonel of Marines, but unable to help himself. 'I mean... No, that's what I mean.'

'Grow up?' she asked him, her eyes on his. 'And make up my mind about things?'

As he said his goodbye, it occurred to him that maybe, just maybe, he meant something to her. Too bad he had so much to do. Too bad armies were on the march. Too bad Laura Brittle stood in the doorway, watching them.

He wanted to clasp Polly Brandon in his arms. He had watched over her on the *Perseverance* and he was uneasy about leaving her without his protection. *Yes, I am proprietary*, he wanted to shout to Laura Brittle. *Why is it your business?*

He did nothing of the sort. 'Stay off the water, Brandon, and you should be all right,' he said gruffly, then turned on his heel as smartly as any Marine on parade, and left her standing alone in the courtyard.

Chapter Seven

Life at the Convent of the Sacred Name answered every wish of Polly's heart. She was busy; she was with a beloved sister; she was doing worthwhile work. In the month since Colonel Junot left her so alone in the court-yard, she was everything but happy.

A sensible woman, she assured herself that the pain of his departure would go away. Even her sheltered life in a female academy had taught her that people come and go, exerting their influence for a brief time. She remembered one dance instructor—an Italian *émigré*—whom all the students had swooned over. He left, after a six-weeks' course of instruction. By the end of the following week, all she could remember about him was his last name and his brown eyes.

Colonel Junot was proving to be more difficult to for-get. True, he was handsome by anyone's standards, made even more beguiling by the unexpected brogue when he spoke. She, who had endured too many years of constant reminder about posture—head up and chin back—could only envy his elegant way of carrying himself. Beyond the superficial, Colonel Junot was stalwart, capable, and kind, and she had never met anyone like him.

That he orbited far out of her sphere was a given, and should have made it easier to forget him. She couldn't, though. She thought she knew why, but there was no one she could talk to, not even Laura, who had seemed relieved when Colonel Junot was but a distant figure in a scarlet coat, far below at the navy wharf.

I should set Laura's mind at ease, Polly thought, as the days passed. *I'm being foolish to even think Colonel Junot has spared a single thought for me since he said goodbye.* Trouble was, she didn't know what to say, so said nothing, choosing instead to throw herself into the work ordained for her in the convent, trusting to time to smooth away any sharp edges. As the days passed, it did; given another year or two, she knew she could forget Colonel Junot.

The Convent of the Sacred Name had been a large community, before the French desecrated its holiest places, and violated and murdered so many of its gentle inhabitants. Most of the surviving nuns had retreated to the safety of their motherhouse in Lisbon. The few who returned were resolute beings, which made them superbly useful in establishing and maintaining smooth order in Philemon's satellite hospital.

Essentially, these were women not afraid of anything. Philemon explained it to Polly one afternoon when he had a moment to sit in the courtyard with his little son in his arms. 'It's a fine line, my dear. People who endure the worst are either broken by it or strengthened.' He ruffled his son's auburn hair. 'I refer you to your own sisters.'

Polly was not slow to understand. 'These young girls I am to teach—they seem to always move in the shadows.

Where do they fall in the spectrum of what you are saying?'

Philemon passed his hand in front of his eyes, as if trying to brush away terrible visions. 'So many women were treated so cruelly by the French. Many took their own lives. Others were turned off by their families, who could not manage such shame, in the middle of other misery. Mind you, loss of what they call "honour" is a terrible thing to citizens of this peninsula. Bless their hearts, most of these girls still love their little ones, even conceived in such a way. I own that I admire women, and these brave souls in particular.'

Polly leaned against her brother-in-law. 'I should be more than a teacher, Philemon?'

'Aye, much more,' he replied firmly. 'Be a friend.'

That was her mandate, she decided, after another night of tossing and turning in her narrow bed. When she rose with the dawn, she decided that was her last sleepless night; there was work to be done. Everyone around her had been affected by war, which made her concerns puny, indeed. War meant sacrifice; it was no respecter of persons. She could understand that. Obviously Colonel Junot did. When he had left her so alone, he had not looked back.

Before she began, she needed an ally. She found her sister sitting quietly on a bench, obviously enjoying a moment of rare leisure. 'You have a look of enquiry, dearest,' she said to Polly, and patted the bench.

Polly sat down. 'I need an ally—someone who speaks English at least a little, so I can communicate.' She leaned close to Laura. 'What do you call these young girls?'

'I've been calling them "little mothers" in Portuguese—*pouco mães*—because they have been helping me so materially with Danny. I remind them I could never do my work without their help.' She sighed. 'They just don't quite believe they have any value. Learning English would be a start.'

'Who can help me?'

Laura sat back, her eyes thoughtful. 'There is only one woman, Sister Maria Madelena. She is a dragon, but she speaks English and Spanish.'

'A dragon?'

'Indeed. I would say she is more Pym than Pym, without the hypocrisy.'

The sisters looked at each other and burst into laughter. 'Where might I find this paragon?' Polly asked.

'Try the old chapel.'

So Polly made her way to the small chapel, which had existed since the Middle Ages. It was dark and redolent of centuries of incense, but there was a small nun, ferociously clicking the beads on her rosary, impatience evident in every contour of her compact body. She must have heard Polly enter, but Sister Maria Madelena did not turn around.

More interested than frightened now, Polly sat down quietly on one of the few benches near the entrance. She looked around her at the simple stations on the cross and wondered how many prayers had risen through the incense-darkened ceiling, low and decidedly pre-Gothic. *What did they pray about then?* Polly asked herself. *The Black Death? Moors at the gates?*

Finally the click of Sister Maria Madelena's beads ended with a finality that made Polly smile, in spite of her fears at approaching Laura's dragon. Polly jumped when the nun slapped the flat of her hand against the stone floor, as if impatient for God to smile down on the Portuguese, who had been getting the short end of some cosmic stick for so many years now. She turned around quickly and Polly swallowed. She opened her mouth to speak, but Sister Maria Madelena spoke first.

'I need your help, Miss Brandon.'

Surprised, Polly stared at her for a moment. 'Actually, I...I...was going to say the same thing to you, Sister,' she managed to blurt out, unnerved by the jagged scar that ran from under her wimple by her ear, across her face under her nose, cut through the corner of her mouth, and wound up on her neck, where it vanished from sight under her habit.

She would have been almost pretty, but for the scar. *Don't stare*, Polly tried to tell herself, but it was too late. All she could do was stare, and wish for the first time that she could telescope herself back through the weeks and into Miss Pym's classroom again, where no one saw such sights.

'I'm sorry,' she said finally. 'I should not stare. Please forgive me.'

If she expected the dragon to suddenly hiss fire at her, she was mistaken. The woman smiled, or at least, it would have been a smile, except that the corner of her mouth drooped, rendered her more sad than terrifying.

'Considering Our Lord, these are burdens easily borne,' she said, the voice of practicality. 'We have not met, but I have heard your name from the *pouco mães*. Sit, sit.'

Her English was excellent, and she wasted not a moment. 'My dear, what is it you want of me?'

Polly had to laugh then. She needed to make up for her

rudeness, and Sister Maria Madelena did not seem to be one to bamboozle. 'You asked first, Sister,' she said, seeing nothing but kindness in the nun's eyes, belying the fearsome scar.

'I did, but you are the guest here in our convent,' she replied graciously. 'Very well, then. It is not a small thing. Would you be willing to help me at night, when the little mothers cry in their nightmares?'

Polly could not help the shudder that ran through her body. 'What could I possibly do?' she asked, when she could speak.

'Hold their hands. Sit with them until the terror passes. I cannot be everywhere.'

It was simply said, as if she had asked Polly to water the flowers in the courtyard. 'I will help you,' Polly said, thinking how Colonel Junot had helped her without a complaint in her worst moments; surely she could do no less. 'Of course I will help. When do I start?'

'Tonight.' Sister Madelena rose quickly. 'Now I have much to do.' She nodded at Polly and starting walking briskly to the low door, where she ducked and paused. 'What was it you came to see me about, *senhorita*?'

It seemed so unimportant. 'I wanted your help in teaching the little mothers English.' Polly stood up.

'Of course I will help,' Sister Maria Madelena said. 'When you have their hearts, my dear, by watching over them at night, you will easily engage their minds.'

It sounded so true that Polly could only nod. 'Your English is excellent, Sister,' she said. 'Where did you learn it?'

Sister Madelena looked at her, as if wondering how much truth to tell. 'I haven't always been a nun, and I am

well named, Senhorita Brandon. I used to be mistress to
an Englishman who managed Sandeman's vineyards. He
thought if he talked English loud and slow enough, I would
learn.'

'How is your hearing?' Polly asked, laughing.

'My English is better. I will come for you tonight
after Compline.'

Polly changed her mind several times before Compline, but when there was a soft tap on her door, she rose
at once.

'Follow me,' Sister Maria Madelena said, returning
with her to the older part of the convent, the section far
away from the satellite hospital. 'At first, Surgeon Brittle
thought the little mothers would prefer to be together, so
we housed them in the old refectory,' the nun said. 'They
kept waking each other with tears and shrieks, so we
decided on the old cells.'

Polly rubbed her arms, feeling the hairs rise on them.
It was the middle of summer, but she shivered. 'Their
children?'

'They sleep with their little ones, those who have children.'

Even though every fibre in her body screamed out to
stop, Polly let herself be led down the corridor to its in-
tersection, where a padded chair had been placed, looking
out of place amid the austerity of a much earlier age.

'Make yourself comfortable here,' Sister Maria Madelena said, as she fluffed up a pillow. 'I will be at the other
end of the corridor. If you hear someone cry out, just go
to the chamber.'

'And do what?' Polly asked, utterly unprepared.

'What your heart tells you to do.' She left Polly alone.

Polly sat, deeply aware of her utter inadequacy. She leaned back carefully, afraid to make the smallest sound and waken anyone from already uneasy slumber. *You could have stayed with Nana*, she reminded herself. It sounded so cowardly to even think such a thing that she felt ashamed. She thought of Colonel Junot then, and the kindness in his brown eyes when he had told her not to sell herself short. She yearned to see him again so she could tell him she was trying, even as she hoped this would be the night when no one cried out.

She did not get her wish. The smell of incense was cloying but comforting, and there was just the hint of orange blossoms and gardenia from a courtyard they had passed. She drew her legs up under her and rested her cheek on her hand.

Polly sat up, straining her ears. The lowest keening seemed to come up from the very stones on the floor, causing her to clutch at her arms in fear. The sound stopped; she was prepared to swear she had never heard it. When it started again, it was louder, and she knew right where to go, provided she wasn't too afraid to get up from the chair.

Shame on you. Suppose Colonel Junot had chosen to ignore you? Polly told herself. She rose, drew a deep breath, and walked down the corridor, pausing at one door, then moved to the next, until she found the right one. She opened it.

The window was tiny, but the moon shone in bravely, casting its light on an empty bed. Alarmed, Polly closed the door behind her, then let out her own cry of terror as someone grabbed her by the wrist.

The young girl had been hiding behind the door,

pressed against the wall. She barely came up to Polly's shoulder, making her wonder what age the French soldiers considered too young to violate. With a great gulp, she swallowed her fear and put her hand on the girl's hand, not trying to pry off her cold fingers, but just to let her know she had a friend. Whether any of that would be conveyed by her almost-involuntary gesture, Polly had no idea, but it was the only tool in her skimpy arsenal.

Since her Portuguese was non-existent, Polly thought of Sister Maria Madelena's well-meaning British lover and spoke as softly as she could. 'You've had a fright, haven't you? You must be tired. Let me help you back to bed.'

She moved, expecting resistance, but found none. Polly wondered if the girl had been sleepwalking. She led her back to bed, tucked her in, and then looked around for a baby. There was no crib. This must be one of the girls without babies that Sister Maria had mentioned. She found a doll made of surgical towels like the one her nephew adored, and tucked it in the crook of the girl's arm. With a sigh of relief, the girl—scarcely more than a child, herself—rested her cheek against it and closed her eyes as she caressed the towel doll. Polly sat with her until her breathing was slow and steady.

Shaken, Polly returned to her chair in the hall. She sat for only a moment, then hurried to another room, where a shriek was followed by a young child's startled cry. Polly ran to the room to find a young woman huddled on her pillow, her eyes wide and staring. She had wakened her child, who sat up in his smaller bed, crying. Polly went to the child first, soothing the little boy until he returned to sleep.

Polly sat on the bed, her mind a complete blank. In desperation, she started to hum a lullaby she had heard Laura sing to Danny. To her relief, the girl's eyes began to close and her head drooped forwards. She resisted Polly's first effort to induce her to lie down. After two more choruses of the simple tune, she did not object to sliding between her sheets again and closing her eyes. She did not release Polly's hand until she was deep in slumber.

'I understand you,' Polly whispered. 'Colonel Junot held my hand when I could have sworn the ship was sinking. Can I do any less for you?'

So it went all night. She went from room to room down her side of the intersecting corridor while Sister Maria Madelena did the same in the other hall. Some rooms she went to twice to console young girls too soon old. One girl could not be consoled until Polly took her in her arms and held her as a mother holds a child. Her horror at such terrible treatment at the hands of French soldiers turned to rage that anyone would harrow up the innocent. When dawn came, Polly knew she would never be the same again, not if she lived another fifty years.

Exhausted in body, one part of her brain wanted to sleep until the war was over. The other part told her she must return every night, until the last victim in the world had been consoled. She wanted to tell Sister Maria Madelena everything she had learned, but she was too tired to do more than nod, when the nun came to her and said it was time to leave.

They walked in silence. Soon Polly was back in the part of the convent familiar to her. She smiled to hear Philemon and her sister in the dining room, laughing over something, ready to begin their own hard days as she had just ended hers. She turned to the nun,

'How can you do that, night after night?'

'I cannot sleep at night.' The nun looked away, as if wondering what to say. 'I know what it is like.'

Polly didn't even try to hide her shock. 'Oh, Sister,' she said, her voice breaking. 'I...I... Oh, I didn't know.'

'When the French came, Mr Wilson brought me here, thinking it would be safe. We retreated to the kitchen when the...the *crapaud* came. She told me not to, but I tried to defend the Mother Abbess with one of the cook's knives. They took it from me, and then all of them held me down for their own amusement...' She couldn't go on.

'I didn't know,' Polly said again, appalled.

'When I thought they were done, they used my own knife against me. I was determined not to die, though all around me were dead.' She shrugged. 'Who else would bury them?'

Polly gasped. 'Surely you did not...?'

'I had help. Not all of the community were murdered. We made our way down the coast to Lisbon and safety. Mr Wilson was killed here in Porto, defending casks of port—imagine how unimportant that is, Polly. I decided to join the order.'

Polly could not detect an ounce of self-pity in Sister Maria Madelena's voice. 'And you are here again.'

'There is work to be done,' the nun said, her voice brusque again. 'Go to sleep now, if you can. Compline will come too soon, I fear.' She peered at Polly. 'You will join me again tonight?'

'Certainly.'

'Excellent!' Sister Maria Madelena nodded and turned towards the sound of children in the courtyard. 'Your nephew Danny and João have turned into such ringleaders! I had better go administer some discipline, or we will be accused of raising wolves in Porto.'

'João?' she asked, remembering the dark-haired child who played most often with Danny.

'Yes, my dear. He is *my* son.'

Chapter Eight

Polly knew she would not sleep, so she did not try. She sat at the desk in her room, took out a sheet of paper, and began a letter she would never send.

She wrote 'Dear Colonel Junot', then paused, because the word 'dear' loomed up at her like a vulgar word, even though thousands of letters began that way, even those from prosaic counting houses. She drew a line through it anyway, then crumpled the page. She reminded herself that the letter was going nowhere, and wrote 'Dearest Hugh' on another sheet.

Freed of that constraint, she said whatever she wanted. She described the long night of comforting sorrow of such a magnitude she scarcely could grasp it. The words poured on to the page, and another like it and another, as she wrote of the young girl who spent her entire night patting the bedclothes and searching the room for her little one, a half-French infant strangled at birth by a midwife in a remote Portuguese hamlet.

She faltered a moment, then wrote of the girls whose troubled minds compelled them to act out their rapes over and over. Maybe even more frightening were the young girls who lay perfectly still in as small a space as they could contort their figures, eyes wide and staring in the dark.

Exhausted and weary with tears, Polly wrote it all to Hugh Junot, her friend, so he would know what a pathetically tiny bit of good she was doing at Sacred Name. 'Knowing you'—she put down the pen, unable to continue for a moment. She picked it up, reminding herself calmly that she did know the man, and knew what he wanted to hear from her. 'Here is what I have learned: it is possible to survive, when all hope has perished.'

She didn't need to reread anything, because the experience of that night would never leave her mind, no matter how many years passed. Polly picked up the pencil again, rubbing it against the end of the wooden desk to get one more sentence from the lead, one more line no one would ever see. 'I wish you were here, Hugh. I would feel more brave.'

'I miss you,' she said out loud as she folded the letter. 'Your loving Brandon.'

Hugh kept himself supremely busy in Lisbon, which was not a hard thing to do, considering the confusion, intrigue, and bustle in the old seaport. Over excellent port, which only served to remind him of the town he had just left, Hugh listened as the Major in charge of the Marine detachment told him of the summer campaigns underway throughout Spain.

'Where are the armies?' Hugh asked.

'Sir, we believe Wellington is drawing out a fight near Salamanca. After that, if he wins, the road is open to

Madrid,' the Major said. He tipped the last of the wine into Hugh's glass. 'Could this be our last summer in this wretched country? Shall we drink to that?'

They did. The major invited Hugh to join him at his favourite brothel, but Hugh shook his head, returning some vague regret about reports to write.

Hours later, restless and tangling his sheets into ropes, Hugh wished he had accepted the Major's invitation. He knew how badly he needed the comfort of a woman's body. Trouble was, he only wanted one body, and its owner was far away, unaware of his admiration.

His thoughts were not chaste. He had never wanted a woman more than he wanted Polly Brandon. He got up and went to the window. *How does anyone explain this feeling?* he asked himself as he watched the Marine sentries below, taking their prescribed steps, about faces, and returns. *I never expected this. How is it I have lived on the earth this long, and never felt this way before?* It was just as well he had not accompanied Major Buttram to the brothel; he would only have disappointed whomever he paid to service him.

He was disgusted with himself. In her polite way, Laura Brittle had made it plain he was not to reappear at the convent in Vila Nova de Gaia. She was a sister watching out for her own, and he obviously did not meet her standards. In misery, he knew that if he paraded his rank before Laura Brittle, the family wealth, and a handsome estate in a charmed corner of Scotland, it would make no difference. Laura Brittle thought him too old, and he was not good enough.

He paced the floor, angry at the unfairness of it all. He

tried to remind himself of the misery around him in this tragic country, which had sacrificed so much, but it didn't work this time. He could only think of his sacrifices, and how this war had cost him wife and children. There was no one he could make love with whenever the mood grabbed them; no bright eyes looking into his as they shared the same pillow; no smile to greet him across the breakfast table, telling him prosaically of bills and schooling; no one to sit with in a pew on Sunday morning; no one to tease him when he stepped on her foot during a waltz, as he invariably would have; no one to turn the page for him when he played the piano; no one. It chilled him to the bone and gave him grief beyond parallel.

He sat at his desk. Laura Brittle be damned; he would write to Polly Brandon, even though it was an ill-mannered thing to do. 'My dearest love' came from his pen. He shared his whole heart to her, page after page, leaving nothing unsaid of an intimate nature. He had never been one to gild a lily, either, and he was too mature to begin now. When he finished, he signed it 'Love from all my heart, Hugh', then immediately ripped it into tatters.

'That's out of your system, you randy goat,' he murmured, and took out another sheet. He began this one 'Greetings, Brandon, from someone with rag manners. I suppose I deserve a slap across the face for being so bold as to write to you, but I am wondering how you are.'

This letter was as easy to write as the first one. He described Lisbon, that dirty, charming city so full of intrigue. He wrote of the Marines he had chatted to, his conversations with the great and the lowly. He told her he wasn't satisfied he had learned enough to write a report yet, but that autumn would probably see him back in

Plymouth, doing precisely that, and chained to a con-
ference table again. 'What, no sympathy from you,
Brandon? You don't like a whiner? Take care of yourself.
Hugh Junot.'

He read it through and found nothing objectionable.
Because he had the liveliest confidence the Brittles would
make sure Polly never received it, should he be so bold
as to send it, he added a postscript on the other side:
'Damn me, if I don't miss you, Brandon.'

He addressed it to 'Brandon Polly, Convent of the
Sacred Name, Vila Nova de Gaia', knowing full well he
would never send it. Still, it looked good on his desk,
almost as though these were normal times and he was
writing to a beloved wife far away. There was no reason
he couldn't just leave it there and return to bed.

When he woke hours later, he saw that the letter was
gone, along with yesterday's towel and last night's slop
jar. After his initial jolt, he found himself surprised that
Portuguese servants were so efficient. He relied on the
Brittles to intercept his bit of nonsense.

Polly knew she would never get accustomed to the
misery of her nightly duty at Sacred Name, but as July
wore on, she learned to adjust to it. Sister Maria Madelena
was right—because of her tender sympathy during night-
time ordeals, the little mothers had no hesitation in sitting
with her in the courtyard during the afternoons and
learning what little English she had time to teach. It went
well; so well, in fact, that she started taking out the letter
to Colonel Junot she was never going to post and adding
on to it, describing the mothers and children and their

efforts to learn English. 'You were right, Colonel,' she wrote. 'I am useful here.'

Her usefulness continued in a way she had not anticipated. She was not even certain she liked the next change—travelling upriver with Sister Maria Madelena to shepherd other young girls to the sanctuary of the Sacred Name.

'How do you learn of them?' Polly asked, as they sat with the children in the afternoon sun.

Sister Maria kissed her son, then sent him back to play. 'There is a network of interested folk who hear things. We take a *barco rabelo* upriver to the village of São Jobim, where we find the young girls waiting for us, some Portuguese, some Spanish.'

'It's not dangerous?'

The nun shrugged. 'Who is safe anywhere in Portugal? There has been no trouble in more than a year, although we always travel with a small detachment of Marines. You will be safe. Ask your sister.'

Polly did. 'I think that is an excellent idea,' Laura told her. 'Sister Maria tells me you already have a wonderful rapport with the young mothers. Perhaps it is because you are so young, yourself.'

'Laura, I am not so young, not compared to some of them. I'll be nineteen this autumn.'

Laura seemed almost surprised. 'Why, yes, I suppose you will,' she murmured. 'I was reminded recently that I am at fault in thinking you younger than you are. You may go upriver.'

Her only regret in the journey was the mode of transportation, one of the flat-bottomed sailing craft used to transport kegs of port wine downriver from wineries farther up the Douro. The war had disrupted the thriving business upriver and the *barcos* were used now to transport people across the Douro to Oporto proper, and to move what wine was available closer to Vila Nova and the ships anchored at the mouth of the mighty river.

'Ships are the bane of my existence,' Polly muttered the next morning to the nun as she allowed a Marine to help her into the craft as it bobbed at the wharf. 'I will claim a spot near the gunwale and try not to make a total fool of myself.'

The wind blew inshore, so the *barco* sailed along against the current, expertly guided by a Portuguese sailor at the long pole in the stern. She and Sister Maria Madelena watched the river narrow and its sides steepen as they travelled through the canyon cut by the Douro. Throughout the morning, Polly watched other *barcos rabelos* coming downstream flying British ensigns. There were wounded men on the deck, with surgeons bending over them. Last week, news had reached the convent of a battle in north central Spain in the Arapiles hills near Salamanca, and Philemon had told Laura over the breakfast table to prepare for casualties.

'My sister tells me even the army sends the worst of the worst to Philemon's hospital,' she couldn't help saying proudly to Sister Maria. 'It was only supposed to be a satellite naval hospital.' She looked closer. 'Oh, Sister, excuse me. I didn't realise you were praying.'

It was dusk by the time they reached the village of São Jobim. 'Ordinarily, we try to leave earlier in the morning, so we can make the trip in one day,' Sister Maria Madelena said, as they approached the wharf.

There were few people about. Polly couldn't see any men at all. She looked at Sister Maria Madelena, a question in her eyes.

'The men have gone with the army or the partisans,' the nun explained. 'So it is, in every village in Portugal.'

What happened once the *barco* docked was a marvel of efficiency, testament to how many times Sister Maria Madelena had made this voyage of rescue. From the Marines to the Portuguese mariners, everyone worked quickly. Escorted by the Marines, they were helped ashore and into the church across the square in a matter of minutes.

'I thought you said we were in no danger?' Polly asked.

'That is correct,' the nun replied, as she nodded to the priest approaching them. 'We are merely careful. Good evening, Pai Belo. Do you have someone for me?'

He did, pointing to a young woman huddled on a bench and shivering, despite the warmth of a late July sun only just now setting west across the Douro. Polly glanced at Sister Maria, as her eyes caught the motion of the priest passing a note to her. It was done so quickly she might have mistaken it. Well, never mind, Polly thought, going to the girl and sitting beside her. She knew enough Portuguese to murmur, 'You are safe now', not touching her, but sitting close.

Sister Maria joined her. 'Pai says she is from across the border, where other young girls have come lately.'

'It's so far,' Polly said, resting her hand gently on the girl's shoulder.

'Not so far,' Sister Maria contradicted. 'I come from beyond the border myself. I have a brother—' She stopped, as if to remember him. 'I have a brother there. It is not so far.'

They spent the night in the church, sharing a frugal

her about the letter, so Polly knew she had neither seen nor delivered it. Polly gave herself a mental shake and went back to work.

Chapter Nine

Hugh knew Polly Brandon would never answer his letter, if she even received it. He felt a little foolish as he listened every day for the drum rolls in the Marine barracks indicating mail call. He was a Lieutenant Colonel; any correspondence intended for him would have been taken to him. Still, he listened for the drum roll.

He had made the mistake of accepting Major Buttram's invitation to the brothel and spent an hour with a languid lass who otherwise would have pleased him greatly, if he hadn't been thinking of Polly. Too soon he found himself wishing that it was Polly's heels digging into his kidneys as he rode her, and Polly's breath warming his cheek, and Polly's head turning from side to side as he satisfied her, or at least, when she pretended so. Something told him Polly would never pretend, not if he was at the helm.

July turned into August and then early September, as he took one short hop to the Mediterranean on a sloop of war and visited the Marines on Malta, always a charming city to visit. He tried to drink himself silly one night, but that was an even greater failure than the prostitute in Lisbon. He had no real liking for any spirits other than grog, which had always been a source of amusement to his brother officers, who generally assumed he was, at the very least, a Madeira man. All he had to show for an evening in his cups was a head as big as all outdoors and Brandon's inability to maintain stuff in the gut where it belonged.

If women and liquor couldn't assuage him, he had more success writing his report back in Lisbon, busying himself with facts and figures. That lasted about three days, until he found himself staring at the wall and seeing Polly Brandon in the stucco. 'All right, lassie,' he said one afternoon to his wall, 'did ye or did ye not even receive my letter? If ye did, congratulations on having superior manners and not responding. If ye didna, well then, I'm nowhere different than I was when I started speculating. Lord, what a chowderhead. Listen to your sister and stay away from Marines.'

And that was that. Or it would have been, if he hadn't decided to take the next frigate north to Ferrol Station for a look around. His only interesting official correspondence had come encrypted from Plymouth. When the translated message reached his desk, he read of Admiral Sir Home Popham's campaign into the Bay of Biscay, with Santander as the hard-won prize. 'Major Buttram, I want to watch our Johnnies in action,' he said the next morning as he packed. 'Is something heading north at least to Ferrol Station?'

Something was—a sloop of war captained by a young Lieutenant. Considering all of his years rubbing shoulders with the navy, Hugh should have known they could not slide by Oporto without stopping, considering the drink-

ing habits of the Royal Navy's officers. The sloop's skip-
per had a heavy purse from thirsty men who wanted to
turn gold into port, alchemy common in the navy.

'We'll be here a day at least, I fear, sir,' the Lieutenant
said. 'I've promised port to ever so many ships. Um, if
you're bored, I hear there are excellent cafés in Oporto,
and the women are the...um...easiest in Portugal,' he
concluded in a rush, his face red.

The women are not easy in Oporto, Hugh thought sourly.
'I'll remain on board,' he said, and turned on his heel.

By early September, Polly had made four trips upriver
with Sister Maria Madelena. Typically, they left before
sunrise, to ensure a quick return that day. There were no
more lighters descending the Douro, bearing wounded,
because the season of campaigning was winding down.
Dispatches had reached Oporto that Beau Wellesley and
his army had marched in triumph to Madrid, and that
several French armies in the region were in motion, as
well, some moving towards the capital city and others
scattering. No one knew what to believe.

'And still there are those who need our help,' Sister
Maria Madelena said, as they came in sight of São Jobim.

Polly knew the routine now. She hurried ashore and
followed the sentries into the church, where the heavy
door swung shut and was barred. There were two girls this
time, one with a baby. Both of them, Spanish sisters,
shrank from the sight of the Marines, even though Sister
Maria Madelena said '*Ingleses*' over and over.

Polly wished she felt less uneasy about this run. Lately,
she had been watching Sister Maria Madelena and the
priest more closely. They almost always stepped aside

where no one could hear, to talk in low whispers, and sometimes exchange notes. They seemed to be arguing this time. The priest shook his head and there was no note.

'We would be a happier country without *any* soldiers,' Sister Maria said as they prepared to leave.

Polly wondered if she should speak. *What could it hurt?* she thought at last, and cleared her throat.

'Sister, did you feel that someone was watching us this time?' Said out loud, it sounded foolish; she regretted her words at once. Sister Maria Madelena would think her a coward. She never asked about the notes; the one time she had, the nun had ignored her.

'What's this?' the nun asked gently. 'Did you feel a prickling of your neck hairs? Fingers along your spine?'

'I am being foolish, I know,' she apologised.

'No, you're not. I felt it, too. I look around, then I remind myself that we are on God's errand.' She shrugged. 'The feeling always passes.'

Maybe for you, Polly thought.

Despite her misgivings, which Polly knew better than to voice again, the trip downriver was as calm as the other ones. She cautiously complimented herself on keeping down that morning's meal, and almost enjoyed the race down to the sea, propelled by a splendid current as the Douro rushed out of the mountains and gradually changed character into a dignified, formidable river that widened with each mile closer to the Atlantic.

They reached Vila Nova as the sun was low in the sky. The slower swells of the turning tide made the bobbing of the small vessel an instrument of torture to her sorely tried equilibrium.

Small, but bristling with guns, a sloop of war was tied to the dock. She glanced at it, then stared, because Colonel Junot stood there, gazing towards the convent. *It cannot be*, she thought first, mainly because she did not want him to see her looking so green under her unlady-like tan, and getting ready to lean over the side of the *barco*. Then, *Perhaps he will not notice me*, she told herself, as she vomited into the river.

If the Spanish girl's baby had not started to cry, maybe he would not have looked around in surprise. When he saw her, he flashed as broad a smile as she had ever seen.

He doffed his hat to her, and bowed.

'I am mortified,' Polly whispered to Sister Maria. 'He probably thinks I get seasick in my bathtub.'

'That is Colonel…how do you say…Junnit? He is the one who…'

Polly nodded. 'I did not really think I would see him again. Perhaps he will not come on shore.'

She couldn't look, but Sister Maria Madelena had no qualms about the matter. 'He appears to be heading to the gangplank, Polly,' she whispered back.

Faster than she would have credited, he was standing beside the *barco*, ready to give her a hand. He helped her over the gunwale and on to the dock, beamed at her, then held out his hand to the young woman with the baby, who hesitated.

'Almira, he is my friend,' Polly murmured in her sketchy Spanish, which changed the girl's worry to relief. Shyly, she handed her baby up to Polly, then took Colonel Junot's hand and let him help her on to the dock.

Suddenly too shy to say anything, Polly stood there with the baby. The Colonel was not smiling now, which caused her to look at him more closely, and then quickly hand the baby over to his mother.

'Colonel?' Something had happened, and she hadn't the slightest idea what it was.

'What were you doing upriver?' he asked, his tone chilly.

She felt like a child under his question. 'We…we retrieve young women from the interior of Portugal who have been…' She hesitated.

'…raped by the French,' he concluded bluntly, as she felt her face flame. He took her arm, a grasp more urgent than angry. 'Brandon, what harsh duty is yours at this convent?'

He took her to a bench and sat her down, then sat down beside her. He seemed to know he was taxing her; she watched him take a deep breath and visibly calm himself. He did not release her arm, but his grip loosened.

She almost wished now she had sent the letter in the bottom of her trunk. It would be easier than explaining to a man what she did. She took a breath of her own. 'Oh, Colonel, it *is* harsh, but not for me. The *pouco mães* wake up at night with terrible dreams. I go from room to room, trying to comfort them.'

His frown only deepened. 'That is not a job for one so young. Is there no one else who can do it?'

She winced, because he had touched a vulnerable place, one that had begun to trouble Laura. 'Colonel, they respond to me, and I certainly have their trust. I sleep in the mornings, and by afternoon, teach a little English here and there, although I must admit I seem to be learning more Portuguese. Some Spanish, too.'

She said that to hopefully make him smile a little, but he did not. What he said surprised her.

He released her arm then and sighed, leaning back

against the railing of the wharf, something she doubted he did very often, considering his military bearing. 'Don't go upriver again, Brandon,' he said finally.

'It's safe, Colonel,' she reminded him. 'Everyone says so.'

'Nothing is safe in the Peninsula,' he replied, and she could not overlook the concern in his voice. 'Armies are marching, and whenever armies march, all kinds of people are put in motion.'

'We don't go so far upriver. Just to São Jobim: six hours up, four hours back, or less.'

'It's too far,' he said flatly. 'Don't do it, Brandon.'

Suddenly, she wanted to agree with him, tell him about her misgivings, and never leave the shelter of the convent again. She might have, if she hadn't looked at Sister Maria Madelena just then, as the nun helped the two sisters with the baby into the back of the ox-led wagon that met every vessel.

She stood up. 'I have to go now,' she told him. 'Sister Maria needs me.'

Hugh had seldom felt helpless in his maritime career. He felt helpless now, because he had no *force majeure* to work on Polly Brandon, nothing a husband would have. He had no tie, no commitment, nothing beyond his feeble effort to get a good woman with charity on her mind to listen to his worries that, for all he knew, were totally unfounded. It was a position he did not like.

Still, he could tell that she left his side reluctantly. For the tiniest moment, he wondered what she would do if he told her he loved her and would she please listen to him? He was being absurd, of course—too bad for her, too bad for him.

Since she seemed disinclined to leave him there, even as the wagon began its slow trip to the top of the bluff, he walked beside her. He noted that her hair was twisted in its funny knot, with a skewer through it. Without thinking, he suddenly pulled out the wooden wand, and smiled when she laughed and hit his arm.

'Laura calls me a ragbag,' she said cheerfully, as she took the skewer from him and wound up her topknot again. 'Nana would scold me and ask how I ever planned to find a husband.'

Just look at me seriously, he thought. *You'd have your answer*. 'It's a good question, Brandon,' he said, thinking how stupid it was the moment he said it.

'Gentlemen never look past my spectacles, Colonel, so it doesn't matter. Philemon tells me to forge my own way, precisely as my sisters have done. Everyone has advice,' she grumbled.

She peered at him then in her kindly way that made him understand, no matter how grudgingly, what Sister Maria and the pitiful female dregs of war already knew: Polly Brandon was good and loyal and not afraid, no matter what she might say about herself to the contrary. They probably did need her. Too bad the thought gave him no comfort.

'Come to dinner this evening,' Polly asked him. 'Colonel? Colonel? When I used to woolgather like you are doing, Miss Pym would rap my knuckles.'

Wordlessly he held out his hand, palm down, and she laughed, even as she blushed. Delightful.

'I must say no,' he replied, as they continued their slow walk to the convent. 'I have already promised myself to the Lieutenant of Marines at the dock.'

She stopped. So did he. A fine frown line appeared between her eyes and she pursed her lips ever so slightly, just enough to make his back break out in sweat. 'Are you avoiding me?' she asked.

'No, ma'am, I am not,' he lied, 'even though dinner with Lieutenant Stephens means the mess hall. It is another opportunity to speak to the men I am interested in hearing from, to complete my report. I have a purpose here, too, you know.'

It came out more sharply than he intended, and Polly had nothing more to say as they walked to the top of the hill. He had shut her down, the last thing he wanted to do, especially when he was so worried.

'Perhaps I could stop by at two bells into the dog watch. That's seven o'clock, Brandon. You need to learn these things,' he added, although why that would be necessary, he couldn't say.

She grinned at him, then hurried ahead to catch up to the cart. He watched her go, admiring her purposeful stride that made her muslin gown sway so nicely, then did an about face and went down the hill.

Hugh hoped he would not see Laura Brittle when he returned to the convent at two bells, full of excellent Portuguese sausage and just enough grog to render him optimistic.

He barely saw Polly. She was lying in the grassy courtyard, dim now with twilight, a child sitting on her stomach and leaning against her upraised knees. The two were silently observing each other, until Polly suddenly darted her fingers into the soft places under his arms and he chortled. Hugh squatted on his heels beside her. The little boy observed him with solemn brown eyes, but did not seem intimidated.

'This is João,' she said. 'João, this is Colonel Junot.'

'You should teach him what my grandmama taught me,' he said. With his forefinger, he began to describe a wide but narrowing circle targeting the child's stomach. '"There was an old bee who lived in a barn, he carried his bagpipe under his arm, and the only tune that he could play was bzzz!"' He aimed his finger at the little boy's navel and zeroed in, to the child's delight.

'Say that again,' Polly demanded, as she raised her hand to do as he had done.

He repeated the little rhyme that every child in Scotland probably knew, as Polly's finger spiralled down, ending in the soft stomach of her totally willing target, who laughed again and made his own buzzing sound, as he tugged at her finger.

'The tough part now is to convince the child he doesn't want to do it any more,' Hugh teased. 'Good luck.'

She smiled at him, which made his heart leap, then continued the finger play. When another child tossed a ball in his direction, João finally moved off. Polly stayed where she was in the grass. 'I didn't think I would see you again,' she said.

'It was a surprise to me, as well,' he told her, as he plucked handfuls of grass and tossed them on her, enjoying her laugh as she let him. 'We are heading to Ferrol Station, where I hope to catch a coastal lighter to Santander. Apparently Admiral Popham has been using his Marines to good effect in taking the town.'

'Is it dangerous?'

He shrugged. 'No more than anything else during a war. When I finish, I will take a frigate to Plymouth.'

She was silent for a long time. He stopped scattering

grass on her and turned his attention to the children at play, obviously getting the last bit of fun out of whatever remained of daylight. He noticed Laura Brittle observing him from the shadows of the colonnade and nodded to her. When he looked back at Polly, she was asleep.

When on earth do you really sleep? he thought, wanting to pick her up and deposit her in a bed of his choosing. *I'm a fool*, he told himself, as he got to his feet, brushed the grass off his hands, and left the courtyard and the sleeping woman who meant more to him than anyone he had ever met.

Philemon sat farther away in the colonnade, holding his son. 'Do that bee thing for me,' he said.

Hugh laughed and did it again. 'It's probably a more popular export than Knox's spare Presbyterianism and oatmeal porridge. Certainly better than haggis, but what isn't?' He sat beside the surgeon.

'You have not been cured of my sister-in-law,' Philemon said, with utterly no preamble.

'No,' Hugh said, amazed at the surgeon's direct approach, but not entirely surprised by it. He had discovered years ago that people with no time to spare seldom wasted words.

'Then you can understand Sister Maria Madelena's need of her. Polly has such a calming effect on those broken reeds she ministers to.' Philemon kissed his son. 'Polly is so self-effacing that she has no idea of her effect on people. Maybe on you, too?'

'You know.'

'Of course I know,' Philemon replied, with all the complacency of a happily married man, damn his eyes. 'I am married to her sister, who has that same effect. I know

Laura Brittle better than any human alive, and I tell you these three daughters of a terrible man are rare and special.'

'Do you want me gone, too?' Hugh said bluntly.

'I don't think so. Don't be discouraged.' Philemon looked at Hugh, as though measuring him. 'I don't know what will happen with you and Polly; wartime is not so amenable to courtship. But things happen.'

'Maybe not right now, though,' Hugh said.

'Maybe not,' Philemon agreed, his voice as kind as one could wish. He nodded to his wife, who was approaching them, her arms held out for her son. 'Laura, take this rascal and put him to bed. I'll see the Colonel to the door.'

He was being dismissed. It was not late, but the Brittles probably wanted Polly to sleep as much as she could, before the midnight hours came when the young women were restless in their dreams.

Philemon was in no hurry to usher him out. They took their time getting to the massive door, with its Marine sentry. Hugh tried one more time.

'I wish Miss Brandon would not go upriver.' He stopped, not mistaking the wary look on the surgeon's face. 'I know, I know! You all think I am being overly proprietary. If the interior of Spain were not in such turmoil this past month, I would say nothing.'

'She's going again tomorrow,' Philemon said.

'No! Don't allow it.'

'We got word at dinner. There was one more girl who made it late to São Jobim. There was some sense of urgency in the communication from the priest.'

'Then insist on more of an escort,' Hugh said.

'Perhaps I can. It's going to be another day trip, that is all.'

'Brandon—Miss Brandon—doesn't have to go, does she?'

'I doubt she sees it your way, Colonel.' The surgeon looked him in the eyes. 'By the way, all mail is delivered to my desk. If Laura had seen the letter you so brazenly sent to her sister, she would have chased you out of the convent with a capital knife.'

'It was cheeky of me,' Hugh admitted. 'Did you deliver it?'

'Guilty as charged, Colonel Junot. You're not such a bad man,' Philemon said generously.

The surgeon's teasing gave him heart. 'Thank you! Now, if you could use your almighty powers of persuasion to convince your sister-in-law to stop those river trips, this Marine could embark for Ferrol Station and then Plymouth with an easier conscience.'

He could tell the surgeon was wavering, but he looked at his timepiece.

'I have to go, Colonel Junot,' he said. 'I'll think about what you suggest.'

Hugh sighed and walked slowly down the hill to the wharf, knowing he would toss and turn all night and probably get even less sleep than Polly Brandon.

Polly had managed to snatch a few moments of sleep in the corridor that night. Before dawn, after a quick kiss on Laura's cheek, she hurried to the wharf. The *barco*, still wreathed in shadows, was the only vessel showing signs of activity. She waited as the three Marines filed on board and sat down near the curved bow. Polly sat near the mast, wrapped her cloak tighter and closed her eyes.

'Goodbye, Brandon. I hope you have a wonderful life, wherever it takes you.'

Startled, she strained her eyes to see Colonel Junot standing on the dock, looking down at her. 'Why, thank you,' she said, wishing she didn't sound so furry with sleep.

He doffed his hat to her and she waved, then closed her eyes again, wishing he had not shown up last night, but determined not to be miserable. As the Portuguese sailor cast off the lines, she felt a sudden thump and a sway. To her utter amazement, she opened her eyes to see Colonel Junot pick his way carefully to the bow. He sat down with the sentries, who looked as startled as she did. He glanced over his shoulder at her.

'I just changed my mind,' he said. His expression suggested to her that he was as surprised as she was to find himself on the *barco*. 'The sloop of war won't get underway until night. You promise me we'll be back here by late afternoon?'

'Certainly. But why…?'

'I have a sudden hankering to see São Jobim, Brandon.'

Chapter Ten

Polly could have told him São Jobim wasn't much of a village. In a peaceful world, one where Englishmen with nothing better to do liked to take the Grand Tour, even the old church was not one of the Seven Wonders.

She couldn't overlook her growing discomfort that he had come along because he was worried about another trip upriver so soon after the last one. She knew he had better things to do, and she doubted he had ever done anything as lowly as escort duty in many years. Still, she had to admit there was some gratification in knowing someone was so concerned about her welfare.

To her relief, she kept down breakfast, which gave her some hope that she could outgrow her tendency to seasickness. *Anything is possible, Brandon*, she told herself, as she leaned against one of the wine kegs lashed to the deck. *Perhaps you can outgrow a certain fondness for the man who was so kind to you. Anything is possible, but it might be easier if he had not been so impulsive.*

She watched the Colonel as he sat with the sentries, impressed, as always, by his military bearing. She watched him gesture to the Private beside him, using what she knew were his considerable skills in getting the sentries to talk to him, man to man, and not as Private to Colonel. In his letter to her, he had told her what questions he asked, and how he was becoming more proficient in the art of interview. *At least I think I am*, he had written. *Perhaps I will show you my list of questions and you can tell me if I have forgotten anything.* Polly smiled to herself, wondering if she had memorised his entire letter.

He couldn't have picked a better assignment for himself, she decided, as she watched all three sentries unbend enough to talk and then laugh. The Colonel had a pad of paper resting on his thigh, and he wrote on it with a pencil, not even looking down, doing nothing to call attention to his actions. She knew it was more than mere command that compelled the sentries to relax enough to talk to Colonel Junot. 'If he says he is interested in what you do, he most certainly means it,' she whispered to herself. 'I could tell you that.'

Lulled by the monotony of motion, she closed her eyes again, relieved for no particular reason that Colonel Junot had decided so impulsively to come along. There was no reason she should feel any safer; unlike the sentries, he carried no weapon. In her brief acquaintance with so august a character, Polly knew he was steadfast. That was enough to send her peacefully back to sleep.

When she woke, he was sitting beside her, gazing out at the shoreline. They had entered one of the gorges where the river narrowed and the current grew stronger. The *barco* had begun to pitch and yaw as the two-man crew accommodated themselves to the new forces at play on their flat-bottomed boat. She sat up, well aware that this was the one place in the river's journey where she felt supremely entitled to her queasiness.

'It looks like a rough go here, Brandon,' was all Colonel Junot said.

She nodded, gratified and not a little touched that he had recognised the fact and come back to sit with her through the canyon. 'You're certain you are never seasick?' she asked.

He smiled and shook his head. 'Brandon, I have been bobbing about in small boats since I was not a lot older than your nephew. Do you want me to tell you about it?'

She did, even as she recognised what he was doing to keep her mind off the tumbling water as the *barco* pushed against the current. 'Indeed, I do, Colonel. Talk away, and distract me from all the waves and toothy things probably swimming around right under the water's surface.'

'You are a silly nod,' he told her, matter of fact. 'I am from a stretch of choppy water near Kirkcudbright, in the western part of Scotland. No one in our current generation has much of a clue how our French ancestor managed to end up in such an obscure place, but we're glad he did, cold knees and oatmeal notwithstanding.'

Her mind partly on the rough passage, but increasingly more on him, she listened as he told her of a childhood she could scarcely imagine: the oldest of three children, and the one always inclined to more adventure than his bookish little brother—now a barrister in Edinburgh—and his sister, who had his same love for tumult but the misfortune of her sex. 'Jeannie should be the Colonel Commandant of the Third Division,' Colonel

Madelena will let you stay at Sacred Name in the future, and avoid this watery purgatory.'

'Perhaps. I am inclined to agree.'

After one more visit to the gunwale, Polly sat back for the smooth portion of the ride, where the Douro widened out slightly, and the canyon was breathtaking in its wild beauty. It pleased her that Colonel Junot seemed to enjoy the view, too. When she returned to his side, he took hold of her again. Although she knew they had traversed the last gorge before São Jobim and she did not need his protective hold on her, she remained where she was in the security of his arms.

'Beautiful, isn't it?' she asked.

'Mostly I am noticing what an advantage anyone with a mind for mischief would have, sniping from canyon walls,' he told her. 'Then I notice the beauty of things next, Brandon. It's what I do. How many times have you made this trip?'

Polly decided he could change the subject faster than most people could think. 'This is the fourth or fifth. Why?'

'In that case, then I am impressed with your own toughness, considering how you feel about the water, and knowing these watery traps are here to ensnare you.'

'I like to make myself useful,' she said.

'I understand,' he replied, after some thought. 'Still, this is a war zone—yes, even peaceful São Jobim—and I worry. There's something about this place... Oh, well, I cannot put my finger on it. Brandon, doesn't a quiet life at home sound appealing to you?'

'I've never actually had a home,' she told him, 'but, yes, it sounds agreeable. It sounded agreeable after my first night in the English Channel.'

Junot told her. 'As it is, she and her husband run the estate west of Kirkie, since our da decided to indulge in a life of leisure in his old age. The estate will be mine some day—hopefully, not too soon.'

'Do you miss it?' she asked, wanting to reach out for him because she knew the upcoming stretch of water was a personal trial.

Maybe she made an involuntary gesture. Maybe he just knew almost as much about water as her brother-in-law Oliver. He took her arm and tucked it next to his side, forcing her to move closer to him, which bothered her not a bit.

'Aye, I miss it,' he told her, his lips close to her ear as the crew manoeuvred the *barco* expertly past the rocks and into a calmer place. 'More lately than usual. Maybe I'd like to drop a line in a trout stream I know about, and sleep in my own bed.'

It was too much. She ducked her head into his shoulder and he pulled her close with his other hand, speaking louder. 'Ah, now, Brandon. Do I have to do the buzzy bee to distract you?'

She tried to laugh, even as she swallowed the gorge rising from her sorely tried stomach. 'No,' she said, wishing she meant it. 'Let go!'

He did instantly, but put his hand inside the collar of her dress, gripping her, as she leaned over the gunwale. 'Brandon, it's a good thing you weren't married to one of Noah's sons. Imagine forty days and nights of this.'

'Don't,' she said as she sat back and he released her. 'I don't even like *reading* that stretch of Genesis.'

He laughed and wiped her mouth with her own skirt. 'I think…this is just my opinion, but perhaps Sister Maria as she could muster. She twisted around and slowly rose to her knees for her first look at the deck, which ran with blood now. So many green-coated soldiers had leaped on the *barco* that the deck canted away from the dock and towards the river, causing the blood from the dead Marines and crew members to pour in her direction as they came closer. How much of it was Colonel Junot's blood, she didn't dare speculate. He was unconscious, with the beginning of an ugly welt on his temple.

Polly knew she would never forget the sight before her. Her wimple torn away, Sister Maria Madelena knelt before her captors, who jabbed at her with their muskets, lifting her black skirt.

'Don't do that,' Polly said, her voice louder.

The soldiers wheeled around in surprise to look at Polly. Her own knees turned to jelly as their expressions went from surprise to speculation, much as a cat cornering a mouse. As two of the soldiers swaggered towards her, one already unbuckling his sword belt, she sat down, mainly because her knees had stopped holding her up. Her eyes on the soldiers, she yanked Colonel Junot into her lap and wrapped her arms around him.

The effort must have roused him. He shook his head slightly, uttering another quiet sigh. 'Brandon, we're in a pickle,' he whispered.

She watched the soldiers out of the corner of her eye, too frightened to look at what was happening to Sister Maria Madelena, but unable to look away. One of the Dragoons jerked her to her feet while another slapped her hard, then slapped her again.

Colonel Junot didn't want her to look, either. 'Keep your eyes on me,' he ordered. His voice tightened as he

'Hold still, Brandon. My God, don't move.'

Her cheek jammed against the deck, she had no choice but to do what he said. Terrified, she strained to hear his even breathing, knowing he must have been hit, and wondering at his own calmness in the face of calamity.

She thought she heard the remaining Marine returning fire, but then there was silence on the deck. To her frightened reckoning, a century or two must have rolled around before she felt the boat sway as men clambered on to the *barco*, shouting in French. She opened her eyes, which she must have screwed shut, and saw with terror that the damp under her cheek had turned pink.

The soldiers were dressed in green tunics, with reinforced trousers and copper helmets with fur lining that reminded her of pictures of Roman legionnaires. Their boots extended above their knees. 'What? Who?' she managed to gasp.

'Dragoons,' Hugh whispered in her ear. 'How's your French?'

'Adequate,' she told him, amazed that she could even get out another word, much less one that made sense.

'Don't move until I tell you. Oh, God!'

Please, please, don't let them shoot him again, she thought. She listened then, hearing what must have torn the words from him, as Sister Maria began to scream and then plead. More men jumped on the *barco* and then the footsteps came closer. Colonel Junot groaned as someone kicked him, and his hands, so tight around her body, went slack.

Turn and face them, she ordered herself as she struggled loose from the Colonel's limp grasp.

'Don't shoot him,' she said in French in as firm a voice

tried to move his arm, the one that must have been hit. 'And if you can think of something... My head...'

Only one feeble idea came to mind, one so puny that on an ordinary day, it would never have seen the light of day. She kissed Colonel Junot on his cheek and then his ear, all the while tightening her grip, looking at the approaching soldiers, who had stopped to watch, wary but interested. 'This is my husband, Lieutenant Colonel Hugh Junot of the Royal Marines. Please do not kill him.'

At nearly the same time she spoke, Colonel Junot did, too, also in French that sounded much better than hers. 'Don't touch my wife,' he said, his voice weak, but with as much determination as she had ever heard from any soul living. 'We are worth more to you alive.'

His eyes so serious, Colonel Junot kissed her cheek. He turned around again and made himself comfortable, his head against her breasts in a gesture both familiar and possessive. The French soldiers squatted on the deck, uncertain and coming no closer.

'Where were you hit?' she asked him softly in English. Then, 'We're married. I couldn't think of anything else.'

'The back of my arm. Nothing much. You can treat it with a strip of petticoat, my love,' he told her. 'As for being married, I couldn't think of anything else, either. I recommend it right now, even though our courtship was amazingly swift.' He took one of her hands that crossed his chest, and slid it inside his uniform jacket in an intimate move.

He sat so calmly that Polly felt herself begin to breathe normally again. 'I don't remember saying yes.' It was the feeblest of jokes in the most dire of situations, but she had to concentrate on him.

'You didn't say yes,' he assured her, settling back more comfortably. 'I told you it was swift. Brandon, we might keep each other alive. I can't think of a better way.' He took her hand out of his uniform front and kissed it. 'Apparently you couldn't, either.'

Sister Maria Madelena shrieked as the soldiers carried her off the *barco*, set her on her feet and stripped off her habit in one wrench, leaving her standing on the dock in her chemise. She dropped to her knees, crouching there with her arms wrapped around her, and looking around wildly.

'We have to do something,' Polly urged, even as the Colonel turned her face gently towards his chest and pressed it there with his hand, shielding her from the terrible sight before them.

'We won't do anything until I see someone above the rating of Private, Brandon. Just hold me. Look at me now. Not at the dock.'

She did as he said, even as she heard Sister Maria Madelena's terrified screams. Her breath must have been coming faster and faster, because the Colonel told her calmly to breathe in and out more slowly.

'We can't help her right now. If we try anything, you will be next,' he said. 'My God, Brandon. What can have happened?'

She shook her head, then looked up when she heard a new voice shouting at the dock. Another soldier ran from the church and was flailing about his own men with his sword, beating them back from Sister Maria Madelena. Polly looked down again, in tears now at the sight of the nun kneeling on the cobblestones, her arms pinned back, her head down.

'It's a Sergeant,' Colonel Junot said, and there was no mistaking the relief in his voice. 'Brandon, help me to my feet.'

Not even sure she could stand on her own, Polly surprised herself by doing exactly what he asked. She hauled him upright, and then braced herself against the gunwale as he sagged against her, then slowly straightened up.

'Don't let go of me,' Colonel Junot ordered. 'Put your hand through my belt. I'll hold you as tight as I can.'

She did as he said, clutching him in a firm grasp. The Colonel leaned against one of the kegs lashed to the deck as ballast. Polly gasped and turned her face into his uniform jacket when one of the soldiers on the dock grabbed Sister Maria Madelena by her arms, slung her over his shoulder and walked towards the church, even as she shrieked and begged for mercy,

'Deep breaths, Brandon,' Colonel Junot said. 'Perhaps I should call you Polly now.'

He stayed where he was, but he stood taller, almost willing himself into his usual impeccable posture and bearing, even though the welt on his face was turning a mottled colour and blood seeped from his sleeve. Polly released him long enough to hand him his hat, then twined her hand through his belt and clutched it.

'Sergeant, I am Lieutenant Colonel Hugh Junot of the Third Royal Marine Division of his Majesty's British maritime forces. I implore your protection for my wife, Polly.'

He spoke calmly, but his voice carried across the bloody deck, where the bodies of the Marines lay sprawled and the *barco* crew was silent in death. Polly held her breath as the French NCO scowled at them.

Decades seemed to pass before he gestured them forwards.

'One foot in front of the other, dear wife,' Colonel Junot said. 'That's how any journey begins.'

Chapter Eleven

Colonel Junot staggered, but Polly held him up, her arm tight around him. She draped his arm over her shoulder and they stumbled across the deck. When they reached the opposite gunwale, the Sergeant nodded to one of his Privates, who held out his hands and helped them to the dock.

'We did not expect to see a Colonel,' the Sergeant said in French. He gestured towards the dead Marines. 'We have been watching, too, for several days. Is the war going so ill for England that Lieutenant Colonels come on patrol? I cannot think you were much help.'

Polly felt Colonel Junot stiffen. 'No, I was not, was I? We are your prisoners, Sergeant.' With some effort, he unbuckled his sword without releasing her and handed it to the NCO, who grinned at the sight. 'I surrender to you and implore your protection for my wife.'

'Not you?' the Sergeant asked, a slight smile on his face, as he accepted the sword, then casually tossed it to a Private, who looked at it and threw it in the river.

'Damn! That was a gift from my father,' Hugh said in English.

The Sergeant laughed at the look on Junot's face. 'Why would anyone want your stupid sword?' he asked in French. 'Why do we even want you, Colonel? Your delicious wife? Now that is another matter.'

'Sergeant, I implore your protection for her,' Hugh said again, his voice softer this time, more pleading. Polly could hardly bear to watch him pawn his dignity, but there was the Sergeant, running the blade of his sword across her breasts now.

The Sergeant apparently had no intention of making anything easy. He walked around them, patting the back of Polly's dress with his sword, then ran the blade slowly down her hips and legs. Hugh set his lips more firmly in a tight line.

The Sergeant continued his leisurely circuit, this time standing too close to Polly and flicking her hair with the point of his sword. 'Here we thought only to bag partisan scum passing information, and what do I find but a Colonel? *Mon dieu*, war is strange.'

She flinched, scarcely breathing. When his words finally settled in on her terrified brain, she wondered if she had heard him correctly. 'Information?' she asked, hoping she sounded much braver than she felt.

Obviously enjoying himself at their expense, the Sergeant smiled broadly as he flicked the blade across the front of her dress, slicing off a cloth rosette. 'And you did not know? Answer this one carefully, *s'il vous plaît.*'

'There was nothing to know,' she replied, trying to slow her breathing so her breasts would not rise and fall so rapidly. 'What can you mean? Sister Maria Madelena and I come to São Jobim to take young women who have been—' She stopped, wondering at the wisdom of saying more about the girls violated by French troops. 'We come here to take young women to a safer place, in time of war.'

The Sergeant was practically standing on her toes now, his eyes on hers. Polly glanced at Hugh, who was breathing shallowly, too. The Sergeant took the pommel of his sword and put it under her chin, raising her face to meet his scrutiny. 'Why is this man along? Your husband, you say?'

'My husband is here because he has been in Lisbon for a month, is headed out on another assignment, and wanted to see me in between. I am certain you understand.'

The Sergeant stared at her. She gazed back, not even blinking. He took the sword from her chin. 'You must be a challenge for him,' he said, stepping back. He looked at Colonel Junot. 'How do you manage her?'

'Very gently,' Colonel Junot said, his voice firm.

'With a whip? How is she to ride?'

Polly felt the blood drain from her face, as Hugh stepped close to the Sergeant this time. 'Sergeant, I resent your foul comments about my lady,' he said, biting off each word, as if he spoke to troublesome Marine Privates, and not the man holding all the cards. 'Do not tell me Napoleon makes war on officers' wives now. I would not have believed him capable of that.'

The men stared at each other. Polly held her breath, waiting for the Sergeant to run the Colonel through with his sabre. At the same time, she felt a spark of pride at Colonel Junot's defence of her, and both of them so powerless.

Hugh spoke first, and his tone was conciliatory now,

although by no means subservient. 'Sergeant, has a mistake been made here? This nun only seeks to rescue those who often get trampled upon in time of war.'

'No mistake,' the Sergeant said crisply. 'None at all.' He shook his sword at Polly. 'We have been watching you.'

'In the greater scheme of things, I can't imagine why,' Polly murmured.

'Oh, you cannot? Let me enlighten you. This way, please, you two. Do you need some help, Colonel?'

'You're so kind to ask,' Junot said. 'My wife will help me.'

Escorted by Dragoons looking hugely interested, they followed the Sergeant across the small square. Polly stopped once when she heard a series of splashes, and looked back to see other Dragoons throwing the dead Marines and crew of the *barco* overboard. 'Sergeant, can they not have decent burials?' she asked, horrified.

'The British? Why, *madame*?' was all he said, sounding supremely bored.

'Don't worry, Polly,' Colonel Junot whispered. 'This is better. The bodies may get snagged on limbs and rocks on the way downriver, but perhaps one of them will reach Vila Nova de Gaia.' He sighed. 'It's puny, but all we have, my dear.'

She was silent then, as the full force of their capture slammed itself home. The village appeared deserted. Who knew what terrors the French had promised to the townspeople if anyone so much as made a peep to the allies downriver? Uneasy, Polly looked up at the Colonel, and was comforted to see him looking at her.

'We haven't had any chance to get our stories straight,'

he whispered in English. 'What say we've been married since June?'

'Where?'

'Vila Nova, where your brother-in-law gave you away.'

Thinking of Laura and Philemon brought tears to her eyes and she looked away. In answer, the Colonel tightened his grip on her shoulder and kissed the top of her head. 'We'll stick together like glue, Brandon,' he assured her. 'I'm not leaving your side.'

They reached the closed door of the church, thick doors that she already knew could muffle any sounds, because she had been inside several times and enjoyed the ecclesiastical quiet within. It was different this time. Shivers travelled up and down her spine as she heard Sister Maria Madelena screaming. Unnerved, Polly stopped, but was prodded from behind. In response, Colonel Junot pulled her in front of him, protecting her with his body.

The Sergeant bowed elaborately and opened the smaller man-gate. 'Do come in, Colonel and *madame*,' he said, gesturing as though he welcomed them to a farmhouse in Gascony. 'Think of this as a wayside shrine on the way to perdition.'

Even at mid-day, the squat building's interior was shrouded in shadow. This was no church of the Renaissance, but a shabby little relic of the Middle Ages, charming in its own way, but not now, and probably never again.

Clad in her chemise, Sister Maria Madelena crouched below the altar, her screams tinged with madness. Before she could react, Colonel Junot turned Polly's face into his tunic. 'Oh, God, don't look!' he said, his voice suddenly filled with horror. She felt his fingers shaking as he forced her against him.

Other hands pulled his fingers away, compelling her to stare at the altar and then up to the large crucifix, where the French soldiers, those students of the Revolution, had crucified São Jobim's parish priest. Naked, pitiful, he hung on the cross, his arms bent at weird angles, his head down as though contemplating the ruin of his pudgy body. In his own death agonies he had moved his bowels.

Polly couldn't help herself. Her knees sagged and it was the Colonel's turn to hold her up. He stepped in front of her, blocking the view, but she knew she would never forget the sight before her. She wanted to close her eyes and keep them shut until the whole nightmare went away and she was back on the *barco*, with nothing more on her mind than negotiating the next stretch of white water. How puny that seasickness had been her biggest fear, how trivial.

Instead, she opened her eyes and looked into the Colonel's concerned face, so close to her own. 'I'll be all right,' she whispered to him. 'The poor man. What did he do to deserve this?'

Colonel Junot shook his head. 'There is a deep game going on here, Polly. I don't think we know even half of it.'

With his help, she stood upright again and turned away resolutely, to find herself looking at Sister Maria Madelena, kneeling and sobbing. Shaken, Polly turned her attention to the Sergeant, who seemed so sure of himself, almost swaggering in his command of this sorry situation. This was probably no more than a typical day for him. 'How can you permit your men to…to…?' She stopped, unable to think of a word to adequately cover what was happening, considering her own genteel Bath French.

The Sergeant mocked her expression, bowed elaborately, and held out a note. 'Perhaps you might consider what she has been doing to *us*!' he declared, triumph in every line of his body.

As she watched, aghast, he stalked over to Sister Maria Madelena and shook her by the hair. Colonel Junot tightened his grip on her when she started towards the nun. 'Don't move,' he whispered. 'These men are wolves.'

'But he's—'

'Stand still.'

She did as the Colonel said, even when the Sergeant tightened his grip on Sister Maria's hair and pulled her head up. 'Tell this Colonel's wife how you have been taking notes from the priest to the Navy docks in Vila Nova,' the Sergeant roared, shaking her head like a terrier with a mouse.

'Sister Maria, you don't have to tell me anything,' Polly said in English, as the Colonel tightened his arms around her.

'Tell her!' the Sergeant demanded of the nun, shaking her again and again until Polly wanted to scream. He looked up at the dead man and let go of Sister Maria Madelena. 'We…persuaded the priest to admit he gave her communiqués to pass on from the interior. Tell her, you whore!'

Polly couldn't stop shaking, not even with Colonel Junot holding her so tight. She leaned back against him, trying to keep the crucified priest and nun out of her sight. 'Sister Maria?' she asked softly, her voice quavering.

The Sergeant released the nun and she struggled into

a sitting position, trying to cover herself with her arms. As Polly watched, horrified, she willed herself into a state of calm and then slowly raised her bruised head and held her hands out, palms up, in supplication.

But it wasn't supplication. Polly jumped when Sister Maria Madelena suddenly clenched her hands into fists. Her tired eyes flashed, and the scar across her face stood out in raw, red relief against her paleness.

'*Viva Portugal e viva España!*' she declared in a loud voice.

'There's your answer, Polly,' Colonel Junot murmured in her ear. 'She *was* a messenger. Is she even a nun?'

'I…I…I didn't know,' Polly whispered. 'I did wonder once…. I thought I saw a note.' She turned her face into Colonel Junot's tunic. 'I do know she was a victim, too, like the young women we cared for.'

'Madame Junot,' the Sergeant said. He was closer to her now, stepping over the nun, who had slid back on to the stones, exhausted and drained. 'Madame Junot?'

'Polly,' Colonel Junot said in English, 'he is talking to you. Polly, pay attention and remember who you are.'

It was her turn to get a firm grasp on her emotions, to dig down deep inside herself where she had never gone before, and pull out more courage than she knew she possessed. Perhaps the Sergeant would not know how terrified she was. He was addressing her as Madame Junot; she would have to remember that and respond.

'Yes, Sergeant?' she said, as she rubbed her cheek gently against the Colonel's tunic as his hand went up to caress her hair.

'Did you know of this deception? Do answer carefully.'

I am no liar, she thought. She continued to rest her head against Colonel Junot, as she realised it was time to think of him as Hugh, the dearest person in her universe. She chose her French with precision. 'Sergeant, on the last trip, the one yesterday, I thought I saw her take something from Pai Belo. It was the merest glimpse. It could have been anything.'

The Sergeant grunted and took the folded scrap from his tunic again. 'This is what he gave me today, just before we hoisted him on high.'

Polly shuddered as she looked at the bloodstained sheet. To her horror, it was covered with numbers, and she recognised the Portuguese words for 'regiment' and the names of Spanish towns.

'We have other messages,' the Sergeant told her, folding the note. 'How many trips have you made to São Jobim?'

'I hope you are not planning to implicate my wife in any of this,' Hugh said.

She wondered at his ability to sound so protective, when he was as much a prisoner as she. 'Hush, my love,' Polly said. 'This is my fifth trip, Sergeant. That is all. I have only been in Vila Nova for eight or nine weeks, visiting my sister.'

'And not your husband?'

She realised her mistake, and fought down panic. *I am no actress, either*, she thought. 'Sergeant, surely that goes without saying. We were only married in June, and this war keeps getting in our way.'

To her relief, he seemed to find her statement funny and laughed. 'Oh, you British!' he exclaimed, his tone almost fond in a way that Polly found more repulsive than a curse. 'What am I to do with you?'

'What will you do with *her*?' Colonel Junot asked, looked at Sister Maria Madelena.

The Sergeant glanced around almost carelessly, as though she was already someone in his distant past. He shrugged. 'I will turn her over to my soldiers. They will make sure she is dead when they are done. You can watch. In fact, I will insist.'

Unable to help herself, Polly sobbed out loud. 'Shh, shh, my love,' the Colonel crooned, his hand gentle on her hair again. 'I have no say in this, Sergeant, but I wish you would just kill her outright. If she must die—if she is a spy, you have your rights, I acknowledge—then kill her cleanly.'

The Sergeant smiled and squatted on the floor by Sister Maria. He lifted her head by the hair. 'Do you hear that? This Englishman harbours a soft spot for guerillas like you.'

'Viva Portugal,' she murmured.

Her heart in her throat, Polly watched the Frenchman as he squatted there, engaged in thought. He rose then, and inclined his head towards them. 'Very well, Colonel. Since you are so concerned, you kill her.'

Hugh made that same huffing sound that had escaped him on the *barco* when he was shot. He took an involuntary step back and Polly had to steady him as he threatened to topple them both.

'Please, Colonel,' Sister Maria whispered from the floor. 'Please.'

Polly reached both arms around the Colonel and held him as close as she could, her hands splayed across his broad back. He buried his face in her hair, and she just held him.

The Sergeant came closer until Polly smelled all his dirt and perspiration. 'In fact, Colonel, I insist. If you do not kill this spy, I will see that your little wife suffers the fate I originally intended for her, and you can watch that.'

'I will do it,' Hugh said immediately. 'Certainly I will. Hand me a pistol.'

The Sergeant laughed as he gestured to one of his men. 'Don't you wish you had not come upriver today, Colonel?'

While the Sergeant took Hugh aside and handed him the pistol to load, Polly gathered up more courage from a hitherto unknown source. Ignoring the soldiers, she walked to the nun, knelt on the floor and wiped Sister Maria's battered face with the altar cloth. She draped the cloth around the woman's bare shoulders.

'I never meant you to be involved,' the nun whispered.

'I wish you had not invited me upriver,' Polly replied, dabbing carefully around the woman's ears. 'How could you put us in such danger?'

She hadn't meant to be harsh, not with a woman about to die, but she could not help herself. *I can repent later*, Polly told herself resolutely, as she dabbed away. *If there is a later.*

'I love my country more,' Sister Maria said. She grasped Polly's arm with fingers surprisingly strong. 'Watch over João for me.'

Polly nodded, ashamed of herself. 'We will treat him as our own son.' She glanced at Colonel Junot, surprised at herself. *He is not my husband, but that came out so naturally*, she thought.

Sister Maria Madelena nodded, her face calm now. 'Come closer,' she whispered.

Polly crept closer on her knees, as though to arrange the woman's hair.

'I never was a nun. Hear me out! My brother is El Cuchillo, a guerilla of León. He said he would always watch out for me...' Her voice trailed off and she looked up at the dead priest above them. 'Perhaps one of his men is watching now. Be ready for anything.'

'Don't give me false hope,' Polly whispered. 'You have done enough.'

There was more she wanted to say, but she knew it would not make her feel any better. Then the moment was gone, when one of the soldiers grabbed her by both elbows and lifted her off the floor. She shrieked, unable to struggle.

'Polly, my love, steady as you go,' Hugh said, as the soldier pinioned her arms behind her back and led her away from Sister Maria Madelena, who crouched and clutched the altar cover, her face calm.

'Madam Junot, you must not struggle so!' the Sergeant admonished. 'I am handing your husband a pistol now. You are my guarantee that he will not turn it on me.' He shrugged elaborately. 'Call me cautious. I have not lived from Jena and Austerlitz by being overly trusting. You understand?'

'I understand,' Polly replied, her voice soft. 'I'm sorry, Hugh.'

His face pale, his eyes so serious, the Colonel looked at her for a long moment, as though willing her to understand that what was about to happen was not his choice. No matter—she knew that, and tried to communicate her emotions with a return gaze as compassionate as his own.

He squared his shoulders and took a deep breath. 'I will

do this my own way, Sergeant, and in my own time. Don't interfere with me or my wife.'

He stood a moment in silence, head bowed, then walked to the altar, where Sister Maria Madelena knelt. He squatted beside her and carefully draped her hair over her shoulder, away from the back of her neck.

'What is your name, my dear?' he asked, his voice conversational.

'Maria Ponce, from León,' she replied in English, 'although my family is originally from Portugal. Your wife will tell you of my brother.'

He squeezed her shoulder gently, stood up, and cocked the pistol. 'God forgive me,' he said.

'He already has,' Maria Ponce said.

Polly tried to look away, but the Sergeant put the blade of his sword against her neck and gently forced her to watch.

'If there is any foolishness, Colonel,' the Sergeant called, 'I will violate your wife myself.'

'I know that,' Hugh said with a certain weary patience, as though he dealt with a child. 'There will be no foolishness. You have my word as an officer and a gentleman, if that holds any merit with a soldier of La Belle France.'

'It's quaint, but I like it,' the Sergeant said. 'An officer, a gentleman, a murderer. Hurry up.'

Hugh pointed the pistol towards the nape of Maria Ponce's neck, then lowered it. 'No. Not this way,' he said, speaking to the Sergeant. 'I don't want my wife to see this.'

'Poor you,' said the Sergeant, when he finished laughing.

'I mean it,' Hugh said. Polly watched as he seemed to stand taller. 'Sergeant, do you have a wife?'

The Dragoon took the blade of his sword away from Polly's neck. She held her breath. 'I do. She is no concern of yours.'

'What is her name?' Hugh asked calmly, with all the force of his rank and age behind the question, to Polly's ears. *You are so audacious*, she thought. *You are trying to bend this man to your will and you have no power whatsoever.*

'Her name is Lalage,' the Sergeant said, speaking as though addressed by a French officer, and not a British captive. Polly could hardly believe her ears.

'Lalage is a beautiful name,' Hugh said. 'Madame Junot is *my* Lalage. She is my love and my life. Would you want *your* Lalage to witness what I must do here? I cannot imagine a loving husband would do such a thing in France.'

Polly reminded herself to breathe as the two men stared at each other. The Sergeant looked away first. He sheathed his sabre and took Polly by the arm, shoving her towards one of his Dragoons.

'Take her outside. Sit with her on the steps.'

'*Merci*, Sergeant,' Hugh said. 'I would ask all of you to leave. Let this be between me and Sister Maria Madelena.'

'I can't do that!' the Sergeant protested, but his voice had lost its edge.

'You can, Sergeant,' Hugh said. 'If this woman kneeling before you is not dead when I come out of the church, you may shoot me next, after I have killed my own Lalage.'

Again the two men stared at each other. Again the Sergeant yielded. He gestured to his troopers, who followed him into the sun. Polly felt as though she stood on blocks of wood instead of her feet. With a look at Colonel Junot, one that tried to convey every emotion she was feel-

ing, she forced herself into motion and left the chapel of
São Jobim.

The sun was hot on her face. She welcomed the
warmth, even as she shivered and knew she would never
be warm again. The Sergeant sat her down on the top step,
then pulled her up gently and took her down several more
steps. He sat down beside her, not looking at her.

Polly steeled herself against the sound of the pistol, but
when it went off, she still jumped and cried out. The Sergeant gripped her shoulder, but it was not the grip of a
captor. He did not release her until she heard Hugh's steps
behind them.

He came towards them slowly, going down each step
as though he weighed a thousand pounds. Polly knew if
she lived to one hundred, she would never be able to entirely erase from her mind his expression. She couldn't
interpret it. She had thought to see revulsion at the terrible
act he had been forced to perform. There was something
thoughtful in his look, instead. If she hadn't known it was
impossible, she would have called it relief.

He sat down heavily beside her and gathered her close
to him, his grip as tender as the Sergeant's had been.

'Where is the pistol?' the Sergeant demanded.

Hugh shook his head and gestured behind him. 'You
can get it. I'm not going back in there.' He looked across
Polly at the Sergeant, wonder in his voice now. 'I pointed
the barrel right at the nape of her neck. Before I could fire,
she grabbed the gun and killed herself.' He began to weep.

It was Polly's turn to gather him close, uttering sounds
of comfort that had no language, as he sobbed into his
hands. To her surprise, the Sergeant and the Dragoons left
them there on the church steps as they went inside again.

'Oh, Colonel,' she whispered into his neck, at a total loss for words.

'From now on, I am "Hugh, love" to you,' he said, after a long moment. 'Never forget it. Our lives depend on it, Polly, dear wife.'

They held hands and sat as close together as they could while the Dragoons finished up whatever business they had in the church. When they came out, the Sergeant gestured for them to stand up.

'What do you intend to do with us, Sergeant, now that Sister Maria has done our dirty work?' Hugh asked.

'Dirty work it is, Colonel,' the Sergeant said. 'Do you know who the whore's brother is?'

'El Cuchillo,' Polly said. 'Sister Maria told me before she died.'

The Sergeant's smile broadened. 'Poor you, indeed, my Colonel! He is a guerilla leader of León, where we are heading.' He sheathed his sword. 'I have always been amazed how word gets around. El Cuchillo will probably assume you killed his sister. You might as well paint a bull's-eye on your back.'

'Perhaps you should just kill me now,' Hugh said, pulling Polly closer.

The Sergeant laughed and shook his head. 'And miss the fun? Never. They say he likes best to kill with a long needle through the eye.'

'Well, into every life some rain must fall, I suppose,' Hugh replied, with just a touch of amusement.

'You're a cool one,' the Sergeant said.

'No, I am not. Actually, let me suggest a very good reason why you should keep me and my wife alive.'

The Sergeant looked down on them from the step

above, perfectly at ease again and in charge, looking for all the world like a cat with cornered mice. 'Colonel, will you never cease to entertain me?'

'Probably not,' Hugh said, his tone equally affable. 'In a word, Sergeant, money. This knowledge is for you alone. You have no idea how rich Madame Junot is.'

Chapter Twelve

'So that is why you married her,' the Sergeant said.

Polly flinched, which made Hugh's heart sink even lower. *Bastard!* he thought. *Damn the man.* But this was no time to argue, so he merely shrugged. 'Think what you will. I am speaking of money. *Dinero, dinheiro, denaro, geld.* Think of all the words for money you have learned as you have tramped through Europe! Imagine that in your pockets.'

He had no idea how this would play. If today was his unlucky day—so far, there was nothing to dispute the notion it could be the unluckiest day of his life—then he had just attempted to bribe one of the few incorruptible men in anyone's army. He stood up, pulled Polly to her feet, and started walking away from the church. One step, two steps, another. The Sergeant did not stop him, but walked at his side. Was it possible even a battle-hardened veteran of Napoleon's campaigns didn't care so much for what had just happened? One could hope; Hugh did. But then,

'A bribe? You want to bribe *me*, Colonel?' the Sergeant asked, putting out his hand to stop them.

I found the only honest man in Napoleon's army, Hugh thought with regret. *Well, then, we have nothing to lose.* 'I suppose I do,' he said frankly. 'One doesn't make Colonel without exercising some initiative. Not in the Royal Marines, at least.'

He knew how that sounded in English. In French, Hugh thought it had a certain Gallic panache. At least the Sergeant hadn't motioned for one of his men to run him through with a sword.

In fact, the Sergeant was smiling—a little smile, to be sure, but a smile. After a long pause, the Sergeant even chuckled. *In for a penny*, Hugh thought. 'It's not for me, especially,' he said. He turned to Polly and gave her a kiss on the temple and a little shake to get her attention. 'And it's not even just for my wife.' He nudged Polly again. 'Shall I tell him, darling?'

He looked her in the eyes and she gazed back through those spectacles that magnified her eyes a little. *Follow me with this*, he thought, trying to communicate through nothing more than a look, something he knew his parents, married years and years, had been quite good at. To his infinite relief, she inclined her head towards him as though the conversation was a delicate one.

'It's this, Sergeant: my wife is in the family way. I especially want her to survive this experience and at least give my estate an heir.'

To her credit, Polly didn't even flinch. He knew she understood his French, because her lips came together in a firm line and she concentrated on her shoes.

'If you can help us, it is worth a great deal to me, Sergeant,' he concluded simply.

They were in the square now. Hugh concentrated all

his attention on the Sergeant, even as his skin crawled at the sound of women and children screaming in some of the buildings. The Sergeant seemed almost reflective, as though he stood in a glade in southern France filled with carnations. *My God, these are hard men*, Hugh thought. He almost hated to interrupt the thought process of a man who obviously had the power to end his life in the next second, but time was passing.

'I know you have a wife, Sergeant,' he said. 'Do you and Lalage have children?' Maybe it wasn't such an unlucky day. While not appearing to stare, Hugh watched the Sergeant's face, and at least thought he saw a slight thawing. He breathed more regularly when the Sergeant gestured with his hand towards a bench and spoke to Polly.

'Madame Junot, let us sit here. You look done for.'

It was probably the understatement of the ages, considering what had just happened in the chapel. Polly nodded, her pale face tinged with pink now, as though she were shy about sharing her *faux* husband's phony admission with a complete stranger, much less the enemy.

Hugh kissed Polly's temple again and whispered in her ear as he sat her carefully down on the bench, 'You're a game goer, Brandon.'

In response, she burrowed in closer to him, shivering in the warmth of the afternoon sun. In a more familiar gesture, Hugh put his hand on her waist and pulled her as near as he could. She responded by resting her hand on his thigh. *Bravo, Brandon*, he thought, enjoying the act.

'Can I get you some wine, *madame*?' the Sergeant asked.

Polly nodded, and the Sergeant gestured to one of his men and made his request. The Corporal shook his head and indicated there was none. The Sergeant merely nodded philosophically. 'We travel light, *madame*. Perhaps he can find something in this pathetic village.'

'Water will do,' she said.

The Sergeant was silent until the Corporal returned with water in an earthen jar. Polly tried to take it from him, but her hand shook so badly that Hugh took it instead and held the jar to her lips until she sipped. A frown on his face, the Sergeant observed her terror.

He spoke at last. 'We have two sons on a farm near Angoulême. It is a small farm.'

Hugh nodded. 'If you will see to my wife's safety, I can promise you your wife will receive whatever sum you consider appropriate.'

The Sergeant nodded, and gazed across the small square of São Jobim, where his men were methodically going through the buildings. He rubbed his unshaven jaw, looking unconcerned as flames suddenly roared skywards from a home. It was just another day in Portugal.

'Of course, I cannot promise anything until we—or she—is restored to Allied lines, but you can trust us to deliver what you wish, and where,' Hugh added, keeping his voice soft, hoping not to distract from whatever the Sergeant might be thinking.

'Because you are an officer and a gentleman?' the Sergeant said suddenly, and his voice was harsh again.

'No. Because I want to be a father,' Hugh said. 'You understand.'

The Sergeant stood up suddenly and slapped his worn gauntlets on his thigh. Hugh had always been a praying man, much to the amusement of his fellow Marines, and he prayed now, as the Frenchman weighed the offer on a scale of delicate balance.

Polly tipped it, to Hugh's everlasting relief. 'Sergeant, what are your son's names? And who are you?'

The Sergeant looked down at her, and Hugh thought he saw pity in the man's eyes, as brown as his own, and something more: a father's love. 'Emile and Antoine,' he said. 'I am Jean Baptiste Cadotte. Colonel, I will help you if I can.'

'I am in your debt,' Hugh replied simply.

'I can promise you nothing.'

'I know that.'

Most of São Jobim was blazing when the Dragoons mounted the horses that had been stabled inside the town hall. Two of the lighter men doubled up and the Sergeant directed Hugh to mount the other horse. He tied Hugh's hands together, then tied Polly's, only not so tight. To Hugh's amusement, Cadotte directed a man to hand her up carefully to sit in front of him. She tried to sit sideways at first, as though she rode a sidesaddle, but gave that up quickly and threw her leg over the saddle, which raised her skirts to her knees. To her credit, Polly scarcely seemed to mind. Directing her to lean forwards, Hugh raised his roped arms and lowered them over her body, resting them against her stomach. The Corporal took the reins and led the horse behind his own.

Polly was still shaking and there was nothing he could do about that. After what seemed like an hour of travel on what was a little-used track, he felt her shoulders lower as her jangled nerves attempted to relax. She said nothing, though, which suited him well enough, since he couldn't think of any words to comfort her. Just as well. Unaccustomed to riding horseback, Hugh felt his inner thighs begin to burn and his buttocks go numb.

* * *

After several hours of steady climbing, Sergeant Cadotte raised his hand and the Dragoons stopped. Everyone knew what to do. In another moment, all the men were urinating into the road.

'My blushes,' Polly said, the first words she had spoken since leaving São Jobim.

Hugh chuckled. 'Boys will be boys,' he told her. 'I hope Cadotte will take a little pity on us, too.'

He did. When the men were standing by their mounts again and eating what looked like hardtack, Sergeant Cadotte sent a trooper to help Polly off the horse. He untied her hands and helped her down, then indicated that Hugh should throw his leg over the saddle and slide off.

'I can't,' Hugh said, looking at Cadotte. 'Sergeant, you'll have to appreciate that I am a Royal Marine and not a horseman of any kind. Undo my hands, please, and I will struggle off and probably fall on my face, to your total amusement.'

Cadotte laughed and told the Private to untie his hands, but was kind enough to steady Hugh as he dismounted. He sank immediately to his knees. All the men in the troop laughed, but Hugh only shrugged and staggered to his feet.

'You meant what you said,' Cadotte murmured. 'Take your wife and go relieve yourselves.'

'Merci,' Hugh said with a grimace. 'Just let me stand here a moment and see if there is any blood in my pathetic body willing to circulate to my ass again.'

'But he is never seasick,' Polly said suddenly in French, which made the men laugh again.

In good humour, Cadotte gestured to the stand of trees.

'Have a little privacy, Colonel. That ought to be worth the price of a few cows at my farm by Angoulême.'

'A whole herd,' Hugh said as he took Polly by the hand. 'Come, my love, and let us find a tree.'

To his relief, the Dragoons turned away and squatted on the far side of their horses, some smoking and others conversing. Wincing at every step, Hugh led Polly into the stand of trees. 'Well, my dear, turn your head and give me a moment.'

Her face bright red, she did as he said. When he finished and buttoned his trousers, he pointed towards a fallen log. 'It's the best we can do, Brandon,' he said, and turned around to face the Dragoons on the road while she took care of her own business.

'You needn't stand so close,' she scolded, when she had finished and joined him.

'*Au contraire, ma chérie*, I'm going to stick to you like a medicinal plaster. If you have any inhibitions about that, I suggest you abandon them right here.'

He watched her expressive face, still red, as she considered his words, then nodded. 'Consider them abandoned, Colonel—'

'No. No. "Hugh, my love",' he teased.

'Hugh, my love, you're trying me,' she shot back, which made him smile and took the lump of fear out of his stomach for the first time.

He draped his arm across her shoulder and gave her a squeeze. 'Adventures never are as much fun as bad novels make them out to be, Polly.'

'I can see that,' she said, as she tucked her fingers in his swordless belt. 'Just don't think for a minute you are going to take advantage of me!'

He kissed her temple and whispered in her ear, 'I already did, Polly. You're going to be a mother, remember?'

'How could I forget such an immaculate conception? I defy even the Pope to be more surprised than I.'

They laughed together, which made Sergeant Cadotte turn around in surprise. With a scowl, he motioned them closer to retie their hands and continue the journey.

They travelled off the beaten track until they came to a deserted village just at sunset. The casual way the Dragoons rode into the abandoned town told Hugh volumes. 'I think this must be where they bivouacked on the journey to São Jobim,' he whispered to Polly. 'Look how familiar they are with it. They knew it was deserted.'

He could feel Polly sigh against his chest. 'We might have been travelling on the moon,' she whispered back. 'This poor country. Does no one live in the interior any more?'

'Precious few, I gather. Only think how many armies have picked it clean, like a flock of vultures dining on one thin rabbit.'

Hugh put his head closer to hers to keep his voice low, but also because he could not deny the comfort he derived from her presence. 'I can't help but think this patrol of Dragoons was a forlorn hope.'

'I don't understand.'

He could see Sergeant Cadotte watching them. 'I'll tell you later.'

With help, they dismounted for the first time since the afternoon, with the same results. In agony, he leaned against Polly, who held him up, then kissed his cheek. 'You Marines are pretty worthless on horseback,' she chided.

'Aye, aye, wife. Just wait until you're back on a ship.'

He wanted her to laugh, but tears came to her eyes. 'Hugh, it couldn't be a moment too soon, even if I vomit from Oporto to Plymouth,' she whispered, her face turned into his chest. All he could do was hold her and silently agree, with all the longing of his deepwater heart.

Expertly, the Dragoons took their mounts into the half-burned church while Hugh and Polly stood in the square, then gradually edged over to a bench, where he spent a long moment trying to decide if sitting down again was worse than standing. He sat down gingerly, grateful at least that the bench wasn't going anywhere.

The evening meal—eaten in a barren interior court-yard—continued to confirm his suspicions about the nature of the French army in Portugal. He knew how fond Napoleon was of exhorting his soldiers to live off the land, but the Peninsula was frail and bare. Dinner was a stew of French hardtack soaked in a broth of wild onions and nothing more, washed down, at least, with excellent port someone must have pilfered from farther downriver. The men were already on starvation rations.

They sat close together in the cool evening air that was beginning to feel like autumn. Rains would come soon enough, spreading enough discomfort around to last a lifetime, if they were still prisoners on the trail. *Or we could be dead, my lady and me*, he reminded himself. It was better not to borrow trouble from tomorrow.

His thoughts were unprofitable, so it was with some relief they were interrupted by Sergeant Cadotte, who motioned for them to rise. He felt the hairs prick on the back of his neck. Was this the end, then? Was the Sergeant going to shoot him and turn Polly over to his soldiers? Hugh forced himself to subdue his rising panic.

He could have sobbed with relief when the Sergeant untied their hands, handed him a dusty blanket, and gestured towards a beehive-shaped stone cairn. 'You two will stay in the granary tonight,' Cadotte said.

He had to go on his knees to get into the granary and Polly bent double. The Sergeant put in a bucket. 'For your needs,' he said gruffly, and to Hugh's ears, almost with an undertone of compassion. 'I have no candle or lantern. And do not worry about mice, Madame Junot. It's been picked clean. See you in the morning.' He closed the door behind him and threw the bolt. They were in total darkness.

Hugh stood up, gratified that the ceiling was just tall enough to accommodate him. He put his arm on Polly's shoulder again, and walked with her around the granary, touching the wall, feeling for any weakness. There was none. From what little he knew of Portuguese history, the villagers' ancestors had built the granary to resist Huns and Visigoths and Moors. *They have come and gone and now we are here*, he thought, as the weight of the whole débâcle clamped down on his shoulders like mortar.

With a groan, he sat down and tugged Polly down beside him. Without a word, he sat cross-legged, when he could force his legs to move, and pulled her on to his lap.

It was all the invitation she needed to do what she had been holding back all day. She put her arms around his neck and sobbed into his tunic, as he knew she would. And somehow, he knew she wouldn't be startled if he joined in. They cried together, and soon, to his own sorely tried heart, she was crooning and rubbing her hand on his back.

'I'm sorry you had to be Sister Maria's witness, Hugh.'

Her soft words, whispered through her own tears, comforted him as nothing else could have. He almost believed her.

'I have dealt out my share of death and destruction, thanks to Boney, but I have never been jolted like that before,' he confessed, hardly able to get out the words.

She sat up in his lap and found his face in the dark, pressing her hands against his temples. 'He shouldn't have made you a party to that!'

Her voice was fierce, and he was glad he could not see her face in the darkness. He was a professional Marine engaged in a long war, and that was his life. Either she was the world's greatest actress, surpassed only by Siddons herself, or this young woman sitting on him in the dark didn't want him to suffer for the shocking death he had been forced to deal out. She seemed to care less for her own safety, than that he not suffer. It touched him.

When her tears stopped, she sniffed a few times, then managed a watery chuckle. 'I'm about to commit such a social solecism,' she said. She leaned sideways and he could feel her tugging at her skirt. In another moment she was blowing her nose on the fabric.

'Uh, I do have a handkerchief in my tunic,' he said. 'You should have asked.'

She leaned back against him again, warming his heart. 'Save it. We might really need it later,' she told him. Her voice faltered. 'At least, I hope there is a "later".'

'So do I, Brandon, so do I,' he said.

'That's "Polly, dear",' she reminded him, and he smiled.

'There is something I should do,' she told him. He heard a rip of fabric. 'Hugh, take off your tunic and shirt and let me bandage your arm.'

He had to think a moment like a village idiot, because his wound seemed to have happened years ago. 'It's not bleeding now,' he said.

'Look you here,' she demanded. 'I ripped off this strip and I intend to use it. Do what I said.'

'You're a taskmaster,' he teased, as he unbuttoned his tunic and removed it after she got off his lap. He unbuttoned his shirt and winced when he pulled his arm out of the sleeve. 'Learn that from Laura Brittle?'

'No. From my dear Nana, when she scolds her three-year-old,' Polly retorted.

She felt along his arm, which made him smile in the dark, then rested her finger lightly on the track of the ball that had slammed into him on the *barco rabelo.* 'We will pretend I am spreading on some of the salve that Philemon formulates,' she told him. 'At least it appears to have merely grazed your arm. Are you bulletproof?'

'Nearly so. Ah, that should do it, wife. You're a handy little wench.'

She laughed softly. 'You are a rascal! There is no one you need to impress in this wretched granary. There now. Put on your coat again.'

Polly made no objection when he pulled her on to his lap again. She was silent for a long time, but he knew she wasn't asleep. When she spoke, her voice was timid. 'I should be braver in the dark, but I am not, Colonel.'

'That's Hugh,' he pointed out prosaically. '"Hugh, darling", to be exact. You keep forgetting.'

Her voice turned apologetic. 'I should beg your pardon

for saying we were married, but I couldn't think of anything else on short notice that might help us both.'

'It was the only thing I could think of, too, on short notice.'

'And now you have got me with child, Hugh…'

'…darling,' he finished.

He felt her laugh more than heard it. '"Hugh, darling", then! We will be in trouble if the French keep us for too many months. Even *they* can count!'

He joined in her laughter, but sobered quickly. 'Setting aside our fictitious fertility, we're in murky water, Brandon.'

She nodded and sighed, and he kissed the top of her head before he realised there wasn't any need in the pitch-black granary to fool any Frenchman. 'I fear these French, but we have reason to be wary of how desperate is their own plight.'

'Desperate?' she asked.

'Yes. I learned a great deal in Lisbon about insurgents. They call themselves *guerrilleros*, and they do not play fair. I am reminded of my Commandant's disgust of Americans in that late unpleasantness in the United States. The rebels shot from behind trees, and dropped logs across roads, robbed supply trains, and engaged in vastly ungentlemanlike behaviour.'

'I thought that was the point of war.'

'Well put, Brandon, you practical chit. You don't think armies should just line up carefully and shoot at each other?'

'Seems a little stupid,' she replied, and he was glad to hear her voice getting drowsy. He didn't plan to ever sleep again, but it would be good if she could.

'Apparently those shadowy armies of Spain and Portugal would agree with you. It could very well be that this squad of Dragoons is in considerable danger from guerrillas. Besides that, I think they are a forlorn hope.'

'You did mention that. I don't understand.'

'This may have been almost a suicide mission,' he explained. 'From what I learned in Lisbon, Admiral Popham's landing north of us at Santander is finally threatening French power in León. I think Sergeant Cadotte's commanding officer is desperate to shut off any trafficking in information, because his position is none too secure. Just a suspicion, mind.'

She digested that thought, then stated calmly, 'It's a good thing you have on a red coat, isn't it?'

'And I intend to keep it on, and you close by me at all times.' He kissed her head again and tightened his arms around her. 'It's this way, Brandon—we truly have to think of ourselves as married. We must trust each other completely and look out for each other. I meant what I said about never letting you out of my sight. I intend to watch over you, as I did on the ship.'

'You are the kindest man I have ever met, but you are probably regretting you jumped into the *barco* so impulsively. Was that only this morning?'

He pulled her back against him and rested his chin on her head. '*Au contraire*, wife. That is the one thing about this day that I do *not* regret,' he declared, his voice firm. 'If I had not been along, there is no telling what would have happened to you at São Jobim.'

'Yes, there is,' she replied quietly. 'We know what would have happened to me.'

'Then it was for the best.'

He didn't think his heart could have felt any fuller just then, except that it did when she found his hand, and kissed the back of it like a supplicant. 'I am for ever in your debt,' she told him, then pulled his hand across her body to her shoulder until she was completely entwined in his arms.

There was no reason for him to feel even the slightest optimism, but something about holding Brandon in his arms lightened his mood. 'You know, Sergeant Cadotte was entirely wrong,' he told her.

'Not about Sister Maria Madelena, he wasn't,' Polly said.

'No, he wasn't.' He compromised, found her hand, raised it to his lips, and kissed it. 'I certainly didn't marry you for your money.'

She was silent for a minute, and then started to laugh. There was nothing of hysteria in her laugh, so he found himself smiling in the dark, and then laughing, too.

'You are more of a rogue than I suspected,' she declared, when she could speak.

'But not a mercenary one,' he added, which sent her into another peal of laughter.

It was easier to settle down then, his arms still tight around her. She sighed, laughed low once more, and then slept. He stared ahead into the darkness, knowing that it would be ages before he would not see Sister Maria Madelena pointing the pistol at her own throat.

'God forgive her,' he whispered into the gloom. 'God protect us.'

Chapter Thirteen

Polly panicked when she woke and could not feel her spectacles on her face. Terrified, she patted the ground beside her, trying not to wake up the Colonel as she searched. She stopped only when he gently took her hand and touched it to his uniform front, where she felt the outline of the glass.

'I took them off you at some point last night. What I cannot understand, Polly, dear, is why these pesky things didn't break yesterday. Do you want 'um now?'

She shook her head. 'No. There's nothing to see. Do you think it's morning?'

'It must be,' he told her. He cleared his throat. 'You'll have to excuse my vast indelicacy, but I need to get you off my lap and edge gracefully around this granary for private purposes. You might hum loudly to drown out the symphony, or marvel at the simplicity of male anatomy.'

'That *is* indelicate,' she agreed, then laughed. 'Just do your business! We're not standing much on ceremony, are we?'

'No, indeed. We cannot.'

She helped the Colonel to his feet when he found he could not stand, after all those hours of holding her on his lap. It took him a moment to stand up straight.

'Good God, Brandon. I will announce to you right now that I am feeling every single year this morning! I am also never going to joke again about men on horseback. How do they do it? I am still in pain from gripping that damned beast. My kingdom for an ocean.'

He stood another moment in silence. She was too shy to ask him if he needed assistance in walking across the granary. After copious cursing under his breath that she chose to ignore, he got himself in motion. In another moment, she heard the homely sound of water against the wall.

When he returned to her side, it was her turn, moving slowly in the other direction until she found the bucket. When she finished, she groped along the wall, following the sound of the Colonel's voice until she ran into him again. When she sat by his side this time, his arm seemed to go around her automatically.

He yawned. 'I think I could eat a whole pig, but something tells me we're not going to be well fed on this journey.'

'I must be philosophical,' she told him. 'I told myself when I came to Portugal that this would be a good time to get rid of what Miss Pym called my baby fat.'

'Miss Pym be damned,' he replied mildly, 'and spare me skinny females. I might remind you that you're supposed to be eating for two.'

'Wretch!' she said with feeling. 'Perhaps to while away the hours, we should play a game of "It Could Be Worse".'
The words weren't out of her mouth before she saw Sister

Maria Madelena, kneeling in the church. 'No. No. Not that.'

'No,' the Colonel agreed. 'We know it could be worse.' He touched her head with his. 'Tell me something about yourself that I don't know already, Brandon.'

She thought a moment, remembering what he already knew about her that she had divulged on the trip across the Channel. 'You already know I am the illegitimate daughter of a scoundrel whom you have resurrected and made into a wealthy man, for Sergeant Cadotte's benefit, if I am taken care of. That was a nice touch, husband.'

'Why, thank you,' he said modestly. 'If raising the dead to provide money in desperate situations doesn't paint me as a Scot, I don't know what would, considering my own French ancestry.'

She laughed. 'Hugh, darling, I would say your ancestors were quick studies.'

'They were, indeed, Polly, dear,' he teased, unruffled. 'There's nothing like political intrigue, plus menace from Queen Elizabeth and her Privy Council, to sharpen the mind, apparently. The original Philippe d'Anvers Junot obviously knew when to fold his tent and steal away. Evidently he also discovered he preferred oats and Calvinism to truffles and popes. What a resourceful man.'

Her laughter bounced back at her from the opposite wall. 'Your French is so good. Does the ghost of Philippe Junot the First linger in your family's schoolroom?'

The Colonel pulled her on to his lap again, and she couldn't think of a single reason to object. 'Our estate is too new to be haunted, Brandon! Your brain is overactive. We "Junnits" have always learned to speak French. It's a family tradition. I was luckier than most—I have no particular ear for language, but in 1803 before that laughable Peace of Amiens, I spent six months cooling my heels in a French prison. What a tutorial.'

Polly squinted into the darkness, trying to see some evidence of dawn. 'I hope you had more light than in here.'

'Light and then some, Polly, dear. That southern coast of France is devilish hot.'

He didn't say anything else, but she suddenly found herself longing for him to keep talking, to distract her from the granary, her hunger and the itch between her shoulder blades, and the fear that seemed to overlay every rational part of her brain.

'I'm afraid,' she said finally, speaking low, maybe not even wanting him to hear her. 'Please keep talking.'

He did, to her relief, telling her about his childhood in Kirkcudbrightshire, where it rained six days out of seven; the gardens of madly blooming roses in everyone's front garden; the hours he spent in small boats in the Firth of Solway; the year he chafed away at the University of Edinburgh until he convinced his father to see him into the Royal Marines; and his years in deepwater service, doing exactly what he loved.

As she listened to his musical accent and soothing voice, she realised how little her life was, in relation to his, how modest and unexceptional. She knew that most women lived quiet lives at home. Her beloved sister Nana waited, agonised, and bore up magnificently under the strain of loving a man too often gone. Her equally well-loved sister Laura had chosen a different path, but it still revolved around her husband and her son, even as she used her own medical skills quietly in the shadow.

'Women don't amount to much,' she said, when the Colonel finished.

'What brought that on?' he asking, laughing.

'I was just thinking about how little I do, compared to you. We women wait, mostly.' She smiled in the dark, casting away whatever of her reserve that remained of the intimate situation in which she now found herself. 'We have husbands and babies, real *or* imagined, and that is all.'

'"That is all", eh? I doubt even Nana Worthy realizes how much her Captain yearns for her. I suspect she is his centre of calm in a world gone mad. He probably even calls her his True North. I would, and I don't even know your sister.'

Leaning back against the Colonel, Polly digested what he had said. Her first reaction was embarrassment, because this man she admired had no compunction about speaking his mind in such a frank way. She was struck also by her own words. 'We women' had seldom entered her mind before, let alone her vocabulary. Maybe her years as a student, and then the cushion, three years ago, of discovering her own protective sisters, had helped to keep her young. Maybe it was the casual way she now sat on the Colonel's lap and how suddenly she was so aware of his arms around her. Something stirred inside her, and it wasn't hunger or fear.

Maybe it had even stirred yesterday on the *barco*, when she dragged the partially conscious Colonel Junot on to her lap to protect him. Protect him from *what*, when women were so easily thrown aside and trampled on? *I thought I could save him*, she told herself in the gloom of the granary. *I felt stronger than lions, just then.*

'Maybe you'll understand better when you fall in love some day, Polly, dear,' the Colonel said in her ear.

She had to think of something to lighten her mood, which was troubling her almost more than the total darkness and the potential brevity of her life. 'You sound like someone who knows,' she told him.

'Aye, Polly, dear, I know what it is to love someone,' he said after a lengthy pause.

I am put in my place, Polly thought, embarrassed. Of course Colonel Junot had a lover somewhere. Why would he not? Who could there possibly be in the universe who did not think him attractive and worth more than gold?

She couldn't think of another thing to say, but it didn't matter, because the bolt was thrown on the granary's small door, and it swung open to reveal bright morning outside. She squinted in the light, then glanced at the Colonel, who was doing the same thing. She also knew she should get off his lap, but his arms tightened around her.

'I wish I knew what was coming, Polly, dear,' he murmured. He loosened his grip. 'Up you get, but I'm going out first.'

She willingly let him, not eager to have a soldier on the outside grab her hand. With a groan that made the soldiers outside laugh, the Colonel crawled through the entrance. Captured by the irrational terror that someone would slam the door now and leave her there in eternal darkness, Polly wanted to race after him. In another moment, Colonel Junot's hand reached for her. She grasped it for a second, then crouched her way out of the granary.

Polly took his hand again and they stood shoulder to

shoulder, watching the enemy, looking this morning like most men campaigning in any army: dirty, smelly, and barely awake. She thought of her brother-in-law Philemon glowering at the breakfast table until Laura brought him tea.

It was obvious there wouldn't be any tea, and not even anything beyond yesterday's hardtack, doled out in a smaller amount. When Hugh asked Cadotte if he could fetch water for all of them from the well in the square, the NCO only shrugged.

'You would not wish it, Junnit,' he replied. 'The well is full of either Portuguese corpses or French ones. I didn't look too closely.'

Polly shuddered and moved closer to the Colonel. Cadotte unbent enough to nod to her. 'Madame Junnit, I do wish we had something more to offer you than hard-tack. I truly do.'

It stung her to think the Sergeant was worried about her non-existent unborn child. All she could do was blush and avert her gaze from his, which—all things considered—was probably the correct attitude. Coupled with her lie, the knowledge of her hypocrisy only stung her more.

'You are too kind, Sergeant,' she murmured.

It was Cadotte's turn to appear uneasy. He frowned and looked away, growling at some fictitious misdemeanor perpetrated by one or another of his hardened Dragoons to alleviate his embarrassment. Or so she thought, as she watched. 'I must keep reminding myself that he is some woman's husband,' she whispered to the Colonel.

'That will render the Sergeant less odious?' Hugh asked, amused.

'Certainly,' she replied crisply. 'Hugh, darling,' she added, which made him chuckle.

Because there was no food, there was little preparation before the Sergeant gave the order for his men to mount. Lips twitching, he watched Colonel Junot heave himself into the saddle with a sigh and a grimace. Without a word, Cadotte tied his hands together again, then tied Polly's together before lifting her gently into the saddle in front of the Colonel.

'I wish you would trust me enough to leave my hands untied,' Hugh grumbled as he lifted his arms and encircled Polly again.

'Trust you enough? I don't trust you at all,' the Sergeant said frankly, as he mounted his own horse. 'We are riding north and east now, covering rough terrain and staying off the roads. If we see partisans, we will hide, because we are a small squad that probably never should have survived our mission to São Jobim, so close to the British lines.'

'I thought as much,' Hugh murmured. 'You were some Lieutenant's forlorn hope, weren't you?'

Cadotte looked down his long nose at them until Hugh was silent. 'That is hardly your business, Colonel. If we encounter partisans and you do anything to attract them, I will shoot you and turn Madame Junnit over to my troopers. Am I perfectly clear?'

'As crystal,' Hugh snapped.

The two men glared at each other. Cadotte handed the reins of Hugh's horse to his Corporal and spurred his horse to the head of the line. The squad began to move at a moderate gait, leaving the deserted village behind and turning away from the Douro.

Polly looked ahead at the mountains and shook her head. 'We're to cross *those*?' she asked.

'It would seem so,' Hugh replied. 'Our Sergeant knows he is in dangerous territory. I'm a little surprised he didn't make me take off my red tunic.' He sighed. 'Of course, any remaining mountain people—*montagnards*—are probably no more fond of the British than they are the French. Portugal is a carcass picked clean.'

'Do you wonder why he didn't just shoot us back there?' Polly asked.

'Polly, dear, I'm actually surprised he let us out of the granary,' the Colonel replied, and tightened his arms around her at her sudden intake of breath. Glancing at the Sergeant, who was watching them, he nuzzled her cheek. 'I don't think he believes I will give him any money for his farm. Men at war tend to be cynical, and who can blame them?'

'Then why are we alive?'

'Polly, dear, I wish I knew his game.'

It was no game, she decided, after three days of weary riding through narrow mountain passes that made her close her eyes and turn her face into Hugh's tunic. Her jaws ached from gritting her teeth as the horses—the big-boned animals that French cavalry used—sidled along nearly imaginary trails far above boiling mountain streams.

She knew the heights bothered Hugh, although he did not admit as much. Once when their horse stumbled, sending rocks plunging down into the gorge, he came close to admitting his own fear. 'Polly, dear, I would trade about five and a half years off my life this moment if we were suddenly transported to the deck of a frigate.'

You must be sorely tried, to admit as much, Polly thought, as she screwed her eyes shut against that awful moment when they would plunge off the mountain face. 'Hugh, darling, you must have mice in your pockets,' she managed to squeak out, when she could talk. 'You know how *I* feel about life on the rolling wave.'

He was silent for a long moment, then all he said was, 'Bless your heart, Brandon, you're a rare one.'

She didn't feel like a rare one. She was grimy, smelly, and hungry, with filmy teeth and a constantly growling stomach. The blood from the noisome floor of the church at São Jobim had stained her light blue muslin dress, which was also torn now, and muddy from a night spent shivering in the Colonel's arms as they were tied to a tree. Still, she decided the tree was better than the claustrophobia of the granary, if only she weren't so cold.

Somewhere, far below in the lovely coastal valleys of the Rio Douro, it was late summer. Here in the *tras o montes* region, autumn had begun, and with it a light mist that fogged the upper valleys and brought relief only to the Dragoons. Now the troopers travelled with caution, but visible relief, because the mist obscured their presence from watchful partisans. They stopped for nothing after the second day, when even the hardtack gave out.

'Tell me, Hugh, darling, are the French so poor they cannot even feed their soldiers?' she asked the Colonel after one noon stop when the only refreshment was cold water from a stream.

'It's not that they cannot, but that they choose not,' Hugh said, as they walked shoulder to shoulder along the bank. 'Napoleon believes that his *Grand Armée* should feed itself in the field.'

'I don't think much of that,' she retorted.

Hugh laughed softly. 'You should demand that Sergeant Cadotte take you to Napoleon so you can give him a piece of your mind.'

Polly glared at him. 'I know you're hungry. Don't try to tell me you're not.'

'I'm hungry,' he agreed, 'but I've been hungrier. Brandon, as long as we get drinking water, we'll be all right. You'll be amazed how long we can last without food.'

'Mostly I'm tired,' she admitted, and stopped walking. 'What can I do about that?'

'Get something to eat,' he said wearily. 'Bit of a vicious circle, ain't it?'

She couldn't help the tears that spilled on to her cheeks then, even though she tried to brush at them. It would have been easy to do that if her hands hadn't been tied. As it was, she couldn't hide them.

To comfort her, Hugh raised his tied hands and dropped them around her, pulling her close to him. With a shudder, she rested her cheek against his chest as his chin came down on the top of her head.

'*Why* did Sister Maria Madelena do what she did?' Polly asked.

'For love of her country, I expect, and fierce anger at the French and the way they treated her,' the Colonel replied. He peered at her face. 'Have you never loved something enough to risk everything, even your life, for it?'

'I suppose I have not,' she said, after some thought. 'Have you?'

'Oh, yes,' he said, more promptly than she. 'Perhaps that is why I am a Royal Marine until I die.'

She thought that over, then dismissed the idea. *Maybe I will understand when I am older*, she told herself. 'But why did she involve me?'

'That we will never know, Polly, my love,' he said.

'It's "Polly, dear",' she reminded him.

'I thought I would change the dialogue a little, Polly, dear,' he replied. 'Variety is, after all, the spice of life, or so I am told. I doubt you want a boring, predictable husband.'

She had to smile then. 'When I get home to England, I am going to vie for the attention of an apothecary or perhaps a comptroller.'

'Too boring by half,' he said, his voice light. 'You'll rue it the moment you get in bed with him.'

Startled, she looked up at him, and saw the laughter in his eyes. He glanced over at the bank. 'Uh oh, the Sergeant is watching.'

He kissed her then, pressing his bound hands against the small of her back and then raising them to her neck. She had never been kissed on the lips by a man before, but she knew better than to draw back or act surprised, not with the Sergeant watching. She returned his kiss, surprised a little at the softness of his lips, since he did not look like a soft man. Their lips parted, and he kissed her again and again, little kisses that made her lean into his hips, to her surprise and embarrassment.

When they finished, he asked in a low voice, 'Is he still watching?'

Suddenly shy, she turned her head to look. Sergeant Cadotte was looking at the water, then tapping his boot with his riding whip.

'You're a scoundrel, Hugh, darling,' she whispered into his neck. 'I'm not so certain he was ever looking.'

She laughed then, and stirred in his arms, which was the Colonel's cue to raise his arms and release her.

'Perhaps he wasn't,' he said with remarkable aplomb, 'but at least you are not so unhappy now.'

She certainly wasn't, she reflected, as they travelled into the afternoon of another dreary day. Only the warmth in her middle, which began and spread downwards when she leaned so close to the Colonel, gave her any satisfaction. That she was out of her element, she knew beyond a doubt. So was the Colonel, and for all she knew, despite their hardness, the Dragoons, too. They were captives riding with hunted men trying to get back to their own lines. Sergeant Cadotte must have been a farmer before Napoleon came calling, yet here he was.

'I can't forgive them for what they did to the priest and to Sister Maria Madelena,' she murmured, half to herself, later that day.

'Nor should you, or trust them for even a second,' Hugh said. 'Still, if we had met these men while strolling in Vauxhall Gardens, we would probably just have nodded and smiled. War changes everyone.' His hands tied, he nuzzled aside her hair with his lips and kissed her ear, biting gently on her earlobe. 'Maybe even you, Brandon.'

She looked around, but the Sergeant was not watching them. 'Hugh, darling, you are taking advantage of me,' she said, feeling that warmth again.

'And who would not, in my boots?' he said complacently. 'Polly, dear.'

There wasn't even a deserted village for shelter that night. They dismounted into mud and gravel. When the rains came, Sergeant Cadotte rummaged in his pack for an oiled slicker, which he draped over Hugh's shoulders. Polly shivered in his arms, unable to keep her teeth from chattering with the cold.

She had not complained when the cold rain started to fall. Come to think of it, she never complained, Hugh realised as he held her close. She said nothing about her empty belly, even though he heard her stomach growl and she winced from the pain of it. She had grown quieter and quieter as the hours passed, and Hugh wished with all his heart that he could make her comfortable, even if for only a moment.

They were not in as bad shape as one of the Sergeant's men, a Private gone unconscious with the cold and deprivation. There was no shelter beyond the dripping trees for a bivouac that night, but two Dragoons had put their slickers together and with some sticks, created a rude shelter for their companion.

'Poor man,' Polly said, as she stood in the shelter of Hugh's arms. 'He's going to die, isn't he?'

'Probably. You'll have to ask your brother-in-law why some men are impervious to a little cold, and others succumb. He's the enemy, Brandon,' Hugh reminded her.

'I know. I know. Still…' She let the sentence trail away.

She surprised him by turning around to face him, burrowing her head into his chest as they stood together, hands tied in front of them. She took his hand and raised it to her breast. 'I don't want to die before I have even lived,' she whispered. 'Don't let that happen to me, Hugh, if you are my friend.'

'I'm your husband, Polly,' he whispered, feeling exactly that. 'I'm proud of you, the way you have borne up under this misery. You're brave and kind.' Unsure of himself, he knew he should make light of what he was saying. 'And an excellent mother to our child.'

She glanced up at him then, her pretty blue eyes so tired and filled suddenly with tears. 'Don't tease me about that, Hugh,' she whispered back. 'I...I don't want to die before I have a child! Don't ever tease me any more about that.'

Words failed him. He raised his bound hands, wanting to pull them free so he could caress away her tears; scrabble in the sparse vegetation to find something— anything—to feed her. In the horror that was São Jobim, he had sworn to protect her with all the fervour with which he had sworn, as a lad of fifteen, to defend King and country. In fact, the two were inextricably bound together in his mind. He wanted to touch her gently until they were content enough in this miserable wilderness where the heavens had opened up. He wanted to assure her that she would not die until she had lived, but he could promise her nothing of the kind.

'No more teasing, Brandon,' he said. 'Don't let me shock you, but I feel exactly the same way about the very same thing.' It struck him then that he understood her completely. 'I...I don't think I have even started to live yet, either, and we know how old I am.'

She hesitated and he leaned closer to her. He thought he knew what she was too shy to ask, this young woman who had been raised properly and carefully, but who must have been aroused as he was aroused when he kissed her ear and then her neck, earlier that afternoon. This was all so strange—no one could seriously fall in love under such conditions.

Or could one? He didn't dare think it was possible. Lord knew he had tried to think of the Brittles' objections to him. But as the rain thundered down, he kissed her with all the fervour of his heart. Because the others were gathered around the dying trooper, this was the most privacy they had enjoyed since the granary. To his joy, she kissed him back, little inarticulate murmurs coming from her throat that made his body yearn for her as he had never yearned for any female in his life. He knew without a qualm that for the rest of his life, he would cherish and protect this woman to the end of his strength. He had sworn to do it, on his honour as a Marine. Was there more? Time might tell, if there was time, and he had his doubts.

He kissed her nose next, then stepped back, shrugged out of the slicker and left it wrapped around his love. Without a word to her, he strode to the circle of Dragoons, calling for the Sergeant. When he had the harried man's attention, Hugh just held out his hands wordlessly. *'S'il vouz plaît,'* he said simply.

Brandon was beside him then, doing the same thing. 'Please, Sergeant,' she said. 'Perhaps we can help your man.'

'And do what?' Cadotte snapped.

Hugh knew that whether seconds or decades would be allowed to pass in the life of his loved one, he would never be more proud of Polly Brandon than he was then. 'I can hold him in my arms,' she said. 'Men are well enough, Sergeant, but women are better. You know they are.'

Cadotte looked at the two of them. Without a word he untied their hands. Polly bobbed a small curtsy that made her look suddenly young. She gave Hugh such a look that he felt his insides begin to smoulder, then shouldered her way through the troop of Dragoons, those men who only a week ago would have raped and killed her, and sat down beside the unconscious Dragoon.

Humming softly, she let one of the men help her lift the dying man into her lap. After only the slightest hesitation, she began to smooth his dirty hair from his forehead. Someone handed her a dry stocking, and she wiped the grime from his face, bending lower over him until her breasts touched his chest. She did it deliberately, wanting the dying man to know he was with a woman.

Hugh watched in humble amazement as his green girl sent her enemy to his death peacefully. She unbuttoned the Dragoon's ragged green tunic and pressed her hand against his chest, stroking him until his eyes flickered open. He tried to speak and she leaned closer.

'Emilie?' he asked, with the smallest bit of hope in his voice.

'*Oui,*' she replied. '*Dormes-toi, mon chéri.*'

With a look of surprising contentment, he died. Polly Brandon closed his eyes and began to cry. As Hugh listened, she seemed to cry every tear that had ever been shed over every soldier in every war since the Lord God Almighty cast Satan from heaven and the trouble really started.

Still enveloped in the too-large slicker, Polly Brandon stood as chief mourner as the troopers buried their comrade. Hugh helped dig the grave, needing the release of hard work to calm the fires in his body. He could have cried at his own weakness, when he had to stop because he was exhausted. No one noticed because all the men, equally starved, were taking turns.

No one said anything over the grave. Polly cried. Hugh

held her close, then turned around, walked to the Sergeant and held out his hands, to be bound again. Cadotte shook his head. He pointed to the foot of a large tree. 'Sleep there,' was all he said. 'We ride at dawn. I'll bind you then.'

Without a word, Hugh wrapped the slicker around both of them and sat Brandon down under the tree. His hands free, he pulled the slicker over them, protecting their heads from the rain, and pulled Brandon close. With a sigh, she rested her head on his chest, her arm possessively around his body. In a matter of seconds, she was breathing evenly.

'Please, Polly, I need your comfort,' he whispered, wishing she could hear him.

She did, which humbled him beyond anything. Without a word spoken between them, without even opening her eyes, she unbuttoned her dress. She untied the cord holding her chemise together, took his hand, and placed it on her bare breast with a sigh. It was warm and softer than he could have imagined. He cupped her breast carefully in his hand as his eyes closed, too. He tried to open his eyes when she put her hand inside his tunic and shirt and stroked him as she had caressed the French Dragoon. All he could do was succumb to his best night's sleep in recent memory, as the rain poured down.

Chapter Fourteen

If the burial didn't change everything, crossing an un-
named mountain stream did. What surprised Hugh about
saving Sergeant Cadotte's life was the ferocious way
Polly Brandon did all he demanded without question.
She had the heart of a Marine, and this unexpected discovery bound him to her tighter than the cords shackling
them. Not only did he love her; he respected her as a
brother in arms.

They had come to the river at dusk one week later.
They had been slowly winding their way down to it for
most of the day on the precipitous switchbacks that Portuguese mountain passes were notorious for. He knew
how terrified Polly was, shrinking back against him as
they travelled the dangerous trail, their hands bound and
at the mercy of the Corporal, who had roped their horse
to his.

One of the Dragoons on the narrow file in front of them
had lost his life around a sharp turn when his horse made
a misstep and trod upon thin air. The man shrieked all the
way to his death. Polly's sharp intake of breath and the

shaking of her shoulders told him volumes about her own state of mind.

She had borne up well against the journey. Even the Sergeant had remarked on that to him the night before, when he had tied them to a picket stake and laid down next to them, spreading his blanket over them all, which had touched Hugh.

'I wish matters were different for your lady,' was all the Sergeant said, and it was quietly spoken, as Cadotte turned on his side to sleep, his back to them.

My lady, Hugh thought, as he cuddled Polly close. He knew her body well by now. His acquaintance with it had begun on the voyage from Plymouth, but he had taken pains not to embarrass her, even as they had to manage private functions in sight and sound of each other. She had accepted their constant closeness for her protection. There was nothing missish about Polly Brandon, which eased his plight. When she had so generously comforted him two nights ago, he knew he was in her debt for ever.

He wished she did not continue to chafe about the impulsive gesture that had caused him to jump into the *barco* in Oporto. He knew it still bothered her that he could be safe downriver, and by now, at Ferrol Station, or even in Plymouth. Not even the reality of her probable fate at the hands of Cadotte's troopers seemed to assuage the guilt she felt at endangering his life, because she had insisted upon accompanying Sister Maria Madelena on the ill-fated journey.

'It's my fault you are here,' she told him after the Dragoon fell to his death.

'Polly, dear, life is strange,' he had said, and it sounded so facile to his own ears, something uttered vapidly in a drawing room to impress fops.

Obviously unimpressed with his philosophising, she had said nothing more to him. It chafed him that she felt so alone in her misery. He knew she liked him, but he also suspected she had not invested her heart in him, as she would have if they were actually married, instead of submitting to a great fiction to stay alive. Something told him she needed to discover how much she loved him, if she even did.

They came to the ford of the stream before dusk. The Sergeant sat in his saddle, his leg across the pommel, in that casual way of his that Hugh could only envy. Cadotte watched the stream for some moments, as if weighing the value of crossing now or waiting until morning. The mist that had been falling on them for days must have fallen as rain higher in the mountains, because the stream boiled along like a river. To cross now or not? Hugh almost smiled to himself; he knew what command decisions felt like.

'We will cross now,' the Sergeant said finally, and gestured his men forwards.

'How?' Polly murmured, into Hugh's tunic.

It was a good question. There was little remaining of the stone bridge that had once spanned the stream, more properly a river now. One army or another had blown it into gravel years ago, leaving behind only stone pillars at either bank. Some enterprising soul had rigged a rope across the expanse. Hugh pointed this out to Polly.

'I suppose we are to grip the rope as the horse does his best,' he told her, trying not to sound as dubious as he felt.

'Then the Sergeant had better free our hands,' was all she said.

The Sergeant seemed disinclined to agree, which

hardly surprised him. What did surprise him was the way Polly argued with the Frenchman, holding her bound hands in front of her and then waving them about, which made the Sergeant's face twitch in what Hugh had decided was as near as the man ever got to smiling.

'You insist?' the Sergeant said finally.

Polly stared him directly in the eyes and nodded vigorously. 'I insist.'

'You have no power to make me do anything, Madame Junnit,' he said.

'I know that, but I still insist,' she replied.

Sergeant Cadotte turned to him and threw up his hands in a Gallic gesture. 'Is she always so much trouble?'

'This and more,' Hugh answered. 'Humour her.'

The Sergeant did, gesturing for his Corporal to untie them. The Sergeant had the sapper find him a longer rope and told his Corporal to tie it around their waists, binding them together.

'We would be safer if you didn't fetter us,' Hugh said.

'I don't care about your safety,' Cadotte snapped, obviously weary of decisions and complainers. 'I want you across the river together, or not at all.'

Cadotte sent half his troopers across the stream. Hugh watched as they guided their mounts into the swift-moving water, grasping the rope as the water tugged at them.

'I do not think it is more than four feet deep. I fear the current. Can you swim?'

Polly nodded, her eyes on the water. 'Miss Pym is a modern educationist. She took us river bathing in the Avon.' She glanced back at him, and he saw the worry in her face take on a calmness that impressed him.

'However, the Avon never looked like this. It's rushing so *fast*.'

He kissed her cheek impulsively. 'D'ye know, Brandon, one of the many things that impresses me about you is that you're not afraid to admit you're afraid, but you plug along anyhow.'

His reward was a faint smile and a shake of her head, as if she thought him two-thirds barmy. Perhaps she did; maybe he was. Who understood women?

The Corporal crossed next, holding tight to the rope and calling for them to do the same, as he kept a firm grip on the rope around their waists. The stream caught them, and Hugh felt the mighty pull of the water. Polly whimpered, then was silent as she glided her hand along the rope. He could feel how tightly she gripped the horse's flanks with her legs.

'You'll do, Polly, dear,' he said loud in her ear, to be heard above the sound of the water.

When they reached the opposite shore, he had to coax Polly to let go, finally just twisting her fingers from their death grip on the rope that spanned the stream. Her face was pale and her eyes huge in her head, as the Corporal tugged their mount on to the bank. Only then did her shoulders slump. 'Thank God,' she said simply.

Hand possessively on her shoulder, he turned in the saddle to watch Cadotte cross. No sooner than it took him to blink, Hugh watched as the Sergeant plunged headfirst into the river as his horse stumbled over rocks slippery with moss. He came up sputtering and grasping frantically for his mount, but he was already downstream of any aid.

'Stand up, man,' Hugh muttered to himself as he quickly undid the knot tying him to Polly. 'It's not that deep.'

As he had remarked to Polly before their crossing, it wasn't the depth, but the current that was playing merry hell with Sergeant Cadotte. He retied the rope around Polly and dismounted, his eyes on the Sergeant, who was watching his startled troopers with desperate eyes. He tried to speak as he was swept downstream.

'Polly, I'm going in,' Hugh said as he took off his tunic and gorget and handed them to her. 'Convince the Corporal to let loose of our horse and follow me along the bank with that rope. Get ahead of me and think of something!'

As he unbuckled his shoes he looked back to see some of the men unlimbering their weapons. *Fools*, he thought. *And the French think they will win this war?* He dived into the water.

There was no thought in Polly's mind except to do exactly as the Colonel said. Scarcely breathing, she watched him make powerful strokes to the middle of the stream, then let the current carry him towards the floundering Sergeant as he tried to swim. Polly pulled at the rope connecting her horse to the Corporal's to get his attention. 'Let me go,' she shouted. 'Then follow me. And for God's sake, stop them from firing. Hugh is trying to *help*!'

The Corporal must have thought she could do some good. After a spare second to stare at her and mull her demand, he did as she said, untying the rope from his pommel and tossing it to her. Grasping the reins for the first time, she dug her heels into the horse and was rewarded with an unexpected burst of speed from an animal probably as tired and hungry as she was. She could hear the Corporal shouting something to her in French, but she ignored him, putting all thoughts aside of what would happen to her if both men died in the river and she was left to face the troopers alone.

To her relief, she heard the Corporal pounding his horse along behind her. She watched the river, which had narrowed and deepened, and the Colonel, who swam with one arm clasped around the Sergeant now. She urged the horse on until they were nearly parallel to the men in the river. In another hundred yards of pounding along the bank, she was ahead of them.

Once through the narrow gorge, the river widened again and the current slowed. She glanced over her shoulder to see Hugh gradually angling towards the shore, fighting the lessening current. He tried to stand up once, but the river yanked them down again.

Polly glanced back to see the rest of the troopers following the Corporal. Her horse was flecked with foam by the time she came to another ford where the bank gradually inclined to a sandy beach. Throwing herself off her horse, she gestured to the Corporal, who dismounted, too.

'Can you swim?' she shouted.

He returned a blank stare, and she realised she was speaking in English. She repeated her question in French, and he shook his head.

It's up to me, then, she thought. *Oh, I don't like adventures*. She handed him the end of the rope tied around her waist, and told him to hang on tight as she went into the stream, recoiling in shock from the cold, and then struggling to stand upright.

The water came up to her chest and the current knocked her over. She struggled to her feet again, then looked at the bank, where the troopers had dismounted and were helping the Corporal with the rope.

Falling and rising several times, and encouraged by the troopers on shore, Polly fought her way to the middle of the stream where the water boiled around a significant boulder. She heaved herself against the protecting rock, letting it anchor her, gratified to see the rope stretching almost taut as the troopers pulled just enough to keep it level, but not to yank her into the stream.

Eyes anxious, she watched for the men. *Please, Hugh*, she thought, *please, Hugh*. It was not coherent or profound, but as she said his name over and over, she realised there was nothing she would not do for this man. He was no longer a Colonel, a Marine, a man she had only met a few months ago. Proper or not, their trials had bound them together tighter than a trussed Christmas goose. He owed her no more than she owed him.

She waited there, her teeth chattering, as the Colonel and the Sergeant swung around the bend of the river. Hugh quickly saw what she had done, and struck out for the space between her and the bank. He grasped the rope with a waterlogged yell of triumph and clung to it as the troopers on shore dug in against the impact.

The force of two men hitting the rope yanked her into the channel again, as she had known it would. She took a deep breath and clung to the rope as the current pulled her under and then downstream. His face a study in concern, Hugh tried to reach for her. She shook her head, and held up the end of the rope that bound them to shore, so he would not worry.

She had no reason to fear. Gradually, the troopers pulled the three of them towards the shallow bank. It was just a matter of hanging on now, and she had the rope tied around her waist. She watched in relief as the two men crawled ashore and slumped on the sand, then let the troopers pull her ashore. She sank face down beside the Colonel, pillowing her cheek against the sand. The water lapped at her legs still, until one of the troopers gently grasped her under her arms and pulled her higher up on the bank. She put her hand on Colonel Junot's back, content just to touch him.

When he was breathing evenly again, he heaved himself on to his back and slowly turned his head towards her. 'Words fail me, Brandon,' was all he said, as he closed his eyes.

Suddenly terrified, she crawled closer, then straddled him, shaking his shoulders and crying. 'Don't you dare die right now!' she sobbed. 'We have miles to go!'

She stopped when he grasped her wrists. 'Polly, dear, I am quite alive.'

She collapsed on top of him then, crying, and not moving until he muttered something about swallowing half of the river, and would she please get off his stomach?

She did as he said, helping him into a sitting position, while he coughed until water dribbled down the front of his checked shirt, torn from his rough passage over rocks and past snags of timber.

She thought of the Sergeant then, but the Corporal was already beside him, turning his leader on to his side as water drained from his mouth. Cadotte opened his eyes and he stared at Colonel Junot in amazement.

'*Mon Dieu*, you saved my life,' he said, when he could talk.

To Polly's amusement, the matter seemed to embarrass the Colonel. 'Yes. Well. Of course I did! Do you take me for someone raised by crofters?'

'But you saved my life,' the Sergeant repeated. He lay back, exhausted, his head against his Corporal's leg.

'Let me assure you, Sergeant Cadotte, I have no love for you at all,' Hugh said. 'Not one scrap of affection. But somewhere near Angoulême there are a woman and two children who think you are worth saving. I did it for them.'

With some effort, the Sergeant managed that twitch that passed for a smile. 'You could have saved yourself some money,' he countered, still stubborn.

'I told you I am an officer and a gentleman. Why won't you believe it?' Hugh said patiently, as though he spoke to a child. 'Polly, dear, are you and our little one all right?'

Drat the man. Why did he have to embarrass her? 'Yes,' she replied, her voice steely.

He patted her leg, then rested his hand on her thigh, giving her a roguish grin and daring her to take exception to his fond, husbandly gesture. He glanced at Cadotte. 'I dare you to submit her name for one of Napoleon's new Legions d'Honneur.'

The Sergeant's lips twitched again and he let out a bark of laughter this time that quickly turned into a coughing fit.

'Lord, you are droll, Colonel,' he said, after his Corporal raised him into a sitting position. 'I will give her something better. You two can ride without your hands tied now.'

The Sergeant surprised her again. He reached across the short space that separated them, took Hugh's hand in his and kissed it, then reached for Polly's and did the same.

* * *

There was daylight left, but no one questioned the Sergeant's decision to backtrack to the bridge and move east just far enough to be among the trees and out of sight. There was even shelter of sorts—a gutted stone farmhouse with interior walls remaining, but no roof. Rendered stupid by exhaustion, Hugh allowed Polly to help him from the horse. Her efforts embarrassed him, but all he wanted to do was lie down and never cross a river again.

'If I see so much as a tin bathtub in the next four or five years, I swear it will unman me,' he told her as she helped him into the wholly inadequate shelter of the tumbled stones.

'You're the one who told me adventures really weren't much fun,' she reminded him.

She was as wet as he was, but he let her help him from his shirt and trousers and wrap him in a blanket smelling strongly of horse. Not until he was lying beside a bonfire, built by one of the troopers, did she think of herself. His men were taking care of Cadotte in much the same fashion on the other side of the interior wall, in what must have been the hut's great room in better days. She cajoled another blanket, looked around to make sure none of the troopers were in sight, and took off her dress.

His eyes could barely stay open, but he watched her stand there in her chemise for a long moment, then sigh and lift it over her head, until she was naked.

'Not a word out of you, Colonel,' she murmured, as she sidled in next to his bare body and pulled both blankets over them. With a sigh, she pillowed her head on his arm, closed her eyes, and slept.

He couldn't help himself. He reached across her body and gently touched her breast. Knowing he deserved a slap to his face, he smoothed his thumb across her nipple, which only elicited a small sigh from her as she burrowed into his warmth. He reminded himself he was an officer and a gentleman as he ran his hand along her rounded hip and stopped there—the spirit as unwilling now as the flesh was weak. He just wanted to sleep until the war ended and he was home again in Kirkcudbright, with his father and sister there to fuss over him.

When he woke several hours later it was dark and Polly was whimpering. Careful to keep the blankets around them both, he propped himself up on his elbow, the better to see her. He watched her expressive face a moment in the faint glow of the bonfire, which had worked its way down to glowing coals, and carefully removed her spectacles. One of the lenses was cracked in the corner now. He set the spectacles on a niche in the wall behind them, a place where a *paisano*'s wife had probably kept her favourite saint.

Polly stirred and cried out, but she still slept. He lay back again, enjoying the feel of her body against his, warm for the first time since he had dived into the river after the Sergeant. As his eyes closed in weariness, he was sure of nothing, except that he relished this woman. How odd it was that in all of his thirty-seven years, he had finally found the woman he wanted like no other, and they were smack in the middle of a war, prisoners, even.

Hugh woke later when Polly stirred in his arms, weeping this time, but still asleep. In his years in both barracks and the fleet, he had heard many a young Marine, newly scoured by battle, do precisely that. His reaction had always been to pat them on the shoulder, so he did that now.

'I'm sorry,' she whispered, as she woke. 'What must you think of me?'

'I think you're magnificent and braver than lions,' he whispered back.

Wordlessly, she turned over to face him and put her arms tight around him, drawing him close as she muffled her sobs against his chest. 'It's too much,' she managed to gasp out, when she could speak. 'Just too much. Is this ever going to end?'

He held her close, cherishing the feel of her breasts against his chest, her hips so close to his. His lust turned to tenderness; all he wanted to do now was touch her shoulder again, as he did his young Marines, and send her back to sleep as he watched over her. It wasn't too much to ask, and God was kind for a moment. She sighed, relaxed, and slept.

He thought she would sleep for the night, but she woke a few minutes later, patting his cheek to rouse him. He looked around in alarm, then settled down when she put her hands on both sides of his face and her forehead against his.

'Hugh, you need to know something,' she told him, her eyes earnest, but with another emotion visible. 'I don't know how you feel about this, but I have to be honest, don't I?'

Mystified, he nodded.

'You may not like it, but I suppose that doesn't matter,' she said. 'How do I say this? Don't let me die without making me a woman.' She put her hands over her face. 'I am so ashamed to say that.'

He took her hands away. 'Don't be. There aren't enough honest people in the world.'

Her words came out in a rush then. 'I know I am probably asking too much. I swear it won't go any further. I mean, here you are, a Lieutenant Colonel, someone of importance, and we know who I am.' She faltered. 'I just wanted you to know.'

She looked ready to apologise further, but he put his fingers on her lips. 'Stop right there, Brandon,' he whispered.

Her face clouded over, but only until he grasped her shoulders and pulled her close for a kiss. She clung to him, her face against his chest, so he kissed her hair this time.

'Brandon, you're not asking too much. Not at all.'

She raised her head to look at him, and he saw her shyness. 'Hugh, I'm just not sure what to do.'

'Nor am I,' he replied, 'except that everyone thinks we're already married.'

'We look like we are right now,' she pointed out, ever the practical one, which he had decided weeks ago was only one of her many charms. 'My goodness.'

'You're not afraid to give up your virginity to me?'

She shook her head, and her humour came back like a brief candle. 'This sort of thing wasn't covered at Miss Pym's, but I have no intention of going to my death without even a memory of a man's love. I refuse to just take the words of poets and sonnets, even Shakespeare's.'

He doubted he had ever heard a more honest admission in his entire life, even as Polly Brandon's eyes closed. She struggled to open them. 'Drat,' she muttered softly. 'Heroines in novels don't fall asleep at times like this.'

Laughing softly, Hugh cradled her in his arms and watched in amusement and love as she sighed and slept. Exhausted, he did the same.

Chapter Fifteen

At peace with himself after Brandon's declaration, Hugh waited until she slept, then left the warmth of her body, careful to tuck the blankets around her. He found his clothes—still damp—and put them on. At least his thorough dousing in one of Portugal's nameless rivers had cleansed his skin and made his smallclothes less objectionable. He smiled in the dark to think of what his Colonel Commandant in Plymouth would think of his filthy state.

I used to be a bit of a military fop, Hugh thought as he buttoned his trousers, which hung loose on him now. Amazing what three weeks on short rations and then no rations could do. He glanced at Polly. He decided that, as much as he admired her, he preferred the Brandon with more meat clinging to her.

He put his gorget around his neck again, always feeling a relief at having it hanging there, as it had for twenty years now. He knew he should wear it outside his uniform tunic, but there was some comfort from feeling the cold metal gradually warm against his skin, as it reminded him who he was. He glanced at Polly again, as unexpected emotion welled up in him. *I wish I had a ring for your finger right now*, he told himself. *Maybe you are not my actual wife; maybe there never will be one, but you should have a ring. Something eye-popping to impress our lovable Sergeant Cadotte.*

He stood a moment looking down at her, suddenly indecisive. If she should wake up while he was gone, what would she do? He chanced it, because he smelled something cooking in the next ruined stone room. Something told him he and Brandon had nothing to fear now from the Frenchmen. Their Sergeant was alive because he and Polly had acted.

Squatting by the fire, Sergeant Cadotte looked up when he came around the corner. 'You see before you a miracle, Colonel Junnit. I do not refer to myself, although I remain in your debt,' he said.

Food. Hugh felt his stomach contract and then release its grip on his spine, where he was certain it had cowered and clung for the last week. 'May I have some?' he asked, squatting beside his enemy.

After a glance at his Sergeant, the Corporal ladled what looked like porridge into a tin cup. Hugh took it from him with no preliminaries, scooping up a spoonful and blowing on it.

'One of my troopers went to take a piss by the sheepfold and noticed the stones,' Cadotte said.

'I don't understand,' Hugh said, after he swallowed a glorious mouthful of the bland mixture. It was wheat, probably cracked with the butt of someone's musket and boiled in river water. He knew he would never eat anything so delicious ever again, not if he lived to be a dribbling old man in a kilt in Kirkcudbright.

Cadotte raised his eyebrows. 'I know Portugal better than you. When they do not feel confident enough to build granaries such as you are already familiar with, the farmers dig grain pits and mark them with a cross of stones.' He finished his cupful. 'I cannot imagine how this was overlooked.' He nodded to his Corporal, who ladled out another cupful of wheat porridge. 'This is for your wife.'

Hugh finished his cup. He wanted to ask for more; for a second, he even wanted to eat the small share meant for Polly. 'Delicious,' he said, taking a swipe inside the cup with his finger and then handing it back to the Corporal.

Before he could take the cup for Polly, he heard an unearthly wail from the other side of the wall and leaped to his feet. He ran around the tumbling wall, the Sergeant just behind him, to see Polly sitting up, keening like an old woman from his home parish who had lost her whole family.

She burst into tears when she saw him. Hugh slid on his knees by her, careful to cover her again, and then hold her close. 'Polly, I was just around the corner! Oh, damn my eyes, Sergeant!'

She held herself off from him for a small second, then burrowed into his embrace with more tears. 'You were gone!' she managed to gasp. Hugh doubted any accusation at the eternal bar of God on judgement day would have even one-tenth the terror for him as her plaintive sentence.

He feared he couldn't hold her any tighter without cutting off her breathing, but she kept pressing closer, her tears spilling down her face until he could not help but cry, too, trying to shield himself from the Sergeant so his enemy would not have cause to gloat over his anguish at leaving Polly alone for even a moment.

He did manage a look at Cadotte, when Polly's tears turned into hiccups. What he saw brought tears to his own eyes again. The Sergeant sat cross-legged, elbows on his knees, his hands covering his face. Hugh kissed Polly's head, looked up at the dark sky. The matter had borne itself home to him more forcefully than any emotion of his life that no matter what happened, Polly was his wife. He had vowed at São Jobim to protect her, and he had just failed her miserably.

Finally she lay silent in his arms, worn out and staring at nothing. His face a study in calm, Sergeant Cadotte leaned across the small space separating them and touched her shoulder. 'Madame Junnit, let your husband help you with your clothes and come to our fire. We have food. He had only left you to get you some, too.'

She nodded, but said nothing. The Sergeant got up and returned to the other side of the wall.

'Can you forgive me for leaving you?' Hugh asked, feeling more wretched than the rawest recruit caught sleeping on duty.

'It's...it's the dream I wake up with every night. I was afraid you had left me to the troopers,' she whispered. 'You would never do that. I *know* you would never do that, but I was still afraid. I'm sorry.'

If she had ripped open his back with pincers and poured lime juice inside, he could not have felt worse, but there was only remorse in her voice, and no accusation. He didn't deserve such kindness.

'I'm the one to apologise, Polly,' he whispered back. 'I will never do that again.'

'Brandon, please,' she told him, with a trace of her former sass.

'Brandon only and always, except in company,' he said. 'Polly, dear.'

She tried to chuckle, but it came out in a sob instead. All he could do was hold her until she pulled away from him and let loose of the blanket. Without a word, she raised her arms so he could pull on her chemise, then let him help her to her feet so he could drop her dress over her head in the same way. He hadn't even needed to unbutton it in the first place, because it hung on her. With her hand on his shoulder, she let him help her into her stockings and shoes again. She stood still, a dutiful woman, as he carefully hooked the curved bows of her spectacles around her ears again.

They stood so close together that when her stomach growled, he wasn't sure if it was her or him. 'That is so unladylike,' she said. 'What a relief that I am not a lady.'

Hugh thought to himself that he would some day like to throttle this Miss Pym, who had been so careful to instruct this dear person in the reality of her illegitimate life, and what little she could possibly hope for. Suddenly, he wanted to consult Philemon Brittle, and meet Captain Worthy, and ask them how they managed their wives, these sisters who were unique in all the world.

'You're lady enough for me, Brandon,' he said gruffly, and kissed her.

Her arms were soft around his neck, then her fingers were in his hair, pulling at it, which he savoured more than he would have thought possible, considering his typical fastidiousness. Neatness be damned, he thought, knowing he reeked and his hair was greasy and he hadn't shaved in weeks. All he wanted to do was kiss Polly Brandon, like a brainless schoolboy.

'And for all intents and purposes, we are married,' he whispered to her, his lips still practically on hers.

She didn't hesitate, but what she said had the power to turn him to jelly. Amazing creatures, women. 'Don't you forget that and leave me alone again, Hugh Junot.'

As she sat close to her beloved, warm by the fire and honestly full of wheat porridge that had nothing whatever to recommend it except that it was hot and filled her stomach, Polly felt something incredibly close to happiness. There was no reason she should feel that way, not with the rain starting again, and sitting across from Sergeant Cadotte, the Corporal, and nine troopers—no, eight now, after the fall this morning. Hugh's arm was around her, and she felt safer than she knew she had any right to.

She looked down at her hands in her lap, wondering if the Frenchmen were sound sleepers, because she intended to give herself to Colonel Junot, that orderly, dignified, maybe a little vain, Marine who had become the man she needed now. For nearly two weeks now, they had lived every day as though it was their last on earth. Something burning deep in her body told her she would not willingly surrender her life in the middle of a war without knowing his love. If they only had one night together, it wouldn't be enough, but it might have to do.

Jesting aside, they weren't married and there was no way they could be right now. Maybe she was her mother's daughter, after all, because she didn't care about the niceties, the banns, the seals, the signatures. She wanted the man beside her. What made the matter so sweet was that she thought he wanted her, too. Outwardly, nothing had changed. He held her as close as he ever did, keeping up their subterfuge with the enemy. He called her 'Polly, *chère,*' as he always did around the Sergeant. Maybe it was the way he looked at her now.

She looked at Hugh and smiled, happy to see the relief in his eyes, and a little embarrassed she had frightened him so badly when she had called out and he had come running. So be it. She had been terrified to wake and find him gone. She would make it up to him. She could do no more right then except turn her face into his shoulder and kiss it, which made him swallow a few times and raise his face to the dark sky.

Maybe he knew what she was thinking. Hugh kissed the palm of her hand and tucked her fingers inside his tunic, which almost gave her the giggles, because it reminded her of a portrait of Napoleon she had seen once. When she patted his chest and withdrew her fingers, he got to his feet with a wince and a groan and tugged her up after him.

He released her and held out his hands, wrists together, to the Sergeant. 'No more, Colonel,' Cadotte said in a quiet voice, one that would not carry to his men, who were starting to bed down on the other side of the fire. 'If I cannot trust you after what happened at the river crossing, then I know nothing about character.'

'*Merci,*' Hugh said, inclining his head in what Polly thought could pass for deference—they were, after all, prisoners. Not even a river rescue had changed that. He turned to her then, and put his hand against her back. 'Come, my dear, let us go to bed.'

Sergeant Cadotte wasn't quite through. He held another blanket. 'The nights are getting colder,' was all he said, as if daring them to thank him.

She knew what she was going to do that night, but was too inexperienced to even frame a declaration. Tomorrow they would probably be joining the main body of the French regiment, and all chance at either privacy or life would be over. When the Colonel handed her the extra blanket, then walked away—keeping himself in her sight—to finish his private preparations for sleep, she spread out the blanket close to the wall. There was little privacy there, but she felt a certain security in the embrace of old stones and rubble.

Hugh stood on the perimeter of their ruined chamber, his back still to her, just looking into the darkness. He must know what she was going to do; it wouldn't have surprised her. By the time he turned around, she had removed her dress and was kneeling on the blanket, lifting off her chemise.

He watched her, a slight smile on his face. After a quick look around, he was kneeling on the blanket, too, removing his clothing. She could have sighed with relief. She was grateful he did not tell her what a supremely stupid idea this was, because giving away her virginity was a serious matter. She was only going to do it once, and thank God it was going to the man she trusted, to initiate her into an experience that might be brief.

When she was naked and unspeakably vulnerable, he helped her tuck the other blanket over her, his face more serious than she could remember, even after these weeks when little had been remotely amusing. Looking into that middle distance again, he removed his trousers and smallclothes and then lay down with her under the flimsy protection of the blanket.

Wordlessly, Polly moved into his embrace. For a long moment, he just held her close to him, running his hand along her arm, which was prickled with gooseflesh from the cool of early autumn in the mountains. With his other hand, he gently touched her body, seeming to find the most enjoyment in tracing the womanly swoop from her hip to her waist, and then to her breast, as she lay sideways, facing him.

The rhythmic motion of his hand relaxed her, then began to frustrate her as she began to grow almost too warm for the thin blanket. Working up her courage, she took his hand and placed it on her breast.

'Touch me wherever you want,' she told him. 'May I do the same?'

When he removed her hand, and raised up on one elbow, she was struck dumb with mortification until he took the moment to remove her spectacles, reach over her body, and place them in the little niche. He put her hand around his still-peaceful member. 'Share and share alike, sweetheart. It's not that I don't want you to see everything clearly, Brandon—oh, you know what a peacock I am! You wouldn't be disappointed,' he whispered. 'I would hate for your spectacles to fall victim to passion, when they have survived everything else.'

She chuckled, disarmed and relaxed. Tentatively, she began to stroke him, enjoying the feeling, but equally amazed by what was happening to her own body, as she touched his. All the blood in her core seemed to be rushing towards her loins as she stroked Hugh Junot—not a Colonel, not a Marine, not a fellow prisoner, but a man with her best interest at heart—and felt him begin to grow under her delicate touch. It was a power she could never have imagined. For a tiny, delicious moment, as though the thought came from another galaxy, she remembered telling him how much she enjoyed making plants grow.

She realised her eyes were squeezed shut, so she opened them to see what he was doing. To her increasing warmth and utter gratification, his eyes were closed and he had a slack look on his face, in vast contradiction to his usual military demeanour. She was a total amateur, and this man of experience was putty in her hands.

She kept her touch gentle, exploring him, running her hand next across the junction where his hip and thigh met. Miss Pym had taken them once to a gallery, where she had admired the cool marble men with sculpted bones and muscle. There was something elegant about the way Hugh Junot worked. Why quibble? All bodies had the same hip-and-thigh junction, but to feel another's skin and bone under her probing fingers was a glory she had not anticipated, in her rush to lose her own virginity. Perhaps this was less about her, and more about them, an epiphany that took away her breath for a moment.

She began to breathe deeper then, because he was touching her now. His fingers were soft as he probed into her body, taking his time as though they had hours and privacy and endless freedom to examine the nature of men and women. She had thought his probing, which grew more insistent, might be painful, until she realised that she was turning into liquid.

'Is this going right?' she asked, wondering for a moment why her mouth didn't work as well as usual.

'Superbly well, Brandon,' he said. She was glad to note she wasn't the only one having a tussle with speech. He sounded less than sober, slurring his words in a way that smacked of brandy.

She had been lying on her side, with his leg thrown over hers. Suddenly it wasn't comfortable; she turned on to her back and put her arms around him. His swollen member grazed her leg now as he gathered her closer, kissing her breasts, and then carefully taking her nipple into his mouth, which made her sigh.

He kissed her lips next, and then her neck. *'Madame Junot, je t'aime,'* he whispered. 'You're the bonniest lass in the universe and I am happy to be your man.'

She pulled him closer, not sure what to do with her body. It seemed almost to be thinking independently, as she felt more heat gather around her loins. *I wish you would enter me*, she thought, then realised he was probably not telepathic. 'I wish you would enter me,' she whispered.

'In a minute, Brandon. Let's have all the fun we can for as long as we can,' he told her.

In small circles, he began to massage her mound of Venus, sitting up so she saw his erect organ and she could watch what he did to her. She could not help thrusting up towards him then, which embarrassed her at first, but not for long. She decided enough was enough, and reached up to pull him down to her again. She clung to him, her fingers splayed out on his spine. She found herself pushing on his buttocks and starting to pant in his ear. She wasn't sure about the protocol, but it seemed a good thing to run her tongue inside his ear and breathe a little harder.

The result amazed her. Who knew that ears were so useful to lovemaking? Not her. Now it was his turn to mutter something indistinct and raise himself directly over her, one hand under her back and the other on his member as he coaxed her legs a little wider apart and slid himself inside.

It wasn't a totally uncontested passage. He positioned her more firmly under him and advised her to breathe deep breaths. It was good advice, because she relaxed after a momentary twinge, then decided on her own to wrap her legs around him, as he went deeper at a sedate pace: no hurry. He must have approved, because it was her turn to discover the delights of a tongue in the ear and reflect— as well as possible, anyway—on what that did to her mind.

And then it was all rhythm, which pleased her enormously. She had always been musical. The rhythm climaxed into a greater stiffening inside her, then a huge relaxation that filled her with peace, even as Hugh bowed over her body and try to stifle his groans into the hollow of her shoulder. She kissed his hair, sweaty now, and felt them turn into one being.

She would have liked the moment to have lasted longer, but as they lay together, she could almost feel the waves of exhaustion pouring off both of them. She opened her eyes to see his closed, his face a testament to fatigue. 'Oh, my dear,' she whispered, her hands on his hair. Eyes still closed, he smiled and kissed her forehead. Still inside her, he turned carefully on to his back, pulling her on top of him. In another moment he slept, and so did she.

He woke her before daylight, and made love to her again, moving slowly because he had little energy. As dawn came, they went through the entire ritual again, this time with more confidence. Their slow, deliberate pace this time aroused her beyond her ability to refrain from crying out in pleasure, as waves of rhythm seemed to spill from her body into his. He quickly put his hand over her mouth, and kept it there as he bowed his head over her, then put his face into her shoulder to silence himself, as he followed her in pleasure.

When they were more entirely satisfied than she ever would have thought humanly possible, he cuddled her close to his side. 'Brandon, I think Cadotte's Corporal will have to sling us over the horse today like meal sacks,' he whispered, and covered her mouth again when she giggled. 'Can you fathom our potential, if we ever get anything to eat?'

'I wish you would not talk of meal sacks! Lord, I am hungry. Let me remind you we have been married since São Jobim.'

'I feel that way, too,' he agreed, feeling reflective. 'Seriously, you know we have to have someone exhort us and counsel us and remind us that marriage is a remedy against fornication, and we have to sign papers and cry banns, and Lord, I have that all out of order. Maybe I should ask someone for your hand in marriage, but who that would be escapes me. Cadotte?'

She smothered her laugh in his bare chest, then grew serious. 'Nothing's happened in the right order. And please don't think I am angling for a proposal. You have not compromised me because I asked for what you gave.' *There*, she thought. *I am honest.*

Hugh reached over and handed her her spectacles, contemplating her. 'Hold that thought, Brandon.'

He kissed her forehead. It was so chaste, so disarming,

that she felt her heart turn over. Polly sat up and put on her spectacles. 'I mean it, Hugh,' she told him quietly.

Again he looked at her in that thoughtful way that she suddenly knew, with a real pang, that she could never tire of. 'Perhaps I should get dressed now,' she said, a little unnerved by his level gaze.

She dressed quietly, and then it was her turn to admire him in the low light. He had not an ounce of extra flesh anywhere, especially now that they were starving, courtesy of the enemy. She wanted to ask him how he managed to maintain such posture; maybe he would tell her that was a requirement of the service. When times were better, she would ask. She decided she had no commentary to make about his manly parts. Maybe Marines were just supposed to be impressive everywhere.

He laced up his smallclothes and put on his black-and-white checked shirt again, tucking the gorget inside, and then doing up the few buttons that remained. The shirt was ripped and well ventilated, and she smiled to herself when he frowned. *You are a vain man, Colonel Junot*, she thought. *Let us hope your hair never dares to fall out.*

She felt no need to look away when he strode to the edge of the ruin laughingly called a room and relieved himself. She felt a sudden breath of fear when he finished and stepped back in surprise. When he did not return to her immediately, she thought he must have trod upon something in his bare feet. He stood there a long while, then backed up a few paces before he turned around.

She wanted to ask him about that, but her eyes were closing again. When he knelt beside her and whispered for her to go back to sleep, she was happy to oblige. He put his lips close to her ear then.

'If I am not here when you wake up, don't worry, my love. I'll just be around the corner, talking to our favourite jailer.'

She nodded, pleasantly aroused again when he ran his tongue around the inside of her ear and took a tentative nibble on her ear lobe.

'Well, well, Brandon, you're a tasty morsel. Let's hope we find some more wheat today, or your succulent accessories might be in danger.'

'You're such a smooth talker,' she said, as the little flame in her body tamped itself down and let her slumber again.

'I am, indeed,' he told her as he lay down beside her once more. 'I'll just rest here a moment.'

He returned to sleep even before she did, to her amusement. Her spectacles were off, so she got as close to him as she could, admiring his face in repose, hoping their children would look like him. She lay back herself then, nearly overcome with the tantalising thought that they might have a future.

And if we don't, at least I have been loved, she told herself, upon reflection. Maybe it took the clear light of dawn to remind her of her place in life. She got up on one elbow to watch him again, knowing she would never tire of her private view, even as she weighed the probability of a real marriage, and not one engineered to fool the enemy into keeping them alive. The realist in her told her such a thing would never happen, no matter what he said when in the grasp of passion. The dreamer in her admonished her to be peaceful and contemplate what she had given away, and received in return.

It was the fairest trade of her life; of that, she had no doubt.

Chapter Sixteen

Hugh hadn't meant to sleep again, not with the Dragoons moving about in the other room. Careful not to disturb Brandon, he raised up on one elbow to watch her lovely face. He lay back for another moment, thinking of his father's letter last spring, admonishing him that it was high time to set up his own nursery.

He yearned to be a father. He had to give Da credit for starting him thinking along concrete lines. His thoughts had begun to solidify at Sacred Name, when he had watched Brandon playing with the little ones in the courtyard. He thought of Sister Maria Madelena and Brandon's promise in the death house of São Jobim to raise João as her own. So be it. They would, and gladly. *There was an old bee who lived in a barn*, he thought, eager for his own father to teach that silly rhyme to a grandson or daughter. Or João. As Scots went, his father was a tolerant man. As Hugh considered it, his father also was dead right about what had ailed him. *I hope I live to tell you, Da*, he thought.

Still, marriage was a serious venture. There was not

one thing Brandon had to offer that he could not get from a lady of higher degree, except her own dear self. Lying there next to her, he contemplated his career in ruins, his peers mocking him in barracks and wardrooms around the globe, his sister shocked and his father dismayed. Or not. *We live in uncertain times, Brandon, dear*, he thought, *and I do not mean the war.*

He rose quietly and dressed, gratified that Brandon did not wake up, and joined his enemies. The Dragoons were tending to their mounts, but Sergeant Cadotte stood by the glow of last night's fire, contemplating the coals as he sipped from his tin cup. He poured Hugh a tin cupful of liquid from the pot and held it out.

Ever hopeful, Hugh looked into the cup. It contained nothing more than boiled water, with what appeared to be a thin smear of wheat from last night's poor banquet. He took a taste. Obviously the French had better imaginations than he did. No stretch of his imagination was going to turn it into coffee or tea. Still, the cup was warm in his hands, and the air had a decided chill.

'Colonel, I am sorry we cannot give you and your wife more privacy.'

Oh, Lord. You must have heard us last night, Hugh thought, and felt his face grow warm. At a loss, he took a sip. 'We tried to be quiet,' he said finally.

'Ah, but I am in command here,' Cadotte replied, with that hint of a twitch around his lips. 'As you well know, Colonel, that means I sleep lighter than any trooper.'

'I understand, Sergeant,' Hugh said, and smiled. The Sergeant was the enemy, but he was also a man.

It was time for a massive change of subject, and Hugh had less trouble with that. The Sergeant was younger than he by many years, but every bit as experienced in the ways of war. Hugh knew he could not offer advice, but he also knew how heavy command could feel, especially when there was no one to talk to.

'Sergeant, we are being followed.'

'I know.' Cadotte gave one of those Gallic shrugs that Hugh knew he could never manage, not after all the family's years in Scotland. 'I think we have been followed since São Jobim.'

'I would agree.' Here was the dilemma. Should he say more? Hugh took another sip, deciding that he liked hot water well enough. 'Sergeant, how close are we to the Spanish border?'

He could tell his question had surprised the Sergeant of Dragoons, perhaps even knocked him off balance a little, never a bad thing with the enemy. *You are wondering why I am not asking you to just let Brandon and me go?* Hugh asked himself.

Hugh had to give the Sergeant points for shrewdness, though.

'Colonel, we are close to the border, which will work in my favour, not yours,' Cadotte replied, regaining his poise. 'When I join up with my Lieutenant and our larger force—hopefully today, if not tomorrow—the *guerilleros* who seem to be content to track us will fade into the background. I think they are not now strong enough to attack us.'

Hugh could think of another reason, and wondered why the Sergeant had not. There was no sense in alerting the man. He went back to the original point. 'Sergeant, why does moving into Spain work in your favour?'

Cadotte almost smiled then. 'Colonel, Colonel! You

know as well as I do that northern Spain is still well populated with French troops. Any hope you have of liberation by your allied troops are getting smaller the farther north we ride.' He replaced the threatening smile with something perilously close to scorn. 'We may have experienced a setback at Salamanca, but—excuse my plain speaking—Wellington is an idiot to besiege Burgos.'

Is that so? Hugh thought. Good thing Cadotte had not been sitting at the conference table in Lisbon last month, hearing of Admiral Sir Home Popham's successful raid on Santander, on the Bay of Biscay. It could be that even as they stood sparring with each other before a fire in a battered Portuguese farmyard, the balance had changed. *Or not*, he had to admit to himself again. There wasn't much about war that was predictable. He thought briefly of the happy times when he knew exactly where he was going in life, and tucked them away as the idiocy they represented.

'I, for one, would not mind if you just left me and Polly here to fend for ourselves.' Surely it didn't hurt to ask.

The Sergeant was silent, so Hugh finished his hot water and handed back the cup. Cadotte shook his head slowly, and Hugh sensed his regret. 'Colonel, I would do as you ask, except for one reason.' The Sergeant looked at his men, who by now had bridled and saddled their mounts. 'Them.'

Hugh understood perfectly, even as his heart sank. 'Ah, yes,' he said, keeping his tone light. 'How would it look if the leader released his prisoners?'

'What would you do in my position?'

You have me, Hugh thought. 'Precisely the same thing, Sergeant. Excuse me now. I will wake up my wife.'

* * *

Still, Hugh had to reflect over the next two days that Sergeant Cadotte was not as confident as he seemed. The Sergeant did not go back on his word to keep them unfettered, which was a relief. They were travelling out of the mountains now, skirting along the foothills, heading for northern Spain. The Sergeant seemed to know precisely where he was going, but he seemed in no hurry to get there, despite the hunger that rode along with them.

'It's odd, my love, but I think our Sergeant is almost daring our invisible *guerrilleros* to attack us,' he whispered in Brandon's ear as they followed the Corporal through the protecting underbrush.

He had told her yesterday of his suspicion they were being tracked, and she had surprised him. 'I thought so,' she had said, in that practical way of hers.

'Brandon, sometimes you amaze me,' he had told her.

'That's good,' she said complacently.

He had let out a crack of laughter at that, which caused the Corporal to turn around in the saddle and glare at them. Sergeant Cadotte even stepped his horse out of line and watched them for a moment, frowning.

'Perhaps he doesn't want us to have too much fun,' Brandon said. After the Sergeant resumed his place in line again, she turned her face into his tunic, lowering her voice. 'What I don't understand is why they have not attacked us.'

'Sergeant Cadotte seemed to think they are a much smaller party than we are,' Hugh whispered back. 'I don't think that's the reason.'

'You think they are larger?' she asked, after a long consideration.

'Much, much larger, my dear,' he had replied. 'I think they are waiting to attack until Cadotte takes them to his Lieutenant and his force.'

'Goodness,' Brandon had said, and nothing more.

Her pointed reminder to him not to underestimate her led him to the only reason for her silence—she knew, or at least suspected, how much more dangerous their situation had become. He could only hug her tighter, aware that she really couldn't know how terrifying a pitched battle would be, when the *guerrilleros* finally decided to attack with overwhelming numbers. Their own chances of surviving such a mêlée were not much better than a snowflake in a furnace, but she didn't need to know that.

The wheat lasted to noon on the second day. By night-fall, Sergeant Cadotte had led his little troop back to his regiment as accurately as a homing pigeon. Before he took them in, he bound their hands again, but not as tight as before.

'The devil we know, dearest,' Hugh whispered in her ear as he settled his bound hands around her again. 'What this will amount to, I have no idea, but we have a new set of captors.'

What it amounted to was a look of amazement on the face of Sergeant Cadotte's Lieutenant, a young man probably in his first command who stared at them, then turned on Cadotte, who had dismounted, along with his troop. After another furious look in their direction, the Lieutenant of Dragoons kneed his horse directly into the Sergeant, practically bowling him over.

'He's an ugly one,' Hugh said into her ear. 'He's never

learned what I learned in my first year as a Lieutenant: it's your NCOs who keep you alive.'

Rubbing his arm, Cadotte kept his face impassive as he took the brunt of the Lieutenant's sharp tongue. 'I can't follow what he is saying,' Polly told Hugh. 'It's too fast for me.'

She felt Hugh's sigh. 'It's what you probably think it is, dearest. He's asking our Sergeant why in God's name he did not kill us at São Jobim.'

Here it is, she thought, surprisingly calm. *After weeks it has come to this. Hugh and I will not live to see the sun go down. I only hope to heaven they are quick.*

'Will we die now?' she whispered.

He kissed the top of her head. 'We might. Polly Junot, you've been the best wife a man could hope for.'

His eyes still on the Sergeant, the Lieutenant shouted an order to Cadotte's Corporal, who walked towards them and held out his arms for her. They had done this for weeks now. Hugh lifted his arms up and Polly swung her leg across the pommel and allowed herself to drop into the Corporal's arms.

The Dragoon settled her on her feet, bending close to her this time to whisper, 'Speak only English, Madame Junnit.'

She knew better than to look at him, especially since the Lieutenant was staring at her, his eyes angry, his hand patting his sabre. She stood still, eyes down, as the Corporal helped Hugh from the saddle. When he stood beside her, she whispered. 'The Corporal told me to speak only English.'

'Then trust him,' Hugh replied. 'I have only one feeble card to play. Tally-ho, Brandon.'

Putting himself between them, the Corporal took them by the arms and walked them towards the Lieutenant. He stopped, but the Lieutenant beckoned them closer. When they were standing close to his horse, he suddenly took his foot from the stirrup and shoved Hugh to the ground.

Polly wrenched herself from the Corporal's grasp and threw herself down beside Hugh, who was shaking his head, as if to clear it. Grasping his arm with her bound hands, she tugged Hugh into a sitting position, as the Lieutenant danced his horse around them, almost stepping on her. She glanced at Sergeant Cadotte, noting the dismay on his face, and the two red spots that bloomed on his cheeks.

'I don't think that was called for, Lieutenant,' Polly said, after taking a deep breath. She put her bound arms around Hugh and hugged him to her.

'Parlez-vous francais?' the officer asked, putting his foot back in the stirrup.

She shook her head. 'Through an unfortunate confluence of events, we found ourselves prisoners.'

'I speak French, Lieutenant,' Hugh said. 'My name is Lieutenant Colonel Hugh Philippe d'Anvers Junnit, of the Second Division, Royal Marines. This is my wife, Polly Junnit.' He hesitated. 'Perhaps you are more familiar with the French pronunciation—Junot.'

Whatever his failings as a Lieutenant, the young officer seemed to have heard of the name, Polly realised, as she watched the man's face. In fact, he grabbed at his reins and stared at Hugh on the ground before him, then dismounted.

'What did you say?'

Hugh repeated himself.

The Lieutenant shook his head in disbelief. 'Junot?'

Hugh nodded. Polly held her breath as the Lieutenant, hands on his hips, glared at Hugh, who smiled back. 'Where *is* my dear uncle Jean-Andoche?'

'Sergeant Cadotte!' the Lieutenant yelled. 'Front and centre!'

Looking almost as amazed as the Lieutenant, Cadotte came quickly to attention, the red spots in his cheeks even more pronounced now. 'Sir!'

The Lieutenant tapped Cadotte's shoulder with the crop. 'Why did you not tell me his name was Junot?'

'Sir, I…' Cadotte began, his voice mystified.

'Help me up,' Hugh told Polly. She did as he asked. He staggered and shook his head again. 'Lieutenant…'

'Soileau.'

'Lieutenant Soileau, it is not your Sergeant's fault. I introduced myself to him as Lieutenant Colonel Hugh Junnit, which is how we pronounce the name in Scotland.'

'Scotland?' Soileau repeated. 'Junnit? Good God. Are you a *spy*?'

'Sir, I am a Royal Marine in his Majesty's service,' Hugh said, drawing himself up and managing to look so masterfully offended that Polly stared, too. 'It happens there is a branch of the family in Scotland, and it is a long story. But tell me, how is my dear uncle? Is he with Clausel or Massena? Does he have his marshal's baton yet?'

Good God, he is amazing, Polly thought. She looked at the Lieutenant, who had the stunned look of an ox banged on the head and ready for slaughter. She watched as he took a moment to collect himself.

'How can I be sure you are who you say you are?'

'Ask my wife.'

The Lieutenant barely glanced at her. 'Bah! She speaks no French, and from the way she is looking at you, she would probably tell me you were the second cousin of Our Lord Himself, if you wanted her to.'

'She is a dear thing, isn't she?' Hugh said agreeably in English. 'Polly, dear, perhaps the kind Lieutenant will untie your hands so you can reach up and unsnap my gorget.' He continued in French, 'My name is engraved on the other side. It's also tattooed on the inside of my left leg.'

The Lieutenant's mouth dropped open. 'The Royal Marines require *that*?'

'Lieutenant, were you never drunk, nineteen, and in a foreign port?'

Lieutenant Soileau shook his head, then gestured to Cadotte to untie Polly's hands. He seemed unaware that the Sergeant's troopers had gathered around, their tired faces lively with interest.

'Thank you, Sergeant,' she said in English, then unbuttoned the top two buttons of Hugh's tunic. He bent down obligingly as she pulled out the gorget he had tucked inside his shirt and unsnapped it from the chain. She held it out to the Lieutenant, who did not take it from her, but read the inscription.

He read it again, aloud this time, and stood another moment in thought. 'As we speak, your uncle is with our glorious Emperor and the *Grand Armée* in Russia,' he said finally, his voice subdued, as though he did not believe his own ears.

'What a shame for me!' Hugh exclaimed. 'I would like to have seen him and exchanged pleasantries. Since the war, family reunions have been impossible.'

Don't press your luck, you scoundrel, Polly thought, as she put the gorget back around his neck and tucked it inside his shirt.

Hugh's lips were close to her ear. 'I'm out of ideas,' he whispered. 'Brandon, this would be a good time to faint.'

With a sigh, she did exactly what he asked. A man couldn't hope for a better wife.

Chapter Seventeen

She must have been convincing. After a suitable amount of time, she moaned and opened her eyes to find herself lying on a camp cot in a tent blessedly warm.

She had known Hugh would catch her on the way down, especially since he had engineered the faint, so never having lost consciousness, it was no surprise to see him kneeling beside the cot, his eyes full of concern, and something else that made her heart leap a little. She touched his face.

She hadn't meant to unman him, but her touch filled his eyes with tears. 'Lieutenant, can you send someone for a little water? Just a sip would be so kind,' Hugh said. He took her hand in his, kissed her palm, and tucked it close to his chest. 'You're better than Siddons,' he said in English. 'Although I suppose after weeks in captivity, it ain't hard to look wan.'

'It's easier than I would have thought,' she murmured to him, putting her hand over his. 'What is this supposed to get us?'

'Some sympathy?' he whispered back. 'Heaven knows, *I* feel sorry for us.'

Lieutenant Soileau snapped out an order and in a moment Hugh was helping her into a sitting position for that sip of water. She took one sip, and with what she hoped was a die-away look on her face, begged her husband to let her rest again.

He did, with a perfectly straight face, and Lieutenant Soileau himself tucked a light blanket about her. He motioned to Hugh and the men withdrew for a brief conference. With a sigh, she resolved to let her husband worry about the pickle they were in, and resigned herself to sleep. At least they were still alive.

When she woke later, Hugh sat in a folding camp chair by her cot, head back, eyes closed. She knew he needed sleep, but she wanted information more, so she put her hand on his thigh and squeezed it. His eyes opened in an instant. He looked wildly around the tent first, as though wondering where he was, then smiled down at her.

'Do we live to fight another day?'

'We do, Polly, dear,' he told her. 'I fear, though, that our good Sergeant Cadotte had to endure a blistering scold for not killing us at São Jobim. I couldn't hear the whole thing, but Cadotte may have even been busted down to Corporal.'

'I *am* sorry for that,' Polly said. 'I should sit up, but for the life of me, I don't want to.'

'Then don't. Lieutenant Soileau graciously consented to your remaining in his tent tonight. He even promised some food, but don't expect much.' He grew serious immediately. 'I think Lieutenant Soileau is taking us along with his force to General Clausel, who had withdrawn to Burgos, where our own dear Wellington is laying him siege. Who knows what will happen then, except that I am so glad Cousin—or Uncle—Junot is somewhere in Russia.'

'You don't even know if he is a relative, do you?' she asked.

'Haven't the slightest,' Hugh replied cheerfully.

'What will Clausel do with us?'

'Probably pass us off to someone else, as Lieutenant Soileau is eager to do.' He hesitated then. Polly knew him well enough to know something else was percolating in his fertile brain. 'I can't gild this, my darling, but I rather think the *guerilleros* who have been dogging our steps will make their move tomorrow. Clausel might be the least of our worries.'

She mulled over that bad news during dinner, which was tough beef in a wine sauce, bread pudding made of hardtack, but soaked in rum sauce with raisins, and excellent port. By the time the meal was over—Lieutenant Soileau had shared it with them—all she wanted to do was sleep.

Lieutenant Soileau had no intention of allowing Hugh to run tame in his tent for the night. So he told Hugh, who translated for her. 'You already know. He is taking me to the detention tent for another of our typical nights in the hands of our enemies, Brandon. I'm sorry.'

She was powerless against the dread of having Hugh Junot gone from her sight. 'Tell Lieutenant Soileau I will go with you.'

The detention tent was no worse than other nights on the trail from São Jobim to this nameless spot in the foothills, and far better than the granary. While Lieutenant Soileau looked askance, Hugh made himself comfortable against a meal sack, obligingly held out his hands to be bound, then patted his thigh. Ignoring the Lieutenant, who refused to bind her hands, Polly sat down beside Hugh and rested her head on his leg, tugging the extra blanket around her. She was asleep in minutes, happy to be where she was.

They were up before daylight, prodded by the sentry, who grudgingly loosened Hugh's bonds so he could attend to his private business and shooed Polly from the tent while he did so. Lieutenant Soileau's blanket around her, she waited serenely in the mist, watching the Dragoons at their breakfast fires. Sergeant Cadotte and his men squatted by their own fires, and she noted with some relief, at least, that the Sergeant seemed to have retained all his rank.

As she stood there, Cadotte brought her a tin cup of what turned out to be chicken broth. She drank it gratefully, surprised there had been a chicken still on the loose in this picked-over terrain. The fowl must have been as determined to live as the Junnits.

'I am sorry we got you in trouble, Sergeant,' she said in French, after looking around to make sure Lieutenant Soileau was not in sight.

He shook his head. 'Junot. Junnit. Good Christ, woman!' Cadotte looked around, too. 'I could not have killed you. It never was the bribe your husband so generously offered, and you may tell him that.'

'Why, then?' she asked, curious.

'That nun was a spy and I did my duty,' he told her. 'You, however, were in the wrong place at the wrong time. God help me, but I don't customarily make war on women.' He looked away, as if contemplating his own family. 'Heartless as I was at Sâo Jobim, God forgive me.'

She handed back the cup. He took hold of it, but did not take it from her. His fingers touched hers. 'Be careful today. I'll watch you two if I can.'

You're my enemy, she thought, grateful for Cadotte. *We owe you so much. 'Merci,'* was all she said.

Cadotte was obviously one of the smaller cogs in the battalion, but he still managed to secure the same horse for them. She noticed he did everything quickly, before Lieutenant Soileau had the opportunity to impose his own regulations. Polly held her hands out to be bound, but Cadotte shook his head. 'Not this time, Madame Junot. Keep your hands low in your lap, and I do not think the Lieutenant will notice. Be watchful and think quickly.'

When he touched his finger to his helmet and turned away, Polly twisted around to look at Hugh, who was watching the Sergeant with his own troubled expression. 'I'm afraid,' she whispered.

'I am, too,' Hugh murmured back. 'Keep your eyes on Cadotte. He'll help us, if he can.'

The column rode into a misty morning, the forest abnormally quiet of birdsong. Although admonished to silence by Lieutenant Soileau, there was no way to totally quieten the creak of harness, clink of mess kit, or the sharp strike of horseshoe against stone. Polly strained for the sound of other horses and men riding on their periphery, but she heard nothing.

The mist gave way to a morning as beautiful as any she had ever seen, the air crisp and the landscape scrubbed clean by the rain that had fallen in the night. They continued their downward path until Polly saw open ground in the distance.

'The plains of León,' Hugh said, and there was no mistaking the relief in his voice. 'I believe we are less than eighty miles from the Bay of Biscay.'

It might as well be a million miles, she thought. Hugh seemed to read her mind. 'Now we will turn east towards Burgos, I suppose,' he said. 'Ah, well.'

Lieutenant Soileau called a rest. When they were in the saddle again, Sergeant Cadotte stepped his horse out of the line and waited a moment until they were beside him.

'This is the last pass to the plains, Colonel,' he said, keeping his voice soft and looking straight ahead, ignoring them. She barely saw his hands move as he placed a knife in her lap. 'Watch for an opportunity and take it. *Bon chance.*' He touched spurs to his mount and moved up into the line, in front of his Corporal.

Polly could not stop the fear that seemed to ripple down her spine. She took the knife, and cut through Hugh's bonds, as he continued to envelop her in his grasp, his hands in front of her. 'Don't drop the knife,' he told her. 'Do what I tell you when the moment comes.'

It was then that she heard other horses and riders, but they were above them in the pass. Some of the Dragoons were looking up, too, and gesturing. It was just a man here and a man there, standing, observing, dressed in brown to blend in with the dry plains of León. When the column turned, she saw Lieutenant Soileau in the vanguard, his head inclined towards one of his Sergeants, who pointed with some emphasis.

'Lieutenant Soileau is too green for this assignment,' Hugh whispered. 'He is in over his head. He's ignoring his Sergeants. Brandon, it's going to be bad!'

He grasped her around the waist then, his hand tight.

At a word from Cadotte, who rode ahead, the Corporal loosed the rope that bound his horse to theirs. Polly snatched the rope, leaning forwards across the horse's neck.

When she tried to rise, Hugh pushed her down again into the animal's mane, and leaned over her. He edged off the path just as the noonday calm erupted in screams and gunfire. 'Get off and slide down the embankment,' Hugh ordered, loosing his grip on her and lifting her leg over the pommel. 'Don't look back!'

She did as he said, as the *guerilleros* seemed to rise like rapid-growing plants from the hillside, and rain down fire. She stood at the side of the road, rooted there in her fear, as the Corporal suddenly slapped his ear, slumped across his horse's neck, then plopped in a heap at her feet, a bullet drilled through his brain.

Polly needed no other encouragement. She slid down the slope, rolling and scrambling up and falling again as the column dissolved in gunfire. Horses screamed and pushed against each other as everyone tried to take cover. Other Dragoons had dismounted, true to their training, and were firing now from positions along the embankment she had slid down.

Scarcely breathing, she watched for Hugh through the growing smoke of the muskets, realising with an ache that he had not been so far from her side in weeks. She began to cautiously climb up the embankment, looking for him. Relief coursed through every fibre of her body as she saw a scarlet tunic and then Hugh as he slid off his horse and tried to follow her down the slope. As she watched in horror, one of the Dragoons pulled out his sidearm and aimed it right at Hugh.

'Hugh!' she shrieked. He had no weapon. She raced up the slope, blotting everything from her mind except Hugh. It wasn't so far, and she suddenly felt strong, despite days of starvation, cold rain, and despair. Suddenly, she knew what it felt like to risk everything for what she loved the most. She understood what Sister Maria Madelena had tried to tell her at São Jobim.

As puny as it was, the Dragoon hadn't expected an attack from the rear. Polly scrambled to her feet and lunged for the horsehair tassel hanging from the man's helmet, jerking it with all her might. It earned her a clout on the shoulder, but he fell backwards, tried to struggle to his feet, then was stopped for ever by a bullet from a musket—friend or foe she had no idea.

Polly sobbed out loud, then shrieked as Hugh grabbed her around the waist and ran down the slope. Not until he found a fallen tree and pulled her behind it did he release his grip.

They lay in a jumble, arms around each other, until the firing stopped. She wanted to say something, but she knew it would only come out as babble, so she was silent, feeling her heartbeat gradually slow, and the tingling feeling leave her arms and legs until she felt as heavy as the log they crouched behind.

'I told you to go down that slope and not look back,' Hugh said finally.

'He came between me and you,' she said, touching his face as though she had never thought to do that again.

He didn't say anything more, but gathered her closer. They lay there, listening, until the voices above them were Spanish instead of French.

'Do you know any Spanish?' Hugh asked.

'Not much. Do you?'

'Precious little.' He sat up cautiously. 'It galls this Scot, but all I can remember is *Ingleses*. I have to tell them I am English.'

'I'm coming with you.'

'You are not!' He took her chin in his hand and gave it a little shake. 'And don't give me that mulish look, Madame Junot! Stay here. I won't ask you twice.'

He sat on the fallen log, brushing futilely at his scarlet tunic, which was torn, stained, and bloody. Most of the gilt buttons hung by threads. He pulled his gorget out of the front of his tunic and settled it where it belonged. He glanced at Polly.

'You're probably going to tell me I'm a dandy and I don't smell very good, either,' he muttered.

'You certainly don't,' she teased, then reached for him. 'Please be careful, my love. My love,' she repeated, enjoying the way it rolled over her tongue.

'Your love,' he mused. 'Brandon, I think—no, I know—your sister wanted you to wait a few years and then fall in love with a solicitor, or maybe a ship builder.'

'Probably,' she replied agreeably, since he was going to be a dunce. 'I will be a sad disappointment to them, but not to me. I never wanted to harm anyone, but Boney gave me no choice. It's my fight, too.'

He looked at her in admiration, then gently pushed her spectacles higher up on her nose. 'I still can't believe they are not broken.' He started up the hill, moving deliberately, his hands up, calling *'Ingleses'* every few feet until he was on the road again. Polly held her breath, fearing a volley of rifle fire, but the only sounds she heard were weapons being thrown on to a pile and the groans of the wounded, followed by shrieks. *Dear God, they are killing the wounded*, she thought. *What kind of men are these?*

When she did not think she could stand it another minute, Hugh came halfway down the slope and gestured to her. She wavered, not wanting to see the carnage on the road, but uneasy to be so far away from her love. Hugh won out, as she knew he always would, and she climbed the slope.

He grasped her arm to pull her on to the road, then held her tight, face against his chest. 'We won't be here long, Brandon. They have no plans to bury the dead or aid the wounded.'

'Are we...?' She couldn't even think of the word. It had been too long.

'Free? Indeed, we are. We are in the hands of General Francisco Espoz y Mina, himself.' He pointed to a tall man, hatless, bending over what remained of Lieutenant Soileau. 'He speaks only Basque, but his Lieutenant, Feliz Sarasa there, speaks Spanish and English.'

She only nodded, her eyes huge in her face, as she watched the killing ground. 'Are they all dead?'

'If they aren't, they soon will be. The *guerilleros* aren't inclined to give quarter. Seems a pity, almost, doesn't it?'

She nodded, unable to take her eyes from the dead, who systematically were being stripped of what clothing might be useful in the guerilla cause, and then rolled unceremoniously down the slope she had just climbed.

Hugh's grip tightened involuntarily. 'Look you there. Sergeant Cadotte.'

She followed where he led, picking her way through

the French until the hem of her skirt was crimson. She knelt when Hugh knelt by the side of the Sergeant, who lay with one leg bent in an odd direction, his hands bloody from clutching his stomach.

'He's barely alive,' Hugh whispered. 'What I would give to have your brother-in-law here, except I fear it would do no good.' He put his hands on both sides of the Sergeant and leaned close until his lips were practically on Cadotte's ear. 'Sergeant, can you hear me?'

The dying man's eyes opened finally. Polly could hardly bear to look at him, but when she did, she saw no fear, only weariness.

One of the *guerilleros* knelt beside Cadotte, too, his knife out. Hugh shot out his hand to stop the man. 'No, *por favor*, no,' Hugh said. *'Este...este hombre...'* He stopped, his Spanish exhausted.

'Su amigo?' the *guerillero* asked, a look of incredulity on his face.

'He saved our lives,' Hugh said, leaning over Cadotte, shielding him with his own body. 'Please leave him to me.'

The *guerillero* obviously didn't understand, but shrugged and moved away, looking for enemies without friends. Hugh turned back to the Sergeant of Dragoons and carefully put his arm under Cadotte's shoulders, raising him up slightly.

'L'eau,' he gasped.

Polly looked around. The Corporal lying nearby still had his canteen attached to his belt. Trying not to look at his ruined face, she cut the canteen with his knife and brought it back to Hugh. He tipped a little of its contents into Cadotte's mouth. The water only dribbled out the corners and from the wound in his neck, but the Sergeant said *'Merci,'* anyway.

She decided she could not be afraid of this dying man and tried to think what Laura would do. She took him by the hand and was rewarded with the slightest of pressure against her fingers. It could have been her imagination.

'Sergeant, we owe you our lives, twice and three times over,' Hugh said, his mouth close to Cadotte's ear again. 'I remember your wife's name, but is there a direction besides just Angoulême where I can send her funds for your farm? Is there a parish?'

The Sergeant was silent. 'I asked him too much,' Hugh said in frustration and near tears himself.

'Lalage.' In spite of his vast pain, Cadotte seemed to caress the name. A long moment passed, then, 'Sainte Agilbert.' He smiled at Polly. 'If…girl, name…Lalage.'

Polly raised his bloody hand to her cheek. 'I promise.'

Cadotte nodded slightly and turned his head a fraction of an inch towards Hugh again. 'Cows. A new fence.' He sighed, as though thinking of the farm he would never see again, and a woman named Lalage. The sigh went on and on, and he died.

His face a mask of pain, Hugh gently released the Sergeant and pulled Polly close to him. 'I wish I had not deceived him.'

'Lalage is a beautiful name,' Polly said through her tears. 'We will use it some day, husband.'

He managed the ghost of a smile. 'No one will understand.'

'Do you care?'

He shook his head and kissed her temple. 'When the war is over, we will mend a fence near Angoulême. There will be a lot of cattle for it to contain.'

Chapter Eighteen

They were in the saddle again in less than an hour, riding at the front of the column now, next to a Lieutenant of Pakenham's division, and dressed like one of Espoz y Mina's ragtag army.

'Wellington has sent a few of us into the hills to ride with the *guerilleros*, Colonel Junot, although I cannot for the life of me understand why,' he said cheerfully as they rode along. 'Good show this morning, eh?'

I wonder what this irritating Lieutenant would do if I suddenly knocked him out of his saddle? Hugh asked himself, his mood sour and his mind dark.

He knew how Brandon felt. As they rode away from the bloody ground, she turned her face into his chest and sobbed, which only made the British Lieutenant look at her in amazement.

'I say, Colonel,' he whispered. 'Doesn't she understand that we have freed you from the French?'

Hugh returned some non-committal answer, knowing it was fruitless to explain to this ninny that in any war, especially one fought as long as this conflict, there comes a time where reasonable men and women have had enough. His own heart was heavy enough, thinking of Lalage Cadotte and her two sons whom she would continue to raise alone. He didn't want to think how many sad little families there were in France, in Spain, in England.

That's it, he told himself, discarding every reason why the world would think theirs a foolish match. *Polly is my love.* He decided then that his home with Brandon would not be a sad one. He longed to take her to Kirkcudbright. He wanted to walk along the shoreline, watch the fishing boats, breathe deep of the fragrance of his late mother's rose garden, and imagine the delight of a young child skipping along beside him. He knew he was duty-bound to the Marines until the war ended, at least, but there wasn't any reason Brandon herself could not be his proxy, and settle into that lovely life he suddenly wanted for himself.

He looked down at her, wondering if she even knew how much she probably loved him, she who would have killed that Dragoon on the slope. If she did, something told him she would never allow herself to be settled so far away from him. He swallowed as his own heart raced uncomfortably at the idea of such a separation. Scotland could wait, as long as she was safely tucked into his quarters in Plymouth. Even then, he thought it would be hard to kiss her goodbye every morning and attend to his deskbound duties a building away. He wondered if a time would ever come when he would feel easy again without her in his line of sight.

They rode as hard as the French soldiers now lying slaughtered had ridden, in that last pass before the mountains gave way to the vast plain of León. At first, he listened with half an ear to the voluble Lieutenant who rode beside him, learning of Wellington's triumphal entry into Madrid, then the need to move north and invest the stronghold of Burgos. There was hopeful talk of wintering in the Pyrenees and moving on France in the spring, rather than enduring another dreary retreat to Portugal and the safety offered by the lines of Torres Vedras and the Royal Navy close offshore.

In late afternoon, the *guerillero* leader the Lieutenant called Espoz y Mina stopped the column and rode with his English-speaking Subaltern along the column, falling in beside the Lieutenant. Through interpreters, he told them his army was taking the road east to Burgos.

'*El jefe* wants you and your wife to continue with a smaller column to the Bay of Biscay,' the interpreter said.

'I won't argue,' Hugh told him. 'After a month in the saddle, this Marine would like to clap his eyes on a fleet.'

'You will, then,' the interpreter said. '*Vayan con Dios.* I will leave you with another interpreter.' He nodded to the Lieutenant on foot, who gave them a cheery wave and peeled off with the long column. The smaller unit watched until Espoz y Mina's army turned on to what looked like no more than a cow trail, but pointed east to Burgos. The new interpreter, a long-faced Basque named Raul Etchemindy, rode beside them.

The smaller column continued north and turned slightly west, as it sought the relative safety of another mountain pass. 'This area is still patrolled by the *crapaud*,' Etchemindy said. 'That will change, God willing, if your Wellington invests Burgos.' He shrugged philosophically. 'If not, then we fight another year.'

The rains came again as the tired horses plodded into a village Hugh never would have seen from the plains below. Small and self-contained, he wondered if it had been guarding the pass since the earliest days of Roman conquest.

Brandon had said next to nothing through the long afternoon, and he was relieved to hand her off carefully when he halted his horse in the village square. His buttocks on fire, he dismounted with a groan and barely had time to blink before the horse was whisked away down a side street. He looked around. All the horses were gone now, hidden from French eyes.

He put his arm around Brandon, who leaned against him. 'I'm so tired,' she said.

Then it was their turn to be taken in hand by Etchemindy and whisked away into a small, fortress-like house. Chattering in an uninflected language he did not understand, two women pried Brandon from his side and led her away. He stood there a moment, indecisive and uneasy to have her gone, then turned to Etchemindy.

'You are safe here,' his Basque said in good, workaday English. 'In the past four years, we have had English visitors. Sometimes they even bring us weapons, but never enough.'

'Perhaps we can change that,' Hugh said, interested.

'Possibly. We are riding to Santander as soon as your wife is able, *señor*. The fleet has brought more weapons for the Spanish army, but we in the hills need an advocate.'

'We can leave tomorrow, and I can help you,' Hugh told him. 'Admiral Sir Home Popham is my friend.'

Etchemindy clapped Hugh's arm as his solemn expression gave way to a smile. 'It is a doubly good thing, then, that we did not shoot you on sight, and wonder later who the man in the scarlet coat was!'

Etchemindy led him into a heavy-beamed room dark with the wood smoke of centuries, sat him down, and offered him a bowl of soup. Hugh felt his hunger pangs increase at the sight of meat floating in the thick broth. His host handed him a hunk of dark bread, which made a heavenly sop.

He ate too fast, knowing he would suffer for it by morning. He was reaching for more bread when he noticed one of the women hovering in the doorway, beckoning to him. *Brandon*, he thought, alarmed, and rose at once.

The woman whispered to Etchemindy, who turned to him. '*Señor*, follow my wife.'

Outside a closed door, the woman spoke at length to her husband, who gestured Hugh closer. 'Your little lady is just sitting in the tub and keeps asking for you.'

Hugh let out the breath he had been holding, relieved. 'It is this way, Señor Etchemindy. We have not been separated for some weeks now, and I confess I am feeling lost without her, too. With all due respect and thanks to your wife, may I go in and take care of things?'

Etchemindy nodded. 'Goodnight. If we are not being presumptuous, we can find some fresh clothing in the village.'

'Not presumptuous at all,' Hugh said. 'It's been a long time.'

The wife whispered again to her husband, who laughed. 'She says she is going to burn your clothing, no matter what you decide.'

'Wise of her!'

When the Etchemindys had returned to their great room, Hugh knocked softly and lifted the latch. What he saw touched his heart. Just as Señora Etchemindy had said, Brandon sat in a tin tub, head down to one side, shoulders slumped. Her hair was tumbled around her shoulders, but it was dry. She just sat there, as though too stunned by the day's events to move.

He just looked at her, seeing again how young she was, how utterly spent. She was a woman with the courage of a lion, who would have killed for him, but there she sat. *Do I sympathise?* he asked himself. *Do I tease her? Do I just tell her I love her?*

'Brandon.'

She gasped and looked around, and the relief in her eyes scored him right to the bone. He felt his own heart lift, and he knew he had been hungrier for the sight of her than that whole bowl of stew, as good as it had tasted. A room without Polly Brandon in it was a room not worth inhabiting. It was a simple truth, but deeper than a well.

He was at her side then, squatting by the tub, his arms around her awkwardly. She didn't try to kiss him or say anything, but clung to him, her arms strong around his neck. She was a woman who would never fail him or tease him or play a missish card. She had a heart of oak, first requirement of a Royal Marine.

He kissed her cheek. 'Brandon, I suppose you will have a thousand objections and try to stop me from sacrificing myself, but here it is. Brace yourself. I love you.' It sounded so good to his ears he said it again. 'I love you.'

Her voice was small. 'Enough to marry me?'

'More than enough. Laura Brittle knew. I knew it, even though I didn't dare say anything. And then I tried to change my mind.' He rested his cheek against hers. 'Are you certain you want to splice yourself to a chowderhead?'

'When I saw that Dragoon point his sidearm at you...' she began. She sobbed and tightened her grip.

'Is that a yes?' he asked, cradling her in his arms and soaking his sleeves.

She nodded.

I daren't be a watering pot, too, he thought, *else she will change her mind.* He tickled her knee instead, content to be easy with the lovely body he already knew. 'You know, Brandon, we will return to Plymouth and I will dutifully take my place at the conference table, probably never to roam the world again,' he said into her ear. 'No more adventuring in foreign waters. I shall leave that to the Lieutenants and Captains in my division. You'll be stuck looking at my sorry visage over breakfast and dinner tables. I can't live without the sight of you.'

'I feel the same way,' she whispered. 'As for roaming the world again, you will, but you will be duty-bound to write me long letters!'

She was patient with him as he poured water over her head and worked soap through her tangled hair, digging with his fingernails until she sighed with pleasure. He washed her hair twice more, then devoted his attention to the rest of her.

It was easy to linger over her breasts, which had lost some of their heft, but none of their attraction. He shook his head at the sight of her ribs. Where had his plump Brandon gone? A few good meals would change that. He had no doubt that his cook in Plymouth would not rest until the Colonel's lady was better fleshed.

She stood when he asked, and let him leisurely lather her hips and thighs and the space between. In fact, she began to breathe hard and clutch at his hair, as he bent to the task. She gasped, pressing his hand into her soft folds, making sure he didn't miss a thing. His thoroughness was gentle. She clutched him convulsively, then kissed the top of his head after she found release.

He rinsed her off as she laughed softly, then wrapped a towel around her and moved her closer to the fireplace. As he dried her, he couldn't help but think how it had all started on board the *Perseverance*, and her so seasick. He had cared for her then and he cared for her now.

'Thank you for saving my life,' he said into her bare shoulder, as she finished drying herself. 'What an inadequate statement, Polly!'

'I would do it again,' she said, turning around.

He picked her up and deposited her in the bed. 'You're my hero, Brandon.'

She blushed becomingly, and held out her hand to him. 'I'd rather just be your wife, and sing lullabies to our children. You can have the adventuring, Hugh. I don't mind.'

'That's fair enough.' He sat beside her on the bed. 'I don't mean to be squeamish, but your bathwater is daunting. Perhaps Señora Etchemindy can get her little Etchemindys—I saw them peeking around the stairwell—to empty this, move it into the kitchen, and fetch some clean water.'

He looked at her. She was asleep, her hand limp on her bare breast. He laughed softly to himself and covered her with the blanket.

Hugh took his time bathing in the kitchen, once the tub had been emptied and moved from the bedroom. Señora Etchemindy had retired for the night, so Hugh entertained his host with the whole story, from his impulsive leap into the *barco* at Vila Gaia to the ambush on the mountain pass. Etchemindy nodded and smoked his pipe.

'That nun at São Jobim was no nun,' Etchemindy said.

'I didn't think so,' Hugh said, soaping up, 'but she had been violated like so many of Portugal's fair women.' He looked at Etchemindy, soap in hand. 'Some women withdrew, some descended into madness, some coped, and some, like Sister Maria, turned it into a great thirst for revenge.'

'No different than men,' Etchemindy commented. 'Sister Maria Madelena passed on valuable information to your navy. She paid a high price.'

Hugh had nothing more than a towel to wrap around his middle when he padded back down the hall, because Señora Etchemindy had taken out everything except his gorget to the burn pit. Her husband assured him that the village wasn't so destitute that it couldn't come up with adequate fabric to hang on his frame, come morning.

The fire had worked its way down to hot coals and a red glow. He breathed in the fragrance of pine oil and pronounced it better than anything he had smelled in weeks. Autumn was well advanced now and the tang of wood smoke reminded him pleasantly of home.

Brandon was sitting up in bed.

'You were supposed to be asleep,' he told her as he discarded his towel and climbed in beside her.

Polly said nothing, but wrapped her arms and legs around him, working her way into his core. She kissed him with a ferocity that stunned him at first, then built a bonfire in his own body. All he could do was show her how much he loved her by easing himself as deep inside her as he could, all the while kissing her open mouth. They were bound up tight in each other arms.

When she cried out, he felt no need to cover her mouth. The walls were thick, and he knew the Etchemindys were understanding. He could have been quieter, too, or maybe not. They had survived; this coupling was a triumphant victory over death, as they told each other of their love and celebrated their survival with their bodies.

Their next coupling at dawn gave them both a chance to watch each other make love. He had never really noticed before that she had a light sprinkling of freckles on her breasts. Maybe, after peace came and he had some free time, he would count each one. He liked the comfortable way she rested her legs on his legs, and massaged his buttocks with her strong fingers.

Drowsy and satisfied, they lay close together later, listening to the Etchemindys moving about in the great room. 'We're going to the coast,' he told her. 'Admiral Popham is there, and we will join the fleet. Brandon, the fleet is big enough to have a chaplain, and when I am on sea duty, my ship is also my parish. Will you marry me there without any further delay?'

She nodded. 'I will probably have to explain a lot to my sisters.'

'I doubt it.' He raised up on his elbow for a good look at her. 'Brandon, do you realize that at every stage of this journey, no one ever doubted we were married?'

She considered it. 'Did we just always seem married?' she asked, caressing him.

'I've felt that way since the *Perseverance*,' he confessed. 'Don't laugh!'

Her hands were soft on his face. He kissed her palm. 'Colonel, you're a looby. You know that's impossible.' She rubbed her nose against his cheek. 'Well, maybe not impossible. I wanted to think along those lines, except that Laura talked me out of it. But I'm young and foolish. How can you explain *your* behaviour?'

He couldn't think of a thing to say. He just cuddled her closer, until Señor Etchemindy knocked on the door, reminded them there was a war on, and invited them to breakfast.

'There is a pile of clothing outside the door,' Etchemindy said. 'I think you will be suitably disguised, Colonel Junot.'

Hugh decided he liked Polly Brandon very well in the ankle-length skirt, white blouse, and shawl of the local woman. He laced up her leather shoes and earned a flick to his head with her finger when his hands wandered farther up her legs than the stockings.

She laughed out loud when he dressed—courtesy of the village priest—in black soutane, cape, and broad-brimmed hat. The priest had thoughtfully furnished a crucifix for his neck and a prayer book. 'Now you must behave, Père Hugh Philippe d'Anvers Junot,' she teased.

'Let us pray no one needs Last Rites,' he retorted, and frowned at his patched sleeve. 'I look better in scarlet.'

'You are a man milliner,' his love accused.

'Guilty,' Hugh agreed affably. 'It used to be my little secret, but I suppose marriage lays one open to all sorts of charges. Dash it all—everyone in the Third Division knows I am a peacock!'

Polly was generous. She kissed him and murmured something about how grateful she was that he wasn't perpetually clad in a bloody apron like Philemon, or smelling of brine and tar like Oliver, her brothers-in-law. 'I could probably even take you to Bath and show you off,' she told him, tucking her arm in his as they went to the great room, 'providing I felt like parading you about in front of Miss Pym, which I do not. I intend to admire your remarkable posture and creaseless tunic without an audience!'

'I'll even take it off for you,' he whispered, the soul of generosity.

He hoped she would laugh and blush, but she surprised him. Unable to keep the tears from her eyes, Polly leaned her forehead against his arm. 'My love, I never thought we would have a chance to laugh about a future, did you?'

'No, I didn't, Brandon,' he replied, as honest as she was. 'We owe Sergeant Cadotte a debt we can never repay.'

'We can repay some of it,' she said. 'Some day.'

Breakfast was bread and blood sausage, washed down with milk. Hugh just sat and enjoyed the pleasure of watching Brandon eat until she finally had to hold up her hands in protest against one more bite.

Not one to be sceptical of any man's opinion, Hugh

still had to ask Raul Etchemindy how an odd couple such as they were now—maiden and priest—could possibly travel north through territory still patrolled by the French.

Raul seemed not at all perturbed. He broke off a piece of bread and dipped it in his jug of milk. 'You're not the only visitors to our village, Colonel. I think I can guarantee you as safe a ride to Santander as you can imagine.'

As it turned out, he did. Hugh decided never again to doubt Providence.

'Wait here,' Raul said. He hesitated at the door, listening intently, which made Brandon tuck her hand in Hugh's and look at him with concern in her eyes. She was even tensed for flight, which told him volumes about her trust for anyone except him.

'Let's see what this new development is, my love,' he told her calmly. 'Raul, don't think I have rag manners, but how *are* we getting to Santander?'

'Would you like a carriage ride with a Frenchwoman?'

Polly shook her head. 'We would not,' she declared firmly. 'No French ever again. I would rather walk to Santander.'

'Polly, let us reconsider your firm stance against anyone of French origin,' he told her, putting his arm around her. He looked at their host, saw the smile in his eyes, and remembered Lisbon. 'Señor Etchemindy, might this lady be of middling height, trim, and with red, curly hair? Young, too? Not much older than my wife?'

Enjoying himself hugely, Raul nodded.

Polly looked at Hugh suspiciously, but he only kissed her hand, so tight in his. 'If this is who I think, I heard of this paragon in Lisbon,' he told her. 'Her name is Madame Felice Sevigny, and she is the answer to more than one of our prayers, actually.'

'The very woman, *señor*. I believe I hear her carriage now.'

Hugh didn't precisely drag his love to the front door of the Etchemindy dwelling, but she did remind him of his favorite hunting dog—when a pup—who had to be coaxed towards open water. 'Trust me, Brandon,' he whispered. 'Our fortunes have turned.'

They were standing in the doorway as a mud-stained carriage came to a halt in front of the house and the door opened. Raul helped down a kindly looking female, not much taller than Polly and barely any older, whom he engaged in conversation. The result was several glances towards them standing in the doorway, then a bow, rather than a curtsey.

'That's odd,' Polly said.

'Not so odd,' Hugh contradicted. 'Ah, here she comes.'

The female in question patted her handsome black hair where a portion of it peeped out from a bonnet that must have come direct from the Rue de Rivoli or a Parisian boulevard close by. She strode across the muddy space to the Etchemindy's front door, and into the house in a businesslike manner, forcing Polly, her eyes wide now, to back up into Hugh's arms.

When she and Raul were inside and the door shut, she nodded to Hugh, and turned her attention to Polly. With a flourish, she lifted off her bonnet, which carried away her hair, too, and bowed again.

'Madam, James Rothschild at your service.'

Chapter Nineteen

Polly stared in astonishment at the young man before her, then clapped her hand over her mouth and laughed out loud. 'Oh, I do beg your pardon!' she said a second later, then turned to Hugh, who seemed to be enjoying her discomfort hugely. 'Husband, you owe me more than an explanation. I think you owe me a lengthy visit to a modiste when we return to England.'

James Rothschild's eyes were merry. 'My dear Madam Junot, I could not resist, so blame me!' He nodded next to Hugh. 'You, sir, seem to know my secret. One for the confessional, eh? Does chastity wear a little thin on a Royal Marine, Père Junot?'

Hugh laughed and turned over his crucifix. 'I attended a secret conference in Lisbon this summer, but never thought to actually meet you. Polly, dear, James Rothschild and his esteemed father in Frankfurt are bankrolling this war through their London office and James's brother.'

'We are, indeed,' Rothschild said. 'Do your fellows know I have set up a house of business in Paris, right under

Napoleon's nose? No? I hide in plain sight, Madame Junot.'

'How on earth…?' Polly began.

'Trade secrets,' he replied, shaking his head. 'Let me only tell you I travel back and forth between France and Spain, a little bullion going to the Corsican's generals, but much more to Wellington and his allies.' His smile was almost cherubic. 'We have an excellent record of backing winners.'

And that was all he would say about that, turning his attention and all of his charm upon Polly then. 'My dear madam, although you are charming in that rustic garb, let me give you another dress, so you can travel as my French companion.' He glanced at the Colonel. 'Your husband can continue in his role as father confessor.'

A nod and a word to Etchemindy sent one of the smaller Etchemindys dodging puddles out to the carriage, where he retrieved a travelling case and hat box. Roth-schild indicated Hugh was to take it.

'Colonel, assist your wife in changing into something more suitable for this next leg of our journey.' He peered into Polly's face with enough intensity to make her blush. 'Something warm in burgundy, if I have it on this trip. She has such lovely eyes.'

'I tell her that often, so you needn't,' Hugh assured Rothschild, which made Polly accuse him of jealousy a few minutes later, when he was unbuttoning her.

'You have me there,' he said. 'Who could blame me?' He kissed her neck. 'He is right; you do have lovely eyes.'

'Even with spectacles, the bane of my existence?' she asked, then felt immediately embarrassed because she had no experience in fishing for compliments.

'Even with spectacles,' he assured her. 'I like them, actually.' He struck a pose, which made her smile, since he was still dressed as a priest. 'Polly, you know me well enough to know I am not precisely a deep thinker, given to introspection.'

'I could disagree,' she interjected.

He bowed. 'Thank you. With or without spectacles, you're obviously an intelligent female. Think how brilliant and wise you will make me look!'

She gasped and thumped his chest, then laughed when he caught her up in his arms again. 'That was the most shallow thing anyone has ever said to me!' she declared.

'But it made you laugh and forget our circumstances for a moment, didn't it?' he teased, then turned immediately serious, or possibly half-serious; she knew she couldn't be sure. 'Brandon, the only problem you might have with spectacles is that all of our babies will want to snatch them off your face. Resign yourself to that.'

'Hugh,' she said softly, and it said the world.

There was no burgundy dress among James Rothschild's catalogue of disguises, so she settled for a dark blue wool travelling dress that screamed Paris-made from every discreet, impeccable seam. It was too big, built for a man's shape, but Hugh looped a sash twice around her waist and called it good. A pelisse of similar hue and a straw bonnet completed the outfit and turned her from a Basque *paisana* into a travelling companion for a distinctly average-looking Frenchwoman with impeccable taste.

After hugs for her hosts, Polly let Hugh hand her into the closed carriage and seat her beside Rothschild, who had replaced his wig and bonnet covering his own red hair. He brought out his tatting. 'My mother taught me,' he said, expertly throwing the little shuttle. 'I have made enough lace to trim petticoats for every sister and cousin I have, and I have a lot of them.' He glanced at Hugh. 'You'd be amazed how something as domestic as this deflects any number of questions from guards and sentries.'

James Rothschild played a deep game, and he distracted her with it through miles of uncomfortable travel, telling them of smuggling goods in all sorts of ways. 'My dears, this coach has a false floor,' he told them. 'And my petti-coats—trimmed with tatting or otherwise—have deep pockets.'

He was only one in a far-reaching network of couriers and spies that spanned continental Europe and spilled into England, where his older brother Nathan had established a branch. 'Our business is money, so we appreciate the value of enterprise and commerce in a free environment. This war will end eventually, and the Houses of Rothschild will reign supreme in Europe,' he said, then made a face when the carriage hit a larger-than-usual pothole. '*Oi vey!* Meanwhile, our backsides suffer. My Hebrew ancestors would tell you it is hard to start dynasties.'

They travelled through two French sentry posts, both well guarded with troops, which told her volumes about the ever-present threat of *guerilleros*. Rothschild, or rather, Madame Felice Sevigny, barely looked up from her tatting, and even handed it to one guard while she searched in her reticule for the safe-conduct pass. His audacity took away Polly's breath.

Nightfall found them in León, also patrolled by the French. With remarkable aplomb, Madame Sevigny asked for her usual room and added one for the priest. They ate in a private parlor, but not until the last dish was removed and hot water brought up did Rothschild remove his wig and hike up his skirts, to rest his white-stockinged legs and chic half-boots on a settle. Hugh tugged at his priestly skirts and did the same thing, which made Polly roll her eyes and throw up her hands.

She started the night on a pallet in the same room with Rothschild, clad in a nightshirt, who had taken a yarmulke, phylacteries, and blue-fringed shawl from some recess in his portmanteau and was rocking back and forth, deep in prayer. She watched him, touched at his devotion and wondering how much courage it took for him to practise this huge deception on Napoleon. Madam Sevigny, née Rothschild, may have tried to let them think it was all for business, but Polly knew enough of men now to reckon that even vain ones like Hugh were fuelled by higher motives. *So am I*, she told herself.

When he put away his religious artifacts, Rothschild climbed into bed and told her goodnight. 'I'm certain if you tap on the next door, there is a priest who would probably do you a bout of no good,' he teased. She blushed in the gloom, blew him a kiss, and left the room.

Rothschild was right. Their bout of no good calmed her nerves and soothed that part of her, somewhere under her skin, that seemed to hum with tension. 'This is disconcerting to the hilt, Hugh, darling, but I only feel safe when you are covering me,' she whispered, blushing as she said it.

'Happy to oblige, even though it's *my* sorry ass

winking at the ceiling,' he said cheerfully, his breathing still ragged. 'At least I weigh less than when our journey began.'

'It seems so long ago now,' she murmured, drowsy. When he left her body, but continued to hold her close, she kissed his arm and pillowed her head on it. 'How soon will we be at the coast?'

No answer. Her hero slept. He even snored a little.

In two days they arrived at Gijón, where Hugh sighed with relief to see the Bay of Biscay, sparkling in the sun. 'God, I love the ocean,' he said.

'We are less than fifty miles to Santander,' Rothschild said, putting down his tatting. 'Here is where I trade *haute couture* for rough trousers and a sweater, and take a fishing smack to La Rochelle.'

'You amaze me,' Polly said.

He shrugged, then tied off the length of tatting, which he handed to Polly. 'Sew this on a petticoat and think of me.' Rothschild took out a handkerchief. With a glance at Hugh, he dabbed at her eyes. 'No tears, Polly! You and your excellent husband will come and see me in Paris when this is over. I never knew a woman to tear up over tatting before.'

The plans changed as soon as Rothschild went on board the fishing boat and spoke to the Captain. After that brief conversation, they were all on board to hear the good news that the British fleet was in no apparent hurry to leave Santander. 'The Captain says he will take us to the fleet, Colonel,' Rothschild said. 'You'll be in Santander by morning.'

Bundled against wind and rain, they spent the night on the deck of the fishing smack. Polly visited the rail several times to retch her stomach out, while Hugh came to the rail to look for the first sign of the fleet. 'I'll feel so much easier when we are on board Popham's flagship,' he told her once, when their trips to the railing intersected.

Morning brought more mist, but not enough to disguise the breathtaking sight of Admiral Sir Home Popham's 100-gun ship of the line, and the frigates and smaller ships, a bomb kedge among them, hovering close by like chicks around a hen.

'Thank God,' Hugh said fervently. 'Polly, we made it.'

They said goodbye to James Rothschild after breakfast, which Polly was wise enough to forgo. After a glance at Hugh, he hugged her and kissed both cheeks, French fashion. 'Be careful, James,' she told him.

Rothschild looked over her head to Hugh in his priest's garments and kissed Polly again. '*Au revoir*, fair lady. We'll meet again in Paris. *Shalom.*' With a wave of his hand, Rothschild returned to his fishing net.

The fishing smack's jollyboat skimmed across the bay to the largest ship in the fleet. Because they approached the flagship as an unknown quantity, they were met on deck by a whole contingent of Marines, bayonets at the ready and commanded by a Captain of mature years who took one look at Hugh the priest and saluted, to the amusement of nearby seamen.

'Colonel Junot! We thought you were dead!'

'A vast understatement, Captain Marten. I do hope my Colonel Commandant in Plymouth has not replaced me yet.' He glanced at Polly, amused. 'My love, I am about to revert to my frivolous ways and ask Theodore Marten, whom I have known for years, if he has some more suitable clothing.'

'I knew you were a man milliner,' Polly said.

Hugh took her arm and led her closer. 'Captain Marten, this is my wife, Polly Junot, and she is abusing me because I am a peacock.'

Captain Marten snapped to attention again for her benefit. 'Sir, I knew right away after that exchange that she was your wife. Who else would treat you that way, sir? Welcome to Admiral Sir Popham's flagship, ma'am. Colonel, allow me to escort you and your lady to the old man himself.'

To Polly's amusement, the old man was as astounded as his Captain of Marines to see Lieutenant Colonel Hugh Junot—thinner, looking more righteous than usual, but obviously no worse for wear.

''Pon my word, Colonel, we have been scouring the coast for news of you,' he said, pouring them each a glass of Madeira. 'And is this Polly Brandon, risen from the dead as well? There is an anxious surgeon's wife on Oporto who has been pelting me with letters, and an equally anxious frigate captain who should be at Ferrol Station but who is patrolling this coast, looking for his sister-in-law.'

'It is Oliver,' Polly said with relief. 'I have so much to tell him.'

'And we have much to tell you, Admiral,' Hugh said. 'But first, there is a delicate matter that demands your assistance and your discretion. May we speak privately?'

They could, after the Admiral shooed away his secretary and other crew members. Hugh quickly explained their situation and requested a wedding in the Admiral's great room at the earliest possible convenience. There were no flies on the Admiral; he summoned his chaplain immediately while Hugh procured himself some clothing from slops—nothing fancier than dark trousers and another black-and-white checked shirt. 'I have my limits, Polly,' he told her, as he patted his gorget, which now lay on the outside of his shirt. 'I won't be married in priest's clothing.'

'I still look better than you do,' she teased.

'You always will, my love,' he told her.

I believe him, she thought, a little surprised at herself, considering what a splendid man Hugh Junot was. *I am the most beautiful woman who ever lived*, she thought, watching her husband—in fact, if not by law yet. 'We have been through more than most, my love,' she said, her voice low, but not low enough that Admiral Popham did not hear, and then turn away, muttering about something in his eye, and complaining that his steward hadn't a clue about dusting his quarters.

They waited while Popham demanded one of his Midshipmen to run up the numbered flags that would summon the Captain of the *Tangier* to the flagship immediately. Then they waited a little longer for Captain Oliver Worthy—anxious at the summons and frowning— to gasp and throw open his arms to embrace his sister-in-law, as soon as he came into the great cabin.

'We needed another witness, Worthy. I thought this was one way to get a lick of work out of you and then send the *Tangier* back to Ferrol Station,' Popham said gruffly. He nodded to his chaplain, who stood ready. 'C'mon, man. This won't wait. Splice 'um! There's a war on!'

Admiral Popham dropped his anchor on her when the ink wasn't yet dry on the marriage lines. 'Mrs Junot, take a long look at your husband and give him a kiss. I'm sending him with Captain Marten and his Marines to Burgos with siege guns for Wellington.'

'Then I am coming, too,' she said, as the blood rushed from her face at the Admiral's news, so drily delivered. 'I...I really don't know what I will do if he is not in my sight.'

'That is not possible, Mrs Junot,' the Admiral said, and she felt her heart slide into James Rothschild's shoes, because she knew he meant it.

'I'll take you to Oporto, Polly,' Oliver said. 'Duty is duty and no one knows that better than your husband.'

She looked at Hugh, pleaded with him with her eyes without saying a word, and saw in his glance that he felt precisely the same way, even as he agreed with her brother-in-law.

'I must obey, Brandon,' he told her.

They all looked at her, each man with some anxiety, and she knew why. She was a woman, weak, missish, and prone to tears. This was their world and she had intruded in it from São Jobim on. No matter how much Hugh Junot loved her, and she knew he did, he was a Marine and the world was at war.

I could cry, she thought, *or I could be the woman my sisters have become; the woman I want to be*.

'I know you must obey, Hugh,' she told him. She turned to Oliver. 'I would love to sail to Oporto with you, or even go back to Torquay and Nana, but I would like to remain here with the fleet, at least until I know what happens at Burgos.' She looked at Admiral Popham. 'I did learn some skills at the satellite hospital, if your surgeon might have need of them. If not, I can stay out of everyone's way.'

'It could be that I must remain in Burgos, or follow the

guns, if we are successful, and winter in the Pyrenees,' Hugh said tentatively.

'Or retreat with Wellington to the lines of Torres Vedras,' she said. 'So be it. Just let me know, one way or the other, and I can return to Oporto on a coasting vessel.'

The men looked at each other, and then at the Admiral, whose decision it was. He removed his wig, scratched his scalp, and replaced his wig. 'Done, madam,' he said. 'You may remain with the fleet here in Santander, until we know where this Marine of yours is headed.' The Admiral chucked her under the chin. 'I suppose I am a fool for love,' he told her. 'Let's send Oliver packing, and find you a berth somewhere on this big ship, shall we?'

'Furnish it with a bucket,' her lover and newly licensed husband said. 'She's my darling, but she is no seaman.'

They laughed. Hugh took her hand and kissed it. 'I'm going now to speak with Captain Marten and find out what the duty entails.'

After he left, and before she had a moment to pine, Oliver tucked her arm in his. 'Polly, if you won't come aboard the *Tangier* and let me take you to Oporto, please write a letter to Laura. I will deliver it inside of a week.'

She took a deep breath. 'I have a lot to say to her.'

It was only a brief letter, because the *Tangier* had to sail. It came from Polly's heart, begging Laura's pardon for doing precisely what she had counselled against, but assuring her sister that she knew her heart, even as she did and as Nana did. '"I trust you will come to love my husband as your brother,"' she wrote, choosing each word with care. '"We will be in Plymouth at the Marine barracks, and you are always welcome in our home."'

She showed it to Oliver, who had been given leave to

relax in the Admiral's quarters and drink the man's Madeira. He nodded, and patted the banquette beside him.

'I wish I could take you back to Torquay, but I understand, truly I do,' he said, then tightened his grip on her shoulder, at the mention of his and Nana's home. 'I didn't tell you the best news. Nana was confined with our son only three weeks ago. Polly, I was there. I was *there*!'

It was too much. He couldn't say anything else. They were still sitting close together when Hugh returned to Popham's great cabin. He sat beside her, his hand on her knee, and looked at them both. 'Should I be suddenly afraid that my new relatives are emotional southerners?' he asked, his Scots accent never more pronounced. 'Oliver, does it take official wedding vows to bring out the fearful truth?'

'Sister Polly, you have married a Marine, a Scot, and a Lieutenant Colonel,' Oliver said solemnly. 'I am not certain which will give you the most trouble.'

'None of them,' she replied. 'I know this man's heart.'

Chapter Twenty

She slept with her husband that night in quarters off the Admiral's cabin, accustoming herself to the motion of a sleeping cot again. They lay tight as sardines, swinging gently as the ship of the line moved on its anchors. He told her of the letter he had sent with James Rothschild, requesting him to forward it through his secret channels to his brother Nathan in London. It was a request for a tidy sum from his banker to be sent through James in Paris to Lalage Cadotte in the parish of Sainte Agilbert.

'Providence sent us the only man in Europe who could actually get that money to our Sergeant's widow before this war ends,' he told her. 'We will still go and see her later, but at least we know she will soon have what we promised her husband.'

'Bless you,' Polly said. 'And João at Sacred Name?'

'He'll come to Plymouth with us, just as we promised his mother in São Jobim, my love.' He turned towards her, his hand inside her nightgown now. 'Give a Marine some comfort,' he whispered, his lips on her breast. 'You're my only girl in a port, and I can't waste a moment. Time management, wife.'

Admiral Sir Home Popham and his Captain commanding kindly allowed her access to the quarterdeck, where she stood at the rail for long hours, looking south towards Burgos. She had said an appropriate farewell to her husband belowdeck as the circumspect wife of a Lieutenant Colonel should, but came above deck to watch the Marines and seamen, aided by brown-suited *guerilleros*, move three eighteen-pounders from the fleet to be used as siege cannon at Burgos. After they were out of sight, she longed to tug at the lace on Sir Home's sleeve and demand to know how long the men would be gone. Instead, she chose discretion and kept her own counsel, as Hugh would want. She passed her nineteenth birthday alone, her mind and heart on her husband, adding his own mantle of duty to her shoulders. She was strong enough to bear the weight of it, and had not a doubt of her own courage.

To her relief, the Admiral had no intention of pulling up anchor until he knew what had happened at Burgos. The rains gave way to unexpected sleet in mid-October and a choppy anchorage, which sent her belowdeck, white-faced and trembling, to kneel over the bucket in her quarters.

Less than a week later, the detail returned, but without the cannon. Even Admiral Popham stared in surprise to see them. ''Pon my word, Mrs Junot,' he said, handing her the

glass and pointing. 'There had better be an adequate explanation!'

There was, and it was delivered by one of Wellington's
aides-de-camp, looking decidedly out of place among his
naval brethren. 'The General sends his compliments, Admiral Popham. I am to tell you that he has lifted his siege
and is returning to Portugal. Your guns are no longer required.'

'Admiral, General Wellington sent his ADC to us when
we were still fifty miles from Burgos,' Hugh added. 'He
couldn't sustain a siege and he decided it was time to
retreat to Portugal.'

Popham frowned and deliberately looked all around
the deck. 'Then where, Colonel, are my flaming guns?'
He stared down his long nose at Captain Marten, his chief
Marine officer on the flagship, who had accompanied the
guns, too. 'Sir? Did they take wing?'

Captain Marten blushed. 'No, sir, not at all. Colonel
Junot suggested we give them to General Espoz y Mina
and his *guerilleros*, who so ably assisted us in the transport.'

'Hmm,' the Admiral said, returning his gaze to Hugh. 'I
trust you have an excellent reason why this was a good
idea?'

'I do, sir,' Hugh replied, not ruffled at all by the stare
from an Admiral of the fleet. 'The rain was bogging down
our own retreat, and Espoz y Mina can find good use for
the guns in his operations here in León.' He glanced at
Polly and smiled. 'Polly and I have seen him and his
troops in action, sir. I think his army is worth three of any
bona fide Spanish army. I take full responsibility.'

'Good of you,' Popham murmured, but with no malice.

'Sir, if I may, any muskets, rifles, and materiel you have not handed over to the regular Spanish army should be given to the *guerilleros*,' Hugh said, pressing home the point. 'Do this, and León will be pacified before winter ends.'

Admiral Popham nodded. 'You guarantee these ragged men can do what a Spanish army cannot?'

'Admiral Popham, no man can guarantee that. My advice is to trust him. Espoz y Mina's brand of hit-and-run war may become a standard of warfare, in future.'

'I doubt that very much, Colonel,' Popham said, after a long pause and much scrutiny of Colonel Junot, who did not squirm. 'Care to make a wager?'

The tension on the quarterdeck vanished when Hugh gasped theatrically. 'Not with my wife standing here, Admiral! She will give me a regular bear-garden jaw, if I gamble away my pay chit.'

'I wouldn't, you know,' she told him later, when they stood on the deck of the frigate *Aurora*, which had peeled off from the fleet towards Oporto with them aboard. 'The Admiral will think I am a shrew.'

Hugh kissed her check, and wrapped his borrowed boat cloak tighter around both of them. 'No, no. He's a married man, too.' He sighed then, and gently rubbed his thumb under her breast, more for comfort, to her way of thinking, than any greater design. 'I don't know what I accomplished during this sojourn in the Peninsula, as far as military matters go. I have a wife—the best one imaginable—but the notes I took from all those interviews must be scattered from here to breakfast. My conclusions about the *guerilleros* will be met with scepticism—you heard the Admiral—because no one understands this kind of warfare yet.'

'You can still write a report about that,' she pointed out.

'I can. I can also urge my Commandant Colonel that our Marines be used here and there among the *guerilleros* as liaison. They'll be better than that ninny from Wellington's army. Certainly more flexible.' He pulled her closer. 'Is it enough?'

'Probably not for you,' she said. 'Will you be content to sit at a desk in Plymouth now and make policy?'

'And not go gallivanting off to the Peninsula?' He kissed her fingers. 'Aye, Polly, dear, because I know that when I come home each night, you will be on the other side of the door.'

She had no resistance to that. After a quick scanning of the deck, she turned around in his arms and kissed him, pressing against his body so brazenly that she was glad his cloak enveloped them both. *Better get the man belowdeck and roger him royally*, she told herself. She knew that as soon as the frigate began its dance on the Atlantic rollers, she would be kneeling by that bucket again, with love a long way from her mind.

He kissed her back with some fervour, but then he sighed, and rested his chin on her head. 'Brandon, I have to tell you something.'

'That you love me?'

Hugh held her off a little, his face serious. 'When we were fifty miles from Burgos, where the ADC joined us, so did El Cuchillo.'

She thought a moment, then tensed. 'Dear God. Sister Maria Madelena's brother?'

'The very same. He came right up to me out of the shadows and stood practically on my shoes. What could I do? I didn't know whether to fight or run, but then he clapped his arms on my shoulders and kissed me on each cheek.'

Hugh couldn't help himself then. He sobbed out loud, trying to smother the sound in her hair. Polly held him closer. 'She spared you!' she said fiercely. 'I'll remind you of that whenever you need to hear it!'

She wiped his eyes, kissing his lips and neck until he could speak again.

'That was what he told me, too, my love. We didn't know it, but the deacon at São Jobim witnessed the whole wicked turn of events from the choir loft. He carried the tale to El Cuchillo, and it was El Cuchillo who took word to Oporto that you and I were still alive. He…he just wanted to assure me he knows the truth.'

'Poor man,' she murmured. 'Did…you tell him of our plans for João?'

'Aye, and he gave me his blessing again. Polly, I want to be a good father.'

'You will be,' she said, running her hand along his face, caressing him. 'And to all our other children,' she whispered.

'Is that an announcement, Polly, dear?' he asked, and he sounded so eager.

'No. It's just a fact,' she said. 'I even predict that when we get to Oporto, my sister will give you a hug and a kiss.'

'I doubt that,' he said. 'She doesn't like me.'

'She will! Philemon will be our advocate, Hugh. Did you know it was Philemon who delivered that letter you so incautiously wrote to me?'

The frigate began its Atlantic roll. He walked her carefully to a nearby hatch and sat down, his cloak still tight around her. 'He did tell me that, and gave me some reason to hope.' He glanced at her. 'Polly, do you think you and I will disagree on things, as the Brittles do?'

'I think you can count on it,' she told him. 'I have a brain; so do you. How could we possibly see eye to eye on everything?' She moved herself into his embrace, wrapping her arms around him. 'I never told you this, but I wrote you a letter, too, only I never sent it. You can read it, when we get to Oporto.' She sighed. 'It's not cheerful reading.'

'It's not a cheerful war. You know that better than any female, Brandon. We're returning to Stonehouse Barracks and I am going back to boring desk duty, where I will write that report—as much as I can from memory—and strenuously argue for the Marines to be used as liaison with *guerrilleros* like Espoz y Mina.' He twined his fingers through hers. 'Maybe there will be time for you and me and João to visit Scotland, but I doubt it.'

'What will I do?'

He kissed her hand. 'You can begin by decorating my quarters. I'm embarrassed for you to see them now, but that can't be helped. And just think—you can spend leisure time playing "There was an old bee" with João.'

'I can,' she agreed, feeling impish. Either the waves weren't rolling too high yet, or she was finally developing those mythical sea legs her Marine spoke of. More immediately, she saw a future belowdeck in a sleeping cot with her husband. *I used to be a lot more circumspect*, she thought, as she leaned closer to him. *Thank goodness that passed.* 'I have a version of my own for you. "There was an old bee…"'

'Brandon, you scamp,' he exclaimed, even as he made no effort to stop her pointing finger, which was more of a caress than a circle, and targeted south of his stomach. 'No one's ever done the bee like that before. No, don't stop.'

'"…who lived in a barn,"' she continued, not even bothering with the circle any more, but touching him where she knew it would do the most good, considering her designs on her husband. She began to undo the buttons on his trousers. '"He carried a bagpipe…"' she began, but he stood up then.

'"…under his arm,"' he continued, as he kept the cloak around both of them and started with her for the gangway. 'So glad you remember that little ditty, except that I may never be able to look at it in the same way again. I believe you are a rascal, Brandon.'

Thirty minutes later, he was deep asleep, cradling her in his arms, as he had protected her from Plymouth to Santander, and apparently back again. She thought about looking for her nightgown, but that was more effort than she deemed strictly necessary. Besides, she might just have to take it off again, and she knew how Hugh, darling, felt about effective time management.

As Colonel Junot slept the good sleep of the thoroughly rogered, she pillowed her head against his chest. So much had happened since early summer, when she had left Plymouth as a green girl. Autumn was almost winter. Wellington and his troops were slogging back to Portugal. The war was her companion, but no war lasted for ever. Duty called her Colonel, and always would, but she expected no less. In the grand scheme of things—where armies marched and tyrants decreed—perhaps nothing had changed. In her heart, everything had. She listened to the ship's bells, content to watch over him.

* * * * *

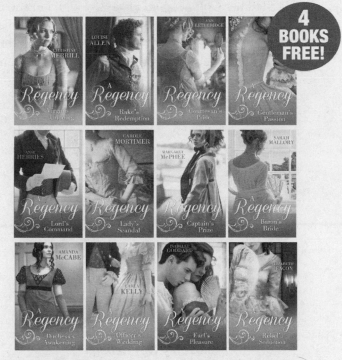

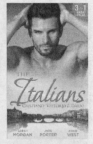

The Admiral's Penniless Bride

Sally Paul is homeless and down to her last penny – so the last thing she expects is an offer of marriage from a complete stranger. Admiral Sir Charles Bright is in need of a wife...but, after marrying in haste, can he convince Sally to enjoy their wedding night at leisure?

Marrying the Royal Marine

Illegitimate Polly Brandon is amazed when the Lieutenant Colonel of Marines introduces himself as they sail for Portugal. In society, Polly knows he would never look twice at her...but with only the ocean for company there's no avoiding their unlikely attraction...

£7.99

ISBN 978-0-263-91769-7

9 780263 917697

e book
also available

ISABELLE GODDARD

A Regency Earl's Pleasure

T2 9 186

1·00

a **MILLS & BOON®** book from

HARLEQUIN (UK) LTD
www.millsandboon.co.uk

MILLS BOON™

Cover design © Harlequin (UK) Ltd. Cover images © Arcangel Images & Fotolia